HERO

Lee Stephen

stone aside publishing

Stone Aside Publishing, L.L.C.

ISBN 978-0-9788508-4-5

Editing by Arlene Prunkl
Cover Illustration by Francois Cannels
Maps by John S. Sirmon, Jr.
Book Design by Fiona Raven

First Printing April 2009
Printed in USA
V1

stone aside publishing

Published by
Stone Aside Publishing, L.L.C.

Dedicated to

GOD

0

WEDNESDAY, NOVEMBER 2ND, 0011 NE
2215 HOURS

EDEN COMMAND

THE LIGHT IN Judge Benjamin Archer's room was subtle. The only significant illumination came from a series of conch lamps mounted along the walls. Archer stood in the center of the room on a deerskin rug. It wasn't a deer that he'd killed; he'd never hunted a day in his life.

Atop his cherry-stained desk sat a small audio recorder. "Message from Benjamin Archer," he began. "Our situation has not changed. Before we proceed as discussed, there is additional information I require. If you cannot supply me with this information, I will be forced to pursue alternate sources."

The judge's amber eyes stared at the conch lamps, but he didn't see them. His focus was elsewhere.

"There is speculation that Carl Pauling, the president of EDEN, will retire in the next four to five months." His words were precisely pronounced; his British accent greatly subdued. "The most likely candidate to replace him is Judge Malcolm Blake, whom Pauling already considers his successor. Blake stands to gain a unanimous vote."

He paced across the room as though it was his own personal amphitheatre. His gaze drifted from the conch lamps back to the recording device. He continued:

"Should this speculation hold true, we shall have the control that we need. I anticipate a fourteen-month campaign, beginning from the point of Blake's ascendancy. By that time, we should be ready—though time has already become critical. As per our agreement, I expect your aggression to cease as soon as we've established control. Until the situation leads elsewhere."

He paused. "I have not heard of the one whom you speak of, but I wish you well in your search. The cohesiveness of our undertaking cannot be compromised. Should we find him, we will kill him at once.

"End of message."

He walked to the recorder and switched it off. Removing the tiny disk from its housing, he placed it on the stand by his bed. He lifted his comm to his lips. "Archer to Intelligence."

Several seconds passed before he heard a response. "Intelligence."

"Have a courier come to my room at once. I have something to be delivered to Kang tonight."

"Tonight, sir?"

"Yes, tonight."

The voice hesitated. "Sir, I believe Director Kang is asleep now."

"I don't care," Archer said. "I expect your courier to arrive within five minutes."

"Yes sir, right away." The comm channel closed.

For the next several minutes, Archer scrutinized himself in the mirror. Despite the late hour, everything about him was precise—his hair, his wardrobe, even his posture and his alert, calculating expression.

When the knock finally came, he looked at the clock. Just over five minutes. He answered the door, where a short operative stood in proper wait.

"Judge Archer," the operative bowed.

"Punctuality is of the utmost importance," Archer said harshly, before his impatient expression collapsed. "I apologize. My tone was uncalled for. This is simply a very time-sensitive message."

The operative lowered his head. "It's my fault, judge. I'll be faster next time. I promise."

Archer placed the disk in the courier's hand. "Deliver this to Director Kang. Deviate for no other task. We are the guardians of an entire species. Every moment of our existence is irreplaceable."

"Understood, sir. Should I tell him it's from you?"

"Tell him nothing. Simply deliver. I want the time of delivery catalogued and confirmed, to the second."

"Yes, sir."

"Tarry not, dear courier."

The operative nodded, turned, and walked hurriedly down the hall.

Archer stood in the open doorway until the courier disappeared around a far corner. Only then did he step back inside.

The new judge did not stay up for long. There were many other important matters at hand—matters that needed clarity of the mind. The kind of clarity only garnered from sleep. He heard nothing from Kang that night, nor from the courier who'd delivered the message.

He heard from no one at all.

PART I

The Fourteenth of Novosibirsk

Clarke, Nathaniel	Captain	Commanding Officer
*Dostoevsky, Yuri	Commander	Executive Officer
*Remington, Scott	Lieutenant	Tertiary Officer
Axen, Matthew	Lieutenant	Tertiary Officer
*Ryvkin, Viktor	Delta Trooper	UNREGISTERED
*Romanov, Nicolai	Delta Trooper	UNREGISTERED
*Broll, Auric	Delta Trooper	UNREGISTERED
*Goronok, Egor	Delta Trooper	UNREGISTERED
Jurgen, David	Delta Trooper	Soldier
McCrae, Becan	Delta Trooper	Soldier
Strakhov, Oleg	Delta Trooper	Soldier
Timmons, Jayden	Delta Trooper	Sniper
Navarro, Travis	Delta Trooper	Pilot
Evteev, Boris	Gamma Private	Technician
Yudina, Varvara	Gamma Private	Medic
Brooking, Esther	Beta Private	Scout (Type-2)
Frolov, Maksim	Beta Private	Demolitionist

*denotes Nightman

1

SATURDAY, NOVEMBER 5TH, 0011 NE
0715 HOURS

NOVOSIBIRSK, RUSSIA

THREE MONTHS AFTER LAKE BAIKAL

THE DAY BEGAN as bleakly as each one before it—at least, each one for the past several months. Leaning over the edge of his bed, Scott cupped his stubble-covered face in his hands. He pushed his palms up against his cheeks, distorting his face for a moment before his hands fell again. He massaged the back of his neck. He'd slept well that night; the nights of restlessness had passed weeks ago. With every sunset, rest came more naturally. His stomach and head knotted less. He could cope.

But waking up was still the worst part. It was always the same process. Pushing himself from the mattress. Mustering the willpower to stand.

Seeing her face for the first time.

Not a day passed for him without looking her in the eyes. Without seeing her smile, frozen in time, staring at him from the boundaries of her picture frame. She was there to find him with every sunrise, every single day.

Scott forced himself to look up—to acknowledge her invisible presence: the woman he'd betrayed. He forced himself to feel her hurt. It tore open old scars and ripped apart new ones. It brought those words to him again. Sinner. Hypocrite. Murderer. That was the hardest part. Knowing the disappointment behind her otherwise happy expression. Knowing he'd lost her forever. It was tortuous to face her, but it had to be done. He had to get it over with, every day.

It was the only way he could move on.

Reaching out without looking, he grabbed the top of the frame, turning it completely around until her smile no longer faced him. Now she watched only the wall.

Scott closed his eyes. It always came on very slow. First, it was a steadying of his heart. Then it was the purpose-laden calming of his breathing. Goose bumps broke across his back, tingling up his spine. His shoulders tensed; the ridge over his eyes lowered. Then he exhaled.

When he opened his eyes again, all sadness was gone. All remorse, all guilt, thrust away. Those were hindering emotions, and they were not allowed in a war.

Rising from bed, he stretched his neck to both sides. Both times, it violently popped. He flexed his shoulder muscles and chest. He turned to his closet.

It waited for him, as it did every morning—the antithesis to the woman he loved. Her rival for affection. It always beat her out. The fulcrum armor beckoned him like an irresistible curse, from its haunting blackness to the bold defiance personified in its horns. It gave him all the companionship he required.

He needed mere moments to don it. Each piece was assembled together like a mechanical monster covering his body. The helmet—a near-featureless black mask without even a face—was the last part to go on. He latched it down over his head with a jarring clank, fastening it into place above his spiked collar. He stared through the interior view screen in front of his eyes.

He could see her through the minute cameras that observed the outside world from the surface of his helmet, which allowed otherwise eyeless fulcrums and slayers to see. Her picture still faced the wall. It always did when this time came around.

This side of him, she wasn't allowed to see.

The morning was shrouded with stagnant fog. The sun wasn't quite ready to appear, which was normal for a Siberian winter. The fog was not quite as common, though in the past few days, it had been dense. No stars could be seen through the mists. The air smelled stale.

The snowfall had been lighter the previous night, but there was still enough to cover the ground. Flakes still drifted in thin, gentle sheets. To anyone else, it might have been beautiful. To Scott, it meant nothing at all.

"Attention!" he barked out in Russian. He'd been in *Novosibirsk* for seven months, the past three of which were spent amid Nightmen. Conversational

Russian had come with immersion. His voice, already booming, was made even louder through the vocally enhanced helmet.

Before him, lined in three perfectly formed rows of six, Nightman slayers and sentries snapped erect. There were no other fulcrums present.

Scott's four slayers—Viktor Ryvkin, Nicolai Romanov, Auric Broll, and Egor Goronok—were in the back row. They were allowed to be there; they had the luxury of staying out of striking distance. Only because they were his.

Scott's faceless gaze found two Nightmen in the front row—a slayer and a sentry. He turned to them. "Front and center."

The Nightmen complied.

Scott paced before them. "Yesterday was a disappointment." He stared at the slayer. "Can you tell me why?"

"Because we did not apply what you showed us, lieutenant."

It was a programmed answer; it sought to appease. "Do I need to show you again?"

"No, lieutenant."

He'd believe that when he saw it. "As you want it," said Scott. "So you two show *me*."

The slayer and the sentry faced each other. They took several steps back, assuming fighting stances. Then they waited.

"Go on."

It took no second command. The two armored Nightmen stalked each other, then clashed together in a mechanized grapple.

Already, Scott felt himself fume. It was pitiful. This might as well have been backyard wrestling. The Nightmen could deliver solid blows to one another, that much was evident. They sparred with more proficiency than EDEN. But just "better than EDEN" didn't cut it. The slayer and sentry had superior ability, yet there was a flaw. Both men alternated between defense and aggression. That was the problem.

"Hold!"

The slayer and sentry snapped erect.

Scott walked in front of them both, though he focused solely on the slayer. Without looking at the sentry, he ordered him, "Fall back and observe." As soon as the sentry had done so, Scott assumed a combat stance across from the slayer. "Attack me just like you did him."

There was a moment's hesitation from the slayer, but he did as ordered. Rushing at Scott, he swung his right hand with a thundering blow.

Scott's counter lasted barely a second. Grabbing the slayer's arm, he twisted it around until he was holding the slayer from behind. The lesser Nightman's arm was pinned painfully behind his back. His entire body tensed outward. He locked up in pain.

Scott made no attempt to speak to his captive. He sought out the sentry instead. "What is so *challenging* about this?" It was a proverb from centuries ago, adopted by a sport he barely thought about anymore: attack is the best form of defense. The best defense is a good offense. "You bring the fight to your enemy, *all* the time! From the moment they see you, they should only feel panic. Every time they press in, every hint of aggression they throw at you, you grab it and turn it around. That is how you dominate!"

The sentry looked at the ground.

"We have gone over this, again and again and again." Scott flexed his arm muscles against the slayer's back. The slayer cried in pain. "The problem is not what you know. You all *know* how to kill. But it's not enough to know it. You have to want it! Then you have to take it. Change your mindset, and your body will comply!"

Scott slammed the slayer down with his knee, still holding the man by the arm. The moment the slayer hit the snow, Scott ripped his shoulder straight out of socket. It popped, and the slayer let loose a blood-curdling howl.

Scott left the slayer—dislocated shoulder and all—writhing on the ground. He made his way to the sentry. "Come at me."

The sentry stared for a moment, then assumed a fighting stance. Lunging forward in a different way than the slayer had, he tried to grab Scott with one hand.

The American fulcrum leaned to the side, grabbing the massive sentry by his extended arm. But instead of twisting the sentry's arm back, something the sentry was clearly expecting, Scott careened an open-palm strike against the Nightman's chin. The sentry's head snapped back.

Then the twist came. Scott clutched the sentry's arm, turned it around, and pinned it straight against his back. He wrenched it ninety degrees, and the giant fell to his knees in torment. The massive man wailed.

Scott's anger turned on the others. "You should all feel this by now! This shouldn't have to be taught. *Learn how to kill*!" His arm clutched the sentry's neck. Lifting the massive Nightman to his feet, he flung him back and over his shoulder onto the snow. It was a sentry almost twice his size, yet Scott threw him as if he were a rag doll.

That was why they listened when he spoke.

Scott kicked the grounded sentry's chest, then jabbed his foot down on his neck. He pushed back the Nightman's chin with his metal-tipped boot.

Scott switched from Russian to pure English—for those who could understand. "For damned men, not many of you seem to care about staying alive." He slowly freed the sentry's neck. "Pair up. Fight until you *get it right*. I will observe."

The fulcrum from America. The black-maned lion. The monster. All were names associated with Scott Remington. In the months that had passed since he'd joined the Nightmen's ranks, he'd become a notorious figure. He was as physically exceptional as any of the Nightmen—that wasn't what made him unique. What made him unique was what burned in his heart. He had vehemence. He had a lust for the infliction of pain. He had a drive for violence that had rarely been surpassed.

Despite his training with Nightmen, Scott was still part of the Fourteenth. He was still their ranking lieutenant. Besides his own slayers—Viktor, Nicolai, Auric, and Egor—none of these Nightmen in his morning sessions could be considered teammates. But they may as well have been—they were the ones he associated with. The only exception was Commander Dostoevsky, who was never present for these exercises. The Russian fulcrum was still in the Fourteenth, but Scott never associated with him. Scott had his own reasons for that.

But with these Nightmen, during these sessions, Scott could unload. He could release every ounce of his wrath and not deal with a moment's regret. He could strike. He could torment. He could beat within an inch of a life. He could take them to hell. And every time one fell prey to his violence, the question surfaced again.

Is this the one?

That question was the crux of it all. With that question, it was all justified. He asked it to himself every time he came across a new Nightman. He'd even asked it about the four slayers from the Fourteenth, though their innocence—at least in the case in question—had long been confirmed. But someone in *Novosibirsk* wasn't innocent. Someone out there needed to die.

But that wasn't the infuriating part. The infuriating part was that no matter who Nicole's murderer was, deep in his heart Scott couldn't hold murder against him.

Because Scott was a murderer, too.

His session ended as brutally as it had begun. The Nightmen, battered and bruised, were forced to endure five laps around the snow-covered track—the same track he'd run on himself the day Nicole died.

When training was over, Scott's public presence came to an end, as it always did. Though he usually accompanied his four teammate Nightmen to the cafeteria, they rarely stayed there. They usually took their food and went their own ways. On occasion, when something needed to be discussed, some of them would accompany Scott back to his quarters. Today was one of those days, as both Nicolai and Viktor followed him out.

The sect of Nightmen had little semblance of a ranking system. It comprised those who ordered and those who obeyed. Slayers obeyed fulcrums. Fulcrums obeyed Thoor, as did the hidden eidola. Sentries—the heavily armored guards—fell somewhere in the middle. That was the chain of command.

Viktor and Nicolai were veteran slayers. Viktor was in his mid-thirties, as was Nicolai, though the latter looked much older with deep crevices on his face. But outside of being long-enduring Nightmen, the two men were nothing alike.

Viktor was slender and tall. He was by far the most arrogant of all the Fourteenth's slayers. He was strikingly handsome, with black hair that shone glossily as it slicked past his shoulders. He was handsome and lethal—and well aware of both.

Nicolai was a walking paradox. He laughed, but at disturbing times. He was brave, yet inexplicably paranoid. He was amiable, and he was obsessed with blood. While few Nightmen openly discussed their rites of passage, Nicolai flaunted his like a trophy. He wore a blackish-crimson-stained necklace he claimed had belonged to the man he'd murdered. He'd dipped it in the murdered man's blood until it crusted. From that day on, it had never been washed nor absent from his neck.

"The session was good today," Nicolai said in Russian. He had a raspy, unsettling voice. "The air was very cold."

Scott had been around Nicolai long enough to understand such disparate correlations. "If it gets any colder, we'll move inside."

"If you desire." Nicolai's head twitched, a habit he repeated unconsciously. It made him look like a lizard.

Viktor's voice, unlike Nicolai's, was smooth and low. "Dostoevsky has informed me that we will be receiving a new medical officer from EDEN."

Scott was surprised, but he took anything heard from Dostoevsky with several grains of salt. "On whose request?"

"On Captain Clarke's."

"We already have two medics," Scott said. "We don't need a third." Though Viktor wasn't officially a medic, he had extensive medical training. He was almost a double-class operative. As Scott reached his private quarters, he opened the door and flicked on the light.

Nicolai leered. "I did not know we had two medics. Viktor and who else?"

"Varvara Yudina is a medic," Scott answered, irritated. "Which you already know."

"Then why doesn't she give more examinations?"

Scott didn't bother to look back. He could picture Nicolai's lewd grin in his head. He walked further inside. "Did Dostoevsky say who it was?"

"No."

"Does he even know?"

"I do not know."

Scott looked at the papers on his desk. Though they had been there for weeks, they were of little significance. They were standard EDEN mailings, all of which he ignored. Except for one folder—a folder that stayed on his desk at all times. It had no label, and was filled with few papers. Reaching down, Scott swept the EDEN mailings into the trash. But the folder remained. "Are we getting just one more operative?"

"I believe so," answered Viktor.

That would give the unit a total of eighteen members. It was growing in size. Scott was puzzled why the new medic wasn't a Nightman. There were more Nightmen now than ever before. They made up entire units. "I'm sure Clarke will inform me." The only time he ever talked to the captain was when business needed to be discussed. All other communication was nonexistent.

"Perhaps we should consider a new epsilon," Nicolai said. "Perhaps one of us."

"Is that what you want? To be an epsilon?"

"If there is a need, I will gladly fill it. As would Viktor, I am sure."

Viktor said nothing.

"Perhaps you should recommend us to General Thoor—"

"No." Scott cut off Nicolai's words. It wasn't the blatant attempt at self-promotion that bothered Scott. It was the other part of the statement. He would *never* speak to General Thoor. "If this unit needs an epsilon,

Clarke will name one. Not you, not me. Not Thoor. Is that why you followed me today?"

"Of course not, lieutenant. I came because I enjoy your wonderful company."

"Get out of my room."

"Yes, lieutenant. If you need me, I am only a comm call away." Nicolai backed out and went his own way.

Scott wasn't sure who made him more uncomfortable, Nicolai because of his strangeness, or Viktor because of his vanity. Neither man made him feel good. He turned to Viktor. "What do you want?"

Viktor wasted no time. "Will Yudina remain in this unit if we receive a new medic?"

"Why does it matter?"

"I am only curious. It is of no consequence."

"So what if she leaves?"

"If she leaves," Viktor said slowly, "then she leaves."

"There's your answer." He watched Viktor for a moment, then walked to his closet. "Is that all you wanted?"

"Yes, lieutenant."

Scott unzipped his black uniform and slid his arms from it. Wearing only a gray undershirt, he turned back to the other man. "Go away."

Viktor acknowledged him and stepped out.

Now alone in his quarters, Scott proceeded with his routine. Viktor and Nicolai were equally disquieting as company. He much preferred Auric and Egor. The German Auric was almost genuinely friendly, as much as a killer could be, and despite Egor's freakish appearance, his fellowship wasn't that bad. If not for his bald head, grotesquely wide eye sockets, long nose, and iron jaw, the man might have been charming.

The hours that followed were newly typical for Scott. His angst mingled with idleness, and he felt the desperate need for something to do. And so he sat. When he became restless he stood, and when standing became uncomfortable he sat again. Only so many times could he wash his face or stare at his desk or look in his closet. Only so many things could occupy his mind. When the battle with bitterness was lost—as it was every day—he lay down on his bed. Though he closed his eyes, he seldom found sleep. Not during the day. But that never stopped him from trying, even after three months.

Her picture remained facing the wall.

* * *

AT THE SAME TIME

THE HALLWAYS WERE vacant. As the fulcrum elite strode through the officers' wing, the only sound he heard came from his own footsteps. Sliding his hands into his pockets, he kept forward.

"Yuri..."

Dostoevsky stopped and turned, staring back down the hallway where the voice had addressed him. Nothing was there. He resumed his businesslike pace, his gaze focused on the ground.

"Yur-ri..."

For a second time, he froze. The voice was closer now—distinct. It was unlike any voice he'd ever heard. It groaned as if it was dead. Dostoevsky's piercing blue eyes again stared uncertainly down the hall. It was as empty as it had been moments before. His heart rate increased.

"Yuri!"

Then he saw them. He saw them move. The shadows themselves, seeming to recede and fold together. Voices emerged all around. Some giggled, some moaned, some cried out his name.

"Yuri! Yuri! Yuri!"

Something grabbed hold of his leg and he was swept off his feet. Then they attacked, teeming, swarming, grabbing him from every direction. He panicked and screamed wildly. He could feel them tearing into him, gnashing their teeth.

They were inside his skin.

Dostoevsky leapt out of bed and scrambled across the floor. He swatted the air all around him, hitting at himself and at invisible flies. He pitched backward until he hit the wall. Then he went still.

He was alone. His heart was pounding against his chest—but he was alone. Gasping for breath, he ran his hand through his hair. It was drenched. Sweat streamed down his face as if he'd stepped out of the shower. Then he looked at his clock. It was a quarter past nine. He'd been asleep.

Closing his eyes, he leaned his head back. He felt reality surface again. He heard no voices; all was silent.

The commander made no attempt to go back to bed. Sleep was the last thing he wanted to do.

2

SATURDAY, NOVEMBER 5TH, 0011 NE
1009 HOURS

DAVID CLOSED HIS eyes and inhaled a deep breath. The spray of hot water crashed against his face and neck as he slowly lowered his head.

Room 14 was occupied yet quiet. It was like that almost every day. It had been that way for three months.

The former NYPD officer turned the shower knob and shut off the water. For a moment he did nothing; he only stared at the tiled wall that formed the back of the curtained stall.

"Move it, Dave," said Becan. "Some o' us are bleedin' waitin' our turn."

David turned his head slightly but said nothing. The only sound that came from his stall was the rhythmic drip of water, barely audible over the full spray from the stall to his left, where the Texas sniper Jayden Timmons was taking his turn. David yanked his towel down from the shower bar.

Most of the other operatives had already bathed. Varvara and Esther were among the first—the women always were. Most of the men had, too. Becan, Boris, and Oleg were typically the last to wash up in the unspoken but often adhered to order of things.

As David wrapped the towel around himself and slid open the curtain, Becan's glare was the first thing he saw.

"It's yours," David said, moving past the Irishman into the room. There was no acknowledgment or thanks from Becan. He simply went into the stall.

That kind of awkward exchange had become normal. Tension was as real as the operatives themselves.

As David sat on his bunk and bent over to tie his boots, Varvara watched him from several bunks down. Only when he'd finished did she approach.

"David?"

He answered her with silence.

She stared with cautious brown eyes. "It ain't going to be as bad as you think," she said with an awkward Russian-Texan drawl.

From her own bunk, Esther looked up.

"You don't know what you've done," David said to Varvara without expression. "This one's on you." With those words, David walked off.

Varvara stood beside his bunk, staring blankly at the abandoned mattress. She looked up slowly, her attention settling briefly on the shower stall where the Texan was bathing. Not even that made her smile.

That was the extent of Room 14's conversation. There was no laughter or banter. Everyone carried out their morning rituals with a kind of grim, stilted seriousness. Every day was the same.

* * *

THE DOOR TO Confinement slid open and Scott stepped inside. Prior to his becoming a Nightman, he'd barely set foot in the Research Center at all. Now he showed up every week. He wasn't asked to, nor was it part of his obligations. But he had to; he had reasons no one else understood.

Gripped firmly in his hand was the blank manila folder—the same folder that sat on his desk. He took it to Confinement every time.

The scientists met him with half-hearted smiles. They were smiles laced with distrust—weakly veiled attempts to seem warm. He'd grown used to smiles like that. As a fulcrum, it was all he received.

"Good afternoon, Lieutenant Remington," said the chief scientist, a man by the name of Petrov. Scott had come to know him during his visits, which worked to his benefit. Petrov let him do whatever he wanted without asking why or interfering.

"Good afternoon, Petrov." Scott's voice was still gravelly and deep.

Petrov always tried to speak English. He was adept. "You are early today, lieutenant. You usually do not come until later."

"I wanted to come early." He glanced at the cells. Aliens were always coming and going. As soon as new prisoners arrived, space needed to be cleared. He knew older prisoners were either transferred or exterminated, but he'd never bothered to ask which it was. "I'm just looking around."

"Please, lieutenant, feel free."

Scott was free whether Petrov liked it or not. He didn't have to ask

Petrov's permission for anything. But with the scientist, Scott was never forcibly rude. He did have his flashes of coerciveness with the staff at times, but so far Petrov had never been a victim.

When Scott was in Confinement, his mind wasn't anywhere else. He was focused. He could think of real things, he could think of the big picture of Earth, he could deduce. It was a welcome escape. At least, that was one of his reasons.

As Scott walked past the cells, his mind filed through the basic questions. What made Earth so important? Were the purple-skinned Bakma and the reptilian Ceratopians working together? Were the Ithini "grays" the ones behind it all? The mystery of everything always bothered him, probably more than it bothered everyone else.

Though he understood little in the grand scheme of things, he'd learned a few things since starting his visits. The personalities of the Bakma were vastly different from those of the Ceratopians. The Bakma—the "purple monkeys"—were noticeably despondent. They bore looks of resigned defeat. That was part of their mystery. They were quick to surrender, but they weren't cowards. They had a reason to surrender, but what was it? To live a life of captivity and interrogation? Was that better than death?

The Ceratopians, on the other hand, were pure brutes. Scott felt a knot in his stomach every time he saw the giant, five-horned lizards. Khatanga was the last time his unit had been assigned a Ceratopian mission. Every mission since had been the Bakma. After a failure of Khatanga's magnitude, The Machine didn't trust the Fourteenth. That annoyed Scott to no end.

As he strode past the cells, he surveyed the inhabitants. His eyes stopped on a brown-furred, unspectacular canrassi. Occasionally orange-furred canrassis were captured. Those had an exotic look, made repulsive only by their pair of spider eyes. Black furs had become rare of late, but that was fine by him. Their viciousness was unparalleled.

His thoughts were interrupted by Petrov. "Will you speak to a prisoner today, lieutenant?"

Scott never actually "spoke" to any prisoners. His visits rarely exceeded staring contests, despite efforts to communicate. That was the disadvantage of not knowing alien languages. "I don't know. I don't guess the new ones talk English or Russian?"

Petrov chuckled. "I am afraid they are never here long enough to learn. And as soon as they learn enough, they are shipped away."

"Off to EDEN Command?"

"Not always. We send many to *Cairo*."

Surprised, Scott turned to the scientist. "Why *Cairo*?"

"*Cairo* is premier base for xenobiology. The good ones go there."

"Huh."

"I wish I could get transferred to *Cairo*."

"Better research?"

"No," Petrov answered. "Because Egypt is warm."

Scott's comm beeped. It wasn't a mission tone; that sound was distinct from any other. This was a communication prompt. Someone was trying to reach him.

As soon as Scott looked at the display, he saw the name of the caller. It was Clarke. Scott felt the knot in his stomach tighten again, but this time for an entirely different reason. It did that every time he spoke to the captain. He almost hated the man. Lifting the comm to his lips, he answered, "Remington."

"Please come to my office, lieutenant."

Scott sighed. "On my way."

Petrov stepped over to Scott's side. "You will be leaving us already?"

"I'm afraid so. Life never ends." It was an unintentionally cryptic statement. At times, he couldn't wait for life to end. But life woke him up every day.

"Then I will see you again soon."

"Yeah, you will." Scott offered the scientist a rare smile; he was one of the few men who received one. Scott left in silence, bidding no other scientists farewell.

Scott knew why the captain had commed him. Viktor had mentioned the arrival of a new medic. The captain didn't know Scott already knew.

He couldn't help but recall Viktor's comment: Viktor had wondered if Varvara would remain. There was an underlying legitimacy to Viktor's concern. Clarke had no use for Varvara at all. The captain used many adjectives to describe her, among them words like *lazy* and *immature*. Scott couldn't help but agree.

The fact that they were getting a new medic meant Clarke might have had enough. There was no reason for a unit as small as theirs to have three medics. In fact, their initial stock of three medics had been deceiving. Svetlana and Galina had been stalwarts, but Varvara had been placed as the EDEN equivalent of an intern, to be trained by the two veterans. But she had never been trained—or she had never assumed the responsibility of learning. Scott had a feeling the latter was true.

Within minutes, Scott stood at Clarke's door. It was not terribly far from his own, but it felt like enemy territory. He grudgingly knocked.

"Come in," Clarke answered immediately.

Scott pushed the door open and stepped inside to find the captain seated behind a stack of papers on his desk. Scott pitied the bureaucracy that must have come with captainship. Every time he saw Clarke's workspace, it was overrun with documentation. It must have driven the fastidious captain insane.

Clarke addressed Scott as soon as he entered. "I saw on the indicator that you were in Confinement. Would you be terribly distraught if I asked why?"

Scott clasped his hands behind his back. "Personal reasons."

"Personal reasons? What personal reasons do you have to be in Confinement?"

Scott refused to feel interrogated. He held the manila folder behind his back and maintained his erect posture. "You wanted to see me, sir?"

Clarke's authoritative stare lingered, as if he was determining whether to pursue his questioning. After a moment his curiosity died. "Tomorrow at 0700, we will be receiving an additional medic."

"I already know."

Clarke looked genuinely surprised. "Oh, really?"

"Yes sir."

"And how, might I ask, do you already know?"

Avoiding eye contact, Scott focused on the wall and said, "It was relayed to me by Delta Trooper Ryvkin."

"And how did *he* come to know?"

"Through Dostoevsky."

Clarke leaned back in his chair. "I see." Silence overtook the captain's quarters. A wooden clock ticking on the mantel was the loudest sound in the room. Finally, the captain went on. "And what else of my business are you aware of?"

"Nothing, sir."

"I see—once again."

Clarke was being coy with his words. It was a British trait—one that annoyed Scott irrationally. His focus remained on the wall.

Resuming his strict tone, Clarke said, "It shall be your task to meet our new medic in the hangar."

That caught Scott off-guard. He had never been surprised in the past when he'd been asked to meet new arrivals, but he was surprised to be asked now. Before, he'd been a soldier of EDEN. Now he was part of The Machine. "I don't think that's the best course of action—"

"I couldn't care less what you think."

Scott was perplexed. Never mind the fact that Clarke had been snide, what bothered him was Clarke's determination. Why would anyone unaffiliated with the Nightmen send a Nightman to pick someone up? "I assume someone else will be coming?"

"No, lieutenant. You'll do this alone."

"With all due respect, sir, I think someone else would be more suited—"

"This isn't a suggestion, lieutenant." Every time Clarke called Scott by his rank, it was laced more intently with gibe. "In military, we call this an *order*."

Scott hated Clarke's sarcasm. He wanted to punch him in the face. "As you wish, sir."

"Thank you, lieutenant. You're dismissed."

Scott turned to place his hand on the knob. Before turning it, he said, "Who am I looking for tomorrow?"

"Svetlana Voronova."

With that revelation, Scott froze. His eyes opened wide. He turned back around. *"What?"*

"Her name is Svetlana Voronova."

Scott's fingers relinquished their grip. He took several steps back into the room. "You mean Svetlana Voronova, as in…?"

"Yes, lieutenant."

"The same medic we used to have here?"

Clarke shot him a cold look. "Have you gone stupid? Is there another Svetlana you know?"

Scott's heart rate increased. "I don't understand—"

"Svetlana is returning to the Fourteenth," Clarke said, cutting him off. "She is returning to active duty as chief medic, based on her past experience. Tomorrow, at 0700, you will pick her up and reintroduce her to Room 14. Being as the rest of us will be at morning session, I entrust her to you. Do you fail to understand these simple instructions?"

Of course he failed to understand. How could Svetlana be returning? *Why* was she returning? She'd left the unit; she'd left *Novosibirsk*. And now, she was suddenly back? Scott opened his mouth, but nothing came out.

"As you wish, then," Clarke said, grabbing his comm. "Axen will pick her up instead."

"No!" Scott's urgency shocked even himself. "I apologize. I'll pick her up."

Clarke set down the comm. "Very well. That's 0700 tomorrow. Please don't forget. You're dismissed."

This time, there was no further questioning. Scott turned and left the room.

The trek to his quarters felt surreal. With only one thought on his mind, he barely noticed the hallways around him. Clarke's words resounded in his head.

Svetlana is returning to the Fourteenth.

He remembered the last time he'd seen her. He remembered the look on her face. She'd been standing in the civilian airbus, ready to depart from The Machine, ready to leave the men and women of the Fourteenth.

He stopped as he came to a door. His mind returned to the present, and he looked at its front panel. It wasn't his door, however. It was a door he'd never seen before. Yet he was in the right hall, in the officers' wing. When he stared at the walls of the corridor, the realization struck him. He'd walked too far. He'd walked right past his own room some time ago and never even noticed.

He quietly backtracked to his quarters. It was in the same place he'd left it. He ventured inside, deciding to leave the lights off. He didn't want brightness, he wanted it dim. He shut the door.

Nicole's picture was still facing the wall. Reaching for it, he turned it around. Her face shone beneath the glow of his lamp. That brown-haired, blue-eyed girl. The love of his life. Beneath her face, beneath her snowy white smile, were the same words he read every night.

I love you!
~Nicole

He felt the pain in his heart hold him tighter. It hadn't hurt like this in some time. He took the picture and lay it face-up on his lap.

Why was he unsettled about Svetlana's return? How could any other woman matter? Svetlana was a friend; she was a teammate. She wasn't Nicole.

He could picture Nicole in his mind. He could smell her skin, taste her lips. He imagined her touch and it tingled over his arms. His eyes closed, but not from fatigue. They closed so her ghost could return.

Scott grinned and glanced at his outfit. Its color was darkened with sweat. She probably wouldn't even touch it. "Do I get a kiss goodbye?"

Her lips curved. "Sure." She leaned into him, propped her hands against his arms, and pressed her lips against his. Scott smiled as the gentleness lingered. He was surprised she touched him at all. When she pulled away, her eyes sparkled. "Do you love me?"

"I'll always love you."

She smiled. For a moment, she said nothing; she simply stared in his eyes. When she finally spoke again, her voice was sweeter than ever. "I'll always love you, too."

"I'll see you in a bit."

"I'll be there."

Then she was gone.

When Scott opened his eyes, he was crying. He felt droplets of tears falling on his hands.

"Why did you go?" His words were barely audible, but spoken as if she were right there. He abandoned the frame and covered his face. It was the first time he'd broken in weeks.

Tomorrow Svetlana would return. And it meant nothing. It meant she was following her own path. Her path was bringing her back there, to the coldness of the place that she'd left—to the bowels of sin. Whatever redemption she hoped she would find, she would have to find it alone.

It wasn't evening, but it didn't matter. Scott laid his head on his pillow, closing his eyes to the rest of the world. He fell quietly to sleep.

Nicole's picture stayed on his chest.

EDEN High Command

Pauling, Carl	President
Kang, Gao Jing	Intelligence Director
Blake, Malcolm	Judge
Rath, Jason	Judge
Lena, Richard	Judge
Torokin, Leonid	Judge
Grinkov, Dmitri	Judge
Castellnou, Javier	Judge
June, Carol	Judge
Iwayama, Mamoru	Judge
Shintaku, Tamiko	Judge
Onwuka, Uzochi	Judge
Yu, Jun Dao	Judge
Archer, Benjamin	Judge

3

SATURDAY, NOVEMBER 5TH, 0011 NE
2100 HOURS

EDEN COMMAND

"AND WITH THAT, our week comes to an outstanding end. You are now *free* men and women!" As President Pauling stepped from the podium, the audience rose with applause. The auditorium lights brightened.

It was the end of a roller-coaster week. Every year, during the opening days of November, the Global EDEN Conference—the GEC—was held. It was always at EDEN Command. Dignitaries from around the globe were invited to attend, along with every top official within the organization. The chance to take a blind flight into the most important facility on the planet was a once-in-a-lifetime opportunity. Even if it came every year.

This year's GEC was especially intriguing. Announcements deluged the conference, from the fast-approaching opening of *Sydney* to the promise of an arsenal upgrade. It was revealed that the Advanced Defensive Fighter—the Vindicator—would finally be replaced with something new: the ADF-2 Superwolf. The craft would be the first to be reverse-engineered from alien technology, straight from the Bakmanese Courier fighter. It would revolutionize air superiority.

Not even Judge Torokin was bored at the event. The week had been enjoyable for the Russian judge. Such weeks were few and far between. Here, he got to meet diplomats from the world over—people who actually mattered. He shook hands with the president of Russia and shared drinks with the emperor of Japan. More importantly, he shook hands with men. Real men, as he perceived them. EDEN veterans whose bodies were scarred, and generals who'd actually fought.

General Bastiaan Platis was among them. Platis knew Torokin well. Though the two had never fought side by side, they had reason to call each other friends. Vector Squad, Torokin's former unit, was garrisoned at *Berlin*, and Platis was their regional general.

Regional generals differed from base generals. The former monitored areas of the globe instead of the operation of an actual facility. Platis's area was in eastern Europe. Though not directly connected with *Berlin*, he'd coordinated Vector Squad many times. For that, he'd earned Torokin's trust.

General Platis was a purist. He was a Greek historian through and through. He was larger than Torokin, but by no means a brute. His hair neatly rounded his head, showing a slight trace of receding. His salt-and-pepper beard matched it well.

Platis was one of the few generals who had his own platoon: the Agèma. Though not as renowned as Vector Squad, it was still a force to be reckoned with. They were an unusually designed group. Every soldier in its ranks was a Greek.

As the general approached him, Torokin said, "I suppose this is goodbye."

Platis shook the Russian's hand. "I suppose it is." English was the only common language the two men shared. "Was today what you spoke of when you talked about politics?"

The ex-Vector laughed. "Yes, it was. Today was not so bad. But usually, this kind of talk puts me to sleep." The last day had been all about Archer. Aside from formally introducing himself, he'd announced to the world his new proposal—his amendment to EDEN protocol regarding interceptions.

"I do not understand how you survive it," Platis said. "There was so much bureaucracy today."

"It can be frustrating, I assure you. Sometimes I want to kill everyone."

"Where is Judge Grinkov?"

Torokin looked through the auditorium's crowd. "I did not see him this evening." He was sure Grinkov was there somewhere. He turned to Platis again. "If you find the vodka, you will probably find him." He turned back to Platis. "What do you think of our new judge?"

The general hesitated. "He speaks very well. He is interesting, but his new policy concerns me."

"How so?"

"It seems an unnecessary change. We are to ask him for permission before we intercept alien spacecraft? It does not make sense."

Torokin looked at the crowd once again. He'd never spot Archer in that throng. But it didn't matter. "The original plan was only for ground intercepts. But it grew to involve combat in the air. I can tell you the real reason for it."

"What is that?"

Torokin wasn't worried about revealing secrets to Platis. The Greek's lifestyle revolved around honor. Nothing would be repeated. "You will not have to worry about this amendment. It was not designed for you. It was designed for *Novosibirsk*."

"For *Novosibirsk*?" Platis was surprised.

"We have reason to believe General Thoor works against us. It is part of…the process of resolution. It is somewhat difficult to explain."

"It took you *this* long to realize Thoor works against you? What is it you do here again?"

"It did not take them this long to realize it," the judge said. "It took them this long to decide what to do about it."

"Is that why General Thoor did not come?"

"I do not know. He has not made one conference yet. I honestly think he does not care."

"So this new policy will not affect me at all?" asked Platis.

"It should not. Your requests should automatically pass. Unless Archer has reason to change them. I do not think he will."

"So you listen to speeches and pass meaningless regulations. Is this all you do?"

"I told you already, sometimes this job makes me want to kill everyone. I was serious." After a shared smile, Torokin went on. "You leave tonight, I assume?"

"Yes." Platis glanced about the room. "This has been enough fun for one week. My flight leaves in four hours, so I must pack."

"Do not forget to look out the window."

The general laughed out loud. "Yes, I must remember that! I did ask for a window seat."

It was a whimsical request. EDEN Command took security measures to the extreme. There were no windows on the transports at all, and rumor had it they randomly altered their courses during flights. Nobody knew where they were going or how long it really took to get there.

"How bad will it be for you, if you find out that you have been living on a beach all these years?" Platis asked.

"I believe that would be too much. That would be a most ironic day. No.

We had better be in the middle of Antarctica, or I will be very upset." Their location was a constant source of speculation. It was the most entertaining conspiracy theory they had. Only Kang—the director of Intelligence—and the pilots who flew the aircraft knew where they were. Not even President Pauling knew. Torokin's hypothesis was that they were in the middle of an ocean. But there was no way anyone could be sure.

Platis sighed. "I must make my leave. I have things to pack. I must bring a souvenir for my wife."

"Do you bring one every year?"

"No, but she fusses me every year to do it."

"Ask the president for his pen. That will make good souvenir."

Platis's eyes brightened. "That is a good idea. That is a *very* good idea, thank you!"

"Tell her it is the most important pen in the world."

"Yes, I will do so. It will be good to see my wife again. I have not spoken to her since I was here."

That was another part of EDEN Command's secrecy. No calls were allowed in or out—not without approval from Kang. With calls, judges could compare time zones with home, whether accidentally or by husband-wife code.

Platis hesitated before turning away. "Before I go, I meant to ask you... have you spoken to Kenner recently? How is he?"

Torokin's face turned sour. "He is as he has always been. I do not miss him."

"The hammer falls heavy on heroes. I, for one, did not blame him."

Torokin bowed his head cordially, then extended his hand. "It is always a pleasure, general."

Platis accepted it. "The pleasure is mine."

With a final nod, the two men parted ways.

General Platis's earlier words to Torokin were true. It was indeed no surprise that Thoor was against them. EDEN had been blind to it by choice. But now that was going to change, for better or worse.

The long-discussed plan had already been set into motion, as overseen by Judge Archer. Black ops personnel were already in place. They'd filtered into *Novosibirsk* through the guise of base transfers and Academy graduates. Torokin heard there were a dozen agents, but only Kang knew who they were.

That was the covert part of Command's espionage efforts. The open part was about to begin. Soon Judges Malcolm Blake and Carol June would visit the renegade Russian facility. They would arrive unannounced; it was meant to catch Thoor unaware. That was for the census—the headcount of who in *Novosibirsk* was EDEN and who was Nightman.

The financial audit had begun long ago, courtesy of Judges Rath and Onwuka. In a matter of days, they'd know where Thoor got his goods. Everyone was getting involved.

Torokin had to hand it to Archer. He had indeed brought the judges together. It had taken recognizing the enemy among EDEN's own to do it.

Little else happened that evening. Torokin found Grinkov chatting with Judge Richard Lena, and the three men retired shortly after. There was no vodka or card game of preferans for them that night—after a long week, rest was deserved. Annual conferences had a way of draining everyone, especially the most important men there. All three of the judges had shaken hands with presidents and prime ministers, and bowed their heads graciously each time. But they knew the truth: *they* were the celebrities to be met. No social camouflage could mask it. They were the judges—the figureheads of Earth. The heroes who defended the human species.

Heroes that desperately needed to sleep.

* * *

LATER THAT NIGHT

ARCHER PASSED THROUGH the security checkpoint into Confinement, and the guards at post offered salutes. He returned the formalities. "Good evening, gentlemen. I trust you're well?"

"Yes sir," answered one of the English-speaking guards. "Are you here to see a prisoner?"

Archer winked amiably. "Interrogations never cease." Stepping past them, he ventured into Confinement, where a scientist met him.

"Good evening, Judge Archer. Something I can help you with?"

"No, thank you. I'll be conducting my own interrogation tonight."

"Very well, sir. We've had moderate success with IC-17 lately, at least in getting him to finally warm up. ICs 19 and 22 are still giving us problems. I assume you won't talk to an IB?"

"Actually, I'll be speaking to one of our Bakma guests."

The scientist looked surprised. For a moment, he didn't answer. "As you wish, but I must warn you. They've been nothing but headaches. Outside of hearing things we already know, we haven't progressed."

Archer's response was cordial. "Then there's a first time for everything."

"Very well, sir. I'll wake up our translator."

"There's no need," Archer said, resuming his walk. "I'll handle translations myself, alone and off record."

"Yourself, sir?"

"*Gaas*," he said without looking back. "That's Bakmanese for yes."

As the door to the Bakma's cell slid open, the alien flinched from its sleep. The interior lights abruptly cut on.

The prisoner was frail for a Bakma, but not for a captive. The moment prisoners were placed in their cells, the luxury of physical activity was removed, causing a dramatic loss of muscle. Few prisoners fought to object—it served little purpose without hope of escape.

"Hello, Nharassel," Archer said in English, stepping inside. He read the documentation in his hand. "According to this, you are a 'well-informed supervisor,' captured seven months ago in South America."

The scientist watched from outside the cell. Archer turned to him. "I'd like total privacy, please. Unguarded."

"Unguarded, Judge Archer? Are you sure?"

"What's he going to do, bump me to death? In seven months, he's lost muscles he never even knew he had. I believe I can manage."

The scientist stepped away from the entrance. Moments later, the cell door was closed.

Archer's focus returned to the alien. "Seven months ago. That's quite some time, isn't it? You've probably forgotten what it's like to breathe natural air."

The Bakma stared in a lack of understanding.

"But what's truly amazing is that in seven months, you've given us nothing. *Nothing.*" Archer was more fascinated than upset. "I find that absolutely astounding. Don't you?"

He continued. "According to this, we've tried taking away your dignity, only to learn that you had none to lose. We've tried depriving you of substance, only to discover that it's what you're accustomed to." He leaned closer. "We've even tried torture. Sensory deprivation, mock executions, public humiliation. Incessant ringing in your ears. And you've given us nothing. Now, isn't that absolutely mysterious?"

He placed his documentation down. “Everyone thinks you’re loyal to your cause. They have no idea who you are.”

Suddenly, Archer’s language changed. It was no longer English—or human. Archer spoke full Bakmanese. “They don’t understand that you’re waiting for the Khuladi.”

The Bakma’s pupils dilated with awareness.

“I am your friend, Nharassel,” Archer went on. “I am your friend, but not because I speak your tongue. I am your friend, because I know the truth.”

The alien rose.

“You want to be rescued. You think that means freedom, but you’re wrong. I can make you truly free. I can give you freedom you’ve never known. I can give you *life*. You will be taken away by the Golathoch. They will hail you as a hero of the galaxy. All you need to do is tell me one thing.”

For the first time, Nharassel spoke. His alien language was distinct and clear. “Who are the Golathoch to you?”

“They are our means to survive—you and me both,” Archer answered. “But like myself, there are things even they do not know.”

“What covenant does your species have with them?”

“My species has no covenant.” He took a step closer. “But I do.”

For several seconds, Nharassel was silent. Then his eyes shrunk to slits. “You corrupt your own blood.”

“I preserve it.”

The Bakma fell quiet. The arches on its forehead furrowed and it drew in a long, rasping breath. “How do I know you can be trusted?”

“I gain no advantage from deception,” Archer answered. “The truth is, you have two choices. You find freedom as a hero of the galaxy, or you die as a prisoner of war, loyal to a cause that you hate. The choice to assist is yours alone. If you decline, I will walk into the cell next to yours and offer the next Bakma the very same thing. And when *he* accepts, he will taste a freedom you cannot comprehend.”

The Bakma looked tempted. He studied Archer with a contemplative gaze. When temptation won, the deal was in place. “What information do you require?”

There was no hesitation. There was no moment of triumph, nor offer of a genuine smile. Judge Archer asked the question immediately.

“How much time do we have?”

The scientist met Archer as soon as the judge left the cell. "Did you have any success?"

Archer shook his head. "No, unfortunately. He was fully uncooperative, as indicated beforehand. I should have listened to you."

"My apologies, judge."

"It's not your fault," Archer said. "You warned me. We'll keep him around for a bit longer, to satisfy my own bullheadedness. I'd like him transferred to a low-end holding cell. He's taking up space here we can use."

"Yes sir."

"Keep up the good work." Without another word, Archer strode past the guards, straight out of the security checkpoints. There was no need to linger. He'd heard what he'd gone there to hear.

4

SUNDAY, NOVEMBER 6TH, 0011 NE
0455 HOURS

NOVOSIBIRSK, RUSSIA

SCOTT SCARCELY SLEPT through the night. He couldn't remember what time he'd gone to bed, but he remembered every hour since. It was 0102 when he'd rolled over and first stared at his clock. It was 0128 when he rose to wash his face. He got a drink at 0244, and rolled over on his stomach at a quarter past three. When the clock read 0450, he completely gave up.

As he left his bed, he searched for some kind of distraction. He fiddled through his desk drawers. He rewashed his coffee mug. He looked for any type of diversion at all—for any excuse *not* to think about why he couldn't sleep. But every task ended with a name. Svetlana Voronova.

Even after deciding she didn't matter, her image forced itself into his mind. What was she thinking? Why was she coming back?

He grabbed his toothbrush and turned on the tap. After rinsing the bristles, he applied toothpaste and furiously brushed. All the while, he stared into the mirror.

She wouldn't even recognize him. Not because of the grizzled stubble he bore, nor because he'd become more toned since becoming a fulcrum. She wouldn't recognize the look in his eyes. The last time she saw him, he'd been a decent man.

Did she even know what he was? Did she know what he'd become? How was he supposed to greet her? He recalled the last words she'd spoken. *Don't let them change you.* He knew he'd failed. He'd become what she'd warned him against: another soul lost to The Machine.

It was 0506 when he finished brushing and washing. It felt as if two hours had passed. It was barely ten minutes. "This is crazy."

He knew how he had to act. Like a professional. Like a commanding officer. Like the man assigned to bring her inside. That was the only option he had.

By 0515, he had already donned his black jumpsuit; the crimson triangle shone over his heart. He fought with his hair to little avail. Moments later, he stepped out the door.

The hallways were always cold, regardless of the heating vents in the walls. They never seemed to warm well enough. For the first time in a while, the chill bothered him.

Why would anyone come back to this place?

For the life of him, he couldn't find an answer. He knew why *he* couldn't leave. This place had created him. As cold and as miserable as it was, it was his own. Where else could he go? Back home? He rarely spoke to his brother anymore. Who would he see? Who would want to see him?

That was the difference between Svetlana and him. She had escaped. She had a home to return to. She had people who loved her. For her to return to *Novosibirsk* made no sense.

Outside it was dark and the ground was covered in the night's snowfall. Even on the sidewalks, a crunch followed each of his steps.

He wasn't sure what to do with his time until 0615, when the Fourteenth would abandon their room for their morning workout. It was still an hour away. He wouldn't go to Room 14 until they were gone. He didn't want to see them, and he was sure they didn't want to see him either.

The frigidity bit at his teeth. He'd grown used to chapped lips and dry skin; it didn't bother him as much as it used to. But the initial bite was always hard.

His early departure from his room afforded him time to grab breakfast. At least it was something to do. The cafeteria was still empty when he walked in. The morning crowd usually came at six o'clock. That was about when the Fourteenth would arrive, too. He would stay in the cafeteria until 0600, then he'd work his way around the back of the barracks. He could avoid passing them in the hallways that way. He could slip into Room 14 from behind. Once he was there, he could wait until 0650. He'd be at the hangar for seven o'clock.

He sat down at an empty table and began to eat. He wondered if Clarke had set him up. He wondered how long the captain had known Svetlana was coming back. He wondered if the unit knew, too. Dostoevsky had known. The Nightmen knew. Or at least, they knew a medic was coming. He wasn't sure if they knew it was her. But that didn't matter—Dostoevsky was the only Nightman who knew who she was anyway.

Why send me to meet her? Then again, meeting Svetlana was partially Scott's own doing. The captain had reached for his comm to call Max, and Scott stopped him. *What was I thinking?* Max should have been the one to fetch her. Scott should have let Clarke make the call. He couldn't blame anyone but himself.

It took only ten minutes to eat. The rest of his time was spent waiting and watching the clock. He was out by 0555.

When the morning rush came and the operatives filed into the cafeteria, the hallways were left clear in their wake. The thought crossed Scott's mind several times that he could have simply waited in his own quarters. But he wanted to see Room 14. He wanted to partake in its silence. He wanted the decent memories it would evoke.

Arriving at the room, he pushed the door open and entered. The familiar smell hit his nose—the odor of habitation. Food left out in the lounge, and laundry piled beneath bunks. It smelled like a dorm. He missed it more than anything.

Walking through the room, he was surrounded by miscellaneous symbols of the Fourteenth. The chess board. Travis's comic books. Jayden's cowboy hat. Only two mattresses were made, both on the same bunk. Varvara's and Esther's.

As he sat on the mattress that used to be his, he ran his hand along its plastic coating. It had been one of the most uncomfortable mattresses he'd ever slept on. This particular morning it didn't feel quite so bad.

The bunks belonging to the Nightmen were in the corner. They slept as far apart from the rest of the unit as they could. Mingling was not a part of their lives.

Scott sat on his bunk for half an hour, just listening to the silence, looking around, and remembering how camaraderie used to feel. He was unaccustomed to the room being silent.

Six-fifty came. It was time to meet her.

He fought the urge to remain sitting. She could find the room by herself; she didn't need a map. He could stay right there, and it wouldn't matter at all. He could let her come to him.

He rose from his old bed. He'd told Clarke he would meet her. What other choice did he have? Giving Room 14 a final look, he set out into the halls.

It was still dark outside, as he knew it would be. It was 0659. She was probably in sight, at least in the sky. He looked upward. Even if her transport was approaching, it was too overcast to make anything out.

When he arrived at the hangar, it was 0702. He was technically two minutes late, but he knew it wouldn't matter. It would take the transport that long to settle down.

Technicians bustled about the hangar as Scott walked past. He cast his eyes to the strip. There were numerous transports arriving, some civilian, others not. Some were already perched on the ground. There was a chance she had already emerged and was waiting amid the throng of people. He might have to actively search.

I should have asked Clarke which transport she was in. I should have been here ten minutes ago, too.

She was somewhere, mixed in with the unexpected frenetic activity of the morning. He sighed, causing vapors to drift from his mouth. He looked at his watch. 0706. Where could she be? He pushed past a pair of technicians and hurried across the hangar.

The heightened activity level didn't make sense. Why were so many people about? Was it always this packed before sunrise? As a mechanic made his way past him, Scott grabbed him by the arm. "Comrade," Scott said in Russian. "I'm looking for a woman. Blond hair, blue eyes. She came in from a transport at 0700."

At first the mechanic laughed, and then he saw the fulcrum's uniform and the crimson triangle attached to it. The mechanic's expression quickly changed. "Yes, comrade. I will help you, right away."

It was 0709. As Scott followed the worker across the hangar, his heart began to beat faster.

"We will get a flight log," the mechanic said. "I am sure it will have her name."

"Why is it so busy here?"

"There is much to do today. We are working with inspectors from Moscow."

"For what?"

"They are doing an inventory check on everything here. The order came from EDEN Command."

It figured. Of all the days for an inventory inspection, it had to be today. He looked at his watch again. 0710. She was lost in the crowd.

The mechanic grabbed a flight log from the wall. "What is her name?"

"Svetlana Voronova."

"Where is she coming from?"

His mind went blank. He had no idea. "I don't know. Not from Moscow." At least, he didn't think so. He didn't remember her being from there. Precious seconds passed.

"Here," the mechanic said, pointing. "Svetlana Voronova. Yes, she should have already arrived."

"I know. I know that. On which transport?"

The mechanic pointed to the other side of the hangar. "That one, on the very far end. It was a civilian flight from Vilnius."

"Thank you very much."

"You are welcomed!" the mechanic called out as Scott raced away. "I will help anytime!"

Scott shoved his way back through the crowd, chastising himself under his breath. *This should have been such an easy thing to do. How could I possibly screw it up?* Had he left Room 14 ten minutes earlier, he'd have been there on time. He was furious with himself.

The civilian transport from Vilnius was waiting as described, but there was no blond-haired woman to be found. It was almost a quarter past seven. She was gone.

Scott hurriedly sought out the pilot. "Excuse me!" The man turned his way. "I'm looking for a blond-haired woman, Svetlana Voronova. Is she here?"

The pilot shook his head. "I do not know. I only fly back and forth. Who I fly back and forth is not my business."

"Do you know where she could be?"

"No."

Scott turned back around, muttering. "Veck." *She's headed to Room 14. She must be.* He strode away from the transport to the hangar's side door. If she wasn't in Room 14 by now, she was probably on her way. Maybe he could catch her. He quickened his pace and left the hangar behind.

If it wasn't so dark, I'd have found her by now. He knew it wasn't true, but his pride was desperate for an excuse. He hadn't found her because he hadn't been there on time.

His footsteps quickened into almost a run. She probably had two full duffle bags. She was probably lugging them by herself.

He tore open the door to the barracks and hastened in. He scanned ahead to Room 14. She was inside unpacking, he knew it. As he neared the room, he saw the door was closed. It didn't surprise him—she would want privacy. But he had to touch base. He swung the door open and hurried in.

No one was there.

Stepping into the center of the room, Scott's shoulders finally sagged. He had no idea where she was. He'd blown a simple assignment for no good reason at all. Squatting down to his knees, he covered his face with his hands. He felt like a fool.

"You Americans have strange customs."

The voice came from the still-open doorway. Scott jumped and turned back around.

She stood alone in the hallway. Her golden-blond hair fell to her chin line, with thick strands caressing the sides of her face. But his focus went straight to her eyes. Straight to those unforgettable, ocean-blue eyes.

"You run into the hangar, you run in circles, then you run away. Now here are you, sitting on the floor." She smiled. "Strange customs, indeed."

"Sveta…" he said ashamedly. She must have been watching him the entire while. "I couldn't find you."

She laughed and stepped into the room, pulling her duffle bag behind her. She only had one. "I know. I watched you as you walked out of the hangar. I was going to shout for you, but you were already gone. You looked very serious."

He laughed out loud—a real guffaw—for the first time in months. It almost felt clumsy. "I thought I lost you."

"You did not," she said, her eyes sparkling.

She looked just as she had in the lounge on the first night they'd met; she smiled in just the same way. Her teeth gleamed beneath her dainty nose. She walked to him, and he met her halfway and opened his arms. She accepted his embrace.

"Hello again, Scott Remington," she whispered.

"Hello, Svetlana Voronova." He remembered the last time he'd hugged her—because she was leaving. Because he'd never see her again.

At that moment, with a start he realized she hadn't met him with a negative stare. Not one word about the black uniform he wore or the emblem over his heart. Not even an utterance of surprise.

She had to have known everything beforehand. Had she not, his new uniform would have shocked her. But she showed no surprise—she wasn't even somber. She was warm. "Sveta..." His tone paved the way for his guilt.

She shook her head and placed it on his shoulder. "No. You don't have to say it. It's okay," she said, squeezing him tightly.

He closed his eyes. *It's okay.* Those were words he hadn't heard in so long.

Her hands slid from his shoulders, and she leaned back to stare at his face. "What is this?" she asked, grinning and feeling his stubble. "Is this new look for you? You are trying to look rebellious?"

He laughed with embarrassment and looked away. "It's comfortable. I guess." It wasn't comfortable at all—it itched—but he had no explanation outside of sheer apathy. He turned again to face her. "What about you?" He brushed a fringe of her hair that hung over one of her eyes. "This is new."

She tried not to blush. "I cut it shorter. But not too short." She shrugged her shoulders. "I thought it looked okay."

It looked more than okay. It looked gorgeous. "You look fabulous."

Her blush won out. "Only so much..."

Scott wasn't sure what else to say. There were questions all over his mind. But for the moment, they surrendered to the comfort of having a friend.

She sighed and took a step back. She scrutinized the room. "Have they ever picked up in here? This looks like same mess when I left." She pointed at the piles on the floor. "It is time to make rules about clean." She bent down to start picking up clothes.

Scott chuckled. Her English wasn't quite up to par, undoubtedly from her time spent away. "Maybe so." He wouldn't correct her vocabulary. She was smart, she'd catch up again. He thought about switching his own words to Russian, but decided against it. "You don't have to pick up everyone's clothes."

"No, I must. I will be living here. I cannot live in mess."

The irony in her words didn't escape him. If she didn't want to live in a mess, why had she come back? The Fourteenth was more than a mess, it was a disaster.

His thoughts returned to the circumstances of her arrival. She somehow knew about him and what he had become. She was prepared to see him as a Nightman. And if she knew he was a Nightman, she must have known why. She knew he was a murderer.

She placed a pile of clothes on one of the beds. "I will make sure to give them clean room code. This is too much to live in."

"I want to talk to you. I *need* to talk to you."

The urgency in his voice captured her attention, and she studied him with her intense eyes. "As you wish. Let us talk."

There was no need to beat around the bush. "Why are you here?"

"Can I not come back? Is that not my choice?"

"There's more to it than that."

"Oh, really. There is?"

"Yeah, there is." One of the last things she'd told him was not to let *Novosibirsk* change him. That was exactly what *Novosibirsk* had done. "I'm a Nightman, and you're not even surprised. How did you know?"

She looked away. "Can I not just be here? Can I not just come back to the war? Why must I—"

"Tell me the truth, Sveta. You owe me that much." She did. He'd saved her life in Siberia at the outpost, and in doing so had risked his own. He'd leapt for her. The truth? He deserved at least that.

Her expression fell solemn, and she brushed at a strand of her hair. When she finally sighed and looked up, her invulnerability had collapsed. "Because three months ago, I received a letter. I received a letter in Vilnius, where I lived with my mother. It was from Varya."

Scott felt his face when it flushed as betrayal burst in his heart. Varvara—she'd gone behind his back to do this. It was all staged.

Svetlana caught him as he tried to look away. "Look at me, Scott. Don't turn away." When he turned back, she went on. "She told me what happened. She told me about you, and about Galina."

"She had no right."

"She had every right. This is her unit. She was medic here. She did what she believed was the best."

"She dragged you back here—for me. I could kill her."

She pointed her finger firmly. "*No.* I don't care if you are not serious, you do not *ever* say that."

He could have killed Varvara right there. "This wasn't her business. This wasn't her call. To guilt you back here is disgusting."

Svetlana grew fiercely defensive. "Varya did not 'guilt' me to come back here. I am adult. I chose to come back here myself."

"So she didn't have anything to do with your coming back? Her letter didn't affect your decision?"

"Of *course* it affected my decision! To know that my friends are living in nightmare, yes, it affected my decision. Scott, what do you want to hear?"

"I want to hear that you didn't come back here for me."

Her mouth hung open, but nothing came out.

"You've got to be kidding me," he said.

She raised her hands in defense. "If you let me explain—"

"You came here for me? Are you serious? Of all the millions of legitimate reasons, you came here for *me*?"

Her shoulders sunk. "Scott, please. I did not come here to fight, okay? I just want—"

"What?" he asked viciously. "What do you want?"

She was silent. Her blue eyes settled nervously on his. When she finally answered, her once-confident voice turned to pleading. "You are my friend, Scott! To know what happened, and what you did for me, how can I do nothing? I know what you are going through—"

"*You don't have a clue what I'm going through!*" His outburst caused her to recoil. "You can't even *begin* to imagine! *Veck*, Svetlana, did you even stop to think?"

"Scott..."

"I don't want to hear it." The anger in his voice reached new heights. "This place damns everything it touches. I don't know what you thought you'd find here, but I promise you it's not what you left."

"Scott, please. I am trying to be calm..."

"I don't want you to be calm. I want you to take the next flight back home."

"Scott, why did this turn so different?" she cried aloud. "Five minutes ago, we were fine! Everything was fine! Why now must it be so different?"

Scott couldn't believe her lack of rationale. She wasn't there for the war. That alone made all the difference in the world. Without answering, he turned to walk out.

"Scott, please, wait!" She grabbed him before he could go. "Varya didn't mean it this way, please do not be mad with her. Blame me. Blame me for leaving here in the first place!"

Blame Svetlana for leaving in the first place? He could never do that. "You had every reason to leave. You had every reason to stay away."

She didn't reply. As her face fell, he turned and stalked out the room.

Scott went directly back to his quarters. Not once did he stop along the way.

5

SUNDAY, NOVEMBER 6TH, 0011 NE
0925 HOURS

TWO HOURS HAD passed since Scott had abandoned Svetlana in Room 14. The process of unpacking took longer than it might have otherwise, as the burden of sunken spirits weighed on her. Every motion of folding or hanging clothes took every ounce of effort she could muster. When she finally finished, she was too exhausted even to have a shower that might have soothed her. And she was too distraught to relax.

The letter—Varvara's letter—lay on the tile floor beneath her. She'd reread it several times from her bunk, before her fingers relinquished their hold.

She was still on her bed when she heard a trample of footsteps from the hall. As she strained to turn her head, the door swung open.

"That's bull, man," said a shirtless Jayden. He threw his towel to the floor. "If you're gonna drive a girl three hours to see some dumb movie, you better get a kiss when it's done."

"Tha's wha' I said," Becan followed in behind him. "But the problem was, tha's exactly how I said it."

The moment they saw Svetlana, their eyes lit up.

"Sveta!" the Irishman blurted, running full speed across the room. He wrapped his arms around her as soon as she stood. He almost bowled her over. "Sveta, yeh really came back!"

Svetlana laughed as she fought to stay upright. "Becan! You are sweaty—stop!" She pushed him away.

"Svetlana's here! Svetlana's here!" he sang.

"Becan, *stop.* That is good enough."

"Yeh don't understand, Sveta," the Irishman said. "You're the reason we're in a good mood for the first time in months."

"Welcome back, ma'am," Jayden said as he approached. Behind them, several others trickled in.

Svetlana touched the Texan's arm. "Please do not call me ma'am. You are same rank as me now."

"Oh. Well, you're probably still older than me."

"Wrong answer," Becan said, coughing indiscreetly.

"Hey, Sveta!" said Travis as he approached her. "It's good to see you back. How was the flight?"

Svetlana turned her attention to the pilot. "Hello, Travis. I knew you would ask about flight. It was a good experience."

Several steps behind the pilot was Max Axen. His own towel was slung over his sweat-drenched shoulder and an awkward smile quivered on his lips. He waited as Travis and Svetlana conversed until a brief pause occurred. "Hey Sveta—"

"Sveta!" Varvara exclaimed, pushing past Max to make her own greeting. "It is so good to see you!" She examined her own sweaty outfit then looked up again. "I want to hug you—is it okay?"

Svetlana gave her a hug. "Becan already got me gross. What more could it hurt?"

As the women embraced, Max backed away.

"I'm so glad to have you back," Varvara said, continuing their Russian exchange. "You have no idea what it's been like here."

"I have a feeling I do."

Across the room, away from the conversation but not oblivious, Esther Brooking watched Svetlana greet her cronies. The black British scout pulled her hair into a ponytail as she continued to observe. Behind her, David placed dirty clothes in his locker.

"Did she really come back for the lieutenant?" Esther asked without turning around.

David looked across the room at Svetlana. He watched the blond woman with expressionless eyes. After a moment, he answered Esther back. "Yeah." His voice was tired as he returned his attention to his clothes. "That's why she came back."

Esther said nothing in reply. She simply watched Svetlana in silence, her eyes narrowing as if summing up a competitor—and being left unimpressed. She resumed her own work.

The others continued to fawn over Svetlana. "Look at you!" Varvara exclaimed. "You look beautiful! I love your hair."

Svetlana brushed aside the compliment. "Thank you. I wanted a new beginning, to start fresh."

Becan cleared his throat and looked around. "Is it me, or is somebody missin' from this scene?"

Varvara too scanned the room. "Where is Scott? Did he not meet you?"

"He met me," Svetlana said, frowning, "but it did not go so well."

"Wha' happened?"

She hesitated for a moment, then looked at Varvara. "He knows why I am here. He knows about the letter."

Varvara winced.

"We will talk about this later. Let us not think of that now."

"We will speak soon," Varvara said. "Captain Clarke wishes to see you, anyway. I will walk you to his quarters when you are ready, and we can talk about it then."

As Svetlana looked away from Varvara, she saw David across the room. The older operative attended to his damp clothing in silence, placing them in bundles at the edge of his closet. He was the only man attempting to be neat.

Svetlana's gaze lingered on him, and then she said to Varvara, "Excuse me." She stepped away, leaving Varvara to change clothes behind her.

As she walked to the other side of the room, several pairs of eyes followed her. The slayers watched her, as did Oleg Strakhov. Esther scrutinized her more intently than anyone.

But David paid her no attention. He did not even acknowledge her presence. Alone, he attended to his towels.

"At least one person here is neat. Hello, David," Svetlana said. Behind and unknown to her, the unit watched the conversation unfold—as if the outcome were already known.

Finally, David turned to face her. "I didn't think you were this stupid."

Suddenly the noise faded. Everyone seemed to expectantly await Svetlana's response. She froze in place, staring, unprepared. When she finally did speak, her voice wavered. "What?"

"They've been talking about this day for weeks," David said, "but I gave you the benefit of the doubt. Guess it just goes to show you—some people are dumber than they look."

"David, what are you talking about?"

"About you coming *back* here—what do you think?" His voice, though low, filled the room. "About getting involved in something that's none of your vecking business. For God's sake, does your brain even work?"

"Don't do this, Dave..." Becan warned.

David looked at the Irishman, then returned to the medic. "You're wasting both your time and ours," he finally said. "But I guess you'll learn that for yourself."

Svetlana looked despondent as David distanced himself toward the lounge. The rest of the room listened and waited. At last her defenses kicked in.

"*You* wait, right there," she said. David kept walking as she marched after him. When it became apparent he wasn't stopping, she halted her pursuit. "You are such a coward."

David turned around.

"Yes, you heard what I said. You are a *coward*, David. You say such hateful words to me, then you walk away before I can speak."

"Save it for some other time—"

"Shut up. Now it is *my* turn to say something to *you*. You do not know me. You do not know anything *about* me. You do not deserve to know me." Her eyes narrowed. "But you do know Scott Remington. And for you to say that I am wasting my time in trying to help him, that tells me a lot about who you are."

Before he could speak she went on. "If you were truly a man, you would stand by your friend when he hurts. You would try to help him."

"Sveta, he's a murderer."

"*Shut up!*" she shrieked. The whole room flinched. "Do not say that word! I never want to hear it—from any of you!" Her eyes flashed around the room. "I know who Scott Remington is. I *know* why he did what he did. Do you think I am a fool?" Before David could answer, she stopped him. "I know already what you think. And I do not care."

"He's a *murderer*!" repeated David. He continued before she could interrupt. "I don't care if you like that word or not. It is what it is. Scott took what he did, and he embraced it!"

Svetlana shook her head emphatically. "You know that is not who he is!"

"Then why doesn't he throw away that uniform?"

At that question, Svetlana was quiet. David took the opportunity to make his case.

"Why doesn't he reject what they are? Why doesn't he put in an order to EDEN for new gear? Why doesn't he leave the Nightmen behind? Why doesn't he do *any* of these things?"

She opened her mouth to reply, but nothing came out.

"You chew on that for a while," David said with contempt. "But in the meantime, don't call me a coward. I'm not the one who tucked tail and ran."

Max stepped in to block David's path. "Watch your mouth, old man."

"Save it for someone you're trying to impress."

Svetlana came to Max's side and glared at David. "Who *are* you? You have changed more than Scott."

"I woke up! I saw through the scat! I saw a holy man exposed for what he was. I can forgive a lot, Svetlana. I can forgive him for hitting a girl."

Esther's eyes sunk.

"I can forgive him for causing Galina to die. I can forgive all of those things. But Scott killed a man. He took an *innocent* life. Maybe you can forget about that in your idiotic little fairy-tale world. But I can't. I have a soul. And so did the boy he killed.

"You think you know so much, Sveta. You think you can prance in here, wave your arms, and make this dung heap smell like red roses. It's not like that. Life doesn't work that way. Whether you choose to accept it or not, he is *not* the man you knew. He *is* someone else. If you haven't seen it yet, just sit back and wait."

Svetlana stood trembling beside Max, tears trickling down her face.

David didn't wait for her to answer. Turning his back to her again, he walked into the lounge. Nobody got in his way.

Varvara touched Svetlana's back. "We will go now, okay? Let us leave here."

On the other side of the room, Esther looked away.

"How could this have happened here?" Svetlana asked Varvara in Russian. "I did not think it would be like this. How could a loving God allow this?"

Varvara eased Svetlana to the door. "We will talk about it. It will be fine. Everything will be fine. Let us go now. Let us talk and walk together."

Max and the others watched as the women walked off.

Svetlana quickened her pace as she approached the hall door. As she turned the corner to make her escape, her footsteps grew faster. Then her exit came to a halt. She ran straight into Dostoevsky's chest, just as he was about to enter from the hall. Their collision forced both of them to stop.

As soon as Dostoevsky saw her, he started back. He stared open-mouthed at her face, his eyes wide with surprise. "Sveta!"

Slap!

He was silenced by the force of her palm.

Slap!

Then she slapped him a third time. Then a fourth and fifth. They came one after the other so fast that the Nightman was unable to react.

When she finally paused, he tried to plead, his face flushed with red welts. "Svetlana—"

"You do not speak to me," she spat, cutting him off. "You do not touch me. You do not say my name."

His mouth hung open.

"For what you have done, you will never be forgiven. You are dead to me, Yuri. You are dead." She pushed past him without saying another word.

The commander watched as the two women walked off and rounded a corner, out of view. His eyes fell despondently.

He never made it into Room 14. He didn't so much as glance inside. He walked right past the door, retreating down the hall.

Svetlana hardly made it around the corner. The instant she was out of Dostoevsky's view, she slumped against the wall, covering her face with her hands. "What am I doing?" Tears cascaded down. "What have I done?"

Varvara knelt by her side and patted her gently. "Sveta..."

"I cannot make a difference here. This is not me. No one liked me before Tolya died, what good am I now?"

"Be quiet. Do not say such things. Why do you say that?"

Svetlana lifted her head. Her eyes were red and puffy. "This unit does not need another medic, it needs a *therapist*!"

"Sveta, you are here because I asked you to come. You are here because I knew if anyone could bring this unit together, it would be you."

"But this is more than I can do! This is not a little problem. This is worse than a nightmare. How was I so stupid to come back?"

"You just had a very emotional conversation," said Varvara. "This is your first day back, and so far it has not been good. But you are here for a good purpose. You are here to get our lieutenant back. You are here for us all."

"But Varya, I am not a comforter."

"Did you not comfort him once already? Or did you make up what happened that night?"

Svetlana said nothing.

"You see? You *can* do this. You have done it already, just in a different way." Her hand slid from Svetlana's knee. "You had a warm welcome in the room, before David ruined it by being a jerk. Do not let one bitter man crush your spirits."

"David is a father," Svetlana said, looking away. For the first time, her tone was controlled. "He sees this in a way the rest of us do not. Maybe he's right. Maybe he's not. I don't know anymore."

"Do *you* believe he is right?"

Svetlana stared at the younger medic. "I believe Scott is a good man. I have told myself that so many times. I have to believe it—I must."

Varvara affirmed. "The rest of us believe that as well. You shared something with Scott that none of us did. You can touch him—reach him. That is why you are here." She tried to smile. "It is not up to you to comfort the rest of us. You worry about *him*. Believe me, if you can do that, it will bring us comfort enough."

"He told me I should have stayed away." Svetlana pressed her hands to her forehead, where her fingers disappeared in her hair. "I did not expect him to say that."

"This will not be easy. I never said it would be. But ask yourself if you want to help him. Do you have that desire?"

Svetlana didn't answer right away. She only stared back, deep in thought.

"Do you?"

Finally, she sighed. "Yes, I do."

"Good. Because if you would have said no, I would have felt very guilty for sending you that letter."

"You should feel guilty." Svetlana offered her a forced grin. "You know I am joking."

A moment of quiet passed before Varvara went on. "You should go see the captain. He will be wondering where you are. You have had too much emotion since you've been here. You need someone to talk about business."

"I will go see him now," Svetlana said, wiping her eyes and nodding.

"Do you want me to go with you?"

"No. I'm okay."

"He will be happy to see you. He might hug you."

"Might he really?"

"He has been desperate for any good news. You're the best news he's had in three months. But most likely, he will just give you a briefing. There is much for him to tell you about."

Svetlana rose to continue her trek. "That's fine with me. At least this will give me something else to think about."

"I will leave you to that, then," Varvara said. "Jayden and I are going into Novosibirsk today, but will I see you again later?"

"Of course."

"I look forward to it." Varvara watched Svetlana for several moments, then the younger medic offered another hug. She whispered, "This was not a mistake. Just keep saying it to yourself, and you will believe it."

Svetlana nodded in silence.

"Now go see the captain."

"I will."

With no further words, the medics parted ways.

When Svetlana arrived at Clarke's quarters, she found Varvara's prediction partially correct. She received a friendly welcome back, minus a hug, followed by a recapping of the past months' events. The meeting was strictly professional, and Svetlana took it well.

She asked for and received full medical records, then left to go to the infirmary. Though she had not seen it since its reconstruction after the *Assault on Novosibirsk*, she assumed it was the best place for a medic to study. She wasn't wrong.

She examined health records, scheduled examinations, and memorized new names. She familiarized herself with her role. She did her job.

It was the first thing that felt real all day.

6

SUNDAY, NOVEMBER 6TH, 0011 NE
1959 HOURS

THAT NIGHT

THE CALL TO ACTION couldn't have come fast enough. Scott stormed into the hangar, assault rifle firmly gripped in both hands, the horns of his fulcrum armor streaking back past his shoulders. Barely a moment after he'd entered, he was caught from behind by slayers Nicolai and Egor.

"What is the mission, lieutenant?"

"A Bakma Carrier and multiple Coneships have landed in Krasnoyarsk."

Nicolai grinned crookedly. "Beautiful!"

Beautiful wasn't the word that Scott would have used. Overdue, maybe. Welcomed, absolutely. The whole day had been a test of his willpower. After avoiding Svetlana and the rest of the unit, and spending the middle of the day grudgingly getting sleep, he looked forward to firing a weapon.

Several others were already waiting by the *Pariah*. Max was the first to approach Scott. "We got somethin' heavy, man. Command says three city blocks are completely engulfed. It's an all-out attack."

It was a frigid night; winter was at its worst. "Where's Clarke?"

"Right there."

Scott turned to the hangar's entrance. The captain was indeed coming in. But he was not alone. Svetlana was walking in step with him. Scott looked away.

"What other units are coming?" Nicolai asked Max.

"We're in the initial callout. But the Eighth, the Thirty-fifth, and the Thirty-ninth are going as well. Thoor's not pulling any punches."

"He never does."

The Eighth. Scott drew a heavy breath. That was William and Derrick's unit, led by Captain Ulrich. William and Derrick still ate with their friends from the Fourteenth, in spite of what happened in Khatanga. But Scott wasn't a part of that group. "Travis, I want a full layout of the target area, down to the cracks in the road."

"Already coming, sir."

Dostoevsky approached from behind. Viktor and Auric were at his heels. "Lieutenant Remington."

Scott didn't grace the commander with a response.

"What are we going into?" the slick-haired Viktor asked.

Nicolai thrust his hand in the air. "Dead bodies! Much fire and blood."

"Sounds like your idea of a date."

"We are going to Krasnoyarsk," Dostoevsky said. "At least one Carrier and several Coneships. They have apparently launched an assault against the city."

Scott had never been to Krasnoyarsk, but he'd heard of it. It was the third-largest city in Siberia—right along the Yenisei River. Forests, hills, and giant rock cliffs to the south surrounded it. The city was heavily built. It used to serve as a military city in the Old Era, though the bases there had been renovated for industrial use. Nonetheless, it had a formidable police force. It was supposedly a breeding ground for Nightman recruits.

When Clarke and Svetlana drew near, Scott deliberately looked away.

"I take it you're aware of our situation," Clarke said.

"Yes, captain," said Dostoevsky. He looked at Svetlana; she glared back without blinking.

"Very well." Clarke walked past Scott into the *Pariah*. Svetlana followed him inside.

As soon as they were gone, Nicolai grinned. "She is very attractive. I am glad she has decided to join us."

Scott tensed. Those words made his veins burn. He looked Nicolai straight in the eyes. "If you touch her—listen carefully—I will kill you."

His words struck the Nightmen like a blow. They all stopped and stared.

Nicolai said nothing for several moments, before finally nodding. "Yes, lieutenant. I hear what you say."

The moment Svetlana stepped inside the *Pariah*, her arms broke out in goose bumps. For several seconds she stood in the bay door. Then she stared at the wall-mounted speaker. The last place she'd heard her boyfriend Anatoly's voice.

Becan was right beside her. "Hey…yeh all righ'?"

She swallowed. "Yes." The words were barely above whispers. "It has been a long time."

Becan squeezed her shoulder and made his way in.

Most of the operatives had already taken their seats by the time Svetlana claimed one of her own. She held her helmet in her hands as the Nightmen filtered in and sat down. Though she occasionally glanced Scott's direction, his eyes never met hers.

Esther watched Svetlana silently from her own seat, until her stare caught the medic's attention.

Svetlana smiled as warmly as she could. "You must be Molly."

Esther froze. Her eyes widened.

"*Molly?*" said Becan.

Svetlana hesitated. "You are Molly, right? Molly Brooking, from Cambridge?"

"*Molly* Brooking?" The Irishman looked puzzled.

"That is the name on your medical records," Svetlana frowned apprehensively. "Is it not correct?"

Esther's face flushed cherry red. She looked down at her boots, furiously tightening her straps. Her voice trembled with irritation. "Yes, it's correct. I'm Molly Brooking."

"Your name is *Molly*?" Becan asked, his voice rising.

"Yes, Becan! I don't think everyone heard you—would you please try again?" Her sarcasm was thinly veiled.

Svetlana covered her mouth. "I am so sorry—do you not go by Molly?"

"I go by my middle name," Esther quietly answered.

Becan slowly put it together. "Molly…Esther."

"Yes," the Briton murmured. "Molly Esther."

"Hey! D'yeh know wha' tha' sounds like?"

"Let me guess! Molly Esther? Polyester? 'Molly Polyester!' Becan, that's bloody wonderful! You're so brilliant. Because believe me, I never heard that for the first *seventeen years* of my life!"

The cabin fell awkwardly quiet.

Scott sat in the back of the troop bay, surrounded by his Nightman comrades. He contemplated the situation in silence, his eyes focused in the distance and his elbows propped on his knees.

According to the log of the mission so far, the city's EDEN stations were occupied with the Bakma Carrier, leaving few forces to defend other areas. Local police were effective but outmanned, leaving several hotspots almost defenseless. That was where the Fourteenth came in. They would hit what the stations couldn't.

He'd seen the map he'd requested from Travis. He knew what his Nightmen would face. They'd be among the first to drop down, on the western end of the city. A strike team of Bakma had captured a multiple-story building. Hostages were involved, but he didn't know how many.

That part made it a challenge, because hostages were not the Nightmen's forte. Their specialty came in outright brutality. Strike hard and violently. That kind of recklessness didn't work well with civilian lives. Already Scott was considering the tools he had to work with.

Egor Goronok. The freak. A tower of muscles so grotesque, the sight of him was enough to cause psychological dread. He was Scott's human wrecking ball. Had he been with EDEN, he would have been a model demolitionist.

Auric Broll. The competent. Unlike Egor, the German slayer wasn't a brute. He was consistent; he could do any job well. Scott only had to tell Auric something once.

Nicolai Romanov. The supplementary. He was their jack of all trades, masterful at nothing but adept at everything. No one made a better complement. No one made more of a creep.

Viktor Ryvkin. The cunning. The slayer-medic wielded his intelligence like a sword. That tenacity made him one of Scott's most able slayers. It also made him the most dangerous.

Then Yuri Dostoevsky. Their commander. But EDEN rank aside, both he and Scott were fulcrum elites. In the eyes of the slayers, both men were equal. But were they equally adhered to? Not even close. Scott was more intelligent—more gifted. Every slayer in the Fourteenth knew it. There was a time when Dostoevsky's physical prowess had been enough to make his authority unchallengeable. But whatever edge the commander still had, it wasn't nearly as much as it had once been. If given a choice, Scott knew whom the slayers would follow. Dostoevsky wasn't even in the running.

Clarke spoke from the front of the *Pariah*. "By this point, you should be aware of our mission. We shall be undergoing a cooperative defense of Krasnoyarsk with the Eighth, Thirty-fifth, and Thirty-ninth."

Becan leaned close to Jayden. "Yeh know wha' I miss abou' Chicago? I could pronounce it."

"We shall divide into three teams for three distinct operations. The first team to drop will be Commander Dostoevsky's."

Behind the captain, the display screen showed their targeted structure. Scott had seen the image up close already. It wasn't as detailed as would have preferred—it never was. Multiple stories, and some kind of tower. For a military city, this wasn't surprising. There were probably lots of buildings with towers. But he was fully prepared for whatever it was.

"A Russian orthodox church has been captured as a stronghold..."

Scott's heart stopped. The captain's remaining words turned to static. Scott spoke without even a thought. "Did you say a church?"

Clarke stopped in mid-explanation. "That's correct."

That was the one thing Scott hadn't expected. His stomach started to ache.

"You *will* go into a church, won't you, Mr. Remington?"

For a moment, he couldn't find any words. When he finally did, his voice was grave. "Of course, captain."

Clarke eyed him before going on.

The rest of the captain's words were completely lost to Scott. His focus fell away from the view screen, and he stared blankly at the floor.

"Lieutenant?" The hushed word came from Auric. The blond-haired German sat at his side. "Are you okay?"

Scott had no explanation for his despondency—at least none he was willing to share. "Yes, I'm fine." Forcing himself into combat mode, he resumed listening to the captain.

Clarke would lead a team consisting of David, Esther, Jayden, and Svetlana into a warehouse. Resistance was expected to be manageable. The warehouse was a tall building, in view of several streets that the Thirty-fifth would be traversing in the distance. It was the perfect opportunity for Jayden to snipe. All the others had to do was secure the warehouse itself.

Max's operation was slightly more difficult. He would be leading Becan, Oleg, Maksim, and Varvara into a federal building with known hostages. It was a coordinated effort with a team from the Thirty-ninth. Enemy presence was expected to be high.

Scott and the Nightmen would tackle the church.

Across the troop bay, Esther aggressively checked her sidearm.

"You all righ', Esty?" Becan asked.

"Of course I'm all right—why wouldn't I be all right?" She tried to slam in a clip, but misjudged her aim. She jarred it in place a second time.

"Well, judgin' from the fact tha' yeh can't seem to properly load your handgun..."

"She did it on purpose."

The Irishman eyed her strangely. "Wha'?"

"I haven't gone by Molly in *years*. Not for applications, not for Academy registration, not for anything."

"Wait, are you still goin' on abou' *tha'*?"

"If your name was Molly Esther, would you want anyone to know?"

"If my name was Molly Esther, I'd have serious testosterone problems."

She turned away. "You're an idiot."

"Esty, they're *medical records*. O' course they'll have your full name. I mean, wha' did yeh expect?"

"Then why didn't Galina or Varvara call me Molly? Why didn't the captain? I filled my forms out with Esther, I introduced myself as Esther. I specifically marked Esther as my *preferred name*. That is what I wanted to be called—it was perfectly clear."

"Well, you an' Svetlana were never introduced, so congratulations! Now yeh are."

"I could punch you in the face."

Scott was examining the mission map when Viktor Ryvkin broke away from the Nightmen. He walked straight to the captain, prompting Scott and the other Nightmen to observe curiously.

"Captain, may I make a request?"

Clarke looked surprisingly at the slayer. "You may, Ryvkin."

"I would like to accompany your team to the warehouse."

The moment Viktor said it, the other Nightmen froze. Dostoevsky rose, and Scott abandoned his map scrutiny.

Viktor continued. "You may need more firepower than you expect, captain. We have enough firepower among the Nightmen. As you know, I am as much a medic as I am a soldier. I would gladly assist you."

Dostoevsky approached them. "Viktor, what are you doing?"

Clarke looked at Dostoevsky, then settled on Viktor. "If you come with us, your fellow Nightmen won't have a medic."

"They could take Voronova."

At the mention of Svetlana's name, the EDEN operatives in the vicinity whipped around. Esther was particularly entranced. Scott was plain floored. But no one looked more surprised than Svetlana herself.

"So you wish to *trade yourself* with Trooper Voronova?" Clarke asked. "You'll excuse me if I'm somewhat confused."

"This unit has gone through enough turmoil," Viktor said. "It is time for us to start working together. Then we *all* will be strong. You do not need to worry about Voronova's safety. She will be more safe with them than anywhere else."

Svetlana drew near. "What is going on here? What are you talking about?"

Clarke continued to look at Viktor as he answered her question. "Mr. Ryvkin wishes to take your place on our team and put you with the commander in his stead." Before Svetlana could speak, Clarke turned to Dostoevsky. "Do you oppose this?"

"Wait, wait," Scott said. "Hold on one second."

"Commander Dostoevsky?" Clarke asked again.

Caught between everyone, Dostoevsky had no counter-argument. "I... do not suppose I would oppose it..."

"Very well," Clarke said. "Ryvkin will accompany us, Svetlana will accompany you."

"Captain!" Scott protested. But Clarke just walked away.

Scott was apoplectic. The Nightmen behind him were almost equally upset.

Svetlana frantically reached for Scott's arm. "I have nothing to do with this, Scott, I promise! I do not understand this."

It was the first time they had made physical contact since her arrival, and Scott felt his heart churning. He was confused, angry. Helpless to avoid the situation. Each emotion was warring against the others and in their own way, each of them won.

"Please believe me, Scott, *please*. I would never try to do this!"

Scott had to look away. He knew what she was saying was true. But that didn't make it easier to understand. "I know."

She didn't look relieved.

Helmet in his hands, he pushed his hair back. This was as much a shock to her as it was to the Nightmen. *Viktor, what in the world are you thinking?* Steeling his jaw in surrender, Scott touched her arm. "Okay. You're going to be fine."

While Scott waited by the bay door to be dropped off, he looked at the operatives around him—the four Nightmen and the woman from EDEN. Svetlana clung to him like glue. He couldn't blame her. For the first time since her arrival, he pitied her. She had *gone* there for him. The consequences of that were too large to escape, and he wondered if she realized it now.

Beside them, Nicolai kissed his blood-encrusted dog tag—the one belonging to the man he'd presumably murdered. Scott would have been disgusted if he hadn't grown used to it long ago. That he was used to it at all made him sick. He looked sidelong at Svetlana. She would never have experienced anything like this before. This was a different situation than the one she'd been in previously with the Fourteenth. Now there were twice as many Nightmen in the unit, and they were ten times more radical than the Nightmen before them, Anatoly and Baranov. This new crew took totalitarianism to the extreme.

At that moment, Scott did something that surprised even himself—he gently squeezed the back of Svetlana's neck. Unspoken reassurance. For a moment, he felt her tension release.

"Prepare to drop!" Travis yelled from the cockpit.

Scott latched on his faceless helmet. It attached to the clamps of his armor. He stared through its interior view screen, where a transparent map of the church appeared. Maps were available only about half the time; thankfully, this was one of those times. He took a moment to study it, as the Nightmen around him got ready.

He watched as Svetlana removed her helmet briefly to pull an insulated layer of rubber over her head. The blond tips of her hair disappeared. She slipped her helmet back on.

The *Pariah*'s inertia shifted. They were about to drop.

Dostoevsky readied his assault rifle. He assigned everyone a shadow. "Remington—Romanov. Goronok—Voronova. Broll—myself."

Scott turned to Egor. The slayer stuck out like a pillar. "Keep her safe."

"I will, lieutenant." The slayer was strapping on a single-barreled 40mm slug launcher, nicknamed a *hand cannon*. It was capable of firing anything from armor piercing to incendiary rounds. The one-handed weapon walked a strange line between grenade launcher and pistol—exclusively a demolitionist's toy.

The bay door whined open. There was no time to be leery of church now. The Bakma didn't care how Scott felt. If he allowed the church to affect him, he'd only be more vulnerable and easier to kill.

There was a thick layer of snow on the ground, and fresh snow was still falling heavily. What the starlight didn't illuminate, his True Color

Vision did. TCV was one of the numerous technologies EDEN shared with the Russian military sect.

The church was grand. Red bricks formed its walls, and reaching to the heavens was a massive bell tower—the same tower Scott could see from the map. For a moment, even through the warmth of his internal heating system, the fulcrum from America felt cold.

Then it began.

Dostoevsky burst from the door. He dove straight from the security of the troop bay and rolled to the church's closed entrance. Plasma blasts exploded at his feet from above. Auric charged behind, followed by Scott and the others. Their dash lasted barely a few seconds—enough time to avoid plasma themselves.

Scott knew where the blasts were coming from—an alien inside the bell tower. It might have been a sniper. The blasts weren't inaccurate, they were just a split second behind. Plasma was a deadly brand of weapon, but its rate of fire was slower than projectile. That was one edge humanity had.

The Nightmen and Svetlana slammed against the front of the church, right beside a set of polished doors. The *Pariah* lurched into the air and turned to depart.

Suddenly, a small metal orb fell to the ground. It stuck in the snow meters in front of the Nightmen. A plasma grenade.

Time slowed.

Nicolai jerked the church door open. Egor pulled Svetlana to his chest. Dostoevsky and Auric tensed. The moment the doors were fully open, all six of them dove.

The boom that erupted behind them propelled them into the sanctuary. Immediately Scott felt a loss of control, then a searing heat against his back and the hail of shrapnel hitting his armor. He saw the ground pass beneath him as he soared facedown into the building, his arms flailing. Then instinct and experience kicked in.

Bend knees. Lower shoulders. Turn head.

He hit the ground in an awkward roll, one that nonetheless brought him upright to his knee. The slayers around him did the same. Svetlana remained cradled in Egor's arms as if he were carrying a child.

Plasma blasts erupted all around.

Scott aimed at the alien attackers, of which there were several scattered in the sanctuary. An exchange of projectile and plasma ensued. The Nightmen dove behind the cover of the available pews as woodchips flew through the air.

"Two on the north side!" Dostoevsky yelled. "Three at the south!" With those words, the counterstrike formed.

Scott popped up and fired a burst at the aliens in the south. The three Bakma there ducked for cover.

At no time did Scott's mind stop racing. *Dostoevsky and Auric have the two on the north. Egor will concentrate on the three on my end.* As if on cue, the oversized Egor launched a blast from his hand cannon. The corner where the Bakma hid exploded, and the plasma fire ceased.

"Two targets retreating," said Dostoevsky, referring to the two aliens on the north.

Scott had no idea if the three Bakma on the south were dead or in retreat. There was only one way to find out. "Nicolai, suppress." He leapt up to charge the enemy stronghold.

Nicolai cracked off several bursts.

The sanctuary, or what was now left of it, was huge and ornate. The space was the size of a gymnasium. A wide stage spanned the front, complete with an altar, pulpit, and baptismal pool. White ceilings arched high above. As he charged, Scott took it all in.

Plasma had a distinct odor. If inhaled too heavily, it watered the eyes. Scott could smell it through his helmet as he rushed the Bakmas' position. Nicolai's bullets whizzed over his shoulders, splintering the wood along the wall and shattering stained glass windows.

The first Bakma emerged to fire a shot. It never got the chance.

Scott was steps away from the doorway when the purple alien popped out—close enough to engage hand-to-hand. Scott raced forward, his armored fist catching the alien's face the moment it appeared. The Bakma flew against the wall as Scott ducked then swung his rifle down the hallway. He opened fire, and a second Bakma was dead before it could shoot.

Nicolai was right behind Scott. Grabbing the Bakma Scott had punched, Nicolai gave the alien's head a violent twist. Its spinal cord cracked in its neck.

"There were three here," Scott said through the comm. "There's one unaccounted." The last Bakma was nowhere to be seen. But there was no telling how many were hiding in the building. By the look of it, the door and adjacent hallway were actually add-ons to the orthodox church building—an entirely different wing. It might even have been an attached seminary.

"Pursue it," Dostoevsky ordered. "Auric and I will pursue the two Bakma on the north. Goronok—take the bell tower."

"Da, commander."

The Nightmen split up.

* * *

CLARKE GRABBED A support rail as the *Pariah* neared its second drop point—the roof of the warehouse they were supposed to clear for Jayden. Fire illuminated the streets in the distance. As the transport lowered to the rooftop, the captain readied his gun. "There's a radio tower attached to this warehouse, Timmons. You should have an excellent view from atop."

"Yessir."

"Ryvkin will accompany you. The rest of us will clear the warehouse from ground floor up."

Behind the captain, Viktor looked mildly surprised.

"Do you object to this, Mr. Ryvkin?"

"Not at all, captain. That will work very well." His eyes panned to the Texan.

"Ms. Brooking," Clarke said, turning to Esther. "Assist Timmons from ground level. Be his second pair of eyes."

"Freedom to improvise, sir?"

"Not yet. Just help Timmons shoot."

A look of defeat replaced her anxious expression.

As the *Pariah* touched down on the roof, Jayden hopped out. Viktor was right on his heels. The Vulture transport lifted away.

"I will clear the rooftop entrance!" Viktor called out. "Do not worry about me. Focus only on the streets."

"All right, man." Jayden turned to the tower.

Viktor watched the Texan for several moments, then turned to the rooftop's only entranceway: an elevated, closed-door stairwell. The slayer positioned his rifle and opened the door.

On the street below, the *Pariah* once again touched the ground—this time to drop off Clarke, David, and Esther. As soon as the female scout stepped outside, Becan's voice emerged through her helmet.

"Mind yourself, Molly-Polly. Don't go doin' anythin' too British."

She scowled as she traversed the warehouse wall. "I'm lucky to do anything at all, besides being a bloody waste of space." Since Khatanga, she'd been kept on a leash. In practice, she was barely a scout at all.

"I guess some people need more time to develop."

"Charming. I don't see *your* plaster bust."

"I had one," Becan answered, "but they accidentally put my real first name, Willard."

"Keep it coming, bollock-brain. Please, I insist."

The next voice to emerge wasn't meant for them. It was Max from the *Pariah*. "We're on our way to the federal building, captain."

Clarke and David stood prepped by the warehouse entrance. "Good luck, lieutenant," Clarke answered Max. Behind them, the *Pariah* rose from the streets. The captain's eyes met David's. "On three?"

"On three."

"One. Two. Three." Taking a single step backward, Clarke grabbed the metal warehouse door and jerked it open. He dropped to a knee as David dashed around the corner inside.

"Room clear," David said.

Clarke followed behind him, quickly assuming the point position. "Stairwell's ahead, second door to the right. First we clear the ground floor."

"Yes sir."

"Follow my lead."

* * *

SCOTT EASED AROUND a corner. He and Nicolai had pursued the third Bakma into the seminary and up a stairwell, right into a hallway on the second floor. Though the two Nightmen had heard the alien running ahead of them and flinging doors open, they had yet to catch a glimpse of it.

Behind Scott, Nicolai crouched and covered their rear. It would have taken an impressive effort for the Bakma to have flanked them, but it was still something they would not leave to chance.

Creeping from the safety of the corner, Scott braced his assault rifle on his shoulder. *There are hostages here somewhere.* Three doors stood in plain view down the hall—two on the left and one on the right. The hall ended with a left turn. Throughout, illumination was dim. The carpet under their feet allowed them to pad forward with stealth.

His map indicated to Scott where the doors led. The first left-hand door connected with the next one farther down, forming one large room. It was probably some kind of meeting room.

He activated his helmet's ExTracker. It was a motion-detecting device capable of tracking and identifying movement in user-defined radiuses. Only certain officers were allowed to use the technology—Scott never had it until he was a fulcrum. Motion detecting was a controversial affair. In an ideal war, every soldier could utilize it. But soldiers were far from ideal. No matter how often operatives were drilled about false senses of security, they fell victim to it just the same. ExTracker wasn't perfect technology. Many an operative had charged through a room expecting no resistance, only to be gunned down by something ExTracker had missed.

Ironically, soldiers on the whole did better *without* the device, which was no more as disastrously apparent than on necrilid missions. Although it was convenient to help detect a necrilid before it attacked, it was that much more panic-inducing to watch a little dot suddenly soaring across the screen straight at you. Smells and sounds were just as important as visible clues, and with ExTrackers, smells and sounds were taken for granted. Thus, ExTrackers had been banned from all but command personnel.

Thankfully, Scott could handle the technology. As soon as his ExTracker was on, he got three hits, all on the right side of the hall. Two in the corner, and one against the back wall. Two humans and a Bakma. According to his ExTracker, nothing was in the large room to his left. *Don't trust it. Look yourself.*

He made a hand signal to Nicolai, indicating to him to investigate the hits in the room on the right.

Nicolai crossed to the right side of the hallway, nearing the door there.

Holding up three fingers, Scott and Nicolai locked eyes. Three fingers became two, two became one, and then there were none. The two men burst through the doors simultaneously—Scott into the room on the left and Nicolai into the one on the right. Scott's room was empty, as ExTracker had predicted.

Across the hallway, gunfire erupted. Scott sprang to his feet and dashed after it. The exchange stopped before he arrived.

Nicolai stood alone in the center of the room. Two dead Bakma were sprawled in the corner. The slayer's shoulder armor was smoldering but intact. Crouched in the corner, behind the dead Bakma, two priests huddled together. The hostages. There had been four beings total in the room—not three as ExTracker had claimed. Thankfully, Nicolai was capable.

Click.

The sound came from the hall. Scott and Nicolai froze. It was a door opening stealthily—in a way not meant to be heard.

On Scott's motion sensor, a new target appeared down the hallway, just beyond the door to the room they occupied. It was identified as a Bakma.

Scott signaled Nicolai to the room's inner wall, the wall shared with the hallway. Nicolai pressed against it. Lowering to a crouch, Scott crept back until he'd placed himself at an angle to the door. The target crept closer.

His mind churned. Nothing had been behind them in the hall. The room on the other side had been clear. This new target must have come from somewhere else. Possibly from the left-hand turn down the hallway.

He heard a new sound—the delicate pad of footsteps on the carpet. Nicolai's body was tense; he must have heard it as well. The Bakma was there, mere meters away, separated only by the wall. Scott was tempted to shoot *through* the wall, but he restrained himself.

It could be another human if ExTracker's wrong.

Scott issued Nicolai another sign—the signal to fall back. Scott wanted this one himself. His hands remained gripped on his weapon as he eased against the wall that divided the room from the hallway. Nicolai fell back, training his weapon on the doorway. The priests remained in the corner.

Scott drew a breath as he set down his rifle. He wasn't going into this one guns blazing. He felt better at close range with a blade. Pulling out his combat knife, he waited a silent three-count. Then he moved.

He dove straight out the doorway, rolling as plasma bolts fought to keep up. It was a Bakma indeed. Scott bent his knees and leapt straight into the alien. The Bakma fell backward as Scott collided against it.

There was no hesitation. Scott jabbed his knife straight into the alien's forehead. The Bakma warrior's body shuddered with spasms.

A new sound emerged from around the corner. Scott released the knife, still stuck in the alien, and ripped out his pistol. No sooner than he'd lifted it up, another Bakma burst into the hall. The alien had scarcely taken two steps before Scott's firearm erupted, causing it to collapse to the floor.

Instinctively Scott turned to his rear. He listened until he was satisfied nothing was there. Then he moved toward the left corner where the Bakma had come from. Instead of edging around it, he burst around it full speed, training his pistol down the next hallway. It was clear.

Scott returned to the room Nicolai still guarded to retrieve his assault rifle. He watched the priests through his helmet's interior view screen. The moonlight through the window made the horns of his fulcrum armor gleam. The priests stared back at him, then one of them spoke. What he said was not what Scott expected to hear.

"You do not belong here."

Behind the shield of his helmet, Scott blinked. It was the first time he'd been told that in a church.

Suddenly, Nicolai lifted his rifle. He aimed the barrel straight at the priests.

The motion was too fast for Scott to prevent. Before he could yell in protest, the Nicolai pulled the trigger. The priests fell backward in horrified shock.

ClickClickClickClickClick!

After several seconds of empty fire, Nicolai's finger relaxed. "Dead God men," he said with mechanized smugness.

Scott lost it. Grabbing Nicolai by the collar of his armor, Scott rammed the slayer back against the wall. The plaster wall cracked with the force. "*Never* do that again."

Nicolai's slumped posture revealed his subordination; he quickly affirmed.

Scott fought off the urge to slay the slayer. But his sense of where he was won out. Releasing Nicolai's collar, he turned to face the priests. "Are you the only two people in the building?"

The men acknowledged him in silence.

"Then follow us out."

Without a word, the four men left the room.

* * *

Dostoevsky barged through the double doors at the north end of the church, with Auric Broll behind him. They were in pursuit of two retreating Bakma. As the two Nightmen emerged on the other side of the doors, they found themselves under fire in a courtyard.

Bushes and foliage decorated ornate columns that surrounded them; fountain water trickled noisily into a heated pool.

Taking instinctive cover behind the false security of hedges, the two Nightmen opened fire then ran. The exchange of energized plasma bolts and orange gunpowder lit the night-shrouded courtyard.

Dostoevsky and Auric found better protection behind a row of columns. The two Bakma were positioned at the center of the courtyard, behind the fountain itself.

"Hold this position," Dostoevsky said, handing his assault rifle to the German. "Do not let them know I am coming."

"Yes, commander." Auric took Dostoevsky's rifle and held it in his free hand. Bracing both rifles against his shoulders, he stood directly behind the column, firing both guns at the same time around both sides of the pillar. Dostoevsky disappeared into the darkness.

Behind the fountain, the taller of the two Bakma fired a volley. Ducking down to reload its rifle, the tall alien eyed the shorter one across the pool. *"Ka-nashga!"*

The shorter Bakma glanced at the other for a moment, then resumed its attack.

With its plasma rifle reloaded, the taller alien once again rose to engage the two humans behind the column. The Earth-born warriors were inaccurate. Of the two steady streams of orange projectile, one on each side of the column, neither was remotely on target. They were downright wild. "U`tasnk," the tall alien said.

The shorter Bakma affirmed, and the two aliens turned to make their retreat. The moment they did, their already bulging eyes opened wider.

Dostoevsky sprang at the Bakma the moment they turned, arms outstretched as both aliens were clotheslined into the fountain. Everyone landed in the water.

The dual gunfire behind the column ceased as Auric charged from his cover.

Dostoevsky shot up from the water. Grabbing the taller Bakma by the head, the Russian used its body as a shield. The shorter Bakma rose from the water, but there was no time for attack. Dostoevsky whipped out his sidearm and pulled the trigger, popping the short alien in the head and neck. There was an eruption of red, and the Bakma toppled backward.

Taking a quick step back, Dostoevsky kicked at the taller Bakma, sending it pitching forward. In the next instant, Auric gunned the alien down. The German skidded to a halt by the fountain, tossing Dostoevsky's assault rifle back to him.

The fulcrum snatched it in midair. "Back to the church."

* * *

EGOR GORONOK stormed through the hallways of the church. Svetlana fought to stay in his wake of destruction. Wooden doors were not merely opened; most were violently unhinged by brute force.

In the trek that took them to the church's third floor, they had already encountered two Bakma. The first had struck Egor in the leg with a plasma bolt, before the slayer blew it to pieces with his hand cannon. Though Egor's leg bled through his armor, he hadn't slowed down. The second Bakma they'd caught off-guard at close range. It was an experience that made the veteran medic gag—she watched the massive slayer crush the alien's skull with his armored hands.

All to get to the bell tower.

Svetlana struggled to maintain the Nightman's pace. Egor didn't need to tell her that keeping up was in her best interest. That part was understood.

Finally, they came to the bell tower's door. As Egor surged ahead like a train, Svetlana paused in the hall. Lowering his shoulder, Egor exploded through the door's ancient frame. Wooden slivers flew in all directions as he stopped at the bottom of a circular stairwell.

The alien sniper did not hesitate. Plasma bolts rained down over the slayer, who quickly pressed back against the stone walls to avoid them.

Svetlana pulled out her sidearm. But there was no need.

The exchange between Egor and the sniper lasted mere seconds. Setting his hand cannon to incendiary, Egor trained it upward, stepped into the open, and unleashed his vengeance. Five bursts of combustible orange shot from the cannon, each one triggering an explosion at the top of the tower. Egor dove into the hallway as an avalanche of fiery rubble rained down. He leapt up, swinging his weapon to the still-falling debris. Running backward, he fired several more rounds. The bottom of the bell tower burst into fiery ruin. The last boom to be heard was the brass bell itself as it crashed down on the burning heap.

Svetlana's mouth hung open as the church's sprinkler system kicked in.

Egor didn't budge. He only stared at the mound of destruction, speaking calmly through his helmet comm.

"Sniper disposed."

* * *

Back at the warehouse, at the second drop point, Viktor Ryvkin made his way carefully down the rooftop stairs while Jayden continued to climb the radio tower. Viktor occasionally looked behind him to keep the Texan in his sight, but his primary focus stayed on the stairs—particularly the T-junction they approached.

He could hear the Bakma below him. He knew exactly where they were. They weren't right there around the corner, but they were close. They were close enough to hear him, too. He remained quiet.

He found them as soon as he came to the bottom; it took only a brief look around the right-hand corner of the junction. There were two of them, positioned just beyond a door at the end of the hall. They were oblivious, probably waiting for Clarke's team below, unaware of the slayer behind them. They would both be easy kills.

Easing up his assault rifle, Viktor aimed at the pair of aliens and fired. Instantly, the two warriors crumpled to the floor.

The Nightman medic took a moment to look behind him. Everything in the hallway was clear. He approached the two fallen Bakma and trained his rifle on their black-and-brown armor. Squeezing the trigger several times more, he riddled their bodies with insurance.

The hallways were silent.

For several seconds, Viktor did nothing. He simply stared at the two victims of his blindsided attack. Then he stared at their weapons—their plasma rifles.

Crouching, he carefully picked up one of the alien guns. His hands slid into a comfortable grip as he took a moment to adjust to its weight. Then he looked back.

When he stood again, his assault rifle was not in his hands. He no longer searched for Bakma. His eyes were trained on the stairs to the roof.

* * *

Plasma fire rocked the *Pariah* as the transport descended to the street. A horde of Bakma from the block ahead fired shots toward it until its nose-mounted cannon burst with suppression. It was time to drop Max's team off.

Max was the first to exit the ship, darting into an alley while the Vulture covered his path. Becan, Oleg, Maksim, and Varvara kept spread out behind him.

The Thirty-ninth—a unit consisting mostly of EDEN operatives—was in their vicinity. One of the Thirty-ninth's teams would be joining Max's efforts in a joint strike on the federal building. Both units were to meet in the middle. Of all the dispatches in Krasnoyarsk, their task had the heaviest resistance. There were multiple teams of Bakma, not only in the streets but in and around the building itself.

The Eighth was there as well, engaging the Bakma farther down the road. They were backup to the federal building strike.

Max's team made its way to the back of the building, where a single metal door led inside. The building itself was four stories of gray brick.

As soon as the others were safely with Max, the coordination began. He adjusted his helmet mic and spoke. "This is Lieutenant Axen of the Fourteenth calling Lieutenant Brunner of the Thirty-ninth. Come in, sexy."

Varvara and Becan both blinked.

A woman's voice emerged. It was foreign, but not Russian; nor was it amused. "You are not dead yet. This disappoints me."

"You'd cry at my funeral," Max said, taking a moment to leer at the Irishman. "She wants me."

"We are at the front entrance," said Brunner. "Are you ready to converge?"

"If that's what the kids are calling it nowadays."

"Converging."

Max stepped to the side of the metal door and readied his rifle. "Maksim, you're with me. Oleg, stay with Becan. Stay behind us, Varya."

"Old *mot*, I presume?" asked Becan.

"I'd answer if I knew what that meant." Max turned to Maksim. "I cover, you counter. Let's go." He shoved the metal door open and leaned around the corner to suppress. No Bakma were in sight. Moving inside, he waited for Maksim to follow. Then he signaled the others.

Though the building had emergency lighting, the hallway was nonetheless dim. Through the vibrant hues of their TCVs, they could make out the building's details in full. Several offices lined the two sides.

Far ahead, an exchange of gunfire was in progress. Its flashes illuminated the halls like lightning strikes.

Max's steps grew hurried, though his voice remained calm. "Ann, give me your status."

"One Ex down," she answered. "Several remaining. We did not get past the front door."

As Max's team emerged from the hallway, they found themselves at

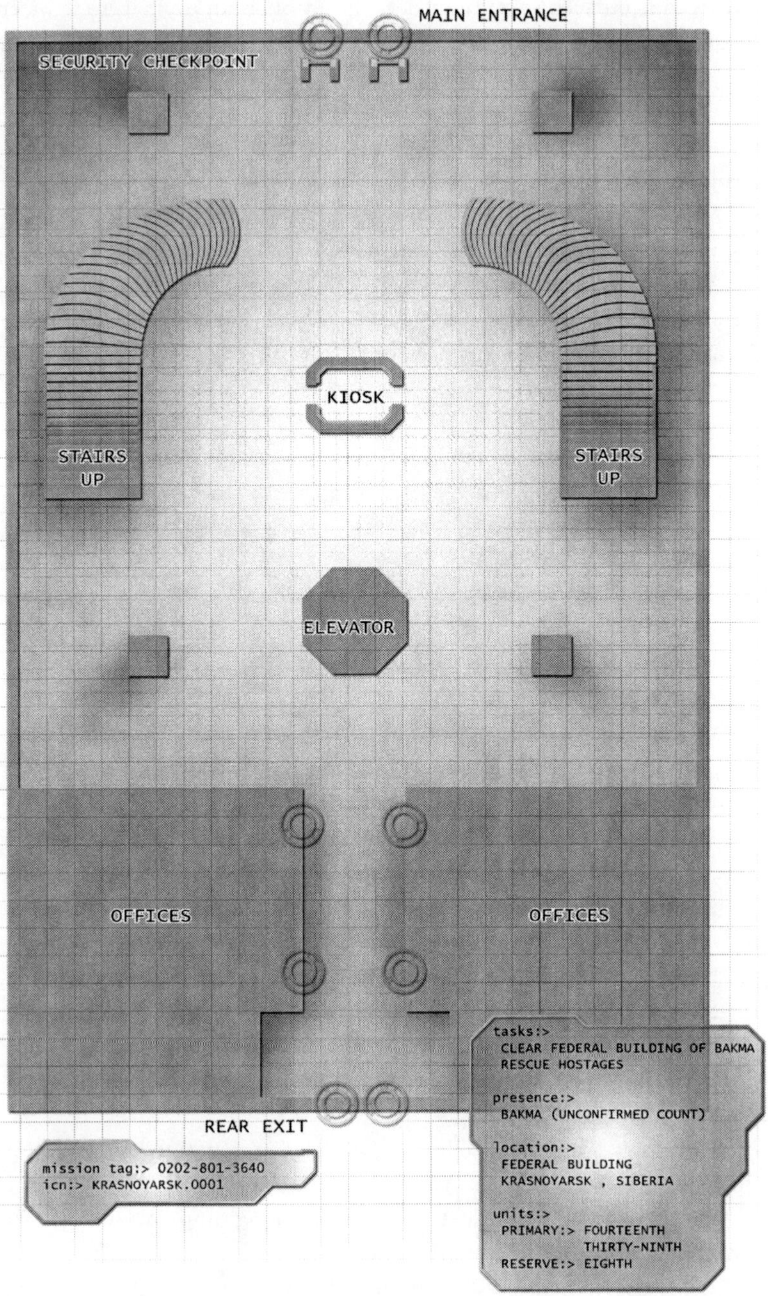
MAIN ENTRANCE
SECURITY CHECKPOINT
KIOSK
STAIRS UP
STAIRS UP
ELEVATOR
OFFICES
OFFICES
REAR EXIT
mission tag:> 0202-801-3640
icn:> KRASNOYARSK.0001
tasks:>
CLEAR FEDERAL BUILDING OF BAKMA
RESCUE HOSTAGES
presence:>
BAKMA (UNCONFIRMED COUNT)
location:>
FEDERAL BUILDING
KRASNOYARSK , SIBERIA
units:>
PRIMARY:> FOURTEENTH
THIRTY-NINTH
RESERVE:> EIGHTH

the back of a large, spacious lobby. Two open stairwells and an isolated elevator sat in the center of a sunken walking area.

They saw Bakma immediately. The crimson-purple aliens were taking cover behind the elevator in the middle of the room.

The Bakma found Max's team, too. No sooner than Max and Maksim emerged, the aliens opened fire against them. Plasma bolts soared down the hall, narrowly missing Becan and Oleg. The operatives dove for the cover behind potted plants and seating areas—but not without casualty. The back of Max's calf was caught in mid-dive, and a bolt aimed for Becan struck him in the shoulder. The Irishman tumbled sideways and crawled for cover. Maksim and Oleg continued their attack.

At the other end of the lobby, the front doors burst open. The operatives of the Thirty-ninth charged inside. The fight lasted mere seconds. Surrounded by both EDEN teams, the Bakma succumbed to quick death.

Becan moaned and tore off his shoulder guard. Varvara rushed over to him, shoving the charred armor aside and ripping off the fabric of his jersey. Becan's shoulder was smoking, and the smell of singed flesh bit the air.

Several meters away, Max hobbled to a stand, propping himself against the wall. Across the lobby, Brunner and the Thirty-ninth spread across the room.

Becan's teeth ground together. "Bleedin' eejit purple monkeys!" He winced as Varvara stuck him with a needle and applied gel to the wound.

"You ain't hurt to the bone," Varvara said. "Stop crying like baby."

Max gingerly hobbled over to them, favoring his left leg. "How is he?"

"I'm bloody *hurt*, how does it look like I am?"

Varvara gave Max an admonishing look. "He will live, even if he thinks he will not. Show me your calf."

"Calf's fine," Max said, ignoring her request. The armor in question had been blown off, exposing an area of burned skin beneath. He limped away before she could examine it.

A woman of small stature approached them. Her face—masculine but not entirely unappealing—stared sternly through the blue tint of her EDEN visor. Pigtails dangled behind her helmet.

As soon as she was within speaking distance, she placed her hands on her hips. "Are you ready to move upstairs, or is your unit too injured to continue?" There was no hint of joking in her voice.

"Of course we can continue. Who can't continue?" Max answered, then he murmured to Becan, "Get up, Becan."

"But I'm bleedin' hurt!"

"Get up, Becan!"

The Irishman bit his lip and rose up.

Brunner took charge. "Shavrin, take Kaligan and Sokolov up the far stairwell. I will lead Axen and his demolitionist up the near one." No room was allowed for Max to argue. "Everyone else, remain at the front entrance of the lobby and monitor the movement of Captain Ulrich."

"Captain Ulrich, eh?" Becan asked. "Tha's just brilliant."

Brunner scrutinized the Irishman. "What is your name?"

"Becan McCrae."

"And you?" She turned to Oleg.

"Strakhov, lieutenant."

"The two of you will fortify the back door from which you came. Your medic will stay with you until needed. We have a medic with us already."

"Uhh..." mumbled Becan, glancing at Max.

"Do what she says," Max said in frustration.

"Righ'."

"There is a safe room on the second floor of this building," Brunner said. "We must assume there are humans inside. We cannot wait—we move now."

The operatives around her affirmed.

"Max," she said, lowering her tone, "are you hurt bad?"

"I'm never hurt," he answered, readying his weapon.

"Good. Then let's go."

* * *

BACK AT THE WAREHOUSE, Viktor neared the corner of the stairs to the roof, the alien weapon still in his hands. He stopped just before the corner, scanning the hallway a final time. No one was present. No Bakma. No teammates.

No witnesses.

The Nightman listened to Jayden's sniper fire from the radio tower. He listened closely as the Texan did his job. A minute passed, then the time to listen came to an end.

Placing the plasma rifle against his shoulder, the Nightman medic rounded the corner. His eyes narrowed as he searched for his target. He pulled the trigger without a moment of pause.

The white bolt struck Jayden from behind. The Texan's sniper rifle flew from his hands as he toppled from the tower.

Viktor didn't see the sniper fall, but he heard the impacts—over and over as the Texan careened against metal crossbars all the way down. Lowering the plasma rifle from his shoulder, Viktor glanced down the hallway once again. He was still alone. He tossed the alien weapon back down the hall, where it slid to a stop by the fallen corpses. He reclaimed his assault rifle and mounted the stairs.

At street level, Esther had been running when she heard the blast. Her nimble steps skidded to a halt in the snow as she turned her head to the tower.

She gasped as she watched Jayden plummet. She screamed through the comm. "Jayden's been hit! I repeat, Jayden's been hit! He's fallen from the tower!"

* * *

AT THE REAR entrance of the federal building, Becan and Varvara went rigid, as if Esther's words failed to register. When they finally did, Varvara completely lost her composure. "Esther, what happened?" she asked frantically over the comm. There was no response.

"Jay!" Becan shouted into his helmet mic. "Jay, can yeh hear me? *Jayden*?"

"Travis, are you still outside?" asked Varvara.

"Yeah," the pilot answered. "I heard what Esther said. Do you want me to take you there?"

Max's voice cut in. "Nobody's taking anyone anywhere!"

"Yes! I am coming!" Varvara said, ignoring Max. She darted for the metal door.

Becan reached out with his good arm and snatched her. "Wait! I'm comin' with yeh."

Oleg watched the two operatives rush away.

Becan readied his M-19 handgun. "Oleg, hold this place for a sec—I'm takin' her ou' to the ship, I won't be gone long!"

"Uh…"

Becan was out the door with Varvara a split second later.

* * *

VIKTOR WALKED CALMLY toward Jayden. The Texan was crumpled in a motionless heap, a deep hole smoldering in the back of his armor. It had easily been a twelve-meter drop. Blood was splattered on the rooftop from where his helmet had hit the ground. Then Viktor stopped in his tracks.

Jayden was still breathing.

Hurrying to the Texan, Viktor watched as his chest moved. He rolled Jayden over, face-up. Jayden's visor was completely shattered inward. His face was a disfigured wreck. But he seemed to have survived the treacherous fall.

Viktor lifted Jayden's chin, exposing the unconscious man's neck. As he lifted his hand to make the kill-strike, he heard Esther. He looked up, flinging his hand back down to his side just as the scout emerged onto the rooftop from a side-mounted ladder.

"Jayden!" In the next instant, Esther was racing across the roof.

Viktor's countenance instantaneously changed. The Nightman quickly felt Jayden for a pulse. He looked only briefly at Esther. "What happened? Did you see it?"

"They struck him from behind!" she said, covering her mouth as she saw the Texan's face. "Oh my God."

"We must get him into a C-collar and onto a spinal board. Help me, quickly!" He removed a portable cervical collar from his kit. "He is not posturing—that is a good sign."

"What does that mean?" asked Esther, breathing heavily.

"It means he is not cringing inward." Viktor got on the comm. "Navarro, bring the *Pariah* here at once."

Becan's voice yelled over the airwaves, "Somebody tell us wha' the bleedin' hell happened!"

"Jayden got struck from behind," Esther answered. "He fell from the tower." Her voice strained to be reassuring. "He's going to be all right, Viktor's with him."

Viktor eyed her for a moment, then went back to work.

* * *

AS BECAN AND Varvara reached the *Pariah*, Travis shouted from the cockpit, "Hold on, we're taking off."

With his good arm, Becan pointed repeatedly. "Go! Go! Go!" He looked back out the rear bay.

Then he saw them. Bakma—right there in the alley he'd just come from. Right past the metal door. Before he could register their numbers, they opened fire on the rear of the ship. Becan dove out across the street as plasma bolts flew into the snow. As he hit the ground, his wounded shoulder surged with fresh pain. He scrambled up and watched the Bakma flood inside. Then the realization hit him.

He'd left Oleg alone.

"Bollocks!" Becan scampered back to the building and readied his assault rifle.

"Becan!" Travis said. "What are you doing?"

"Scram! Go after Jay!"

The next sound Becan heard made him go rigid. Plasma fire exploded from the back of the federal building, engulfing the lone spray of an assault rifle. A five-second ruckus of sound ensued, followed by silence. By the time Becan got to the door, it was too late.

Jerking the door open, he burst in, aiming his weapon. He thought he was prepared for the worst, but nothing prepared him for what he actually saw.

Blood was everywhere. The walls were stained with scorch marks and holes. Death pulsed through the air. But it was not human death.

A stranger was standing in the hallway, the broken bodies of six Bakma scattered around him. The man's hands were poised to strike. His fighting stance was eager and cold. It was a stance Becan had never seen before. In one hand, the man's knuckles were anxiously protruded. In his other, his assault rifle loomed. When he turned to the door where Becan stood, chills broke over the Irishman's skin.

It was Oleg. The expression on his face was unfathomable, vile.

The two stared at one another for a mere second before everything about Oleg changed. The killer's posture snapped into a kind of alarmed subordination. His butcher's gleam transformed into innocent shock. He became the man Becan knew once again.

For several moments, they stared at each other. Then Oleg bent forward and heaved. He spoke in the same soft voice he'd always adopted. "What a rush…"

The Irishman stood motionless in the open metal door, his M-19 still in his hand. Then he lowered it. "Yeah…what a rush…"

* * *

MAX PRESSED AGAINST the second-floor wall as a flurry of plasma flew past him. Maksim rolled forward from behind, awkwardly crouching and firing an armor-piercing round from his own hand cannon. The Bakma fled around the corner in retreat.

Lieutenant Brunner had flattened herself against the opposite wall. She barked out orders through her comm. "Shavrin, do you know the location of the safe room?"

"Yes, lieutenant."

"There are civilians there. Retrieve them."

A Bakma warrior emerged from the corner and fired. It narrowly missed Brunner, who countered with a shot of her own. The Bakma was struck in the side and slunk back in retreat.

Brunner was on her feet again. "Max, I am going ahead. I am taking your demolitionist with me. Make sure nothing comes from behind you."

Max gritted his teeth and hobbled forward. "No, *I'm* going with you. Maksim, you stay here and cover the rear."

"This is not the time or the place to prove you're a man," she snapped back. "You will do as I say." She looked back at Maksim. "Are you ready to go?"

Maksim exchanged a conflicted look with both lieutenants.

Max growled and fired a shot in frustration. "Draggin' bull-headed woman. You wanna play it your way, go get killed. Go with her, Frolov."

As Maksim took to Brunner's side, she said to Max, "You had better watch the rear well."

"I'm watching! I'm watching! Freakin' *go*!"

Brunner and Maksim charged the corner.

* * *

SCOTT HAD BEEN leading the priests outside when the overhead sprinklers kicked on in the church. The moment he left the building, he saw why. The top of the bell tower, where the alien sniper had once been, was engulfed in flames.

He had heard the announcement about Jayden over the comm. But there was no time to think about that now. He had two dripping wet priests in the middle of a snowfall.

On the other side of the street, on an adjacent corner, stood a row of residential housing. Only one thought came to Scott's mind: warmth.

"Across the street," he said to the priests. "Come on, *move*!" Grabbing one by the arm, he dragged him along.

Nicolai had been directly behind Scott until something else caught the slayer's attention. Down the street, several blocks ahead, a canrassi lumbered around. The Nightman raised his weapon to fire.

As soon as Scott reached the first doorway, he tried the knob. It was locked. *There's no time for this.* Taking a step back, he struck out with his foot and bashed the door in. Gunfire struck him immediately. He flew back through the air. It wasn't plasma—that much was revealed by the clattering sound of metal against his armor. It was something more brutal. As Scott landed back-first in the snow, gasping for breath, he registered the way he'd been hit. The wind was completely knocked out of him. He looked into the house. Huddled in the far corner was a terrified family, shielded by an old man with a shotgun. When they saw his gleaming horns, they froze.

It took every ounce of strength to fight off his pain, after which Scott grabbed the two priests and hurled them inside. He was too winded to talk, but it didn't matter. The family would know what to do. He heaved a rasping breath and turned to the street.

His fulcrum armor now bore a dent, though by the looks of it, no pellets had pierced it. The armor had likely saved his life. Taking another moment to fill his lungs, he lifted his head to find his teammate.

As Nicolai pressed the trigger, in the middle of the street the spider-eyed canrassi made its charge. It lasted mere moments. A hiss came from the church doorway as a smoke trail soared at the beast. The front half of the canrassi exploded. Its bloody carcass crashed to the snow.

Egor emerged from the building, smoke rising from the barrel of his hand cannon.

Scott was there moments later, and he pointed to the fire in the bell tower. "What the hell happened?"

"I had few options," Egor answered. "That was the safest one for my life. Buildings can be replaced. I cannot."

Svetlana appeared in his wake. Behind the sky-blue tint of her visor, she appeared overwhelmed.

Scott knew why. She was fighting alongside Nightmen for the first time. Not a Nightman who was her boyfriend, who would always show her his best side. True Nightmen. People who would burn down a church at the first inclination it might get the job done, without giving it a second of thought.

Dostoevsky and Auric arrived next. The commander wasted no time. "I will go to the warehouse to assist Captain Clarke. Auric and Egor, you will come with me."

Svetlana's mouth fell open. "But what about this church? Will we just let it *burn*?"

"We are not firefighters, Svetlana."

"We are the fire," Nicolai said cryptically. He was silenced by a hard look from Scott.

She shook her head in disbelief. "This is not right."

Scott fought to stop his thoughts from becoming words. *You're surrounded by murderers. Of course it's not right.*

She set her eyes squarely on him. "Scott, this is not what righteous men do."

Those words hit him strangely. They didn't hit him because he felt righteous—he hadn't felt righteous in months. They hit him because they were laced with, of all things, sincerity.

She still considers me righteous.

Dostoevsky turned to Egor. "Come. And Broll, you come, too. We will go to the captain." The commander turned to Scott. "Remington, you have time to assist Lieutenant Axen. Travis can transport you. Will you go, or will you remain here? Whatever you choose, you will take Romanov and Voronova with you."

Scott wrestled with his options. The wrestling match was short-lived. "Travis," he said through the comm, "where you are?"

Svetlana turned away from him.

"We're approaching the roof of the warehouse," Travis answered.

That made Scott remember. *Jayden.* Now the Texan was forefront in his mind; now worry had time to sink in. "Ryvkin, how is Timmons?"

Several moments passed before Viktor replied. "He may have serious back injuries, lieutenant. I will get him on a stretcher."

"How critical is time?"

"Time is always critical, lieutenant."

Time was always critical. For a moment, memories of Galina flashed in his head. She was sent back to *Novosibirsk*, too. Not even that had saved her. Jayden was worth taking the chance again.

"Captain," Scott said, "with your permission, I'd like Travis to take Jayden back to the base. The rest of us can hold our own here."

"Granted, lieutenant," Clarke answered. "Navarro, take Timmons back to base."

Viktor interrupted the transmission. "I will go with him. Ms. Yudina can come as well if she wishes."

"*Yes!*" Varvara's voice cut in.

Clarke's grew irritated. "Denied. We're not sending two-thirds of our medical crew home."

Scott switched to a private connection. "Captain, he's right. Varvara's useless right now. Do you think she'll be able to concentrate here? And do you really trust her with Jayden's life by herself?" It was a heartless comment, and the hurt look in Svetlana's eyes showed it. But it was still true.

"Point made," Clarke answered. The comm chatter returned to public frequency. "Very well, Ryvkin. You and Yudina may escort Timmons home."

"Thank you, captain," Viktor answered.

Scott looked at the church. There would be no meeting with Max's team now. Not with the *Pariah* leaving the scene.

"Lieutenant," said Nicolai, approaching him, "are we really going to try to fight this fire?"

Behind Scott's faceplate, he was glaring. "Absolutely not." He went back on the comm. "Travis, contact every fire department that you can. If any of them have any vehicles to spare, send them to our position." Entire city blocks were already engulfed. There were probably fire and rescue vehicles everywhere.

"Boris is already on it."

Scott turned to Svetlana. "In that first residential building, there are two priests. Go make sure they're not hypothermic."

She stared at him for a long moment, then left.

"What will *we* do, lieutenant?" Nicolai asked.

"We're staying here. There could still be Bakma about. Or even canrassis." Just like soldiers weren't firefighters, firefighters weren't soldiers. If a fire truck arrived, its occupants would need protection as well.

"Goronok, Broll, come," Dostoevsky said. "We will meet up with the captain." Egor and Auric acknowledged, and the three men left, too.

Scott and Nicolai were alone.

* * *

THE MOMENT THE *Pariah* touched the roof, Varvara burst from its doors. She was upon Jayden in seconds. When she saw the Texan's butchered face, she covered her mouth.

Esther was fast to turn her away. "Varya, don't look. Jay will be fine, Viktor's taking care of him."

Varvara shoved her away, diving to Viktor's side. "Will he be okay?"

"Get the spinal board and prepare the high-flow oxygen," the slayer said. "And get him ready for hypothermic suspension!"

Varvara bolted into the ship.

At that moment, Clarke and David appeared. They emerged from the same stairwell where Viktor had been. They too were beside Jayden in seconds.

"What happened?" David asked. It was the first time in weeks he sounded concerned about anything. When he actually saw Jayden, his face became pale.

"He got shot from behind," Viktor said, shaking his head. "I know nothing more. Esther says she saw him fall. I was in the building."

Clarke stooped down beside them. "Did you kill those Bakma on the top floor?"

"Yes, captain. Then I heard the blast on the roof. I ran to him as fast as I could."

"Is he going to survive?"

"I do not know the extent of his injuries," Viktor answered. "I cannot know until we return him to base. I am taking every precaution. I am assuming this scenario is worst-case."

Varvara returned, pushing the stretcher. Tears streamed down her face. They moved Jayden onto the bed.

Esther took David aside, where she whispered. "He's going to be fine. We have to believe that. For Jay *and* for her."

David said nothing.

The bay doors lifted as soon as Jayden was on board. Varvara whimpered and knelt by his side.

From behind, Viktor fastened his eyes on Varvara, where his gaze lingered faintly on the curves of her body. Then he reached out. Placing his hand on the back of her neck, he gently gave her a squeeze.

"He is always so careful," she cried in Russian. "He always knows what is going on all around him." She began to break down.

"Varya," Viktor said softly, "I want you to hear me. He will survive. That is my promise to you. Look at me, Varya." He placed his hand on her chin and tilted it to him. "I *promise* you—I will not let him die. Do you believe me?"

She stared at him for several moments, then her shimmering eyes settled back on the Texan. "Yes."

Viktor watched her for a moment, then smiled. "That makes me glad. You stay where you are. Hold his hand. I will do everything else."

She entwined her fingers around the Texan's.

The *Pariah* took off.

7

SUNDAY, NOVEMBER 6TH, 0011 NE
2134 HOURS

AT THE SAME TIME

MAX WAS ALONE on the second floor of the federal building. Lieutenant Brunner and Maksim had gone ahead to confront the Bakma deeper in the facility, leaving the battered technician to watch the balcony alone. Everything on the first-floor lobby was quiet.

"Missile!"

It took a moment for Max to recognize that the shout was not a part of radio traffic. It had come from directly beneath him—from one of Brunner's men in the first floor. By the time he realized it, it was too late.

The outer entrance of the lobby exploded. The blast reached the second floor, where Max was thrown off his feet at the top of the stairs. He howled as his back hit the wall.

Bakma warriors poured into the first floor like rampaging pirates, their plasma rifles bursting with white flashes.

As flakes of ceiling and wall debris drifted down on Max, his senses fought to recalibrate. He scrambled to his feet, wincing as he stood on his wounded leg, and grabbed his assault rifle from the rubble around him. Stumbling to the rail, he looked down on the first floor.

There were too many Bakma to count. They were everywhere. Their plasma blasts engulfed the sparse EDEN operatives below. Max opened fire from above.

Becan and Oleg witnessed the entire episode from the back of the building, where they'd been waiting in the hallway that opened up into the lobby. They saw the blast. They saw the men from the Thirty-ninth get blown through the air. They saw the Bakma storm in.

Oleg swung up his assault rifle and Becan followed suit. Together, they dashed to the lobby.

Max was instantly surrounded by plasma. The white bolts crashed against the ceiling and walls. Chunks of debris flew over his head. As he dove for any cover he could find at the top of the stairs, he pulled out a grenade and flung it below.

Becan watched Max's grenade as it exploded. It sent several Bakma flying to their deaths, but the Bakma were too spread out for a single grenade to kill them all. Of the half dozen men from the Thirty-ninth who had just been in the lobby, only three scrambled to their feet; the others were motionless heaps. The survivors fled to join Becan and Oleg in the hall, and all five men struggled to return fire.

A plasma bolt struck Becan as he was trying to reload, hitting his chest just inside his shoulder. He flew back and rolled across the floor.

Oleg was fast on the comm. "One operative down."

"That better not be you, McCrae!" Max answered from the second floor. In response, Becan screamed in pain.

As Max scrambled to avoid plasma death, Brunner and Maksim appeared from behind.

"Max, what is happening?" Brunner asked.

"What the hell's it look like? What about the second floor?"

"It is clear!" She and Maksim joined the defense.

As soon as Max had a moment to breathe, he was back on the comm. "Strakhov, who's down?"

"McCrae, lieutenant."

"Veck." He turned to Brunner. "Were any of those guys in the lobby medics?"

"No," she answered. "Kaligan is up here."

Moments later, one of the operatives from Shavrin's team—the team on the opposite balcony of the second floor—toppled backward to the ground as a plasma bolt tore through his armor.

Brunner stared at the fallen operative, then gravely spoke. "That was Kaligan."

Max snarled viciously under his breath, "Thanks, God."

Meanwhile, Becan writhed to escape his half-melted chest plate. Finally, he fought his way free. Tugging up his jersey, he looked at his injury. The left side of his chest was still sizzling as the stench of burned flesh bit his nostrils. He growled through clenched teeth.

"McCrae," Max shouted through the comm, "please tell me you're alive."

"Yes, I'm bleedin' alive!"

Suddenly, another of the men from the Thirty-ninth was caught by a plasma bolt. He dropped like a brick.

"Veck!" Becan hollered as Oleg and the remaining two men held the hall. The Bakma had taken the lobby completely, leaving the hallway as the only EDEN-held area on the first floor. Becan crawled to the fallen man. The soldier's chest was blown apart—he hacked violently to breathe. "This guy just got reefed pretty bad!" Becan said through the comm.

Brunner's voice emerged. "Who is it?"

Becan read the soldier's nametag. "Jacobsen."

"How bad is he hurt?"

Becan stared at the wide-eyed young soldier. He wasn't unconscious. On the contrary, he contorted with terror. Becan lurched forward to hold him down. "He needs someone *now*."

* * *

IT SEEMS ALMOST *peaceful*, thought Scott for the first time that night. Sounds of explosions still rang in the distance along with the echo of projectile and plasma. There was even the frenzy of fire trucks tending to the church. To anyone else, it'd have been anything but peaceful. But Scott saw it all in different light.

None of it involved him.

He and Nicolai had been guarding the street for some time. There were no signs of Bakma, and aside from the lone canrassi that Egor had destroyed, there'd been nothing at all. Scott found it ironic that amid the chaos of a war and a raging fire, he could find serenity. It put his life in perspective.

Svetlana hadn't returned from the residence. He wasn't sure if that was a good thing or not. He'd watched her go through the door he'd kicked through. Thankfully, she'd escaped any shotgun blasts.

He knew he'd be bruised from the shot he'd taken to the chest. But it was better than being pounded by plasma bolts. A shotgun wound, he could survive.

For the first time since her arrival, Scott was glad for Svetlana's presence. He didn't know anything about the priests' conditions, but he knew they were in capable hands.

His thoughts stopped right there. How did he know they were in capable hands? He didn't know if Svetlana was a capable medic—he'd never actually seen her in action. All things considered, he barely knew her at all. It all was so paradoxical. He felt as though he knew her so well.

Nothing ever makes sense.

Turning back to the residence, he watched as the battered front door opened. Svetlana emerged and approached him. His thoughts churned again.

Of course she was capable. She was more than capable. She was a professional. Why else would she have been chief medic? She had even held authority over Galina.

I had just one good conversation with her. Just one, that night in the lounge. Did that really mean so much?

Apparently enough to convince her to return.

"How are they?" he asked.

Svetlana sighed. "They will be fine. The family knew more about hypothermia than I do. If you live here, I suppose that you must."

Silence settled between them. Scott could tell before she spoke that he was in trouble.

"Scott, if Jayden had not been shot and there was no need for the *Pariah* to leave, would you really have left this church unprotected?"

He didn't know how he should answer; the question made him uneasy. Finally he said, "Egor had it right. A church can be replaced. People can't."

She shook her head disapprovingly. "You are wrong, Scott. A church is not just another building. It is a house of God."

If it's a house of God, where is God? Where has He been all this time? Where is He now?

The comm channel crackled, and Max yelled over the airwaves. "We need a medic to the federal building *now*!"

Clarke was the next voice they heard. "The *Pariah* already left with Trooper Timmons."

"Max, what's wrong?" Scott cut in.

"We're in the middle of a trashin' war zone! Some guy from the Thirty-ninth got hit bad! Among other assorted emergencies!"

Scott felt his heart sink. With the *Pariah* already gone, there was no way to fast-track it to the building. "How bad is 'bad?'"

"Like 'he's gonna die' bad!"

* * *

Back on the warehouse roof, Esther was listening to the conversation unfold. She'd stopped doing everything else.

"Do we have any other transports in the area?" Scott asked through the comm.

From his position on the rooftop, Clarke shook his head. "Negative, lieutenant. Jurgen's been trying. Every other unit's overwhelmed."

Esther listened for several more seconds. Then she turned and walked to the edge.

"Max, how far are Remington and Svetlana from your location?" the captain asked.

It was a while before the technician answered. "About a kilometer, maybe more! But it's not a straight line, and there's a half-meter of snow the whole route."

Esther began scanning the streets of Krasnoyarsk below. She scanned the corners and alleys. She scanned the sidewalks and curbs. She scanned everything in a five-block radius.

"We're going to run it," Scott answered through the comm. "Svetlana wants to know how he got hurt."

Becan's voice came moments later. "He got shot through the chest. He has a hole!"

All of a sudden, Esther stopped searching. Her eyes focused on a sidewalk in the distance.

Meanwhile, Clarke growled in frustration off-comm. "I shouldn't have let both medics leave. Stupid, worthless Yudina."

David frowned.

Clarke was back on the comm. "Traverse it as well as you can, Remington. Axen, have you contacted Ulrich?"

"Piece of scat's ignoring my signal."

"*Bloody hell!*" Clarke said, tearing off his helmet.

David sighed heavily beside him. "Because of Khatanga."

"Clarke to Captain Ulrich." Silence. After several moments, he attempted again. "Clarke to Captain Ulrich, bloody come in!" He shook his head in disgust and turned to find Esther. But Esther was gone. "Where...?" Clarke's question trailed off into silence as he and David surveyed the roof.

On the snow-covered street far below, Esther's feet churned furiously forward. When she finally came to her goal—a snowmobile parked on a side street—she knew what to do. In a matter of seconds, the snowmobile roared to life and Esther was gone.

* * *

SCOTT RAN AS hard as he could. He knew it instinctively: someone's life depended solely on them. It went even beyond that. Max had said they were in the middle of a war zone. There was no telling how many people were hurt—and were likely desperate for additional help. Behind him, breathing laboriously and struggling to keep up, Svetlana plodded through the snow-covered street. Nicolai had stayed behind by the church—someone had to stand guard.

Curse you, Ulrich. Scott was fuming. *We didn't pull Khatanga on the Eighth on purpose. You're so close to where they are now. Just go get them!*

Scott could tell by Svetlana's labored breathing that she was worn out. This was her first mission back since her time away, and she wasn't in mission shape. The lull with the priests had probably hurt more than it helped. Her adrenaline was gone.

"Scott..." she panted behind him. She said nothing else, but her intention was clear. She wasn't going to make it.

"We have to run," Scott called back to her. "Sveta, we can't stop!"

She fell on the ground and vomited.

Scott slid to a halt. *I've had enough.* His face flushed behind his helmet as he screamed in the comm. "This is Lieutenant Remington of the Fourteenth to Captain Ulrich of the Eighth. We need *immediate* assistance at the federal building. We're not the only unit in trouble!" It wasn't someone in the Fourteenth Ulrich was punishing. It was someone from an innocent squad.

"I can make it," Svetlana heaved. She wiped her mouth and stood up.

"Captain Ulrich!" Scott lost any shred of composure he might have had left. *"Don't let them die!"* This was vengeance at its worst. This was an innocent error being repaid with betrayal. All because a scared rookie forgot how to work her comm in Khatanga. All because of—

The mechanical whine came from nowhere. In the moment it took for Scott to whip around, it was already upon Svetlana and him. They dove to the ground as a tidal wave of snow doused them both.

The snowmobile skidded to a stop, its lone rider straddled brazenly on its seat. For a split second, Scott didn't recognize who it was. Then Esther pulled off her helmet.

She stared at Scott with borderline cockiness, her brown ponytail swaying. With a one-handed flip over the bars, she was off the snowmobile and crouched in the snow. "Get them back."

Scott leapt on the snowmobile immediately. He didn't even wait to ask questions. "Hold on to me," he said to Svetlana, sparing her a moment to climb on. She wrapped her arms firmly around his waist. Scott curled his wrist, and the snowmobile surged through the snow. In seconds, it was gone.

Esther stood alone in the center of the street, staring at the fresh snowmobile tracks. Snowflakes had collected on her face and hair, creating a faint shine as they melted. She didn't bother to wipe the moisture away.

Placing her helmet back on her head, she turned and walked to the church.

* * *

Max jumped as a plasma bolt struck his assault rifle. It spun out of his hands and fell down the stairs.

"Veck!"

Beside him, Brunner and Maksim fired. Maksim's hand cannon, set to armor-piercing, consistently blew holes in the walls. But few Bakma were struck.

"I do not understand!" Brunner yelled. "Why does Ulrich not answer us?"

"Because Ulrich is a worthless sack of scat!" Max spat. "To hell with the Eighth!"

Rising from her crouched position, Brunner fired off another round. Two Bakma toppled to the floor far below. She dropped back as Maksim took her place.

"Shavrin," Brunner said through her comm, "what is Kaligan's condition?"

"Kaligan is dead."

Brunner swore in Dutch. "We cannot hold this building." She spoke through her comm once again. "There is a second-floor exit in the rear corridor. It leads to an outer stairwell. Do you know this?"

"Yes, lieutenant," Shavrin answered.

"Fall back to muster point Bravo. Take the civilians. We will follow your retreat."

Max grumbled, pulling out his handgun to fire. He unleashed several shots into the lobby. "Maksim, go with her."

Brunner shot Max a cold stare. "You say that as if you are staying."

"I got a man down on the lower level, too, Ann. I'm not leaving him here."

Maksim reloaded his hand cannon. "I will stay with you, lieutenant."

Brunner gritted her teeth. After a second of indecision, she reloaded her gun. "Shavrin," she said through the comm, "we will not be following you. Continue to Bravo alone."

"Lieutenant?"

"*Do not question me,* gamma private! Fall back to the muster point *now*!" She knelt next to Max and fired a round. "Come together, go together."

Max reloaded his gun.

* * *

SCOTT DECELERATED as he reached the federal building. The snowmobile skidded to a halt by the rear entrance. The moment Svetlana disembarked, Scott brandished his assault rifle and took the lead.

A map of the federal building had been transferred his way. He already knew what to expect. The metal door—the one they were approaching—opened into a wide hallway. That hallway opened into a lobby. That's where the Bakma were. His ExTracker would be useless now. He could hear the chaos on the other side of the back door. It sounded like hell.

An outer stairwell rose above the back door. He looked up, where three operatives from the Thirty-ninth were in retreat. They appeared to be protecting several civilians. They began to fall back down the stairs into the alley.

Those operatives have citizens to tend to. We'll be on our own to help the others. He jerked the metal door open and went inside.

Gun exhaust choked the corridor. Ahead, he could see two EDEN operatives firing through the smoke. Then he spied Becan and the fallen soldier.

The armorless Irishman turned and saw Scott. His eyes were reddened with pain—he was holding back tears. Scott saw why. There was a scorch mark burned into his chest. But the fallen soldier from the Thirty-ninth was worse off. He didn't have a scorch mark, he had a hole.

Svetlana rushed to Jacobsen's side.

Scott turned his focus to the battle. Charging past Svetlana and Becan, he joined Oleg and the remaining soldiers from the Thirty-ninth. "Strakhov, how many are there?"

"I do not know, lieutenant! Too many!"

Scott laid down cover for the wounded behind him. "Max, where are you?"

"On the second floor, above the lobby! Are you here?"

"I'm downstairs, Svetlana's with me."

"Did you find Becan and half-dead guy?"

"Yes."

"Can they be moved?" Max sounded relieved.

Scott turned to Svetlana. She was already answering. "Becan will live, but we *must* move Jacobsen. We have no choice. He will die here."

A plasma bolt whizzed past Scott's shoulder. He heard it crash into the metal door behind him. Retaliating with suppression fire, he barked out his orders. "Strakhov, escort Svetlana and Jacobsen outside. Get Becan out of here, too!" He had no idea if the injured man could be transported on a snowmobile, but there were no other options available.

"Yes, lieutenant."

Taking Oleg's position in the hallway, Scott opened fire at the Bakma ahead. He was helped by the two remaining soldiers from the Thirty-ninth—both capable men. Though the smoke made it difficult to see, he still fired on.

"Max," Scott said through the comm, "we're getting them out of here. Are you in a position to fall back?"

It wasn't Max who answered. It was a woman. "This is Tanneken Brunner of the Thirty-ninth. We have a muster point not far from here. Some from our unit are already en route. If we meet you outside, can you follow us?"

"Yes," he answered. Anything to get out of there. Though he could scarcely see them, he could sense the Bakma getting closer. And if he wasn't mistaken, he heard something that sounded unsettlingly like a canrassi. "We're falling back now!"

"Lieutenant..."

The troubled words came from behind him. Scott fired a quick burst then turned around to find Oleg standing awkwardly by the door. Scott saw the problem before Oleg could explain.

The door was completely welded shut.

Scott felt his stomach invert. His eyes locked onto the metal door, where the plasma bolt that had whizzed past his shoulder only moments before had hit the door's metal frame. The seam had melted together.

This just got bad.

Turning back to the fight, he rejoined the EDEN soldiers from the Thirty-ninth. "We have a problem."

"Battering ram!"

The booming words made Scott jump. It wasn't Brunner at all. The lobby of the federal building erupted as a Grizzly crashed through the wall. Even through the gun-smoke fog, its giant metal hull was impossible to miss. As Scott stumbled back, the ground trembled.

"Y'all call for backup?" asked a second voice over the comm. Scott knew it the moment he heard it. It was Derrick Cole of the Eighth. The first voice became clear.

"Hey guys," William said, "where y'all at?"

The emotional rush Scott felt could scarcely be contained. The adrenaline alone caused his eyes to well. "We're at the back of the building. How many of you are there?" *Thank you, Ulrich,* Scott thought. *You came through for us after all.*

A moment of silence passed before William answered. "Umm…well… two."

Scott's face fell.

Max interrupted the chat. "Did you just say *two*?"

"Yeah…" William said. "Me and Derrick just kinda broke orders."

Scott lowered his head. *I take it back, Ulrich—you're still trash.* The question then struck him. *How'd they get a Grizzly?* No time for that. He opened his comm. "Strakhov, we need you back up here! Max, Brunner, we're going on the offensive into the lobby. Do you have a way out of here?"

"We still have access to the outside from the second level," Brunner answered. "We will stay to cover you while you run for the Grizzly."

That was all Scott needed. Oleg hurried to his side. Further into the smoke, Scott could hear William and Derrick engaging the Bakma. Scott flashed a look back to Svetlana. The injured soldier, Jacobsen, was angrily fighting her off. Scott recognized the look in his eyes right away. *He looks just like Galina did.* A knot formed in his gut. Becan, though hurt himself, was holding Jacobsen as best as he could.

"We are behind you, Scott," Svetlana said.

Scott wasted no time. Bursting forward through the exhaust and debris, he dashed straight into the lobby—straight into the enemy force. His boldness was met with hot plasma. Two shots ricocheted off his shoulder armor, thrusting him backward to the ground.

Assault rifles exploded behind him. Oleg charged through the fray, diving, tucking, then coming to a crouch next to Scott. The soldier fired until his final clip was gone, at which point he flipped out his pistol.

Scott didn't have time to check his shoulder for damage. He saw the canrassi he'd heard—the massive spider-eyed beast towered just meters away. It spewed saliva as it lurched his direction.

William fired his hand cannon from the top of the Grizzly. On the second floor of the federal building, Maksim did the same. Their armor-piercing rounds blew holes in the canrassi's back. The war beast succumbed.

Without a second's delay, Scott thrust himself once again in the midst of his enemies. Three Bakma converged on his position.

Suddenly, Oleg was there. The bearded Russian slid beside Scott, handgun blazing as a melee ensued. One of the Bakma cut a backward flip as Oleg shot it in the face. The former member of the First felled a second with a hard, sweeping kick.

Scott's Nightman instincts took over. He focused on the third Bakma, grabbing it and wrestling it to the ground. Several more were suddenly near him. Some were gunned down by unidentified soldiers. Others, he took aim at himself. Bullets and plasma flew in every direction.

The men from the Thirty-ninth fired frantically. All the while, they pressed farther into the lobby toward William and Derrick's Grizzly APC.

"Man down!" Max yelled from above.

Scott knew it was Maksim without asking. But he didn't have time to look up. His E-35's ammunition ran out, and with no time to grab his sidearm, he had no choice but to engage hand-to-hand.

A plasma bolt struck an operative from the Thirty-ninth. He fell to the ground.

Nonetheless, the plan was working. They'd burrowed a hole through the Bakma stronghold, clear enough amid the chaos to get to the Grizzly, where William and Derrick were firing from its roof.

Svetlana was right behind Scott. She and Becan fought to push Jacobsen through the chaos. They were moving too slowly.

Get to the Grizzly, Sveta! Diving forward and sliding behind a desk, Scott finally had a chance to unholster his pistol. But he was blindsided by a Bakma before he could shoot. Scott twisted and threw the alien off, only to be broadsided by another.

William screamed in pain from the Grizzly.

If this carried on, they wouldn't survive. It was almost impossible to tell who was where. The gun exhaust formed swirling blankets, and the sound was so loud it was painful. White bolts and orange streaks whizzed past everyone's heads.

Finally, Svetlana's voice came. "We're at the Grizzly! We're climbing aboard!"

"Fall back and retreat!" Scott commanded. A Bakma latched onto him from behind—but this time he was prepared. He grabbed the alien and spun it around. He shot the Bakma before it could rise.

Scott searched for the injured operative from the Thirty-ninth and saw that he was already being helped away by his comrades.

Where's Oleg?

As if on cue, Oleg was there, ducking, rolling, and diving to avoid getting shot. The Russian was holding his own. He didn't even look hurt.

The Grizzly's massive engines revved to life. William and Derrick were nowhere to be seen. Both men must have gone back inside the armored vehicle.

"Veck!" Max screamed. "I think Maksim's dead!"

There was no time for concern. Scott and Oleg scrambled desperately for the Grizzly. Scott felt his shoulder burn with every flex, but slowing down wasn't an option. Ahead of him, Oleg leapt athletically up the side of the APC. Crouching and spinning around, the Russian fired from beside the porthole entrance.

Scott scrambled up the Grizzly behind him, pushing the delta trooper down through the hole. Scott dove in behind Oleg's wake, and quickly slammed the porthole shut. "Go! Go! Go!" The behemoth's wheels spun in reverse.

The cabin was in chaos. Svetlana huddled over Jacobsen while Becan shivered in a sweat-riddled state. William was bleeding from his thigh. The other injured operative from the Thirty-ninth clutched his side in agony. Only Oleg, Derrick, and one man from the Thirty-ninth remained uninjured.

For the first time, Scott examined his shoulder. The skin beneath his armor was charred, but he'd avoided the severity of a direct hit. It still burned, but he could work through the pain.

"This ain't gonna be smooth!" Derrick warned. Plasma fire rocked the hull of the vehicle.

Brunner came over the comm. "We have a transport en route. We are exiting from the back of the building."

"Max," asked Scott, "what about Maksim?"

"Like I told you, Maksim is dead."

Scott didn't have time to register remorse. The Grizzly's front end whirled around as Derrick manhandled the wheel. The swift motion threw the occupants of the cabin to the wall. In a burst of acceleration, and the metal monster thundered down the street.

* * *

DAVID AND CLARKE were alone on the warehouse roof, sitting criss-crossed opposite one another as they took in the idleness around them. They'd exchanged few words since Esther's departure, and with the lack of activity in their area, nothing needed to be done. Their purpose had been to secure the radio tower for Jayden. With the Texan out of the picture, and with less resistance than even they had anticipated, their excursion had become a non-event.

The captain looked tired. His eyes sagged with invisible weights and his hair stuck up in odd places. He had the appearance of a man who no longer cared. When he spoke, his voice was laced with disgust. "We were both weak today."

David lifted his head as explosions drummed in the distance. "What, sir?"

"Remington and myself. The two of us were weak."

David said nothing.

Clarke stared at the darkened sky. "Scott is a fearsome leader and a formidable fulcrum. But he still has a flaw." He exhaled a heavy breath. "He still cares too much."

David looked at Clarke with an odd expression, but remained quiet.

"One of his friends was injured tonight—Timmons. And to save one man—one friend—he sent four of us home. Ryvkin. Yudina. Our pilot and our technician. The whole bloody ship, all to save one." His gaze got lost in the distance. "And I let him to do it."

Clarke's monologue went on. "That is my flaw. That is my weakness. No one else here understands the confounding frustration in being a powerless leader. In knowing that your rank doesn't matter—that what you've accomplished amounts to *nothing.*" His words turned to spite. "I am the captain of this squad, but I am subordinate. So why am I here?"

No answer was given.

"I am a husband and a father. Yet I remain here, in this unit over which I have no control. And I give, and give, and give, and get nothing in return. Yet, I choose to remain. I am expected to lead."

David turned to the battle in the distance—to a red sky that was not from a sunrise.

They heard footsteps from the stairwell. David and Clarke turned around as Dostoevsky and his slayers appeared on the roof.

The commander stared at the captain for several seconds. Then he approached. "Captain. We are ready to fight."

"Go fight," Clarke said flatly. "Go fight your bloody battles—go worship death. Do what you're destined to do—rape, pillage, and plunder in the name of The Machine."

Dostoevsky stood motionless, his expression hidden by his faceless fulcrum's helmet.

Clarke's voice was devoid of all emotion. "You haven't a clue what you've done to this planet, Yuri. You've corrupted our chain of command. You've destroyed our cohesion. You wield power at the cost of our humanity." He rose. "Well, you can have your power. You can have your savagery. You can have whatever you want, you despicable chimp. But you will not have this unit."

With those words, he turned to walk away, stopping briefly before reaching the stairs. "When you grow tired of Remington, give him back. We could use someone who cares—even too much."

David said nothing as Clarke left the rooftop, disappearing in the stairwell. He said nothing as Dostoevsky watched the captain go, the fulcrum's own face hidden in blackness.

* * *

As the Grizzly traveled, Scott crossed the cabin to Svetlana's side. Most of the operatives in the APC had removed their armor by that time, as the prospect of reentering the battlefield seemed remote. The ride had grown considerably smoother as the vehicle distanced itself from the plasma-cratered streets.

"How is he?" asked Scott, kneeling beside Jacobsen.

Svetlana looked worried. "He is in shock. His pulse rate is still over one hundred. I have treated this kind of injury many times, and I have seen worse, but we must return him to *Novosibirsk* as soon as possible. He needs infirmary care to survive."

William watched them from several meters away. His own thigh was wrapped thick with gauze. "Is he gonna make it?"

"The sooner we get him back, the better the chance. I cannot make guarantee, but...I think he will survive." She looked over at Becan, then briefly at Scott. "I must tend to the others." She quietly slipped over to the Irishman.

"How did you get a Grizzly?" Scott asked William. That question had been on his mind since they'd first arrived for the rescue.

William's face was stoic. "There was an EDEN station not far from where we landed. We took it."

"You *took* it?"

"Come on, man, we just saved your life."

Derrick looked back from the cabin. "You know Ulrich's gonna be ticked, right?"

"Forget Ulrich," William scoffed. "That guy is a jerk."

Scott wondered what made Ulrich a jerk to William—if he was referring to his behavior in Krasnoyarsk, or if he'd been brash all along. He considered delving more, but he wasn't given the chance. William elaborated before Scott could ask.

"Couple of months ago, I had this big five-gallon bucket of barbeque sauce shipped to me from Memphis. It was gonna be awesome." He shook his head. "Ulrich confiscated the whole thing...every last bit. So now we're stuck eatin' the Russian crap they serve here."

Svetlana cleared her throat noisily, but it was ignored.

"So yeah," William concluded, "Ulrich's no good. He's the kind of guy who goes straight to hell."

Scott had no words.

It took several minutes for the news of the Fourteenth's casualties to spread around. It took even longer to find out where everyone was. Esther had met up with Nicolai at the church, and the two were en route back to the warehouse. Together, they would catch a ride back to *Novosibirsk* with Clarke and a Vulture from the Thirty-fifth.

Max would go home with Brunner and the Thirty-ninth—or at least, the operatives of her unit that remained. Maksim's body would be taken back with them.

The Thirty-ninth had suffered the worst. At least thirteen operatives were dead across the unit; numerous others were heavily wounded. Two of their officers had been killed.

Contact had been made with Travis and the *Pariah* not long after the Fourteenth's Vulture arrived back at *Novosibirsk*. Jayden had been rushed to critical care, though his current status was still unknown.

Jacobsen aside, the Grizzly's other occupants suffered only non-threatening injuries. The skin on Scott's shoulder had crisped, but it wasn't an incapacitating wound. Becan was in considerable pain, but his kind of injury was common with plasma, much like Scott's except to a worse degree. He'd be out of action, but not for too long. William's thigh was moderately burned, but it was nothing some time off wouldn't fix.

Lieutenant Brunner arranged for them to ride back in the Thirty-ninth's other Vulture—the larger squad possessed two. The Fourteenth was one of the few units that could fit in a single troop transport. It was one of the smallest squads on the base, even despite its recent growth. Brunner directed them to one of the Thirty-ninth's alternative muster points, where they were loaded aboard.

Little was said during the flight back to The Machine. William and Derrick exchanged occasional words, but at times even they appeared forced. Too many other things occupied their minds. There was Jayden, and to a lesser extent, Becan and William. Then there was Maksim's demise. There was Ulrich's refusal to help. There was so much.

The ride back to *Novosibirsk* ended up being one of the quietest Scott could recall. For a squad like the Fourteenth, that said a lot.

8

SUNDAY, NOVEMBER 6TH, 0011 NE
2347 HOURS

BACK AT NOVOSIBIRSK

CLARKE WAS THE first to step from the Thirty-fifth's Vulture. Viktor was waiting to meet him.

"What's Timmons' status?" the captain asked.

"He is in surgery, captain. Varya is with him."

"I don't bloody care where Varya is, I want a rundown on Timmons."

David hurried over to hear the explanation as Viktor drew a preparatory breath. "Do you want the good news, or the bad news?"

David spoke up. "The bad news—"

"The good news," Clarke interrupted. "Let's start with a smile."

"I cannot express how fortunate Timmons is," Viktor answered. "We took every precaution, we treated him as if this was the worst." He took a moment to formulate his words. "His spine is not even *fractured*. He has cuts and bruises and some broken bones, but nothing that will threaten his life."

"He fell twelve meters," Clarke said. "How is that possible?"

"He must have fallen down right with the structure, impacting it all the way down. That is the only explanation I have. The impacts must have slowed his fall."

"That *is* good news. Now let's have the bad."

"He has deep lacerations on his face, apparently when his visor struck the tower. He will need major cosmetic surgery. Both eyes experienced severe corneal abrasions…"

"Which means?"

"…more than likely, he will be blind."

David turned away in disgust. Clarke said nothing.

"Captain," Viktor said, "I wish there was more I could say. This is terrible, terrible tragedy. I wish I could have been able to prevent it."

"Is it absolute fact that he will be blind in *both* eyes?"

"I do not want to say. It is not good to speculate on such things. We can hope for the best."

Clarke stared at the slayer-medic for several moments, before he turned slowly away. "We shall see. Thank you, Viktor, for all you've done. You're one of the good ones."

Viktor was quiet for a moment. Then he bowed his head in reverence. "You are welcomed, my captain."

Dostoevsky and the other slayers exited the Vulture. The fulcrum elite had said nothing during the flight home—not since Clarke had confronted him in Krasnoyarsk. Helmet in hand, he crossed the hangar floor behind the others. It wasn't until Viktor approached him that he showed any emotion at all. "What in the hell were you trying to do?" he asked in Russian. "Why did you go with Clarke?"

Viktor said defensively, "Perhaps I want to end this bickering between us and EDEN."

"Shut up. You are not honorable enough for that. You had a plan."

"Perhaps it was *he* who shot the sniper," said Nicolai smugly. "Were you not asking about Yudina two days ago? Perhaps someone wanted her to be single before Clarke transferred her away."

Viktor suddenly glared Nicolai's way. "Watch your words, you perverted cannibal. I would slit your throat for the joy."

"From this moment on," Dostoevsky said, "you will bring your assignment requests *only* to me. Clarke is not interested in us."

"I disagree," Viktor answered. "He told me that I was a good man."

"He does not know you well enough," Auric said quietly.

"I am still a fulcrum, and you are still a slayer," said Dostoevsky. "Do I need to remind you what will happen if you break rank again?"

"No, commander," said Viktor. "I now understand." After a moment of uneasy silence, he took a step back. "May I be dismissed, my commander?"

"Go."

"Thank you, commander." Without another word, Viktor left the hangar as the other slayers looked on.

Only after he disappeared did conversation resume. Nicolai turned to face Dostoevsky. "I do not think he likes you."

Dostoevsky scoffed under his breath. "If I were hated by the entire world, would it matter?"

"You are not hated by the world. I like you very much."

Dostoevsky stared at Nicolai, who flashed him a dirty-toothed grin. He waved the slayer away. "Go be sick somewhere else."

Clarke was inspecting his armor when a Vulture taxied into the hangar. The captain knew it belonged to the Eighth. His eyes flared. As soon as the transport stopped, the rear door whined open. Ulrich was the first to emerge.

"*Captain Ulrich!*" Clarke shouted angrily.

Ulrich turned to face Clarke's wrath. His own expression twisted into a scowl.

"What in bloody hell was that?" Clarke went on. He stood face to face with the rival captain. "You had *no right* to leave us abandoned!"

"I am so sorry," said Ulrich smoothly. "Did you try to contact us? I suppose we had a 'comm malfunction' too."

"*Rubbish!*"

David and Esther rushed to the confrontation.

"Do not make a mockery of my intelligence," Clarke said. "Two of your own operatives broke rank to save us. Would you care to explain that?"

"Do *you* care to explain how you destroyed half my unit in Khatanga? Or was that not premeditated?"

"*That was not premeditated and you bloody well know it!*"

Before Ulrich could respond, Esther stepped forward. "Captain Ulrich, I was the one who made the mistake in Khatanga. If you're angry, take it out on *me*—"

Esther had no chance to complete her thought. In a motion too quick to prevent, Ulrich punched her square in her jaw. The scout toppled backward to the floor.

The scuffle was on. Clarke surged forward, tackling Ulrich where he stood. David dove to Esther's side, as several operatives from the Eighth jumped on Clarke's back. He was surrounded in seconds.

The fight was emotional, but short-lived. Before too much blood could be drawn, the mechanized shout of a Nightman sentry halted the brawl.

"*Do not move!*"

The operatives turned to the lumbering Nightman. Behind him, a second sentry approached. They ploughed forward like tanks, their metal boots hitting the cement floor sharply as they prepared their assault rifles.

"You will cease all unwarranted activity," the sentry said, his Russian accent thick. "Speak no more words."

On the floor behind Clarke, David helped Esther to her feet. The scout's lower lip was split open. She wiped it on her sleeve.

Ulrich straightened his uniform and exhaled. "I request an audience with General Thoor at once—"

The sentry aimed at Ulrich and opened fire. Every operative jumped as the barrel discharged. Bullets rippled across Ulrich's stomach and chest and blood sprayed from his mouth. It took seconds for the barrage to fell him; then the sentry ceased.

Everyone froze. As the suddenly lifeless body of Captain Ulrich lay sprawled across the floor, their eyes were wide with shock. Silently, they turned to the metal enforcer.

"Dispose of this corpse," the sentry said to an operative from the Eighth.

Terrified, the operative stared back, opened his mouth to affirm, then stopped himself short. He simply nodded and grabbed the dead man.

* * *

THE FLIGHT FELT as if it were the longest of Scott's life. He knew they weren't far from The Machine; he'd heard the pilot exchanging words with NovCom—*Novosibirsk* Command. But every second still felt like a long minute.

When she wasn't tending to the wounded, Svetlana was sitting right next to him. He couldn't blame her for sticking to his side—not after what they'd been through.

He had listened to the radio long enough to hear the latest status of the federal building. To his satisfaction, he discovered that the rest of the Thirty-fifth had finished the job. All Bakma in the building were dead. He was frustrated that he couldn't complete the task himself, but at least it had been done. Better by someone else than by no one at all. If any Bakma stragglers remained in the city, they wouldn't last long. While local authorities skimped out when it came to battles, they did an excellent job of cleaning up. They would be assisted by the city's local EDEN stations once they'd wrapped up their job with the Carrier. Krasnoyarsk would be safe, if not half burned to the ground.

"I forgot what this was like," Svetlana said softly.

Scott looked her way.

"I got used to being a civilian. It was nice." She laughed pathetically. "This is not so nice."

That's why you should have stayed home. He couldn't stop the thoughts from forming, but he held them back. Instead of speaking, he looked at the floor.

"Scott, you there?"

The voice came from Scott's handheld comm. He immediately recognized it as Max.

"Scott?"

Rising from his seat, Scott took the comm to the back of the Vulture. Lowering the volume for privacy, he brought it up to his lips. "I'm here."

"Ulrich's dead, man."

Scott's face must have registered his surprise, for his comrades were all staring at him. He resumed his covert exchange. "What happened? Did he get shot?" The obvious answer had to be yes. Unless he fell out of a Vulture. Nonetheless, he was surprised he hadn't heard it over the open channel. News like that tended to spread.

"A sentry killed him."

"A sentry? I don't understand."

"I don't know all the details. Clarke just commed me. Something happened back at the hangar."

Ulrich dying in the hangar? What could possibly have happened that would induce a sentry to kill him? He had a feeling Krasnoyarsk was part of it.

"How's Becan?" asked Max.

Scott turned to the Irishman, who was in less pain now thanks to morphine and burn gel on the wound. Svetlana had done well. "I think he'll be fine," he said. He could hear Max sigh with relief.

"At least only *one* of us died," Max said.

Max's words struck Scott as heartless until he had a moment to think them through. Maksim was dead. That was indeed terrible; the young demolitionist had been cursed from the start. But that *only* Maksim was dead—that was a minor miracle. He tried not to think about God, but only halfway succeeded.

"All right," Max said. "I'll see you back home."

The comm channel closed.

Scott lowered his head. Maksim Frolov. Though the demolitionist had

had several good missions after Khatanga, he'd been more in the background than anywhere else. What a wasted career. *I should have taken more time to know him. Now it's too late.* He forced himself to think about something else. Maksim wasn't the mission's only loss.

Ulrich was dead. The Eighth was leaderless. He wondered how William and Derrick would take it. He wondered how he would tell them. Returning to his seat, Scott lowered himself next to Svetlana. She looked at him with curiosity.

"Scott, what is the matter?"

How would he even begin to explain it? It wouldn't even matter to her. To her, Ulrich meant nothing. He was a Russian name, nothing more. She hadn't been there in Khatanga. But to William and Derrick, he meant their careers. He glanced at them. Both men were watching him with apprehensive stares, and as soon as it became apparent that the news concerned them, they approached.

"What is it?" Derrick asked.

Your commanding officer was just murdered. How else was he supposed to say it?

"Scott?"

Just say it. Just get it out. "Ulrich was killed by a sentry."

Neither William nor Derrick said a word; they simply stared. Then William reacted, his gaze falling to the floor for a moment as he lost himself in deep thought. Then his eyes settled on Derrick. When William spoke, his voice was thick with new purpose.

"Dude. I bet we can get our barbeque back."

* * *

Back in the hangar, Max was carrying Maksim's body bag out of the Vulture and prepping it for departure. It was a tedious task usually carried out by several people, but Max was the only member of his team there. There was no captain, no commander, no one else from the Fourteenth. It all fell on him.

"Veck," he said under his breath.

Brunner approached him from behind. Like Max, she was out of her armor. Her brown pigtails dangled behind her head. "What is wrong?"

"There's no one else here and I gotta make a report."

"Report about what?"

"About casualties, Ann! I got one man dead and one injured, and it's my doggone fault."

"Max, it was not your fault."

"Then who the hell's fault is it? You see anyone else from my team standin' around?"

"Max..."

"This was just a bad mission. That's it. Just one of those missions from hell. We get a lotta those in this squad."

Brunner was quiet for several moments, then her jaw set firmly. "Thirteen of my teammates are dead. By the end of the night, there may be more." She stared as he looked the other way. "And you are feeling sorry for yourself because you lost *one*. Shame on you, Matthew."

An awkward silence ensued, and she turned to walk away.

"Ann!" he called after her. She walked on without stopping. "Veck, Ann, I'm sorry! Gimme a chance to say something here!"

When she turned and saw the sincerity in his eyes, her anger relented. "I will pray for your men. I expect you to do the same thing for mine."

Max sighed. "All right, fine."

She acknowledged and left.

* * *

DAVID AND ESTHER stood alone in the infirmary. It didn't matter that surgeons and nurses were bustling past them or that they were periodically forced to step aside to allow wounded through. In the midst of the clamor, they were alone.

No word had come back about Jayden—not since the initial report. They were forced to endure the anxiety of having no news. They could do nothing but wait.

Varvara was somewhere in the infirmary. Supposedly, so were Travis and Boris. No one else's whereabouts was known.

Not once had Esther shed a tear, despite the knowledge that two of her comrades had fallen either to death or heavy casualty, and despite the fact that she'd just been punched in the face. Her lower lip, swollen and torn, was Ulrich's final mark on the Earth.

"You saved that guy Jacobsen's life today," David said, his voice barely a murmur. "You did good."

She watched him for several seconds, scrutinizing his expression. Finally she spoke. "I just did what I did."

"Esther..."

Surprisingly, the voice wasn't David's. Esther turned to find the source of her name. It was Varvara. The ragged medic was running toward them. The moment she reached her friend, she buried her face in Esther's shoulder. Tears poured as Esther pulled Varvara in close. For the first time since they'd arrived back, Esther's British stoicism faltered. "It's okay. It's okay."

"What did you hear?" David asked.

Varvara didn't answer.

"It's okay," Esther whispered again.

Travis and Boris appeared down the hall and approached them. "There's good news and bad news," ventured the pilot.

"The bad news," said David firmly.

Travis frowned. "Boris and I didn't get to go in, but we saw photos. Jayden looks like a wreck." He kept his voice low, concealing it from Varvara. "Apparently, he hit metal railings or something all the way down from that tower. Hard enough to slow down the fall and save his life, but it jammed his visor into his face like a cookie cutter."

"What about his eyes?"

"His left eye is gone. They said it was beyond anything they could do. But his right eye...they think it has a chance."

"Is that the good news?"

"Yeah."

"If one eye gets better, that's good enough," David said. "God, I'm not even worried about his career. I just want the poor boy to see."

Travis agreed. "This was the worst thing that could have happened to the best possible person."

"It's not like him not to see a Bakma like that. He's never missed one before."

"Speaking of Bakma," the pilot sighed, "Jayden's got a nasty plasma hole in his back. It couldn't have been a better shot, it hit him straight on. He's lucky he still has a spine."

"Viktor said something about broken bones?"

"Yeah." Travis looked at Varvara again to ensure their privacy. "You name it, he's got it. Foot, fingers, toes...his legs and arms...I heard more bones I couldn't pronounce than in my whole life combined. He's messed up, man."

David grew more concerned. "How bad are we talking about?"

"*They* said all of it's recoverable. The plasma hole, too. They said it's possible for him to actually be at one hundred percent in two or three months, minus being totally out of shape. They said he's the luckiest man on the face of the Earth."

David scoffed.

"I guess we're just at 'wait and see.'" Said Travis. "It all depends on that right eye."

David did not respond.

Clinging to Esther's jersey, Varvara repeated her near-garbled words incessantly. "How could this happen? How could this happen?"

Esther stroked the medic's hair. "He's going to be all right."

For a moment, Esther caught David's eye. He stood beside Travis and Boris, his expression revealing his despair. For her part, Esther remained stubborn. She gently shook her head, mouthing the words, "Do not give up."

David's reaction was faint, but evident. He almost looked ashamed.

* * *

JACOBSEN WAS CARRIED out of the transport while Svetlana clung to the injured man's side despite the fact that he was from another unit. She'd monitored him constantly during the flight, as she had the other injured operatives. Now the injured were being removed. Becan was among them.

It was one of the strangest missions Scott had been on. Though his role in it had been smaller than that of his mission in Chicago, for some reason this one felt larger. It felt as though he'd been on several missions in one.

As Scott stepped into the hanger's open area, he took a moment to observe the chaos. The hangar was bustling as rarely before, undoubtedly due to casualties from Krasnoyarsk.

"Lieutenant."

Scott turned to see Oleg approach. The battle-scarred operative smiled through obvious fatigue.

"Thank you for saving us, lieutenant. We would not have survived without your rescue. Becan and Jacobsen would surely be dead."

Scott answered Oleg with silence. Almost for the first time, instead of fawning, the delta trooper's flattery sounded sincere. "Go find Brooking. Thank her, instead." If not for Esther's arrival on the snowmobile, they'd have never reached the federal building in time. He had no idea where she'd found the vehicle, but she'd done a good thing.

The delta trooper looked puzzled, but acknowledged. "As you wish, lieutenant." He turned and walked away.

Scott recalled the federal building battle. He remembered everything from the moment they entered through the metal door to the moment they were driven away in the Grizzly. He remembered Oleg in particular. Scott had never seen the soldier fight like that before, and he'd never seen Oleg so adept. Prior to joining the Fourteenth, Oleg had been with the First—supposedly the most elite unit in *Novosibirsk*. It was now obvious why.

Every time I turned around, Oleg was there. Shooting. Attacking. Avoiding the enemy. He never got touched. Perhaps there was something untapped there. Perhaps Oleg was epsilon material.

Scott turned back to the hangar, where he found the *Pariah*. It was parked in its regular space at the opposite end. He walked toward it.

It was a mistake to send Travis back.

The cursed transport had been home for quite some time. From the looks of things, it was already prepared to launch again. Reaching out with his hand, he felt the ship's hull.

I never thought I'd miss you.

He stared at the image of the feral dog painted on the Vulture's tail wing. More paint had chipped off, yet the dog still snarled with rabid ferocity. Was the ship cursed? Maybe. But it was theirs. During the entire return ride in one of the Thirty-ninth's Vultures, Scott felt as though he didn't belong. Flying in any other craft just didn't seem right.

His thoughts were interrupted as footsteps emerged from the ship. Stepping back, Scott looked at the rear entrance. Max made his way through the door and down the stairs.

The two lieutenants locked eyes in an awkward moment. Both men were exhausted. Both looked beaten. The soreness in Scott's chest where he'd been blasted by the shotgun was affecting how he walked. Max had a noticeable limp, too.

"I didn't know you were in there," Scott said. Max looked more weary than Scott could ever recall—in fact, he looked lost.

"Yeah," Max answered. "Just wanted to walk through it. For some reason."

Scott understood. There was familiarity with the *Pariah*. "We should have kept it out there. I screwed up." He caught himself at the end of that statement; it sounded uncharacteristically responsible. At least, uncharacteristic as of late.

"Nah." Max looked up at the ship from outside. "I would've done the same thing."

If the ship had stayed in Krasnoyarsk, we might have reached the federal building sooner. Lives could have been saved. Was one sniper worth it?

He hated himself for asking the question, even if only in his head. The emotional side of him said *absolutely.* But the logical side disagreed. He wondered what would have happened had someone else made the decision. Clarke could have made it, but the captain had left it to Scott. He knew what Thoor would have done, but Thoor was too vicious to even matter. *What would Colonel Lilan have done?* For a fleeting moment, he missed Falcon Platoon. Scott was snapped out of his thoughts by Max's next words.

"I'm a horrible lieutenant."

The statement stunned Scott.

"Some people have it," Max continued, "and some people don't. I apparently don't."

Max, what are you talking about? What happened to you? This was the same man who had beaten him senseless in a sparring match the day he'd arrived. Who had mocked his religion to his face. This was his rival. *Is it because I'm worse than you now? Do you feel we're somehow at the same level of crudeness?*

Max ran a hand through his hair, his fingertips disappearing beneath snow-dampened blond spikes. "Sometimes I could die."

Scott still said nothing. Those were words he could understand—but from his own point of view. He had felt the same sentiment many times.

Max stepped away from the *Pariah.* As he strode past Scott, he slowed down. "If you tell anyone I said that, I'll bash in your face. Fulcrum or not." The technician-turned-lieutenant walked away.

Scott watched as Max disappeared. *I'll bash in your face.* That sounded like the Max he knew. For a moment, he considered saying something. But no proper words came to mind. Instead, he queried himself.

When was the last time I actually reached out to someone like Max? Am I really so different now than I used to be? He shook his head. *I'm not different at all. I was always this way. It just took Novosibirsk to prove it.*

Scott touched the *Pariah* a final time before stepping back and turning away. He was ready to go somewhere else, somewhere dark, where he could be alone. He still needed to check on Jayden, but that could come later. The Texan would be in surgery for a couple of hours. Hours, if not days.

Scott made it all the way to his quarters without encountering anyone he knew, and without having to talk to a soul.

That felt familiar, too.

9

MONDAY, NOVEMBER 7TH, 0011 NE
0535 HOURS

EDEN COMMAND

JUDGE TOROKIN'S entire body quivered as his right forearm flexed into a rocklike bulge. He dangled just a half-meter from the ground in one of EDEN Command's many weight rooms. It was an irony that any of the rooms existed at all. He was one of the only men who religiously used them.

He clenched the pull-up bar with white knuckles, lifting himself with one arm. It was a slow motion by design. It was meant to be painful. His chin eased over the bar.

"Seven," he counted in Russian. The word was barely audible as he inhaled a short breath. Exhaling, he lowered himself.

As usual, there was no one else present. On rare occasions, Judge Richard Lena would join him in the mornings. But more often than not, he was alone. Taking a preparatory breath, he once again pulled himself up. His teeth were clenched in focus. As he lifted, his face flushed bright red.

"Eight."

Of all the judges in the High Command, only Torokin could have picked up a weapon and rushed into battle with little to no warning. With office jobs often came physical laziness. He refused to succumb to the same out-of-shape fate as the rest of his fellow judges and staffers.

For a ninth time, his chin edged over the bar. He could feel the muscle fibers tearing in his chest and arms.

"Nine." Then down again.

The routine was always the same. Ten one-handed pull-ups with each arm. This would finish off his entire set. He had been in the weight room for over an hour already. His sweat-soaked hair and gray T-shirt were evidence of that. It was a rare night when he got more than six hours of sleep. Sometimes even six felt like too much.

Closing his eyes and drawing a breath, his forearm flexed one final time. His lips parted to reveal still-clenched teeth. A week of GEC-related activities had set him behind. He felt out of shape.

His body began to tremble frantically as his chin hovered just beneath the bar. His legs bent up by the knees. He groaned softly.

Someone was behind him. He could sense it, even in mid-lift. Someone was watching him from the door of the weight room.

His subtle cries turned into moans of sheer agony, as he bellowed out loud from deep in his throat. He was still beneath the bar.

"You can do it, comrade," the observer said.

He recognized the voice of Grinkov, his friend and fellow judge. Nonetheless, he ignored the man and strained to pull up. His knees bent farther and his lower torso twisted. Finally, he released the bar, his right hand burning. He landed on his feet, cursing out loud.

Grinkov laughed. "So close, but so far."

"How many one-handed pull-ups can *you* do?" Torokin retorted.

"How many did you do just now?"

Torokin crouched down in exhaustion. "Nine."

"Ah. Last time, I did ten."

The ex-Vector scoffed. The day Grinkov could do a single pull-up of any kind would be a day worth inscribing in history. "What do you want?"

Grinkov was wearing a gray and blue sweat suit. It made him look fatter than he already was. The overweight Russian had been attempting to jog himself into shape. He averaged two runs a week. The large judge held out a newspaper. "The GEC is officially a success—Mariner is mocking it."

Torokin grunted in disgust and reached for the paper. "Let me see."

"Page six."

The sweaty judge took the paper, turned to page six, and began to read from his crouched position on the ground.

There was a notable absence at EDEN's annual global conference. Group Captain Jon Mariner of Atlanta's Flying Apparatus Squadron was a surprising no-show, considering the announcement of a new interceptor fighter at the event. When asked about his absence, Mariner was brief in response, stating only that he had "more important things to do."

Torokin threw the paper aside. "More important things to do. Like what? Build a statue of himself?"

"He probably already has one."

"He probably does."

Jon Mariner was as household a name as Klaus Faerber—for good reason. There wasn't a better pilot on the face of the Earth. There wasn't a bigger ego, either. Mariner was well aware of the fact that he'd redefined modern air tactics. His personal squadron—the Flying Apparatus—was the Vector Squad of the sky. He was one of the most peculiar personalities in all of EDEN, known for one-word answers and cold-shoulder arrogance. He embodied everything Torokin hated about pilots and Americans combined. Mariner thought he owned the sky. The worst part was that he practically did.

"He will be the first to get a squadron of Superwolves," Grinkov said. "Wait and see."

Torokin didn't doubt it. EDEN Command had probably asked Mariner's permission to design a new fighter in the first place. He had probably helped design it.

"He makes me sick," Grinkov added. The fat man walked into the weight room, eyeing the pull-up bars briefly. His focus returned to Torokin. "Would you like to run with me today, Leonid?"

Torokin brushed back his hair, then looked at his hand. It glistened with sweat. "Not this morning. I need to go take a shower before the meeting."

"You do not need to shower. Tell them you just got back from a mission. I am sure they will believe you."

"Right," Torokin said, laughing quietly. "I am sure they would." The meeting later that morning was one of necessity. It was a progress report on *Novosibirsk*'s financial audit. Torokin already knew what would be covered—he'd heard the grumblings for weeks. It had been a total failure. Nothing conspicuous had been discovered. No wrongdoing at all. Judges Rath and Onwuka hadn't found a money trail anywhere. It was as if Thoor and his Nightmen were forging their equipment from scratch. For all anyone knew, maybe they were.

"I *am* losing weight," Grinkov said. "I have lost four pounds in two weeks. That is progress. I think I will ask Tamiko on a date. It has been a long time since I have been out with a beautiful woman. Even *you* are beginning to look attractive."

Torokin couldn't restrain a chuckle. "Go run your laps. I am done talking to you."

The larger Russian walked to the door. "I will see you at the meeting." Several moments later, he was gone.

Torokin stayed crouched for some time, his heart finally catching up with his slower breaths. Another day, another meeting. It was like that every day. They were allowed ten days off a year, and he had yet to use any. He was tempted to blow them all at once. The Caribbean sounded pretty nice.

For all he knew, he could already be there.

Approaching the pull-up bar once more, he gripped it with his right hand, closed his eyes, and drew a breath. Flexing determinedly, he tucked his knees and pulled himself up. As soon as his chin passed the bar, he let go and fell back to his feet.

"Ten."

Walking away from the pull-up bars, he felt as if he'd just gone through a dirty washing machine. His body was on fire. But something felt wrong.

He stopped, looked at the pull-up bar again with an irritated stare, and tightened his lips. Marching back under the machine, he reached up and clenched the bar again. Without giving doubt a moment to rise, he flexed, growled in agony, and pulled himself up. After a brief struggle, his chin crossed the bar.

Falling back to the floor, he almost toppled, but maintained his balance. He allowed a brief sigh.

"Eleven."

The sense of something wrong was now gone, as he walked to the weight room bench to claim his towel. He ran it over his hair and face then flung it over his shoulders. He turned to exit the room.

The next day, the pain would set in, especially after that last extra pull. He'd barely be able to get out of bed. But he knew it was necessary. He wouldn't be able to sleep had he stopped at ten—eleven simply had to be done.

Just in case Grinkov had been telling the truth.

* * *

LATER THAT MORNING

THE CONFERENCE ROOM quieted with President Pauling's call for attention. Every conversation drew to a halt.

Torokin stretched his head all the way back. The numbness from his workout was already starting to penetrate. The pain was going to feel soothing.

"I want to thank all of you for a wonderful week," Pauling said. "The GEC couldn't have gone better. I almost hate getting back to normal business."

"There's no need to rush," said Judge Blake. "I'm more than willing to push *Novosibirsk* back another month."

The judges laughed, all except for Torokin. Judges Blake and June wouldn't be leaving for Russia for another week, and Torokin couldn't help but feel they were lagging behind. Nonetheless, their timing didn't matter. Thoor had no idea the visit was coming. They had already hit The Machine with a surprise inventory count. It worked like a diversion to the judges' real plan: to go there themselves. Thoor wouldn't expect two surprises in a row. He probably wouldn't care, either.

"I received a message this morning from General Fuller," Pauling said. "He expressed his appreciation for everyone's hospitality at the conference. He plans to come here again soon."

Fuller was the general who would operate the new base of *Sydney*. Torokin had had an opportunity to chat with him briefly. He seemed like a nice man. Torokin hated him.

"This is the most cohesive we've felt in months," said Pauling. "I couldn't be more proud of our progress. With that said, let's get right into business." He turned to Jason Rath. "What's the word on the audit?"

Rath swapped a worried look with Judge Blake. He then turned to Judge Uzochi Onwuka, though his words were directed to Pauling. "Uzochi and I have scoured literally everything. There is no record of *any* spending outside of what *Novosibirsk* is allotted."

The smile on Pauling's face melted away.

"Obviously, we know they're spending *something* to get Nightman equipment, but..."

Judge Onwuka finished the statement. "General Thoor is a very smart man." His Nigerian accent was at times almost impossible to understand. "It is not surprising that all of his deals would involve the black market. We know that he's as rich in reputation as he is in finances. But no money is coming in or out of *Novosibirsk*. We have to consider that they could be forging their own armor, and transporting the material there by some other means."

"There is the case of the 'Citadel,' as some of them call it," Rath explained. "According to our agents, it's their secret base of operations. But as for where it is, that's anyone's guess. They could be operating a forge there."

Pauling looked thoughtful as he listened to their report. After several moments of absently tapping his pen on the table, he finally replied, "If they're forging their own armor, and they're not using EDEN funds to do it...is that breaking the law?"

Onwuka frowned. "Unless they are selling it for profit, it is legal. It would be no different than if you had made something for yourself in your room, like carving a wooden doorstop. You are not selling it for profit, and you are not using EDEN's money to carve it. All you need is your own wood, your own knife, and your own time. It is perfectly legitimate."

Torokin sighed from his chair as he listened. He had mixed feelings about the whole mess. The Council was going through so much trouble to pin something on Thoor. Was Thoor even the right enemy? *Novosibirsk* was effective for a reason. This all struck him as a waste of time.

The Machine. A modern marvel of terror, dominated by one of the most ruthless tyrants the world had ever known. But what if that was what Earth needed? What if the ends *did* justify the means? Was it better to survive with Thoor—the Terror—or potentially die without him? As horrible a human being as Thoor was, his ability to muster an army was almost beyond compare. The fact that one man at one base was such a topic of conversation said it all.

He snapped out of his reverie and refocused. The judges were still talking about finances and forges, and Rath was still trying to soften the blow of the financial audit's failure. Torokin knew the end result. They'd find nothing on Thoor—he was too smart for that. There was only one way to challenge a general like him: face to face. Thoor would cover everything but the front door. He *wanted* EDEN to come knocking. Torokin refused to believe anything else.

"Don't stop looking yet, gentlemen," Pauling said to Rath and Onwuka. "Even if they do forge their own equipment, they have to get resources from somewhere. Who is their supplier? Payment could go beyond monetary means."

Castellnou spoke for the first time. "What happened to the talk of attacking him? Has that just disappeared? Why are we still talking about audits and resources?"

Torokin reverted to his own thoughts again. Castellnou wanted to attack Thoor. Castellnou was an idiot, but he was brave—at least he could be credited for that. EDEN versus The Machine. That would be an interesting brawl—and a complicated one. The ex-Vector had a feeling it was inevitable, too.

Conversation stopped when Torokin rose to his feet. Every judge and the president turned to the Russian. "Where are you going?" asked Pauling.

Torokin was tired of the infighting. He was ready to focus on the alien threat—the one that actually mattered. "This goes nowhere. Over and over, we talk about Thoor. Why must we do this?"

It was Archer who issued the retort. "Do you not believe it's necessary? We must face our enemies with a united front. If Thoor divides us, we will certainly fail."

"That is fine, whatever. Malcolm and Carol go there in a week. Let us talk about it when they return." He motioned cordially to Rath and Onwuka. "The financial audit has failed. There is no other way to put it. Why must we continue to discuss it? We should move on."

Pauling let loose a sigh. "Leonid—"

"I know, Mr. President," Torokin said. "You think this needs to be discussed. So, discuss it as much as you need. Invite me back when you are finished." He was sick of it, and there were too many other important topics at hand. Like the Alien War. He pushed in his chair.

"I respect Judge Torokin's opinion," Archer said, looking at Pauling for a moment, then at the retreating judge. "We look forward to your return."

With no further words to deter him, Torokin left the room.

As he walked through the halls of EDEN Command, Torokin felt his soreness strike again. He couldn't get enough of it. He almost wished it hurt more. The ache of battle. The burn of striving to make a difference—that was what he needed. The politics, he could do without.

He was halfway down the hall when he suddenly stopped, his mind struck by an unexpected thought. *Since when does Archer give me permission to leave?*

After a short pause he resumed his walk. In the grand scheme of things, it didn't matter. Archer loved politics. So did Pauling, despite the fact that he'd once been a soldier. It was only natural that their kind shared the spotlight.

Maybe Archer thinks he will be president.

That thought brought Torokin a smile. Archer as president. That was almost cute.

When Torokin arrived in his quarters, he resumed his workout. Push-ups. Sit-ups. Leg raises. Lunges. He did everything—the more ways he found to hurt, the better he felt. That was how he wanted it to be.

The other judges did not call him back.

10

MONDAY, NOVEMBER 7TH, 0011 NE
0800 HOURS

NOVOSIBIRSK, RUSSIA

SCOTT SQUINTED AS his alarm clock went off. With an almost instinctive slamming of his palm, he shut off the device. His room was silent again.

Closing his eyes, he brought a hand to his face. The motion was painful, and the burn marks on his shoulder caused him to groan. Rubbing his hand across his forehead, he exhaled slowly.

Was yesterday real?

The moment he tried to sit up, he winced. His stomach felt as if it were being ripped apart. Lifting his shirt, he looked at his bruise. It stretched almost clear across his torso. It looked like he'd been hit by a log.

I guess yesterday was real.

Gathering the mettle to sit, he carefully leaned his neck to each side. After a series of satisfying pops, he leaned his head back. It didn't feel like morning. It didn't feel like anything familiar. It felt as though he was existing in a personified premonition of horrible news.

Jayden and Becan are hurt. Maksim is dead. What other tragedies await?

He'd heard no updates from anyone upon returning to the base—not that he'd sought any out. He couldn't help but recall the last time one of his comrades was in the infirmary. Galina. He'd learned of her death when David knocked on his door. When David told him he no longer cared. There was a part of Scott that was convinced another knock would come at any moment. But none did.

Pushing up from his bed, he stumbled to his closet. Removing his Nightman uniform from its hanger, he dressed methodically. He gave little attention to his grooming, sparing nothing more than a quick look in the mirror to ensure that he didn't appear completely unpresentable.

Partially unpresentable was okay. For a moment, he actually considered shaving. But the moment came and went without action.

As he crossed the room, he looked briefly at his desk. The manila folder still sat there, untouched since he'd last taken it to Confinement, but not out of his mind. It never was. Scott opened the door and stepped into the hall.

Krasnoyarsk hadn't been the largest battle he'd ever fought, nor the most important. His entire contribution had involved only two buildings, and not full buildings at that. Next to the *Battle of Chicago* or the *Assault on Novosibirsk*, it paled. It would probably not even be named for historical purposes. Nonetheless, it had been one of the hardest to endure—a war unto itself.

No one else was in the infirmary when Scott entered—at least, no one else from the Fourteenth. He wondered for a moment if he was the first to arrive, but he knew better: he was probably the last.

He made his way to the nurses' desk, where he learned of his teammates' conditions. Becan was expected to recover, though he would remain in the infirmary for at least two weeks, which was longer than Scott had initially thought. Plasma had burned much of his chest, and his body would forever be scarred. There'd be skin grafting involved. That was as much as Scott wanted to know.

It was the news Scott heard next that hit him in the gut. Jayden would be at least partially sightless. His left eye had been removed, and his right eye was still on the verge. The question was not whether the Texan could return to active duty; it was whether he'd be able to see at all. His family had already been contacted, and preparations were being made to send him home after his recovery. After that, none of the nurse's words registered as real. Scott felt as though he were dreaming again.

Jayden was not allowed visitors. Not even Scott's fulcrum status could garner him rights. According to the nurse, Jayden was being kept sedated while under their care. Scott was instructed to return in two days.

It wasn't until several minutes later, as Scott was returning to the officers' building, that the information he'd received actually processed. Jayden might be totally blind. Jayden—his friend from *Richmond*. Their first encounter replayed in Scott's head.

He was slender, though height compensated for a lack of size. His arms were folded across his chest as he leaned against the doorway arch, and his shadowed gaze scrutinized them beneath a tuft of dusty brown hair.

"Who's that?"

"No idea." Scott shook his head.

"Hey there!"

Startled, the stranger shifted bodily to face them. Everything about the motion was uncomfortable, and his body language immediately withdrew. His gaze darted down to the floor, and he mumbled a response. "Howdy."

He had to be from Texas.

Scott stopped when he came to his door. That memory seemed like so long ago. Like a forgotten time. When life still felt warm and with a point.

He knew there'd be business that day. On these kinds of days, it was inevitable. There were things to discuss and decisions to make, on more than a few topics. He knew it wouldn't be pleasant.

Scott ate a light breakfast that morning—only what was there in his room. His appetite was simply nonexistent.

* * *

SVETLANA CRINGED AS her body touched the ice water for the first time. She gripped the sides of the metal tub, easing her descent just above the surface. She muttered in Russian.

Her morning had been laden with pain. From the muscles in her calves to the small of her neck—everything hurt. It was a soreness she hadn't felt since she was a cadet. Having grabbed her turquoise swimsuit from her Room 14 closet, she'd made her way to the gymnasium-sized pool. After changing in the locker room, she filled one of the soaker tubs with ice water. It was her best option to provide immediate relief.

Finally she mustered the courage to submerge her body, shivering as she did so. It took several seconds for the initial shock to subside, then she leaned her head outside the tub.

No one had accompanied her to the pool. That suited her just fine. She wasn't in the mood for socialization. She lifted her head, passing a wet hand through her hair. The alone time felt good. It felt needed and long overdue.

"Svetlana?"

The British voice caught her unaware. She turned her head to the side of the tub. The voice had come from her comm; it was unmistakably Clarke's.

"Svetlana, are you there?"

Closing her eyes for a moment, she bit her lower lip. She fought back the temptation to curse. Gingerly reaching down for the device, she brought it to her lips. "Yes, captain?"

"I'm about to have a meeting with the officers. I'd like you to attend."

As soon as she heard it, she rolled her eyes. Her arm drooped outside of the tub, carrying the comm with it. It took her several moments to reply. "As you wish, captain."

"Lounge. Five minutes." The comm channel closed.

For several seconds, Svetlana didn't move. She only stared dull-eyed at the wall, still holding the comm to her lips. Finally dropping it back on the floor, she closed her eyes. "Lounge. Five minutes," she muttered mockingly. Sliding forward, she sunk her head beneath the water's surface.

It was the only place she could be left alone.

* * *

SCOTT WASN'T SURPRISED that he'd been called to Room 14. What surprised him was that it was so early in the day. At least, it was early for Clarke. The captain had been a procrastinator as of late. It was unlike him to address anything immediately.

In the short time that Scott had been alone in his private quarters, he'd taken a few minutes to adjust his appearance. He'd fixed his hair enough to look passably respectable, and he'd actually taken a few moments to shave after breakfast. The smooth skin felt good.

It felt odd having an officers' meeting. Over the past several months, they'd had few. They usually happened when something significant was afoot. This definitely qualified as one of those times.

Scott scanned Room 14 as he stepped inside. The only operative present was Esther. The scout lifted her head from a book as he entered. "Good morning, lieutenant," she said, placing her book down.

Scott offered a cordial nod. "Good morning, Brooking. What are you reading?"

She hesitated. "*In the Custody of Angels.*"

"What is that? Religious?"

"...gothic romance."

"Oh." He had no idea how to respond. If nothing else, he found it unique—and a little dark.

Esther's face tinged a deep shade of red. She awkwardly raised the book from her lap.

A legitimate question came to Scott's mind. "Yesterday, did anyone tell you to do that?"

She looked at him oddly.

"The snowmobile."

Her countenance changed. She stopped short of a frown. "No, sir. I apologize."

She was apologizing? For what? "You made an excellent decision. You don't need to apologize for that."

She looked at him strangely, then smiled. "Thank you, sir."

Nodding, Scott reached for the door. To give someone praise felt refreshing. He hadn't done that in months. He twisted the knob, but stopped short, turning back to her. He had to ask. "Is your name really Molly?"

She immediately looked embarrassed. "Yes, sir. Molly Esther 'Polyester' Brooking."

Scott couldn't hold back his amusement. "That's cute."

Her deep shade of red surfaced again. So did her grin. She watched as Scott left for the lounge. As soon as he was gone, she plopped her head on her pillow, closed her eyes, and let loose with an *ugh*.

Moments later, Svetlana entered from the hall. She was in her uniform, a bathing suit folded in her hand. Her blond hair was still damp. As she made her way through the room, Esther's eyes tracked her every step.

"Hello Esther," Svetlana said, forcing a smile.

"Hello, Svetlana." Esther's smile was unabashedly fake.

Svetlana stepped through to the lounge.

Esther continued to stare for several seconds, even after Svetlana was gone. Finally, she returned to her book. "Yellow-headed tart."

The officers were already seated when Svetlana entered. The moment Scott saw her, his surprise was evident. Dostoevsky and Max were also taken aback.

Clarke cleared his throat immediately. "I've asked Ms. Voronova to join us. As chief medical officer, I value her opinion."

She nodded apologetically. "I am sorry to be late," she said, taking a seat across the table from Scott.

The captain wasted no time. "To say we have much to discuss is an understatement."

Scott turned his attention to Svetlana. He wasn't sure if Clarke legitimately valued her input or if he was still trying to force her upon him. Either way, Scott realized he didn't mind. She had done enough in

Krasnoyarsk to earn her the privilege of contribution to the meeting, even if she was out of mission shape.

Suddenly Scott realized he was staring. He quickly looked back at Clarke.

"I received an update this morning from infirmary," the captain said. "There is some good news—we can expect McCrae to return in about two weeks. His injuries are quite recoverable." He was quiet for a moment. "With that, our good news comes to an end."

Max shifted uncomfortably in his chair, the metal casing of an unlit sprig held between his fingers.

"As you know," Clarke continued, "Frolov is dead. His body is being flown home today. I don't know the exact time, but if you wish to know, just contact NovCom."

Scott lowered his eyes. He wondered if anyone would be there to see Maksim off. Few people had really known him.

"The additional awful news is about Timmons. Is anyone else already aware?"

No one made any indication. Scott looked around the table, slowly acknowledging with a raised hand. He was certain he wasn't the only one who knew something.

The captain's frown was genuine. "Timmons is fortunate to be alive. He will walk, and he will talk. Let's take that good news just as that. Some of you may already know that his left eye has been lost. Barring a miracle, his right eye will be, as well. For a sniper, that can't quite do."

Clarke almost sounded smarmy. Scott knew it wasn't intentional, but nonetheless the captain's tone seemed less than compassionate. He wondered if anyone else had heard it that way.

"As much as it pains me to say, we have to move on. The Fourteenth has never been without a sniper, and Ms. Brooking was sent here specifically to supplement—"

"Hang on," Max interrupted, "back up the short bus. Don't tell me we're about to start talkin' about replacements..."

"That's precisely what we're talking about."

The technician threw up his hands. "You said 'barring a miracle!' For God's sake, let's wait for the miracle!"

Scott sighed. This was where it would begin—the downward spiral that would ultimately doom the meeting. It was already happening.

"Lieutenant Axen, please understand that Timmons' career with EDEN is effectively over. That he's alive is a blessing in itself."

"Who says it's over?"

"That would be the man we call *surgeon*."

"To hell with surgeons—give the guy a freakin' chance to improve!"

Scott, Dostoevsky, and Svetlana simply watched. It didn't feel right to try and force a word in.

"Understand the word that I'm saying," explained Clarke. "*Blind*. This is the word that describes Jayden Timmons."

Max shook his head. "He ain't totally blind yet, he's still got one good eye."

"And one eye is a problem!"

Max threw the unlit sprig to the floor. "Is this really how fast it ends? Can we give the guy a day of respect before we throw his career in the trash? Can we not give it *one more day* to see if somehow this thing turns around?"

"Will the Bakma give us a day of respect? Will the Ceratopians?"

"Captain, that's not the point."

Clarke's nostrils flared for the first time. "*The point is that I am captain of this unit! If I say we move on, we bloody move on!*"

Even Scott jumped. He'd never heard the captain's voice like that. Not even in his worst moments.

Max stood up from his chair.

"Where are you going?"

Max's frustrated glare did not waver. He swiped his sprig from the tiles below. "To hell with this unit." He stormed out of the lounge, slamming the door. The others looked on blankly.

"What is it with you Americans?" Clarke asked, glaring at the door Max had slammed. "The irony of this is that he didn't even give me a chance to bloody finish."

To finish what? What irony? Scott looked at Svetlana and Dostoevsky. They looked as confused as he was.

"By now, you're aware of our situation with the Eighth," Clarke said. "You know about Ulrich. What I had *intended* to explain to Mr. Axen is that we require additional operatives to fill now-empty roles. In the aftermath of Ulrich's demise, Commander Plotnikov has control of the Eighth. His first executive decision was to 'remove' William Harbinger and Derrick Cole."

Scott sat up straighter.

"I am giving you the option. We can attempt to replace Frolov and Timmons with a demolitionist and a sniper from somewhere else, or we can 'adopt' our friends from the Eighth. Due to the personal nature of this rubbish, I was going to let you decide."

Scott was surprised. Clarke was actually giving them the power to choose. Granted, it was a choice with a blatantly stacked answer, but it was a choice nonetheless. It was democracy at its most British.

Svetlana seemed uncertain. She looked uncomfortable to be included.

"Personally," Clarke said, "I'll be properly shocked if this vote isn't unanimous. Does anyone *not* prefer Harbinger and Cole over two altogether new people? I'm accustomed to having a sniper, but Cole will suffice. And Harbinger would fill our demolitionist role well."

No one opposed.

"Then the matter is resolved. Remington, would you kindly inform your acquaintances from the Eighth?"

"Yes sir." William and Derrick, in the Fourteenth? That was the best news he'd heard since Svetlana had come back. Once again he looked at her.

"Thank you." Clarke motioned to some papers on the table. "These are their medical papers, Svetlana. I anticipated this result." He pushed up from his seat.

"Now...hard as it may be to believe, I miss my wife terribly at the moment. I had planned for this to be a constructive conversation, but apparently that was a foolish idea. Shame on me. Dostoevsky, the unit is yours."

The commander uttered a quiet affirmation, at which point Clarke stepped from the room. He offered no goodbyes.

It was the quickest exit Scott had ever seen from Clarke, and he had a feeling he understood why. The captain was frustrated to new heights—he had been met with resistance even while trying to do favors.

"I need to read Harbinger and Cole's medical papers," said Svetlana, pushing back her chair. "I do not know them like you."

Dostoevsky reached out to pick up the papers himself, but before he could grab them, Svetlana snatched them away.

"I will read them," she said. "Not you."

"Sveta..."

She glared at him. "Nothing has changed, Yuri. Do you think I have words for you? I do not." Turning away from the table, she walked out of the room with the papers in hand.

Scott and Dostoevsky—the two lone fulcrums—stood awkwardly in her wake. For several moments, neither man spoke. Dostoevsky finally broke the silence.

"I was going to hand them to her so she didn't have to reach."

Turning to the commander, Scott found himself caught in the sudden realization: he was sitting with Dostoevsky as though they were comrades. As though they were friends. He felt nauseated. Like Svetlana, he had nothing to say to the man who'd arranged his fiancée's murder. Dostoevsky might as well have been dead. Scott stood and walked out of the room.

Dostoevsky was left alone once again.

"Sveta," Scott said, hurrying to catch her in the hallway. Svetlana stopped and turned around.

Something had been hovering over Scott's conscience since the mission. Something Svetlana had told him about righteous men. "I want to tell you something."

"Well?" she said when he didn't elaborate.

"A church is a building. That's it."

She pressed her hand to her forehead and looked down. Strands of hair fell through her fingers.

Clearly she was not understanding what he was trying to say. It completely escaped her. "I'm trying to be respectful," he said. "It's not the brick and mortar that makes it holy or not holy. It's what happens inside." He wanted to justify himself. That was it. He didn't want to be blamed for something that really wasn't his fault.

For several moments she stared at him, saying nothing, distanced in thought. "Do you really believe that, Scott Remington?"

Of course he believed it. He wouldn't have said it if he didn't. "Yes, I do."

"Then apply it to yourself."

Scott blinked. Her statement took him aback.

Svetlana offered no other words. She simply turned and walked away.

Then apply it to yourself. The words resounded in his mind. *Then apply it to yourself.* He tried to pretend he didn't know what she meant, but he did. He could not help staring down at his uniform—his black Nightman exterior. His own brick and mortar.

He looked up again. Far ahead, she rounded a corner and disappeared. *That's not fair, Sveta.* That was a low blow. A sucker-punch to the gut of his soul. That one would linger.

He made no more attempts to catch up to her, nor attempts to reconcile his emotions. In the aftermath of the soft-yet-stinging confrontation, Scott forced her words to the back of his mind. He could wait to deal with them when he felt like tearing out his own heart.

At least that was something he was good at.

11

MONDAY, NOVEMBER 7TH, 0011 NE
1157 HOURS

WILLIAM'S EYES opened wide. "Are you serious?"

"Yes, I'm serious."

"That's *freakin'* sweet!"

Scott had gone to the cafeteria directly after his exchange with Svetlana. The task was a welcomed escape. He knew William and Derrick wouldn't be in Room 8; the Eighth would already have kicked them out. Of all the places in *Novosibirsk* they might have been, the cafeteria was the most likely. He had been right.

It was a pleasant surprise to see William up and moving. His leg was bandaged, but he looked otherwise unhindered. He would be ready for action in a matter of days.

"Shoot," said Derrick, chewing on some beans. "That's gonna be awesome. Being with the Eighth flat-out sucked."

"Yeah," William said. "We were like, the only people who spoke English. You guys have the unit to be in if you're an American."

It always struck Scott how normally William and Derrick treated him, even after he'd gone to the Nightmen. The fact that he wore a crimson triangle didn't seem to faze them. He leaned back in his chair. "You know not everyone in the Fourteenth is American?"

"I know," answered William. "But everyone there speaks English. We tried to learn Russian, but that language sucks."

Scott considered whether he was offended. He'd felt more Russian than American lately. He liked the language, especially since he'd become fluent.

"I heard about Jayden, man. Is he really gonna be blind?"

Scott's face fell slightly. "We're holding out for the slim chance he'll still see out of one eye. Supposedly it doesn't look good, but it also didn't look good when he fell. We'll just have to wait."

"If he can see out of one eye, he can stay, right?"

"It'd be tough," said Derrick. "He's a sniper, man. He needs to have two eyes."

"Man, whatever," William made a stupid face. "A sniper doesn't need two eyes. It'd just be like he's aiming all the time."

Scott was barely listening to the exchange. His mind was still fixed on the Texan. He had to wait two days before he'd be allowed to visit. Two days seemed like an eternity.

"So when can we move in?" Derrick asked.

Scott refocused on the chat. "You can move in right now. Where's all your stuff?"

"We hid it in the snow."

Scott actually caught himself in a chuckle. The statement was an odd brand of humor. It was unmistakably William and Derrick's. That was the part of camaraderie that he truly missed. But when he realized Derrick wasn't smiling, he stopped. "You were kidding, right?"

"No, I'm serious. It was this moron's idea."

"There was nowhere else to put it, man," said William. "You know they woulda stole it."

Scott's mouth fell. "So you hid it in the *snow*?"

"Don't worry, we taped garbage bags around it. It'll be fine."

Garbage bags. That was hilarious. Though he never doubted the two would get along fine in Fourteenth, it was conversations like this that made the decision seem golden. The unit needed people like them to lighten the mood. He couldn't recall the last time anyone in the Fourteenth had looked like they were enjoying themselves.

But Scott was enjoying himself now. The moment he realized that, the question rose in his mind. Why didn't he feel guilty about enjoying himself? Guilt constantly nipped at his heels—after every inadvertent smile or laugh. After every moment of anything other than darkness and depravity, guilt and bitterness were always right there. He couldn't even be happy that an old friend like Svetlana had returned, or that he'd just saved the lives of two priests. Every white cloud had a miserable lining.

He decided to ask the question that had been lingering in his mind since finding William and Derrick in the cafeteria. In truth, it had lingered much longer. "Why are you both so comfortable around me?"

Both other men stopped eating.

Scott felt the urge to continue. "I really want to know. Why?" He knew they both had strong feelings about the Nightmen. A Nightman had murdered one of their own. That was how Joe Janson had died—by the Silent Fever. They must have felt something.

Derrick hesitated before answering, his voice deadly serious. "Scott, man…you got this all wrong. You killed someone. Yeah, you murdered someone, and it sucked. But it'd be totally different if you'd wanted to do it."

I did want to do it, Scott thought. *Just to a different person.*

"I mean, shoot, someone killed your fiancée," Derrick went on. "And *why* did they kill your fiancée? To get to you, 'cause they knew there was no other way you'd do it."

"If I was in love," William cut in, "and someone killed her? Man, I'd kill every Nightman in sight."

"We talk about this all the time," said Derrick. "We talk about it with Becan and Jayden and Max. There ain't a guy in our group who wouldn't have done the same thing." He hesitated for a moment. "If I'm bein' honest, man…I *still* hope you catch the guy who did it. He deserves to be killed."

The words cut Scott deep. A day did not pass when he didn't wonder who the real killer was. He'd wondered about it when Viktor, Nicolai, Auric, and Egor joined the unit. Every time he met a new Nightman, he wondered. But for the life of him, he didn't know what he'd do if he found Nicole's killer. There was a part of him that still wanted to kill, but another part of him was afraid. *What if I kill the wrong person again?*

"There's a difference between you and someone like Dostoevsky," said Derrick. "Whatever he did, it was 'cause he wanted to. I never seen anyone so sold out to the Nightmen. You're not like that."

Scott sighed. He thought about the other Nightmen, too. What if they'd all made mistakes? What if they were all victims of conspiracy? Even though he knew it couldn't be true, the thought remained.

Nonetheless, Derrick's words had merit. Nightmen like Dostoevsky were the backbone of The Machine. Ruthless murderers—some of them worse. Scott wasn't like that. But he wasn't like EDEN, either. Everything about life seemed like gray areas. The line between hero and villain was scarcely a line at all.

He had no idea who he was.

"I like you, man," Derrick said. "That's just the truth. I know why you did what you did. I don't hold it against you."

William nodded. "I like you, too. In the way a guy can like a guy, without being like, romantic."

Derrick stared at him.

"Derrick's not being romantic, either."

"Do you ever ask yourself if you sound dumb?" Derrick asked.

Scott laughed again. Just briefly, but it was there. He'd never thought about things the way these two described them. He wasn't sure he could accept their view, though; it seemed too easy a way out. But God—it felt so good to laugh.

"So!" Derrick said. "We better dig up our stuff." The two new additions to the Fourteenth rose from their chairs.

As they grabbed their trays, Scott said, "I appreciate what you told me, guys." He could feel something in him about to bend, but he wasn't sure what. He'd felt a quick spurt of pleasure, briefly, but bitterness still lurked treacherously underneath. His soul still felt robbed.

"Don't mention it," answered Derrick. "We'll see ya soon."

"Later, suck-fist," said William.

Scott laughed as the two men left. Evidently, William had never forgotten Scott's first sparring match—the humiliating defeat against Max and Dostoevsky. Scott had a feeling the demolitionist never would.

For several minutes after William and Derrick had left, Scott remained behind in the cafeteria, sitting and thinking. *Maybe I've approached this all wrong.* All of it. His reaction to Nicole's death. His reaction to becoming a Nightman. His reaction to the Fourteenth over the months.

He was still a fulcrum—a symbol of murder. But for the first time in a long while, he thought he sensed something over the horizon. *Maybe Svetlana was right.* He still wasn't sure—his own black brick and mortar ran deep. Still, something was there, something better than what he'd become. Something better than despicable.

It seemed like a good place to start.

* * *

It was past noon. Hands on her knees, Varvara sat nearly motionless in an infirmary chair. She'd been there since before the sun rose. It didn't matter that she wasn't allowed into critical care; she was determined to stay put.

Updates on Jayden had been rare, even considering she was a medic from the same unit. She'd asked numerous times, but the surgeons simply weren't obliged to talk.

"Varya?"

The voice startled her. She looked up, turning her head to the infirmary's entrance doors. It was Viktor. The slayer-medic stepped hesitantly into the foyer.

As she watched him approach, she tried hard to smile but the effort failed. Instead, her face twisted and moisture brimmed in her eyes. Her head dropped and tears came forth in heaves.

"Varya..." Viktor said, kneeling beside her. He placed his hand on her knee. "It will be okay."

"Why does God allow this to happen?" Her words barely escaped. "Anyone but he deserved this. I deserved this!"

"I do not know."

"If he becomes blind..."

The slayer was quick to take over. "Jayden will persevere. He is strong, just like you. There is a reason you found one another."

"But what if he leaves? What if he goes back to America?"

Viktor fell silent for a moment. He bowed his head briefly, then spoke. "Then you must go with him. If you truly love him, it should not be a question."

She covered her face with her hands. Doctors, nurses, and surgeons passed through the entrance hall, but she was oblivious to them.

Viktor sighed. "This is not good for you. It worries me greatly. Will you come with me, anywhere else? You have been here for too long today."

"He is suffering!" She looked up from her hands. Tears streaked down her face. "How can I leave now?"

"Varya." He squeezed her leg. "I know this is not easy. This could be the hardest thing you have ever felt. But what good are you to him, if they wake him and you have gone crazy? He needs you to be the girl he knows and loves. You cannot be that if you spend all your time here."

He frowned. "I am not asking this as a medical professional. I am asking this as your friend. Give yourself one hour with me. One hour, away from this place. We can go wherever you like. When you come back here, you will feel *so* much better. I *promise* you that." When she didn't respond, he forced her to look into his eyes.

"Varya, I am here for you."

She hesitated before turning to stare down the hall and brushing the tears away. Sniffling, she nodded her head.

He smiled. "This is good. This will be a good thing. You will see."

She awkwardly rose and turned to face him fully. Her eyes were still moist. "Thank you, Viktor, for saving his life. Thank you for this. I can never thank you enough."

"It is okay. I understand. We Nightmen are not *all* evil, are we?" When she cracked a faint smile, he laughed softly. "At least, I hope that is what you believe."

Her smile lasted for a moment, then faded and was replaced with an expression of guilt.

"Let us go. He will be here when you return." She nodded and they walked out together through the infirmary doors.

Several minutes later, a doctor entered the foyer of the infirmary. His apron looked recently washed, despite being spotted with old stains. Stopping in front of the now-abandoned chair, he looked around, puzzled. He returned to the main desk and found the attendant. "The young woman. Did she leave?"

The woman looked at the doctor, then through the main doors. "She left, not even five minutes ago. She left with another man."

Sighing, the doctor placed his hands squarely on his hips. "That is very unfortunate."

"Is something wrong?"

For a few moments, the doctor did not respond. Then he said, "No, actually, it is not wrong at all. I wanted to give her the news."

"What news?"

"His right eye. We ran some tests to determine progress. We were surprised at how good it looked. There is a good chance it can be saved."

"That is wonderful!"

"He has been under anesthesia since he came in. I was going to wake him and let her come see him. I am sure he will be confused when he wakes, so I thought she would be the best person to greet him."

Both of them fell silent. More surgeons and doctors passed through the hall. Occasionally a nurse pushed a cart.

"I will go back, then," the doctor finally said. "I will explain to him myself what happened." Offering a nod to the attendant, he turned and walked away from the desk. The attendant resumed her work.

No one else visited the infirmary that morning. Varvara never returned.

12

WEDNESDAY, NOVEMBER 9TH, 0011 NE
0702 HOURS

TWO DAYS LATER

As Judge Blake stepped out from the transport on the icy airstrip of *Novosibirsk*, he rubbed his arms together. "Frozen hellhole." Carol June, the auburn-haired judge, appeared equally cold. She stepped out of the transport behind him.

Blake looked in the hangar's entranceway, where two Nightman sentries hurried to intercept them. "Here come the welcoming committee."

The first sentry spoke. "You were not authorized to land." Then he froze. His zombified stare caught the judges' insignias.

"Yes, well," said Blake, "I'm afraid we're authorized to land wherever we please. What is your name?"

For a moment, there was no response. The two Nightmen stood like metal statues, apprehension detectable in their stances. When one of them finally answered, not even his mechanized voice could hide his anxiety. "Mikhajlov, judge..."

"And your counterpart?"

The other man spoke. "I am Petrenko..."

"Very well. My name is Judge Malcolm Blake. This is my good friend, Judge June. Now that we've been properly introduced, Mr. Mikhajlov, might you be so kind as to escort me to Alien Confinement? And Mr. Petrenko, might you be willing to entertain Judge June while she asks you a few short questions?"

The sentries stood in unified hesitation. Then Mikhajlov replied. "Of course. It would be my pleasure, Judge Blake. Follow me, please?"

"By all means, lead the way."

As Mikhajlov turned to leave, he cast a final look back to Petrenko.

They exchanged bewildered hand gestures before they were forced to break apart from each another.

Carol June looked at Petrenko. "Mr. Petrenko—jog your memory for me concerning the *Assault on Novosibirsk.* And while you're doing so, fetch me some tea."

* * *

"DOSTOEVSKY IS still *feared* as a fulcrum," Oleg said, "but the unit's respect for him has diminished. Clarke addresses him only when necessary. He and Remington have no relationship. His role as commander has become awkward."

General Thoor stood, arms folded, along a wall of the Inner Sanctum. "The commander has not asserted himself as I had hoped. He has allowed the Fourteenth's leadership to fall into question. That makes the Fourteenth useless to me."

"He will never assert himself, general. He is suffering from a disconnect. He still has the capacity to lead, but his fervency is no longer there. He no longer has passion."

"And Remington?"

"There is a problem with Remington, general. It is the woman, Voronova. She should not have been allowed to return."

"Elaborate."

"She has had an effect on the unit," answered Oleg. "She has had an effect on Remington himself. He *feels*, now. I observe him from a distance, and I see it in the way he carries himself. He does not like what we have made him."

Thoor stepped into the illuminated portion of the room. "Do you like what I have made *you*, Strakhov?"

Oleg responded instantly. "Yes, general. I do."

"Monitor her actions. If she becomes a nuisance, relinquish her of her breath. Her return may have been EDEN's prerogative, but I will not allow her to become an obstacle to my will."

"Yes, general."

Thoor was silent for several moments, letting the background noises of the Inner Sanctum come into prominence. When he spoke again, his voice cut through the room. "My patience with Dostoevsky has worn thin. If he will not lead by choice, he will lead by necessity. Exterminate Clarke."

Oleg bowed his head. "I would be honored, general."

Before any more discussion could ensue, the doors to the Inner Sanctum burst open and a slayer hurried inside. Thoor and Oleg turned his way.

"General!" the slayer said, huffing as he knelt before Thoor. "There is an urgent situation at hand."

"Speak."

"It is EDEN Command, general. They have sent two of their judges to *Novosibirsk*. They are here now!"

"And this concerns you?"

The slayer blinked. "But general, they are freely roaming The Machine. One has gone to Confinement, while the other interrogates our sentries."

"Interrogates them concerning what?"

"The *Assault on Novosibirsk*, general."

Oleg turned to Thoor.

Once again, the noises of the giant room became louder. The general's eyes grew threateningly cold. "Let them roam. Let them interrogate. Let them bask in their own inferiority. They wish to intimidate us with their presence. They do not yet understand where they are."

The slayer bowed his head reverently.

Thoor turned to Oleg. "Send word to the eidola. Lift our veil of ignorance. Deliver EDEN's informants to me."

"Yes, general."

"Leave at once."

The two Nightmen—Oleg and the slayer—offered closing salutes to General Thoor. They strode down the crimson carpet of the Inner Sanctum, opening the wooden doors and stepping out. Their footsteps disappeared into the Hall of the Fulcrums.

* * *

"AND THESE ARE *all* of your specimens?" Blake asked. He turned to Petrov, the chief scientist in Confinement.

Petrov hesitated. "Yes, Judge Blake."

Blake turned to the cells. Several aliens peered from their glass prisons. "So *Novosibirsk* possesses no Ceratopians?"

"That is correct, sir."

"Mm-hmm." Blake pulled a notepad out of his pocket and scribbled a few words. "And if you were to recover a Ceratopian, what would you do with it?"

The scientist hesitated a second time. "We transport all Ceratopians to *Cairo* within one week of capture. That is what EDEN has instructed us to do."

"Do you always do what EDEN tells you?"

Several other scientists standing along the walls and watching the episode swapped leery looks. Mikhajlov, the sentry who'd escorted Blake, listened intently.

"Of course, judge," answered Petrov. "We are a part of EDEN, are we not?"

"Of course." Placing the notepad back in his pocket, Blake turned to one of the Bakma prisoners. He stared at the captive's face. "Mr. Petrov, why are you lying to me?"

"I do not know what you mean, my judge."

Blake broke away from the Bakma. "You are just aware as I am that this is not the only Confinement in *Novosibirsk*. This is not the Confinement I wish to see."

"But Judge…"

"I wish to see the one in the Citadel of The Machine."

At the door to Confinement, Mikhajlov gasped.

"That is what you call it, correct? Or is that something I'm not supposed to know?"

Petrov fumbled for words. "The Citadel of The Machine, yes, I forgot about that, but…"

"But what?"

"But that is not so much a Confinement, it is more like…" His words trailed off again. They never returned.

Blake walked to him. "More like a *what*, Mr. Petrov?"

Petrov looked back at the sentry helplessly, wiping newly formed sweat from his brow. "It is a different kind of Confinement."

"Then I would like to see your 'different kind of Confinement,' if you would be so kind as to take me there."

"I—"

"Take me there *now*."

Petrov glanced at Mikhajlov once again. After a moment of silent deliberation, the sentry nodded his head. Petrov said to Judge Blake, his voice quaking imperceptibly, "As you wish, judge. Please, follow me."

The two men led Blake from the room.

* * *

CAROL JUNE SCRIBBLED in her notebook as another Nightman entered the chamber. It was a room she'd requested, a small one that wasn't in use. The lights were low. She was there by herself, except for the Nightmen. They came in, one at a time, as she asked for them. This was the fifth one she'd addressed.

As the latest Nightman to arrive stood before her, she sipped her now tepid tea. "Tell me your name."

The Nightman hesitated before answering. "My name is Petr Radin."

"And do you have a rank?"

He turned his eyes from her. "I do not, judge."

"So you're unregistered?"

"...that is correct."

She scribbled in her notebook. "So tell me, Mr. Radin, where were you during the *Assault on Novosibirsk*?"

"Where was I?"

"That's right. This battle came suddenly. Surely you must have been somewhere other than the airstrip."

After several moments of silence, he answered. "I was asleep in my room, judge."

Taking another sip of tea, June leaned back. "So when the attack took place, you were asleep in your room. I assume that when the alarms went off, you and your comrades immediately rallied to the airstrip, correct?"

The Nightman said nothing.

"Please answer my question, Mr. Radin."

"Yes, judge. What you say is correct."

"Really? You immediately rallied to the airstrip?"

"Yes, judge."

"That's what I thought you'd say," she said, eyeing her notebook, "because so far, that's what every Nightman has said." She unfolded a paper from her lap. "Until of course, I mention our official log of the event. That's when everyone's story seems to change."

Eying him suspiciously, she revealed the paper's contents aloud. "The assault came at 0136 hours. Your Nightman comrades charged the airstrip at 0225. That's forty minutes—hardly what I'd call an immediate response." She paused to let the information sink in.

"So *you* say you immediately rallied to the airstrip, but evidence says that's not quite the case. Tell me, Mr. Radin. How's *your* story going to change?"

* * *

WITH EVERY PASSING step through The Machine, Petrov and Mikhajlov grew more perturbed. Judge Blake, on the other hand, was fearless. The bald judge walked behind them, hands clasped confidently behind his back. Their path first took them across the outer grounds of the frozen base, then into the halls of the officers' building.

Finally, the men stopped walking. Blake stepped several paces in front of them, then stopped to look around. They stood in a hallway no different than the ones they'd been traversing. Doors lined both sides of the hall.

"I'm tired of walking in circles," said Blake with irritation. "Take me to the Citadel now."

"Judge," Petrov said, "we have."

Blake gave both men an uncertain look.

"The three doors on your left, judge. Open one of them."

The judge suspiciously eyed the doors. There was nothing remarkable about them—they even were numbered in sync with the rest. Reaching the first door, Blake cautiously took the knob and twisted it. As the door swung open, his eyes widened in awe.

It wasn't a room. It was a dimly lit staircase descending straight down. Blake turned to the men. "Does this lead to the Citadel?"

"That is correct, judge."

Blake no longer hesitated. He strode purposefully down the stairs, with Petrov and Mikhajlov behind him.

The stairs continued down until moldy discoloration replaced the painted walls. Finally, they reached a landing, where it gave way to a narrow stone passage, devoid of all but yellowish institutional lighting. At the end of the passage was a wooden door.

Blake pointed. "Where does that door lead?"

"To the Hall of the Fulcrums. It is the main corridor of the Citadel. From there, you can go anywhere."

"And what do you people call 'Confinement' here?"

The scientist hesitated. "The Walls of Mourning."

For several seconds, nobody spoke. Blake turned to the scientist with an expression that walked a line between suspicion and willful ignorance. Then he whipped around, swung the wooden door open, and strode through.

They entered an enormous corridor. Torches lined every wall, accompanied by ancient chandeliers on the ceiling. Except for the lighting, the room was Spartan. Nightmen milled about everywhere—slayers, sentries, and fulcrums. As soon as Blake appeared, they all froze.

The stalemate didn't have time to turn awkward. The EDEN judge spoke at once. "Take me to the Walls of Mourning. No delays."

"Yes, judge," Petrov said. "Follow me."

The trek to The Machine's version of Confinement took a mere minute. Ignoring the Nightmen who watched warily from ever corner, the three men crossed the Hall of the Fulcrums until they came to a single iron door. Nothing on it revealed its identity. Blake pulled the door open.

The room had depth. There were no separated chambers, no other doorways or hallways. Instead, iron-barred cages stretched far ahead along every wall, placed one right after the other.

The first thing that hit Blake was the stench, but what he saw made him cover his mouth. Blood. Everywhere. On the walls, on the floor, even on the ceiling. The headless corpse of an Ithini was nailed to the wall with iron spikes. It had apparently been there for some time. Miscellaneous weapons lay strewn about—swords, axes, and maces, among other things. Chains hung from the ceiling. The whole room reeked of decay and death.

Bakma prisoners lolled in the cages, many with missing limbs and missing eyes, some twitching in near-lifelessness. Ithini in separate cages appeared in much the same state. Some were bleeding as they writhed in mute agony. Not an alien in the room was unscarred.

Blake was speechless. His formerly defiant expression had faded into pale shock. His mouth hung open; his arms hung limply at his sides. He didn't breathe.

Several other Nightmen moved around the room; all were bloodstained and occupied. One by one, they looked at the door. When they recognized Judge Blake, they stopped.

"He knew," Petrov explained to the Nightmen in Russian. To Blake, he said, "Do you not torture at EDEN Command?"

For the first time since entering, the British judge spoke. "This isn't torture. This is sadism."

Petrov walked forward as Blake followed. They came to the first cage, which held a Bakma. Both of its arms had been removed, and the trauma appeared to have gone almost untreated. The creature writhed in pain on the floor, surrounded by blood.

"This is Lu'tikmanassa. He is a soldier. We thought he knew more than he did. He will not live much longer."

The Bakma evidenced no indication that it was aware of their presence.

Petrov stopped at the next cage. Another Bakma sat on the floor inside, but this one's limbs were intact. Its body was grotesquely malnourished. "This one is Tauthinilaas. He is an officer. He was captured during the *Assault on Novosibirsk*."

As Blake leaned closer to the bars, the Bakma looked up at him. The alien's skin dangled loosely as if a once muscular body had atrophied beyond repair.

"We are sustaining him for questioning, though he has not given us much. If he does not cooperate soon, he will be killed."

Blake interrupted him. "Do you have any Ceratopians?" His voice broke. His eyes stayed locked on the Bakma's.

"...yes, judge," Petrov confessed. "Come with me."

The Bakma was left to its emaciated state.

Blake was directed to the opposite side of the room, in the far corner. There were two Ceratopians present, but only one seemed conscious. The other lay crumpled on the floor.

"This is Gag`hraffthra," Petrov said, pointing to the better-kept brute. "It is a hard name to pronounce, but they all are. We received him very recently, and we're considering our options."

Blake turned to the other, worse-off alien. One of its horns had been removed, and the wound had festered. But the alien was alive. "What is this one's name?"

"H`gath. He was wounded when we recovered him from a crash."

"Is that how he lost one of his horns?"

"No..."

Blake stifled a gag. "I've got to get out of here."

"Are you all right, judge?"

Blake waved Petrov off and hurried back to the iron door. The Night-men in the room exchanged dark looks.

As soon as Blake was in the hallway, he placed a hand on the wall to steady himself. "This is evil," he whispered under his breath. "This place is pure evil."

Petrov and Mikhajlov were right behind him.

"Take me out of this place," Blake said. "I've seen enough."

The men affirmed and escorted him out.

* * *

EDEN COMMAND

THIRTY MINUTES LATER

THE VIEW SCREEN on Archer's desk flickered on as Blake's face appeared. His typically amiable expression was absent behind a veneer of disgust.

Archer sat alone in his suite. "Don't you look lovely?"

"If you'd seen what I've seen..." The statement was left unfinished. "Forget every preconceived notion of civility you thought this place might have had. These are barbarians."

"Is he there?"

Blake frowned apologetically. "No."

Archer's face noticeably altered. He fought hard not to scowl. "This does not bode well, Malcolm. We do not have as much time as we thought. He must be found."

"I understand."

"What of Thoor?"

"We haven't seen him. We've succeeded in catching him off guard, that much is for certain. You should see the looks we've been getting. They're definitely unprepared."

"Good. Has Carol made progress?"

Blake attempted a smile. "You know Carol."

"Have you spoken with her?"

"Not yet. I want to make sure it's the right time. I want everything to go smoothly. If I don't find the opportunity to speak with her here, I'll talk with her during the flight home."

Blake paused and continued. "As ironic as it may be considering where we are, they've made our accommodations quite comfortable. We've been given neighboring suites in their officers' wing. One of the entrances to

Fort Zhukov is just down the hall. I'm not sure how long we'll stay. Possibly several days, possibly a week. Much of that will hinge on Thoor's responsiveness. But we won't leave until we get the job done."

"Stay as long as your obligations permit. Find out all that you can. *Novosibirsk* is a threat we can't afford."

"As you wish."

"That's all for now."

Blake acknowledged and the view screen went blank.

For several moments, Archer simply sat there, his arms folded as he stared at the blank screen. Eventually, his gaze moved to the conch lamps that provided the room's dim illumination. "Carol June, you sour little witch. Come to the light."

13

WEDNESDAY, NOVEMBER 9TH, 0011 NE
1342 HOURS

THAT SAME DAY

SCOTT RARELY VISITED the infirmary—for any reason. A certain uncomfortable feeling accompanied him whenever he was forced to make the trip—one unmatched by anyplace else. He recalled his own time there after his first mission in Siberia with the Fourteenth. He knew how confining it felt to be restricted to a bed. It was like being in a prison cell.

Two days had passed since he'd attempted to visit Jayden. This was the day they'd instructed him to return. Despite the fact that he hadn't seen the Texan since Krasnoyarsk, he had received several updates through Svetlana. Those were the only times when he and her had talked.

According to Svetlana, the surgeon had awakened Jayden from his multi-day slumber, sadly, alone. Jayden learned of his condition not through the gentle words of Varvara or any other friend, but from the man who'd removed his left eye.

He had broken bones over his body. In a strange twist of fate, however, none of the breaks were major. Considering the fall he'd taken, it was a sheer miracle. Had he no other problems, a full recovery could have been expected in a matter of months. But unfortunately, broken bones were the least of his concerns.

His face had been torn apart by his visor. A local cosmetic surgeon had come to base specifically to stitch him up. Supposedly, this was Jayden's first day without his face wrapped up in bandages. Though Scott hadn't yet seen him, according to Svetlana the surgeon had done very well. But the truth could not be denied: he'd never look the same again.

Then there was his vision.

Scott had specifically asked Svetlana to refrain from describing the gritty details. Scott had overcome his initial queasiness when it came to blood and grown accustomed to seeing gruesome things on the battlefield, but the fact that it was Jayden made the subject taboo. Scott wanted the gist of things and nothing more.

Jayden's right eye, after all, had fared unexpectedly well. It was being treated with antibiotics and something Svetlana called a *cycloplegic* to reduce inflammation. He'd need to wear an eye patch for a few days, but the outlook was optimistic after that. At that point, the members of the Fourteenth would take any degree of optimism they could get.

That was all Scott knew when he walked into the infirmary. He was aware of the fact that, no matter how prepared he was to see Jayden for the first time, reality was liable to shock him. What he saw when he entered the room made him cringe. The Texan looked like a mummy. His entire body, save his face, was wrapped in plaster casting. He was thoroughly immobilized.

His face looked like a swollen patchwork quilt—a labyrinth of stitches and puffy, discolored skin. Both his right eye and vacant left socket were covered with patches, leaving him effectively blind as he was. Had Scott not known it was Jayden beforehand, he'd have never recognized him upon entering the room.

Walking to the edge of Jayden's bed, Scott placed a hand on the sniper's cast arm. As softly as he had ever spoken, Scott said, "Hey, Jay." For the life of him, he had no idea how to sound confident or even professional.

What Scott saw next almost broke him. In the midst of his wretched condition, Jayden smiled. He smiled at the sound of Scott's voice. Scott was moved nearly to tears.

"Hey, man," Jayden said quietly. His voice was barely audible, but it held a faint trace of enthusiasm.

Scott wasn't sure if Jayden had made a deliberate attempt to whisper or if that was the extent to which the Texan could speak. He thought it best not to ask. Instead, he blurted, "How do you feel?" He regretted the question the moment he asked it. What a stupid thing to ask.

"Good, man."

Good. Of all the miserable ways Jayden could have answered, he'd said *good*. Scott couldn't help it—he bit his fist as his eyes started to well. *I pale next to someone like this. If I'd gone through life with an attitude like his, I wouldn't be a fulcrum.*

He swallowed his emotions before they could become audible; he didn't want Jayden to hear him break down. "You had a lot of company?" He couldn't think of anything else to ask.

"Clarke came earlier," Jayden mumbled, slurring his words slightly. "And Svetlana and Esther. Becan, too."

Scott caught the omission of Varvara. Surely she must have visited him by now. If an injured Becan could make his way over, surely Jayden's girlfriend must have come, too. The Texan had probably still been unconscious at the time.

"What's Varya doing?" Jayden asked.

He didn't know how to answer. "She's been busy with everything going on. It's been pretty crazy." It was an absolutely meaningless answer, and a lie. He had no idea what Varvara was doing. But whatever it was, it apparently hadn't been with her boyfriend—at least not when he was conscious. *You better have visited him, Varvara.*

"Man," Jayden said, "I'm so glad you came. What's been goin' on?"

"Heh," Scott said without answering immediately. So much had happened. He wasn't sure where to begin. "William and Derrick are moving to the unit."

"Yeah, Clarke told me. I think that's great."

The simplest of conversations, but it made Jayden happy. Scott honestly felt good about that. He decided to leave out the details of William and Derrick's addition, which was the execution of Ulrich. The Texan may have already known anyway.

"I think I'm gonna be able to fight again," Jayden said. "The doctors told me there's a chance."

Scott's good feeling quickly turned to rot. Jayden would be able to *fight* again? That wasn't what he'd heard at all. "Just take it easy. Worry about getting better first."

"I'm serious, man. I really think I can do it. I've been asking a lot of questions."

Scott waited for the out-of-place statement to be furthered, but it never was. So Scott prodded on. "What kind of questions?"

Jayden never answered Scott's inquiry. Instead, he repeated his earlier statement. "Svetlana came. Man, it was so good to see her. Clarke and Esther came, too."

Scott knew it right then. The Texan wasn't in his right mind—there was no telling what he imagined the doctors had told him. He was probably drugged up. "They did, huh?"

"Yeah. Svetlana said I was gonna get better."

Scott tried to sound well-intentioned. "I guess that means you'll get better. She knows her stuff." He felt sick with disgust.

"Yeah." Jayden stared without eyes at the ceiling, but his grin never left. "I'm gonna get better."

You just told me that, Jay. It became increasingly difficult for Scott to maintain his smile—until he realized his friend couldn't see anyway.

"I'm gonna get better," Jayden said again. But this time it was different. The look on the sniper's face drooped slowly. His body started to tremble.

Suddenly Scott understood the Texan's repetition. He wasn't speaking out of his mind. He was speaking in denial.

Finally Jayden broke down. His patchwork face froze in open-mouthed anguish. He began to moan—a low-pitched whine.

Oh no...

Scott leapt to his friend's side. He placed his hand on the Texan's arm. "Jay! Hey man, it's all right. It's gonna be all right."

Saliva dripped from the corner of Jayden's mouth. His words poured out like liquor. "I didn't see him. I didn't see him," he repeated. His slurred accent broke more with each word. "I don't even remember..."

He was talking about the mission. He was talking about the Bakma that had hit him.

"I'm sorry I got hit."

Tears streamed down Scott's face, but he tried to sound strong. "We're going to get you out of here. Just give it time." He understood now the role of false hope. Jayden was desperate for any hope at all.

The Texan's expression was still frozen in pain. "I don't wanna go home..."

Scott lowered his head, closing his eyes. This wasn't fair.

"Please let me stay. Please, I'm gonna get better. Please let me stay."

Scott had no idea how to respond. He couldn't even speak.

Jayden violently cleared his throat with a guttural grunt. "I'm gonna get better." He words were stocked with forced intensity.

"I know. I know." As Scott spoke, he was praying in his heart—for the first time in months. *Don't let him go out this way, God. I deserved what happened to me. Jayden didn't deserve this.* It was the first time he'd prayed since he'd become a Nightman. He couldn't think of a better time to restart.

The emotions Jayden conveyed from his immobile position in his bed were so intense they were palpable. He seemed desperately determined, lost to everyone but himself. The Texan drew in a breath—made heavier by his prior outburst of emotion—then swallowed hard.

He breathed out slow, regular breaths. He seemed finished with his efforts at speaking.

Realizing Jayden's silence meant he was giving Scott permission to leave, Scott reached down and touched his friend's hand. It was a brotherly instinct. He didn't know what else to do.

Rising from his stooped position over the bed, Scott took a step back. He offered Jayden no parting words. He simply patted the Texan on the leg and turned to leave. That was all Jayden needed to feel.

As Scott exited the infirmary, he felt something he hadn't felt in a while—something he'd grown accustomed to lacking. It was a measure of camaraderie. Barely a measure at all—but it was there.

Nothing else needed to be done—no other pressing duty needed to be filled. At the end of one of the longest two-day stretches of his life, that suited Scott fine.

* * *

SEVERAL HOURS LATER

ESTHER'S FOOTSTEPS tapped rhythmically on the infirmary's tile floor. Her brown ponytail, glistening with the sheen of fresh, melting snow, bounced on her back as she surveyed the rooms. In her hand was a sealed envelope.

Bad weather had not relented all week, and a meter of snow had collected on the outskirts of the base. Maintenance crews were kept busy clearing the sidewalks, and the airstrip was under constant care. The pristine cover of virgin snowfall had long since vanished. The grounds were muddy and messy. Esther, like her comrades, had grown used to feeling chilled and uncomfortable most of the time.

As she rounded the corner into Becan's room and approached his bed, she waved the sealed envelope at him. "At least *someone* apparently loves you. Though I can't fathom why."

Becan looked miserable in his thin, standard-issue hospital gown. Outside of a few small scabs on his face—scabs that would fade away with time—there was nothing outwardly wrong with the way he looked. The gown covered his half-charred chest.

The moment the Irishman saw the envelope, he lurched upright and snatched it from her grasp, wincing at the pain of the sudden motion. The movement was too quick for Esther. She watched as Becan stowed it away. "For a moment I thought I was getting a kiss," she said saucily.

"Ara be whist."

"Is that Irish for 'I'll take a rain check?'"

"That, or 'shut the hell up.'"

The scout placed her hands on her hips. "Who writes you without a return address?"

"Tha's none o' your business, now, is it?"

"Do I get a bloody thanks?"

"Thanks."

"You're welcome, twit."

Becan said nothing.

Esther approached the chair by his bed. She sat and crossed her legs, leaning her head his direction. "So, who is it?"

"Who is who?"

"The letter!"

Becan responded with a bland look of his own. "I just told yeh it was none o' your business. You're actin' all jealous."

"My apologies. It's just that I'm so wildly attracted to you. It must be your ridiculous charm."

"Guess it must."

She glared at him. "You know, I've come to visit you every single day since you went and got pasted. Not to mention I saved your silly life. You could at least show me a granule of appreciation."

"Wha' do yeh want? Yeh want me to polish your nails? Yeh want a complimentary massage? I already said thanks."

Esther tightened her lips.

"Righ'. I'm sorry."

"I deserve better. Do you think I've nothing better to do than be your sodding postwoman?"

Becan threw his hands up helplessly. "I'm sorry, Esty, wha' else can I say? It's been a flatulent week if yeh haven't already noticed."

She sighed. "I saw Jayden earlier. He's in good spirits, all things considered."

"I need a favor from yeh. I need yeh to find ou' if annyone from the First is in the infirmary."

"The *First*?"

"The First."

"Why do you want to know that?"

"I've got me own reasons." His expression grew serious. "There's just somethin' I have to know. Can yeh find ou'?"

Esther smirked and said, "I've been privy to such things before."

"You have."

"Does this have something to do with the Nightmen?"

"I'll tell yeh after the fact. I cross m'heart."

"Fair do's."

"Thanks, Molly-Polly."

As she rose from her chair, she bit back a retort. "You want this soon, I presume?"

"I do. As soon as yeh can."

"You owe me."

His face remained deadpanned. "I'll give yeh tha' kiss you were beggin' for."

She rolled her eyes and walked to the door.

"Hey Esty…"

She stopped just outside the door and turned, arching an eyebrow.

"Thanks for comin' after us. I do owe yeh for tha'."

Neither of their expressions revealed any sign of jest. After a moment, Esther sighed. "Cop some zeds. I'll be back soon enough."

"Away with yeh."

For several moments after Esther left, Becan lay motionless in bed, his eyes on the doorway as his ears listened to her footsteps fade away. Then he waited a minute more. Only when he was sure that she had disappeared did he slide the envelope from under the covers. He gently eased the seal open and slipped the letter out.

Suddenly Esther emerged from around the corner. "Come on, just tell me *where* it's from!"

"Wick!" Becan frantically shoved the letter beneath his blanket. "Wha' the hell are yeh, some kind o' faerie?"

She scoffed and disappeared again.

"Nosey little tinker."

"I heard that!"

"Scram!"

The infirmary received no other visits that day. As evening wound down into bedtime, the operatives of the Fourteenth collected in their rooms to settle in for the night.

* * *

SVETLANA LAY ON her lower bunk. Having showered and donned her nightwear, she was already under the covers and ready for sleep. Her hair, too short to be tied into a ponytail, was held by a simple blue band that pressed back her bangs. As she waited patiently for the room's lights to go out, she passed the time reading pages of Scripture in Russian. No name identified the brown-covered book—only the wear and tear that came with age and neglect.

David occupied the bunk to her right. Their proximity had been unintentional; she'd simply chosen her current empty bunk when she returned, and it happened to be right beside his. As David retrieved a pair of photos from under his bunk, Svetlana shifted her eyes in his direction. Though she couldn't make out the fine details of the images, it was easily apparent what they were. They were photos from home. Photos of his sons.

Svetlana observed David quietly for a moment, her Scripture still opened against her knees. After careful consideration, she gently cleared her throat. "Are those your children?"

At first, David didn't respond. He continued to stare at the pictures. When he did speak, his voice was subdued. "Yeah."

"Do you mind if I see?"

His response was again delayed. Finally he nodded his head slightly. Reaching over, he handed the photos to her.

Svetlana looked at the first one in greater detail. It showed two small boys smiling in a yard, a football in their hands as their father knelt beside them. David looked younger, despite the recent date on the photo. His face looked less tired.

The second photo was similar but older. David was blowing his lips against one of the little boys' necks. The child was laughing hysterically. Behind them, far in the distance, a diaper-clad newborn crawled across the floor.

"They are beautiful. How old are they now?"

"Timmy, he's the oldest. He's nine. Stevie just turned seven."

"What is Stevie's birthday?"

"October 15th."

She smiled. "My birthday was October 27th. I turned twenty-six."

David offered a faint smile in return. "Happy belated."

"Thank you." She handed the photos back. "You must miss them very much."

"I do."

"You must miss your wife."

David's eyes grew momentarily distant. It took him a moment to respond, "Yeah."

Svetlana grew more serious as she led the conversation down another path. "David, I need your help. If I am to do this, here with the unit, I cannot do it alone."

"Do what, exactly?"

She frowned at his tone of voice. "If I am to make improvements to this place." After he didn't respond, she spoke again. "I am serious."

"I know why you're here."

She became quiet as he spoke.

"You're a good person," he went on. "I know you're here with the best of intentions. If I made it sound otherwise, I was wrong. But Svetlana, a place like this can't be saved. Getting stationed here isn't a calling. It's a curse." He placed the photos facedown on his chest. "You're a young, beautiful woman. You have every opportunity in the world. You should look after yourself."

"If I leave, who will look after Scott?" When David didn't reply, she said, "I understand why you feel the way that you do. You are a father, and a young boy here was murdered. Scott made a mistake." She placed her hand over her heart. "But there is only so much I can do. He needs more than a medic. He needs a father figure as well."

David's gaze trailed off to a faraway place. He still said nothing.

"You may be right. Perhaps I am stupid girl. Perhaps I should have stayed home in Vilnius. But what can I do now?" She laughed mirthlessly. "I am here. I have done this. It is too late. I can only hope that you will forgive me and be my friend. And if that happens...maybe Scott will find forgiveness from you, too."

As David remained silent, other sounds of the room filtered in. Travis flipping a page in his comic book. Chess pieces moving on the board occupied by Boris and Esther. The slayers mumbling among themselves. Svetlana continued staring at David until he returned her attention.

"Will you try?" she asked softly.

David slowly nodded.

Svetlana gave him her warmest smile.

An hour later, Boris, the last man left awake, turned off the light. It was slightly past curfew. It was the earliest they'd fallen asleep in quite some time. No one spoke or showered or visited the lounge. The bunks gave way to the soft whisper of sleeping breaths—and nothing more. Night brought a rare peace to them all.

14

MONDAY, NOVEMBER 14TH, 0011 NE
1334 HOURS

FIVE DAYS LATER

CLARKE'S FIRST words made Scott nervous.

"Ladies and gentlemen, we have a unique situation."

It was mid-afternoon when the Fourteenth was called to the hangar. The sky was overcast, as it usually was during winter. Sunlight glowed eerily from beyond the gray clouds.

Scott knew before Clarke said anything else that something was different about this mission. He could tell by who was *not* present. Max wasn't expected to be there; he was still recovering from his injured calf. The same went for Becan and his wounds. Varvara wasn't there, but that didn't surprise him, either. Clarke was always eager to leave her behind. None of those absences surprised him. It was the absence of Egor and William, however, that struck him immediately.

They had no heavy hitters.

"Approximately twenty minutes ago," Clarke said, "the Bakma launched a full-scale invasion of northern Europe."

Every pair of eyes opened wide.

"Stockholm and Copenhagen were assaulted simultaneously by over two dozen Carriers. There have been Bakma Courier fighter sightings over Belgium, the Netherlands, and eastern Britain, along with a full assortment of Coneships and Noboats. Forces from *Berlin*, *Leningrad*, *London*, even *Cairo* are working cooperatively in the defense. Even Vector Squad is involved."

As Scott listened, something felt wrong. For an event of this magnitude, it made no sense for demolitionists not to be present. And Clarke's tone wasn't exactly indicative of an impending urban brawl.

"We will *not* be partaking in the defense."

The adrenaline in the air thinned a little.

"Due to the extraordinary circumstances facing Europe," Clarke continued, "we are forced to respond to a smaller incident that would otherwise have been assigned to some other base. Three days ago, a pair of Ceratopian Cruisers were intercepted over Pripyat, in the Chernobyl Zone of Alienation. Several units out of *Leningrad* assaulted the Cruisers. The operation was a success.

"Yesterday, a group of civilians were driven to Chernobyl Nuclear Power Plant as part of an historical expedition. They were examining reactor number four."

Scott's stomach started to turn. He already knew what Clarke was going to say.

"They never returned."

This was a bug-hunt.

Scott glanced around at the other operatives. David's head was lowered. The Nightmen looked untypically apprehensive. Svetlana looked confused.

"There have been efforts to communicate with the team via radio, none of which have been successful. We have reason to believe that necrilids from the Cruiser escaped and sought shelter in Chernobyl. That they picked reactor number four is purely coincidental."

Flashbacks sparked furiously through Scott's mind.

"Colonel, we've got something."

"Sir...why don't we have any medics?"

"Human remains and a hole in the ceiling."

"Are you questioning me?"

"Because if you get caught by a necrilid, you won't need one."

His recollections paused, as the words of his former colonel replayed in his mind.

"Because if you get caught by a necrilid, you won't need one."

Scott snapped back to the present. He spoke aloud without even thinking. "Svetlana shouldn't come."

Clarke stopped in mid-explanation. "I'm sorry?"

"Svetlana shouldn't come. We won't need a medic."

The operatives around Scott stared at him. Svetlana looked alarmed.

"Lieutenant Remington," Clarke said, "there may still be civilians alive. This is not a recovery—it's a rescue."

Now David spoke to the captain. "Scott's right. We have Viktor, he's medic enough as we'll need."

Scott looked at David, surprised. The older man agreed with him? He'd taken Scott's side against Clarke, even if cordially. And he was recommending a slayer for the job, though that shouldn't have surprised Scott. Viktor had earned everyone's trust. Added to that, Viktor could fight.

David continued. "You might think this is a rescue, sir. But it's not. This is a hunt and *nothing* else."

Clarke eyed them both. When he spoke again, his tone was considerate. "There comes a time when empowerment should give way to experience. You have both been in close-quarters combat situations with necrilids. I confess to having not.

"Yet in that same line of thought, there *are* civilians involved. There are loved ones. Real human beings. I understand your unique perspectives, but it isn't that simple."

"This isn't like fighting the Bakma," Scott said. "These things won't fire from afar. They come fast. They come from anywhere. If you don't look one direction for a *second*..."

"She is *not* good enough," David said. "Not for this."

At that comment, Svetlana frowned.

"This is a gray situation," said Clarke. "You have experience, which I truly trust. Yet there is still the possibility, even if remote, that someone is alive. With all due respect to Mr. Ryvkin, I have worked with Svetlana for several years. She is the most accomplished medic I know." He turned to face her. "Sveta, I have asked you many times to put yourself in danger. You have never hesitated to be selfless. You're aware of the intricacies of this situation. You're aware of the danger, of the possibility that no one is alive. I would have you go on the mission, but out of respect for their experience and your life, I will ask you this..."

Svetlana wiped sweat from her hands.

"What are you confident you can do?"

Before she could answer, Scott said, "Anyone missing is dead, Sveta. You have to understand that. Anyone missing is dead." It was one of the few times Scott was thankful for Clarke's soft style of leadership. Had Thoor, Lilan, or even he been in command of a mission, any such interruptions or dissidence would not have been tolerated.

It felt like a full minute passed. As Svetlana visibly weighed her options, the tension in the hangar continued to mount. Everyone else—the Nightmen, Travis, Boris, Derrick, Esther—they all remained disturbingly quiet.

Finally, Svetlana spoke. "If you say there may be a remote chance that someone is alive, then I must go."

Scott knew what a mistake she was making. "Sveta, I know you want to be brave, but—"

"Scott, this is what I am here to do. One does not take this job to stay safe."

"You don't understand."

"No. I understand. I do." She tried to smile. "I will be fine."

Scott held his tongue and looked away.

"Lieutenant Remington," Clarke said, "I am giving you executive officer status for this operation. No offense to the commander, but you have experience he simply does not. Unless the commander has been on a bug-hunt like this one?"

Dostoevsky shook his head. "I have not, captain."

"Settled. Remington has secondary command. Into the *Pariah*."

The next few minutes felt like two lifetimes. As the chosen operatives of the Fourteenth climbed aboard, they reluctantly donned their armor and weapons. No one spoke.

Scott wished they would have been called to the defense effort in Europe. In a strange way, that would have felt safer. Urban warfare was dangerous, but nothing was as bad as a bug-hunt. He remembered his first and only true bug-hunt, at the high school in Arkansas, when he was with Charlie Squad. It was the first time he'd thought of his experience there as a rare asset. Not even Clarke had experienced something like this. Shooting a wounded necrilid at a crash site and stalking one in dark corridors were two different worlds.

"Lieutenant?"

Scott was jerked from his thoughts. Esther stood readied before him.

"I want you to know I'm prepared, sir."

Scott could see the good intentions in her eyes. She was trying. But she had no idea.

"I'm here if you need me."

How was he supposed to respond? The fantasy she saw in her mind and the reality of what lurked in Chernobyl weren't the same. If she couldn't handle Khatanga, how could she handle this?

As the *Pariah* cut through the sky, Scott focused on the setting itself. The Zone of Alienation was the region abandoned in the Old Era when Chernobyl had blown its top. Originally, it was supposed to have been uninhabitable for centuries, before de-radiation had been introduced. Now it was supposed to be clean. Still, no humans had returned.

He thought about reactor number four, the one that erupted. The radioactive fallout had covered several kilometers. Trees glowed red. Animals mutated. Human beings died. It was as legendary as it was horrible, because it was true.

Travis's voice broke over the speakers. "We're over Pripyat now."

Scott peered out the transport's porthole window. Stretched out below was the wasteland of the abandoned city. It had been the city meant to house the Chernobyl plant's workers. Now, under the ice, everything looked old and forgotten by man. He wondered what kind of beasts were roaming the weed-infested streets. He wondered if they'd soon find out. Then, just like that, Pripyat was behind them.

The *Pariah*'s forward motion changed, replaced by the gut-shifting lightness of descent. They were on their way down.

"Coming up to the plant," Travis reported. "It's gonna be cold."

It would be more than cold—it would be freezing. Scott turned on the internal heating system in his fulcrum armor, as the other operatives around him did the same. Outside the porthole, he could see the surrounding area of Chernobyl. Everything looked exactly the same. Decrepit buildings surrounded by decayed forests. A vast expanse of ruins. The *Pariah*'s landing gear whined down.

Though he couldn't see it, he knew reactor number four was in front of the ship. Travis was probably looking at it now.

Necrilids. Not mammals, not reptiles, not insects. Just *bugs*—a term used to describe a monster from a child's worst nightmare. Necrilids had a tendency to seek out the warmest environments—typically the bowels of the largest structures around. This place fit the bill perfectly. The animals' body heat alone would warm the tight quarters.

Scott envied the operatives who weren't present. They would escape these horrors. Scott wished he could escape them, too.

Across from Scott, Dostoevsky and Viktor checked their weapons. Auric and Nicolai did the same from further down. Glancing to the front of the troop bay, he saw Captain Clarke closing his eyes. Scott wasn't sure if it was prayer or concentration. It needed to be both.

The *Pariah*'s momentum shifted again and the ground drew nearer.

They hovered meters from touchdown. Leaning to the porthole again, Scott finally saw the plant's fossil remains.

The sarcophagus.

He couldn't think of a more appropriate name for a structure that symbolized death and decay. A massive rectangular column of metal and concrete, it completely covered reactor number four. Prior to de-radiation, the plan had been to build new sarcophagi as the old ones fell apart. They were designed to keep radiation inside. This one's huge, rotting shell stretched as high as a tower, like a gargantuan gravestone.

The cabin rocked gently, and then they were down. Travis spoke again. "We've got one van, parked by the main gate. Plant's entrance is sixty meters ahead."

"Rad level?" asked Clarke.

Scott looked at the captain. There shouldn't have been radiation anywhere.

"Less here than anywhere else on Earth," the pilot answered.

Scott breathed a sigh of relief. Having a panel of scientists tell you de-radiation worked was one thing. Actually being there and finding out for oneself was something different.

"Lowering the door."

Scott rose and walked to the rear entrance. Donning his helmet, he watched as Chernobyl appeared through the view screen inside of his featureless faceplate.

The *Pariah* had landed nose away from the plant, with the bay door opening toward it. Was that intentional on Travis's part? If it was, it would be the first time he'd gotten it right. There were no plasma bolts or neutron beams to hit them when the door went down, as had been the case in Khatanga when Travis had landed the wrong direction. Maybe the pilot was learning. Scott stepped from the Vulture and took in the environment.

They were parked inside a concrete barricade that separated the plant from the rest of the world. Cracks and tangles of dead foliage adorned the barricade. Nothing was spared from neglect—not buildings, not equipment, not even the giant smokestack of reactor number four. It stretched skyward with all the grotesqueness of a dead hand reaching from the grave. Its red and white stripes were faded, and the passage of time stained its surface.

There was a good half-meter of snow on the ground, its untouched surface a stark contrast to surrounding deterioration. To the left, he could see a railcar's unloading arm. There were probably tracks under the snow.

Looking behind, Scott surveyed the concrete barricade. It was as he'd suspected—not a trace of graffiti. To the rest of the world, this place didn't exist.

"There used to be engineers stationed here," said Dostoevsky, standing beside him. "Before de-radiation. They were here to monitor the plant's progress after the explosion." He hesitated. "I could not work here."

Though Scott said nothing, he agreed. He allowed his sight line to travel down the smokestack. It looked frail, as though it could fall at any moment.

"Has anyone here been to the plant before?" Clarke asked, stepping from the *Pariah*. No one answered, and he turned to Esther. "Go investigate the van by the gate. Find anything to indicate where they are."

She affirmed and hurried away.

Clarke's attention returned to the structure. "I don't think I've seen anything more depressing in all my life."

The statement's profoundness struck Scott. This, coming from the captain of a torn-apart unit. From someone who lived in The Machine. Scott agreed with him.

"Oh, *veck*, it's a wolf!" Travis stood at the top of the *Pariah*'s rear bay door ramp, pointing to the structure ahead.

"Where?" asked Clarke. He engaged the zoom on his visor, as did several others.

Scott was among them. The sarcophagus and adjoining building grew large in his vision until he could see them in full-fledged detail. Scanning the area, he stopped at the structure that housed the smokestack. That's when he saw the creature lying on the ground in front of the door, barely visible, its head lowered between outstretched front paws.

"That is not a wolf, you idiot," said Nicolai. "That is a dog."

The slayer was right, though at first glance, Scott couldn't fault Travis for his error. The animal had all the lupine characteristics.

"All right," said Travis, "then tell me why there's a dog in the middle of Chernobyl?"

"Maybe the research team brought one with them," answered Dostoevsky.

The animal was lying motionless in the snow. The only indication it was alive was the fact that its ears were straight up.

Travis looked at the captain. "What are we gonna do, sir?"

Clarke glared at him. "It's a bloody dog, Navarro. We don't need to alter our approach." Taking several steps toward the structure, he motioned to the others. "Guns at the ready. Let's go."

With every step, the enormity of the structure became increasingly evident. If necrilids indeed were inside, it would take a full-fledged expedition to find them.

"If that is their dog," Clarke said to the whole group through his comm, "we know which door they went through. Obviously."

"Why do you think it's sittin' here by itself?" asked an uncharacteristically quiet Derrick. It was the first time he'd spoken all mission. "It looks dead."

The dog wasn't dead—just lifeless. As Scott drew within ten meters of it, he slowed to a stop. The others did as well.

The animal was medium-sized, its fur a patchy mix of brown and gray with a trace of white under its chin. It lay motionless, staring at the group. Its ears tilted forward slightly.

"That is a laika," said Dostoevsky. "Looks like East Siberian."

"Look at its face," said David.

Scott zoomed in on the dog until it took up all of his view. The moment he did, he knew what David meant. The animal's large brown eyes were wide open. Its brow was arched across the center of its forehead. It was the most worried look Scott had ever seen from any animal.

"That dog's scared to death."

Svetlana moved forward, but Dostoevsky grabbed her by the arm. "Sveta, stay back."

Irritated, she shoved his hand away. "Do you see the dog? Does it look like it wants to attack? Did you ever think of why the dog is here and not inside the building?"

Scott considered her words. Why *was* the dog there, waiting at the front door of the plant? Why wasn't it inside? When he thought about the answer, he felt chills. Dogs were more loyal than people. For a dog to abandon its owners…

Svetlana took another step forward. Crouching in the snow, she spoke softly in Russian. *"Kommnye. Kommnye. Iji shudah, shch nawk."* She made several clicking sounds with her tongue.

Nicolai scoffed. "What good is a dog that is a coward? A worthy dog would not be hiding by the door. We should kill it. It would make wonderful welcome mat for the room."

"*Zatknis*. This is only a *puppy*." She held her hand out to the animal. "You do not know what horrible thing this dog has seen. Do you not wonder *why* it is so afraid?" Clicking again with her tongue, she took a careful step closer. "*Kommnye. Kommnye.*" The dog's tail swayed back and forth limply.

Clarke spoke through the comm. "Brooking, what have you found?"

After several seconds of silence, Esther replied, "There's nothing, captain. No bags, nothing in the glove box, nothing anywhere. There's not even a map of the reactor. I'm sorry."

The dog slowly pushed to its feet.

"Very well," Clarke said. "Return to us. Boris, I want you here as well."

"Da, captain."

As Svetlana reached out her hand, the dog approached her, sniffing cautiously. She laughed as it stopped at her leg. She rubbed her hands gently on its belly and back.

Scott watched as the dog's tail finally wagged.

"You are a *good* boy," she whispered, this time in English. She rubbed the sides of its face, and its pointy ears folded to the sides. "You are a cute little flopper."

"Well, Ms. Voronova," Clarke said, "kindly take 'Flopper' back to the ship. Do it quickly."

"Yes, captain." She carefully scooped the dog into her arms.

Scott turned back to the plant. It was time to refocus on the mission. "What's the plan, captain?" There was no immediate response. Instead, Clarke scrutinized the structure. He was figuring out where to begin.

Scott refused to hold ignorance against the captain. Not for something like this. Scott's first bug-hunt had been nothing remotely like Academy training. In training, you knew you would live. If you flunked out, that was as bad as it got. You wouldn't be eaten alive.

"I will take lead."

Scott raised an eyebrow in surprise. The captain's courage was unexpected; Scott was impressed.

Clarke readied his E-35. Several of the other operatives—David, Derrick, Nicolai, and Auric—sported combat shotguns instead. Giving his assault rifle a quick check, Clarke said, "We move as follows. Jurgen behind me. Followed by Strakhov and Cole. We will clear the initial chamber, or corridor, or whatever we're faced with."

There'd be no map for this one, something that happened more than

Scott liked to think about. There was a running joke among civilians that if someone claimed to be lost, they must be from EDEN. It wasn't EDEN's fault—it was the result of a war of global dimensions. Consistently accurate mapping was needed, yet impossible when a summons to anywhere on the planet could come at any time. Corporations were always redesigning their buildings. Some buildings were torn down completely. New roads were built; old roads were renamed and redirected. With near-exponential corporate growth, schematics regularly became obsolete. Especially for a heap like Chernobyl. New parts fell apart every year.

"TCVS on," the captain continued, engaging his own. "There will be nothing resembling power of any kind." He looked back at Scott. "Was your first bug-hunt in total darkness, too?"

Scott silently nodded.

Without another word, Clarke stepped through the entranceway with David, Oleg, and Derrick following behind him. Scott waited until Esther was back with them before leading her, Boris, and the other Nightmen inside.

15

MONDAY, NOVEMBER 14TH, 0011 NE
1452 HOURS

AT THE SAME TIME

SVETLANA STEPPED into the ship, cradling the adolescent pup in her arms. She knelt by the cabin and placed the dog down. "Travis will take good care of little Flopper."

"Flopper?"

She gave him a flat look and said, "Just watch the dog." She turned to leave.

The dog watched as Svetlana walked away, standing up briefly as if to follow. After taking two steps in her wake, it stopped and simply stood still, its eyes following her every move.

Travis got out of his seat. "Hey, Flopper." Crouching beside the animal, he scratched the top of its head. Without warning, the young dog jumped forward, arched its head, and let out a howl.

"Whoa, whoa, hey there…" Travis said quietly, rubbing the dog's back. "It's all right." He leaned into the cockpit and closed the bay door. The dog howled until the *Pariah* was sealed.

"Corridor clear," Clarke said over the comm.

Scott took a position in front of his team of operatives. Staring into the darkness, he engaged his TCV for the first time. The passage came into view.

It wasn't a natural corridor. By its appearance, it had once been a room or perhaps even a front lobby. It was impossible to be certain; the walls had all but completely crumbled. Debris, some of it twisted and half melted, stretched across the ceiling and floor. Age had taken over. *If I were a necrilid, I'd choose this place, too,* he thought. *If for no other reason, to make people too afraid to come after me.*

Everything reeked of oldness. Ancient, scarred walls framed rotten tiled floors. Disconnected cables and fixtures dangled from the ceiling. With every breath he took, musty dust particles were sucked into his helmet.

"Radiation level, still zero," said Boris.

The technician stayed close behind Scott. Esther had crept behind him, too, and he heard her inhale sharply. "Disgusting filth," she muttered to herself.

Paying special mind to Clarke's team ahead, Scott examined every corner, even the ceiling. It was almost impossible to walk stealthily. With every step, the floor creaked and snapped. At least the temperature was low. He didn't know if that would have a sluggish effect on the creatures, but anything remotely advantageous would be welcome.

Behind Scott, the other operatives filed in. Boris fell back to the rear with Svetlana upon her return. Ahead, Clarke, Oleg, and Derrick waited; the three of them had taken positions outside of another doorway directly in front of them. The door had long ago been blasted open, and the large metal frame lay on the floor. Scott continued creeping forward, sensing the walls all around him. He felt almost claustrophobic.

Clarke moved through the door, with his three teammates following. Esther stayed close to Scott, gripping her pistol firmly.

"Commander Dostoevsky," said Scott, stopping and turning, "you and Auric take the rear. Nicolai and Viktor, behind me. I want Sveta and Boris in the middle." Everyone followed orders. Scott passed through the torn metal doorway—the one Clarke had passed through moments before. When the next room came into view, it was more of the same—damaged ceilings, walls, and floors.

Once again, Clarke and company were stationed ahead of Scott's team, again at both sides of an open metal door—this one intact. When the captain pulled at the door, a piercing screech hit the air.

"Boris," Clarke said, "oil this door."

"Yes, captain."

Through all the tension, Scott nearly laughed. *Oil the door, Boris.* Of every operative in the unit, no one was as misunderstood and underappreciated as Boris Evteev. He was as able a technician as Max, minus the cockiness. He worked the *Pariah*'s cannon, which was actually Travis's job. In the rare event that a weapon actually broke, he was usually able to repair it. But even in the midst of a task as intimidating and monumental as Chernobyl, he still managed to come across as unassuming. And to receive the singular job of oiling the doors.

Moments later, Boris returned and took his place next to Svetlana again. Ahead, Clarke opened the door without sound.

"Nice work, Evteev," Scott said, smirking on the inside. *Way to be useful.*

"Thank you, lieutenant."

The building was quiet. The door to the outside world was still relatively close, but soon that would change.

"Next room is identical," Clarke informed them. "Moving forward."

That made three rooms, each patterned the same as the one before it, and each reduced to ancient ruin.

"Halt." They all froze. "We've got something," Clarke said through his comm. "Stairwell in the third room, along the left-hand wall. The west wall. Leading down."

Scott knew what the captain's next words would be.

"Brooking, scout the sub level."

Esther breathed steadily as she made her way slowly through the second metal door, into the third corridor with Clarke. Scott wondered if she'd ever trained for something like this. Surely she must have, but he could see she was afraid.

Clarke wasn't being a coward, he was using what he had. It made no sense to send half the team down if the sub room was just that—a single room. That would be a waste of both energy and time.

Scott looked back at the outer door. It looked a lot farther away.

"We're continuing forwards," Clarke said over the comm. "Remington, assume our previous position by the stairwell. Wait for Brooking's report, then use your judgment."

"Yes sir." Scott couldn't help but wonder what was going on in Stockholm and Copenhagen. He wondered if the cities were being defended. He wondered if EDEN was winning and wished he could see for himself.

He realized he'd allowed his mind to wander. The battles in Europe might have been important, but here, they were nothing but distractions. Distractions on bug-hunts could kill.

He turned on his ExTracker, but no dots appeared on the grid. It hadn't worked perfectly in Krasnoyarsk, but he was willing to give it another chance. *Esther isn't an officer, but she could use one of these. She'd know how to handle it responsibly.* It was a crime that it wasn't already standard scout equipment. But most rules were written by people who'd never fought.

Scott and Nicolai arrived at the top of the stairwell, where Scott looked down for the first time. It descended only one floor, where it leveled off and continued straight west. Esther was nowhere to be seen.

As if on cue, the scout's voice emerged. It quivered slightly. "There's serious damage to the corridor, from the walls and ceiling. There are a lot of openings. It continues about thirty meters, branching off in numerous directions. No signs of life." Her breathing grew heavy.

She was going too far. She needed to stop. "Esther, hold," Scott said, turning to the others. "Commander, take Auric and Svetlana to Brooking's position. Start a methodical sweep of the lower level." Dostoevsky and Auric were competent warriors; Svetlana and Esther would be safe with them.

He watched until all three of them had arrived at the bottom of the stairwell. Then they were gone. Nicolai, Viktor, and Boris remained behind Scott. "Romanov take rear. Ryvkin, you're behind me. Boris, stay in the middle."

They affirmed and the foursome moved on.

Clarke was not far ahead of them. The captain had apparently waited for Scott and his group before moving ahead any farther. As soon as Scott reached him, he realized why—the pathway was about to divide once again. One route was ahead of them, to climb a single rusty ladder through a hole in the ceiling. Beside them now was an open corridor leading west.

"Lieutenant," Clarke said, "please lead your team up the ladder to the next floor and investigate. We'll remain on this floor, following this corridor west."

Scott was surprised. As perilous as scaling the ladder would be, this level seemed more dangerous. The ladder and the porthole above it were clean, and no holes had been torn in the ceiling. A greater chance of necrilid presence existed where Clarke was going. Scott wondered if that was intentional on the captain's part or if it was an oversight.

David, Oleg, and Derrick would be with the captain. David and Oleg were capable, but it was time to find out where Derrick stood. He was sure the southerner had never done this before. Demolitionist units didn't get bug-hunts.

Placing his hands on the ladder, Scott tested its strength. It seemed secure, though it moved slightly as he put weight on it. *Just don't fall apart.* Placing his hand on the rim above, he began to hoist himself up.

He wondered for a moment if this was how Becan had felt, slowly crawling through a hole in the ceiling in the Arkansas high school. There was a certain rush about it, but Scott wasn't afraid.

With only his head sticking through the hole, he looked around. The next level was a large, open room containing dozens of ancient computer consoles, each covered in dust. He looked in every direction. The north, south, and east walls were solid, but the west wall had two branching corridors. *Everything leads west, on every level.* Each corridor appeared to lead into the complex. *Two teams of two. One of them has to have Boris. I'll take him with me.* He didn't trust the slayers with Boris's life. He gripped the ladder tighter and prepared to climb all the way through.

Movement! Still propped on the ladder, Scott thought he saw a sudden motion in the room. *What was that?* From the corner of his eye, he perceived something dark, blurry, flitting across his peripherals. But when he turned, nothing was there.

The atmosphere turned thick. His mind rationalized what he saw. *If that were real, I'd have heard something. Claws on the floor. Breathing. Something. This is just paranoia.* Necrilids had retractable claws—they could move in almost total silence. Nonetheless, bounding across a room would surely make noise. Now he understood the Irishman's fear. It was so real he could taste it. *Lilan had Becan doing this on just his second mission. That colonel had ice water for blood.* Scott slowly flexed his forearms and pulled up the rest of the way. Nothing else moved.

Dostoevsky, Auric, and Svetlana finally reached Esther. She was standing motionless meters before an intersecting corridor that ran north and south. With rigid compliance, she'd followed Scott's order to stop.

"Brooking, get behind me," said Dostoevsky. "Sveta, behind me as well. Broll, take the rear." The commander warily eyed the intersection. "Everyone, hold." Assault rifle at the ready, he crept cautiously first to the corners, then to the middle of the intersection. He looked around and said, "Intersection clear."

Esther and Svetlana approached. Auric stepped backward, watching the rear.

Dostoevsky crouched in the intersection. "Four directions," he said. "Broll, remain here. Make sure nothing comes back this way. I will take Voronova and Brooking with me down the south corridor. We will see where it goes."

Auric joined him in the intersection, knelt down, and readied his shotgun.

Dostoevsky didn't wait. He was already stalking down the south corridor, as Svetlana and Esther followed behind.

"Commander," Esther whispered, "I can go another route. I can go north, the other way."

After several seconds, Dostoevsky answered. "Very well. Go north. We will all stay in one another's view."

She stepped away.

"She is brave," the commander commented once Esther was out of earshot.

Svetlana did not reply.

Back by Scott's team, Nicolai scaled the ladder. The twitchy slayer was the last one to climb up, as Scott, Viktor, and Boris waited. They pressed their backs to the east wall, leaving the hallways on the west wall in plain view.

"Romanov, Ryvkin, check the left hall," said Scott. "Boris, come with me down the right. Watch for holes in the ceiling. If you smell anything, say something quick." They affirmed.

Motioning to Boris, Scott moved to the right hallway and approached the edge of the wall. After glancing around the corner to ensure its safety, he crept around it. "Stay behind me, Boris. No matter what."

Boris breathed heavily behind him. "Yes. I stay behind you. All the time."

Dostoevsky and Svetlana were halfway down the south hall on the lower level when Clarke's voice came over the comm. "All teams, hold."

Both of them froze.

"We've got a hole in the ceiling on our level. It doesn't look Old Era. Remington, watch your position—it's nearest to you."

"Affirmative," Scott answered through the comm.

Despite the frigid cold of the structure, sweat drops dripped down Svetlana's face. From behind her visor, she stared at the commander.

"Continuing forward," said Dostoevsky.

Auric's voice suddenly cut through. "Commander...I do not know for certain, but I am looking down west corridor and I think I saw something."

Dostoevsky continued moving ahead. "You must be more specific."

"It was like a movement, very fast. Like it was shadow. Far ahead, but I cannot be sure. Maybe it was trick of vision. I wanted you to know."

"Which way did it go?"

"Across an intersection far ahead. It was traveling north."

Esther spoke up. "I've heard nothing on my end. Are you *sure* to the north?"

"That is what it looked. It was there when I blinked. I do not know."

"Commander," said Esther, "I'd like to regroup."

Dostoevsky stopped. Far ahead of him, the corridor turned. "It could have been trick of vision, as he said. Continue to go forward."

"Yuri..." Svetlana whispered behind him.

Esther spoke again. The waver in her voice was growing heavier. "I know I said I could go alone, sir, but..."

Svetlana touched Dostoevsky's arm. "We should not leave her by herself."

"...I'm not sure I want to move ahead now," finished the scout.

Dostoevsky motioned Svetlana away. "Go back to Auric. I will go ahead alone."

For the first time since returning to *Novosibirsk*, Svetlana looked at Dostoevsky with urgency and concern. "No!" she whispered. "Come back with us, please. We will do this together."

"We are less than five meters from the turn, Sveta. I must see what is around it—"

Auric interrupted. "I just saw it again. Again, it appeared, then went north. There is something there."

"I'm falling back," Esther said. "I have to fall back. I'm not staying here."

"I am here, Esther," Auric answered her. "Come to me."

Svetlana tugged on Dostoevsky's arm. "Please, Yuri. I beg of you, please. No one should go alone."

His eyes lingered on the corner ahead. Finally, he muttered, "As you wish. Go. I am behind you."

"Thank you, Yuri."

Nodding a single time, the commander remained facing the south corner. Instead of approaching it, however, he carefully backed away.

Captain Clarke and his team had passed through several rooms, most of which housed lockers and tables. Various ancient instruments—gas masks, dosimeters, field instruments—were strewn about in disarray.

"Tell me, Jurgen," Clarke asked, "how did your first bug-hunt feel?" The captain continued to move forward, hitting corners hard when he reached them.

David mirrored the captain's every action. "It felt a lot like this."

Behind them, Derrick and Oleg covered the rear.

"But we didn't see a hole in the ceiling first," David went on. "We smelled human flesh."

Derrick's mouth fell open. "Are you serious?"

"Then we saw blood on the walls. Then we saw the corpse."

"Aw, shoot."

Oleg, who had been silent up to that point, finally spoke. "Perhaps we should all be quiet, yes?"

Clarke slipped around another corner. David did the same. Only when the new halls were visibly cleared did David respond. "It doesn't matter if we're quiet or not. They already know we're here."

Svetlana was the first to meet Auric and Esther. "What did you see?" she asked Auric.

"I only saw it for a second, twice the same thing. Just a shadow that disappears to the right. But it could have been nothing."

Dostoevsky finally joined them.

"We should tell the captain," Svetlana said to him. "So he knows what Auric saw."

"Nothing has been confirmed," the commander said. "He *thought* he saw something dark. Everything is dark here, even with TCVS—I have already seen movement several times. But I know it is not really there."

"We still should say *something*."

"What will we say? That we saw shadows in the distance? None of us have heard a single thing."

Suddenly, as if on cue, a human voice wailed. It came from directly beyond the corner Auric had been watching. It was a female voice—a voice in pure agony.

All four of them froze. The hair on the backs of their necks stood on end, as chill bumps exploded on their arms. The wail lasted for several seconds before fading away.

Svetlana reached for her belt. "There is someone alive."

Dostoevsky listened, but no further sound came. He addressed Auric without looking. "Broll, did that come from where you saw something move?"

"Yes."

The sound came a second time—a drawn-out, tortured moan. Then it was gone.

"It is definitely from the right, around that far corner," Svetlana said as she prepared her medical kit in one hand and pistol in the other. "We must go, quickly."

Dostoevsky readied his weapon. Auric did the same. But neither they, nor Esther, took a step forward.

Svetlana turned to Dostoevsky. "Yuri, if we do not hurry, this woman may die. This is why we are here. We *must* at least try to save her."

Dostoevsky focused down the corridor again. "Auric, stay here. Sveta, Esther, stay directly behind me. We move slowly." He turned to Svetlana again. "Let us go."

Nodding her head confidently, Svetlana stood at the ready. When Dostoevsky moved, she mirrored his pace.

Two other intersections preceded the one from which the scream had come. Leaping into the first one, the commander pivoted his assault rifle in every direction.

The woman wailed again. The chilling cry was louder; they were noticeably closer.

Svetlana stayed low, her handgun poised and her eyes focused ahead. "I may need time to work on her. Esther, can you hold one direction if Yuri holds the other?"

"Yes."

"I do not know what condition she will be in. It may not be good to look at. Just watch the hall."

"I said yes, didn't I?"

They approached the second intersection—the final one between them and the woman. Dostoevsky secured it, and they were one turn away. The woman wailed again; now she was around the very next corner. The tortured pain of her voice reverberated along the corridor walls, just as it had time and time before.

Esther suddenly slowed, right behind Dostoevsky and Svetlana. "Wait, wait! Everyone freeze!" They all stopped in their tracks.

Esther's muscles were tensed. She stared straight ahead, hardly breathing. "It's always the same."

Dostoevsky looked at her oddly.

"Every time she screams. It's always the same."

For several seconds, not an operative moved. Only their breathing made noise. Suddenly Dostoevsky gasped in realization. Grabbing Svetlana, he yanked her behind him.

She stumbled but maintained her balance. "Yuri, what are you *doing*?"

"That is not a woman screaming," he answered, aiming at the corner ahead.

From around the next corner, the voice wailed once again—lingering for several moments then fading away.

With Svetlana and Esther behind him, Dostoevsky hurriedly backed away from the corner, forcing the two women back farther.

"I do not understand," Svetlana said.

"Your woman is dead," said Dostoevsky. "That is the last sound she made. We are being lured."

Suddenly, a new sound came from the corner. It was not the voice of a woman, but it was trying to be. It was a series of whimpers and moans. It was unmistakably alien.

Something skittered in the opposite direction.

"Auric," said Dostoevsky through the comm, "look around you. There is more than—"

Auric fired his shotgun. Dostoevsky turned just in time to see the discharge. In the next instant, the German was gone. The sound of claws against armor rattled out of view.

The second attack came moments later. As Dostoevsky turned his head away, a necrilid leapt from the corner ahead, striking the commander in the chest. The fulcrum was knocked off his feet.

Svetlana screamed and fell backward, dropping her pistol while Esther aimed with her own. From the corner behind them, out of a view, Auric fired another shot.

Dostoevsky howled as claws stabbed through his armor. With a frantic swing, he punched the creature in the side of the head. The necrilid was thrown to the wall.

Esther fired. Several shots pierced the necrilid's body, and it leapt from wall to wall. It disappeared around the next intersection, its screeching claws echoing.

Dostoevsky groaned, thrust himself up, and reclaimed his gun. "Where did it go?"

"Down the hall," Esther answered. Eyeing the fresh trail of blood, she said, "Shall I pursue?"

"No. Wait."

From around the corner behind them, they heard something new—the sound of stumbling boots.

"Get Broll," Dostoevsky said, waving the two women away. He staggered as blood seeped from claw holes in his armor. "I will get the necrilid." Down from the intersection, where the creature had fled, came the frantic tearing of claws.

Auric emerged from the corner before either woman could seek him out. Claw marks were etched on his armor, but he still gripped his shotgun firmly.

Clarke's voice came over the comm. "We heard gunfire—what's going on?"

Dostoevsky readied his assault rifle again. He was hunched over in pain. "Two necrilids," he answered through his helmet comm. "One injured, the other..."

"The other is dead," Auric answered.

Dostoevsky grunted. "We are in pursuit of the injured creature."

Svetlana stopped him before he could move. Her voice was shaking. "We must get you back to the *Pariah*. You are hurt."

"I am fine," he answered gruffly. "It did not go deep. This armor is good." His attention returned to the comm. "Captain, be advised—they are mimicking human sounds."

"They're doing *what*?"

"It sounded like a woman. It was drawing us close. Perhaps it was a woman it killed."

"Noted, commander. Remington, are you getting this?"

"Yes sir," Scott said. "That's good to know."

Esther grabbed Svetlana's pistol from the floor and jammed it hard into her hand. "Do you know what this is?"

"Of course—"

"Then next time, *use* it."

Dostoevsky and Auric rounded the next corner, where a freshly clawed hole had been torn through the ceiling. Flakes of debris fell to the floor.

"Captain," Dostoevsky said, "the necrilid has gone one level up. It may be near you right now."

On the level above, Clarke stood still. Around him, David, Oleg, and Derrick fell silent. "Understood, commander." As soon as the captain was off-comm, he turned to the rear. "Jurgen, Cole, return to the entrance. Make sure it's not flanking us. Be watchful."

The two men were about to go when another sound stopped them. It was a loud shriek from deeper in the complex.

David stepped back. "Sir, we need to stay together."

Clarke shook his head. "No, we don't. Go back and cover the entrance. Strakhov and I shall proceed ahead."

"Captain, you're seriously underestimating—"

"I am a *captain*, Jurgen. I know a little bit about combat. Go back to the entrance." He turned to Oleg. "I shall continue at point. Cover my back."

"Of course, captain," Oleg answered.

David and Derrick reluctantly backtracked.

Oleg's stare lingered on Clarke from behind. For several moments, he simply watched the captain in silence. Finally, he turned to check the rear, and together, the two men walked ahead.

On the upper level, Scott was moving ahead with the other Nightmen and Boris. Most of the rooms they passed were offices and storage rooms; some contained outdated computers. Cobwebs adorned every console, and everything was covered in a thick layer of dust.

Dostoevsky's words over the comm replayed in Scott's mind. The necrilids were mimicking human sounds. At least to some extent. He'd never heard of that before and wondered if it had ever been encountered.

"I smell blood."

They were Nicolai's words from across the hallway, where he and Viktor crouched. Both Scott and Boris stopped their advance.

"I smell it as well," said Viktor. "There is someone dead here. There is no doubt."

If they said there was no doubt, there was no doubt. Death was something Nicolai and Viktor knew well. *You know death well, too, Scott.* He quickly repressed his thoughts.

Scott hadn't been with the David in the Arkansas school when the older man had experienced the stench of the mutilated body. But now, it was approaching Scott's turn. "Proceed forward. Everyone on high alert." Glancing back, he looked at Boris. "Check our six."

"Yes, lieutenant," the technician said nervously.

For some reason, Scott's mind flashed to the dog they'd rescued earlier. He wondered if it had smelled blood, too. He wondered if the animal had watched it spill.

"Lieutenant!" Boris whispered frantically.

Scott turned.

It was staring at them from the circular hole in the floor—from the very ladder they'd climbed minutes ago, where his ExTracker was coming up blank.

It was a pair of yellow eyes.

It didn't move. It didn't flinch. If Scott hadn't been staring right at it, he wouldn't have believed it was real. But there was no mistaking the top of a necrilid's head, watching them silently from the hole. How long had it been there? Why had it not been detected? How had they not heard it? There was no time for answers.

Scott swung up his assault rifle and unleashed a blast of projectile. Sparks popped against the metal rim around the hole. He heard something thump, and the yellow eyes were gone.

Nicolai and Viktor scurried from the next hall. "Lieutenant?"

"Necrilid, by the ladder. Hold your position."

David and Derrick were almost back to their starting point when they saw it. It began as a small black blob that darted into their hallway. Moments later, its yellow eyes fixed on them.

Derrick screamed and jumped back.

David's heart leapt, but he kept his composure. As the creature bounded from wall to wall toward them, the older operative steadied his shotgun. He took a half a second's aim before pulling the trigger.

The necrilid was stopped in midair. Its body contorted backward, and it fell to the floor. It twitched for a moment, then was still.

"Oh shoot, oh shoot, oh shoot…" Derrick said breathily.

David stared at the dead alien. He took a step toward it and fired. The creature's head blew apart.

"Oh shoot!"

David spun around. Behind them, bounding again from wall to wall, was another pair of eyes. This time there was no time to fire. David flinched in unexpected fear as the necrilid leapt at them both. Derrick was knocked to the floor as the creature landed claws-down. Its hands pounded on Derrick's thighs. The southerner screamed.

David hoisted his shotgun and pulled the trigger. The necrilid cut a flip backward as the blast slammed into it.

Derrick scrambled away. "Oh God!" The soldier's leg was torn open.

The second necrilid twitched on the floor, then finally lay still.

"Two Ex down," David said through the comm. "Derrick is hurt."

Farther ahead, Clarke drew to a halt. "Did you just say *two*?"

"Yes, sir," David answered through the radio.

The captain stopped moving. "That's three confirmed dead and we've barely begun to look." His next statement was almost a question to himself. He turned to Oleg. "Could that possibly be *right*?"

Dostoevsky's assault rifle remained trained on the ceiling as the sound of creatures skittering echoed above. Auric stayed at his side, surveying the halls with his shotgun pointed. Svetlana and Esther remained in the intersection.

Something shrieked, but it wasn't from the ceiling. It came from deeper into the structure.

Dostoevsky and Auric exchanged a stunned look.

"No way," said Esther. "That came from farther in..."

"There are *this* many necrilids in a Cruiser?" asked Auric in amazement.

Gravely, Dostoevsky said, "Captain, we have multiple targets in our immediate area."

Scott crouched by the hole and the ladder. The necrilid he'd fired at was nowhere to be seen. Had he killed it? It had to be somewhere. Turning around, he motioned to Boris. "Stay right where you are. Don't move."

Boris was breathing erratically.

Grabbing the sides of the ladder, Scott dropped to the ground level. He swung his assault rifle in every direction, but there were no targets. Reaching up, he switched off his ExTracker; it was going to get him killed. "Ryvkin, have either of you seen *anything*?"

"Negative, lieutenant. But we still smell blood."

"Don't move any farther. Fall back to the ladder. Stay with Evteev." He wasn't about to leave Boris alone.

Scott searched the area again. *Where did it go?* There wasn't even blood. He must have missed it completely—yet it had to be there somewhere.

He tracked cautiously up the hall. It was only a matter of moments until he'd reached David's position. He immediately saw Derrick on the ground. The soldier was wounded, his EDEN leg armor ripped open. The necrilid was dead on the floor.

David looked up. Nine times out of ten, there would have been awkwardness between the two men, but this time it was absent.

"Where'd it come from?" Scott asked.

David motioned with his head. "Same direction you did."

Scott felt a sense of relief. The one David killed *had* to be the one he'd seen on the ladder. He checked behind again just to be sure.

"That's not the only one we killed," said David. "There's another right there down the hall. I just heard Dostoevsky say he's after two more."

"I heard, too. That's five, and we haven't seen half this place."

"Six," David corrected. "We heard one with the captain before we separated."

Six necrilids. That was almost too much to believe. Something was very wrong.

"Scott….how often do people come to this place?"

How often did they come to Chernobyl? He had no idea. There were no engineering crews assigned to it anymore. Outside of adventurers such as the ones they were supposedly rescuing, there couldn't have been many visitors at all. "I wouldn't think often."

"What if EDEN was wrong?"

Scott tilted his head.

"What if these necrilids *didn't* come from the Cruiser EDEN just shot down? What if they've been here for months?"

A knot formed deep in Scott's gut.

"What if this is a nest?"

Oleg followed Clarke silently, his eyes lingering on the captain from behind. He hadn't spoken a word since they'd set out on their own.

Clarke's eyes peeled ahead. "I haven't heard a thing." His voice wavered, but barely.

Oleg quietly reached for his belt, where he slid his combat knife from its sheath. His kept his eyes on Clarke. Then he stopped, his hand frozen on the knife in his grasp. He inhaled to smell the air. The knife slid back into place as he swung around with his gun. "Captain…"

Clarke stood back to back with the operative. "I smell it, too. It's very close."

Something shuffled in the hallway ahead. Oleg's attention remained fixed on the rear. A new sound appeared—the scratching of claw against floor. Then it was there.

When the captain saw it, his eyes bulged. The black monster appeared out of nowhere, bounding from one wall to the next. Clarke opened fire.

Something else crashed through the ceiling behind them. It rasped loudly and bared its sharp teeth. Oleg sidestepped to the wall. He fired, and the second creature was struck.

Clarke dove forward to avoid the first necrilid just as it was struck by his bullets. He staggered to his feet and turned to fire again. There were two necrilids in his sight—one dead and one injured. It was impossible to tell who had done what.

Oleg aimed at the injured creature and fired. The alien's squirming ceased.

Something new hissed. The captain spun around, trained his rifle, and fired. Another creature dropped from the ceiling. He fired again. The alien toppled over, attempted to stand, then was gunned down permanently.

When stillness hit the hallway, it was almost surreal. Clarke breathed furiously as his sweaty hands gripped his assault rifle's stock. His whole body shook. "Bloody *hell.*" He turned to find Oleg.

It happened in less than a second—before the captain could think. The blade of Oleg's combat knife flashed in the darkness. Fresh incisions crisscrossed Clarke's throat. He was spared no time for a last gasp. Oleg slammed his palm straight into Clarke's forehead, and the captain collapsed to the floor. He gagged a single mouthful of blood before he went still.

Not a sound could be heard. Through the sky-blue visor belonging to EDEN, the man who was not EDEN's stared in malevolence. Pulling out a black, unmarked comm, Oleg uttered the Russian words.

"Strakhov to Thoor." His voice never wavered. "Clarke is exterminated. The Fourteenth is Dostoevsky's alone."

Several seconds passed before a reply came. The Terror's droning voice was the next thing he heard. "Message received."

No more words were exchanged. Pulling a rag from one of his leg guards, Oleg wiped his bloody blade clean.

"What's he mean, what if this is a nest?" Derrick asked Scott from the floor. "How fast can they make a nest?"

Scott recalled Lilan's explanation. "Necrilids can conceive in hours," he answered, paraphrasing his former colonel. "They can lay eggs and hatch them in a matter of days. All they'd need is food." While humanity had left Chernobyl alone, it was a well-documented fact that nature hadn't. Animals flourished in the Zone of Alienation. More than enough sustenance was available for predators to thrive.

"If we continue this operation," David said, "we're all going to die."

Scott stared at the floor under his feet. They'd been operating under the assumption that six, maybe seven necrilids had been present. A nest was altogether different. There could be dozens, if not a hundred.

Scott's mind was churning. *There's no way we can accomplish this as a large group. There's no strength in numbers at all.*

He knew what the correct course of action would have been. To flee. Head back to The Machine and throw in the towel. Just as they'd done in Khatanga. And Krasnoyarsk. And now Chernobyl. That was why they were never sent on serious missions—because they never got the job done. Not even this was a serious mission when compared to the invasion taking place in Europe. This was a junk job.

He was sick of losing those, too.

"David, take Derrick back to the ship." No more sneaking around. No more easing around corners like a terrified kid. It was time for a different tactic—time to hit this place hard.

David stared at Scott, then his mouth fell. "Wait a minute—don't tell me you're—"

"Get Derrick back to the ship. This mission's not over."

"Scott, personal feelings aside, this is *not* a smart decision—this is out of our league."

He faced David head on. "I completely agree."

David stared blankly. When he realized what Scott was saying, his countenance fell. "You're going to come back in with the Nightmen."

Scott said nothing.

David stepped back in wary concern. "This is not the right thing to do, Scott. I am begging on *behalf* of the Nightmen—don't make them go in there. They will not survive."

David didn't understand. He *couldn't* understand. There wasn't a doubt in Scott's mind that this could be finished. "Take him back to the ship," he said a final time, turning away.

Dostoevsky's team was tracking deeper into the sub level when Scott's voice broke through the comm. "All units, attention. We have reason to believe that this is an established necrilid nest. I advise *everyone* to fall back to the plant's entrance."

Far ahead of them down the corridor, something new skittered. Auric and Esther trained their weapons at the sound. Nothing was there.

"I hear you, Remington," Dostoevsky answered, motioning the operatives behind him to retreat. "We will find you outside."

Oleg stood motionless over Clarke's body. He listened to the conversation with concern.

"Captain?" Scott asked over the comm.

Oleg remained quiet.

"Captain Clarke, did you receive my transmission?"

From farther ahead in the compound came an inhuman howl. Oleg turned its direction, but nothing could be seen. Kneeling, he picked up Clarke's body. He hoisted it over his shoulder. "The captain is dead."

Upon first hearing them through the comm, Oleg's words failed to register with Scott. Only after Scott repeated them in his mind did he realize what he'd just been told. *The captain is dead. Clarke was dead.* Their leader was gone.

Perhaps it was Scott's determination to finish the mission. Perhaps it was his inner frustration, or the fact that his capacity for grieving had already been drained. Whatever the reason, at the announcement of his captain's demise only one thought entered Scott's mind: *he* was next in command. The captain had given him temporary executive control over Dostoevsky.

For this mission, the Fourteenth was his.

When Svetlana heard Oleg's announcement, she covered her mouth in shock. Esther was more composed and quickly resumed her defense. Dostoevsky's shoulders slumped.

They could hear Scott's voice over the comm again. "What happened, Strakhov?"

"He is dead," Oleg repeated, stepping carefully backward up the hall. "A necrilid killed him."

A hissing sound came from the ceiling above him. The eidolon's attention shot upward, where the ceiling tiles shifted.

"Oleg," Scott said, "get out of there now."

The tiles erupted and gave way, and a necrilid crashed through to the floor. Oleg fired his assault rifle and the creature jerked backward.

As soon as Scott heard the gunfire, he swung in its direction. Without looking at David, he ordered, "Get Derrick back to the ship."

David helped Derrick to his feet.

"Romanov, Ryvkin, where are you?"

The two slayers were still on the upper level. They were crouched behind Boris at the ladder.

"We are here, lieutenant," Viktor answered. "We have seen nothing so far."

"We're leaving the plant, Ryvkin," said Scott. "Fortify the main entrance. Hold there until everyone is out."

"Yes, lieutenant."

"Romanov, come to me and assist."

Nicolai shot Viktor a smug look. "This is turning out to be an interesting day."

Boris jumped through the hole.

"Wait for us, you coward!" Viktor shouted. He dove down in pursuit with Nicolai behind him.

Dostoevsky backpedaled on the sub level. Auric, Svetlana, and Esther followed suit.

"The stairs aren't far," Esther said. Her breathing was growing weary. "One intersection behind us."

Svetlana's heart rate was out of control. Her chest heaved laboriously.

Far ahead, deep into the structure though impossible to miss, yellow eyes materialized in the blackness. Without warning, the aliens sprang to attack.

The two Nightmen lifted their weapons, firing simultaneously. Bullets ricocheted everywhere. One creature fell.

"Go!" Dostoevsky shouted. "Run for the stairs!"

Svetlana and Esther bolted for the stairwell. Only Esther paid mind to the last intersection.

Auric's shotgun blast hit a necrilid as it lurched toward him. Momentum sent the creature skidding past. More eyes appeared in the distance.

The two women reached the stairwell together, turning to spot their Nightman comrades. Dostoevsky and Auric sprinted for the stairs as the necrilids behind them leapt closer. Esther took aim, firing at will. Dostoevsky and Auric ducked. One pair of eyes skidded to a stop; the others kept on. Svetlana fired several times, but none of her shots connected. As soon as the Nightmen reached the stairwell, all four operatives united to fire. A tidal wave of projectile ensued, and the necrilids catapulted out of view. That was all the operatives needed. They fled up the stairs.

Scott could see Oleg ahead in his TCVS; the Russian soldier was firing in all directions. He could see Clarke's body over his shoulder.

We are not here to protect humanity.

Scott crouched and raised his rifle to fire.

We are here to destroy all who oppose it.

The creatures appeared. They were bouncing into view from side passages, snapping and rasping as they careened from wall to wall. Scott didn't wait for Oleg to move from his line of fire; he unleashed his assault rifle without caution.

Bullets streaked past Oleg as he dove to the ground. Clarke's body rolled across the floor.

Scott swiveled the barrel of his gun purposefully from one necrilid to the next, to the next, then to the next. Never in his life had he focused with so much precision. It almost felt spiritual, but in a way he'd never felt before. This was pure killer's lust. As the last necrilid fell, Scott checked his ammunition. He was still good.

Oleg looked up from the floor. Behind the tinted visor of his EDEN helmet, a surprised pair of eyes beheld Scott. The fulcrum from America stood firm.

Footsteps appeared behind them. It was Nicolai. Without turning, Scott issued his orders. "Watch everything behind me. I've got point." His next words went to Oleg. "Get Clarke out of here."

Both men affirmed, as Oleg picked up Clarke's body. He began to make his way out. The trio fell back.

Boris was the first out of the plant's entrance, even surpassing David and Derrick. The technician sprinted back to the ship.

Viktor appeared moments later, but he held his ground outside the door.

As the *Pariah*'s door lowered to the snow, Boris flew in right over the dog.

Travis snapped a look back, as the technician leapt into the copilot's seat. "What? What's going on? What happened?"

Boris was shaking too much to talk.

In the troop bay of the ship, barely having avoided Boris's flight, the rescued dog laid its chin down.

It wasn't long before everyone was out of the plant. Uncomfortable stares were cast at Oleg as the soldier carried Clarke's corpse to the ship.

Scott didn't care. His thoughts were solely on the new situation. This was a task tailor-made for the Nightmen. In their black metal suits, they didn't look human. They looked like dark war machines. They looked fearsome. That was the new point.

Speed. Aggression and speed. Make the necrilids fear us for a change. Scott wouldn't offer Dostoevsky the reins back, at the risk that the commander might actually take them. "I want everyone back in the *Pariah*," Scott said, "except us." The Nightmen turned his direction.

Svetlana's mouth hit the snow. "What are you doing?"

"He's going back in," said David, having returned from bringing Derrick to the ship. "And anyone who goes with him is a fool."

"You're going *back*?"

Scott's focus went solely to the Nightmen. "We're going to hit this place with tactical speed. I will take the point position, flanked by Romanov and Ryvkin surveying the perimeter. Dostoevsky and Broll have the rear." He would give Dostoevsky credit where it was due. Only the commander could keep them safe from behind at the level of skill Scott required.

David cut off Scott's commands. His attention turned to the slayers. "If any of you listen to this, you're insane. You don't stand a chance."

Esther crouched quietly in the snow.

Scott's teeth clenched. He was about to charge a necrilid nest—he wasn't about to be intimidated by David. "This isn't up for debate."

"You're doing to them *exactly* what Thoor did to Anatoly in Siberia," David said. "You haven't learned a *thing*!"

At the mention of her dead boyfriend's name, Svetlana turned David's way.

"Nothing good came out of Siberia, Scott!" said David. "Siberia is why you're a Nightman."

Svetlana blinked. A look of total shock hit her face.

Scott's patience with David was gone. "You're about to cross a line you do *not* want to cross."

"I want to go with you," Esther said. The scout rose to her feet.

David's jaw dropped. *"Esther!"*

"I'm not afraid, sir. I can do this."

"I appreciate your interest," Scott answered, "but this isn't for you."

Esther lowered her head, looking away.

David turned to Svetlana and scowled. "Everything you told me, everything you said about friendship, and fatherhood, and forgiveness..."

this is what you haven't seen!" He looked at her while pointing to Scott. "*This* is what you can't comprehend. This is our hell!"

Svetlana said nothing. There was nothing she *could* say.

Scott ignored David completely. He spoke only to the slayers. "Forget everything you were taught about necrilids, because this won't be pretty or precise. Our objective is shock and awe."

The slayers watched him expectantly.

"We go in as one, we move as one, at pure assault speed." He foresaw the whole thing in his mind. He foresaw their whole charge as if it was a vision. They tore through the necrilids like chainsaws. They ripped them apart with their bare hands. They switched the roles of predator and prey. He'd had his fair share of sneaking around. It was time to bash in the door.

Svetlana turned to Scott again, but remained mute. Nonetheless, her eyes gave her feelings away. Behind the featureless faceplate of Scott's helmet, he could read her. This wasn't what she had expected—or understood. *This* was who he was now. This was the man he was created to be.

He stared at the plant's entranceway, feeling his anger take control once again . *Three.* They would not lose this fight. *Two.* They would not lose again.

One.

16

MONDAY, NOVEMBER 14TH, 0011 NE
1524 HOURS

SCOTT BURST THROUGH the front door, his legs churning as he stormed down the hall. As he hit the stairwell, the Nightmen followed.

He plunged down the stairs, landing in a heavy roll that brought him crouching on his knees.

The wait was not long. The moment he landed, he saw them—four of them—two near and two far. The creatures whipped around to face him.

Scott held down the trigger and the two nearest necrilids fell. The farther ones began their attack run. With their yellow eyes burning, they leapt frenetically from wall to wall.

Nicolai and Viktor landed at Scott's side. Both of them fired their weapons, and the last two necrilids were cut down.

At the top of the stairs, Dostoevsky and Auric opened fire. The double-pop of impacts hit the halls.

"Four Ex down!" Scott yelled. He made no attempt to be quiet. He wanted the necrilids to know they were there.

"Two Ex down," Dostoevsky said from above.

"Moving forward!"

Scott's heart was pounding through his armor. It was fear and adrenaline, fight over flight. He darted ahead to the first intersection, flashing his gun wildly. Nicolai and Viktor followed in sync. Above the ceiling, more creatures skittered. As Viktor fired mercilessly at the sound, a necrilid corpse fell straight through the hole to the floor.

Just then, Dostoevsky and Auric appeared. Scott turned back to the corridor just in time to hear a howl from deeper within. His pace quickened as he moved forward.

A necrilid leapt into the intersection ahead. All three Nightmen barraged it with shells.

"Is this as far as you went?" Scott asked Dostoevsky.

"Yes."

That was all Scott needed to know. *"Come on!"* he shouted at the top of his lungs. The words were not meant for his comrades—they were meant for the beasts. *They need to hear us. They need to know we're not afraid.*

"Weapons away," he said to the Nightmen. They complied without protest, slinging their weapons over their shoulders.

The necrilids need to know what it feels like to lose.

It happened in an instant, in tune with Scott's thoughts. As the corridor opened into a new room, a necrilid leapt into view. It rasped loudly and dove after Scott. In the next second, Scott propelled himself through the air, hurling his entire shoulder around and plowing the full brunt of his strength against the necrilid's head in the form of a single, solid fist. The creature smashed into the wall.

Scott didn't wait for the alien to rise. Grabbing it by its head, he rolled forward and hurled it over his shoulder into the room ahead. As the creature flipped upright, it screamed in anger and pain. What Scott did next silenced it cold.

He screamed back.

Propelling himself forward, Scott pulled back his fist and swung at the beast. But to his surprise, he struck only air. The necrilid had moved out of harm's way.

It was a moment so liberating that shockwaves pulsed through Scott's veins as he landed again. The creature had leapt away. It had darted halfway across the room to avoid him.

It was afraid.

The other four Nightmen—Nicolai, Viktor, Dostoevsky, and Auric—charged into the open. Together, the five black knights stood in unison, the horns of the fulcrums stabbing through the dark. They stood like a pack of metal wolves.

Suddenly, something happened that none of them had ever heard or witnessed before. The necrilid let loose with an eerily long howl—a terrible, anguished scream.

Scott cocked his head with comprehension. *You're telling them, aren't you? You're alerting the others. You're warning them of an imminent threat.*

The necrilid bounded away.

"Oh my God," said Viktor. It was the first time he'd ever sounded stunned.

No one challenged a necrilid. They were horrible creatures, made of razor sharp teeth and terrible claws. They were aggressive, rapacious monsters straight out of a nightmare. No one challenged a necrilid—until now.

"Weapons out," Scott said, as he re-aimed his rifle. The Nightmen around him followed suit. There was no need for unarmed bravado now—they'd needed to prove their point only once. Now the necrilids knew real danger. Danger that could beat them one on one. Scott bolted in pursuit of the retreating creature. He knew he couldn't literally catch it—necrilids were faster than anything else. But he had a feeling deep in his gut—a feeling it was fleeing to the nest.

They met almost no resistance through the twisting corridors of Chernobyl. On occasion a necrilid surfaced, but lone necrilids were no match for five Nightmen. They fell without resistance.

"Lieutenant," Esther said over the comm, "do you need any help?"

Scott answered immediately. "Radio dark." He didn't want to hear Esther's voice, nor anyone's from the surface. This wasn't EDEN's mission—it was theirs. The slayers around him assumed radio silence, and no more transmissions came from the team outside.

The terrain inside the plant was impossible to predict. Oval rooms flowed into half-melted halls, which declined into ladderless tubes. Only one direction mattered at all: straight ahead full. The Nightmen surged down a solitary hall, longer than most they'd traversed. It opened ahead into a much larger space.

The screaming began. It came from every direction—from the ceiling and floor, from behind and in front. Bloodthirsty, predatory screaming. A chill passed up Scott's spine.

"Fortify, three-sixty!" Scott shouted. Behind him, Dostoevsky and Auric about-faced and dropped to their knees, while Nicolai and Viktor did the same, but remained facing front. Scott stayed in the center. Every direction was covered forward and back. With the freedom of the middle position, Scott could fire anywhere. They were a fortress of metal.

The screaming around them continued. Howling, snarling, and shrieking.

"*Come on!*" Scott challenged the beasts. He thrust up his E-35. "Amplify your helmets." The Nightmen affirmed, adjusting their volume controls. When Scott spoke again, his mechanized voice blared like a megaphone.

"Come on, we're right here!"

Two necrilids appeared from behind. Dostoevsky and Auric cut them to the ground. Another pair appeared from in front, and Nicolai and Viktor opened fire.

This is it, Scott thought. *This is the end.*

They descended like a black avalanche. Two necrilids. Then ten. Then ten more. Assault rifles and shotgun blasts erupted from both sides as creatures sprang up, then toppled to the ground. Scott's rifle blazed in every direction.

The attack went on for several more seconds before the rush of necrilids ceased. Their screaming continued, but no new creatures emerged.

Their first plan just failed. Keep on the offensive. "Reload and advance!"

There was a burst of stomping and slamming, as assault rifles and shotguns were refreshed. The Nightmen fortress marched forward. Scott remained in the center as the larger room loomed ahead. Then he saw it.

It was cowering far down in the hallway—he almost missed it at first. Its small size made it harder to see. Then it was gone.

A necrilid hatchling.

"The nest is ahead!" Scott bellowed. "State your count!" One by one, the Nightmen called out.

"Eight!"

"Six!"

"Five!"

"Eight!"

Scott himself had killed six. Overall, their fortified guns had dropped over thirty. They'd probably killed forty since they'd arrived at the plant.

The Nightmen pressed onward and the large chamber loomed nearer.

A pair of necrilids appeared from behind, and Dostoevsky and Auric opened fire. Above Scott, the ceiling gave way. He knelt, aimed upward, and fired. Another necrilid fell through to the floor.

They're coming from above now. They're dropping on us.

Panning his rifle in both directions, he fired a steady stream of waves through the ceiling. He could hear them scatter.

"They're in the ceiling! Open fire!"

He hadn't needed to say it. The Nightmen swung their weapons high, unleashing a barrage of assault rifle and shotgun fire into the ceiling. Chunks of bloody debris cascaded around them. Corpses and body parts were littered about.

Proactive. Stay proactive! Stay one step ahead.

"Advance forward!" The formation once again marched ahead. But Scott knew what was coming next. *Their attack from the sides and through the ceiling failed. Their next step is the floor.*

It was a worst case scenario—and inevitable. The necrilids would destroy the humans' footing, then tear them apart before they could stand. If they did that, the Nightmen were dead.

"Burst forward, five meters!" It was a move they'd practiced innumerable times but never used in the field. "Move!"

Every Nightman leapt to his feet. They lunged forward like armored gazelles, diving into the large room ahead.

Behind them, innumerable claws tore away the floor, causing it to fold and collapse.

The five Nightmen hit the ground rolling—and still in formation. When they came out of their rolls, they were once again crouched on their knees, Scott once again in the middle. The entire fortification had moved. The moment Scott looked around, he knew it'd been done.

They'd just bashed in the door.

The room was crawling with necrilids, every one of them caught off-guard by the five raging knights. It was like charging a den full of lions and bludgeoning the predators before they could react. Without a moment's hesitation, the Nightmen opened fire.

In the first ten seconds of the assault, necrilids catapulted in every direction. They dropped from the ceilings and walls. Hatchlings scurried for the protection of their parent monsters, only to be mowed down themselves. Bulbous eggs, clustered in heaps in the corners, exploded as projectiles shattered their shells. Unborn aliens oozed lifelessly to the floor.

All at once the necrilids' panic came to an end. The adults, their numbers decimated in a matter of seconds, roared and leapt at the humans. Bullets struck the creatures in midair and some rolled lifelessly across the floor. But not all.

The first necrilid to break the fortification had come from the corner. Its desperate lunge had not gone unnoticed, but there was no time to take aim. The creature crashed into Viktor from behind, pushing the slayer-medic into the open. Immediately Nicolai shot the necrilid and Viktor fell back into place.

Next Scott was struck from behind. His rifle nearly flew from his grasp as he suddenly found himself on the floor, claws stabbing into his back. A shotgun slug saved him, and he took his place in the middle again.

The battle lasted for almost a minute. Necrilids were chopped down by streams of firepower, even as the fortress was breached. The fortification fought to hold on.

Then, as suddenly as everything had begun, everything ceased. Aliens stopped screaming, monsters stopped lurching. Skittering gave way to silence.

Scott froze as he scanned the room. Through the fog of gun exhaust, he could make out mangled necrilid bodies strewn across the floor. Their entrails pooled in the floor's low points. But even more nauseous was the smell—a mixture of gunfire and innards. It was the sickest thing he'd ever inhaled. The silence was oppressive.

Auric was the first to speak. "Is that it?"

No one answered. It seemed too sudden to be over, and Scott knew better. Necrilids were smart enough to flee. They wouldn't simply stay to be slaughtered. He asked the impossible question, "Does anyone have a count?" No one did.

As the smoke rose to the ceiling, the room began to clear. It was the bloodiest carnage Scott had ever seen. He felt surrounded by evil. Evil they'd annihilated, but evil all the same.

A hatchling emerged from the corner. Auric's shotgun blew it away. All was still again.

Scott considered the situation. *They aren't all dead. They can't all be dead. Some of them would have tried to escape.*

"I think we killed them," Nicolai said, sounding surprised.

"Stay in formation." Scott had no idea how many necrilids still remained in the plant. Even an exact body count would mean nothing. What if this was one nest of ten? He knew exactly what he had to do.

Comm The Machine.

He adjusted his helmet and opened the link, ending radio dark. "This is Lieutenant Remington of the Fourteenth. We have uncovered and isolated a necrilid nest in Chernobyl Nuclear Plant. Requesting instruction."

What to do next? Somehow, storming the rest of the compound seemed premature. He hadn't had a chance to think this far ahead.

NovCom was quick to reply. "Hold your position, lieutenant. The Tenth is en route to your location."

The Tenth. That was the four slayers' original unit. Scott knew why they were coming, and he was willing to bet that a team of scientists was coming, too. *Novosibirsk* didn't want to clean out Chernobyl. They wanted to own it.

Once again, Scott listened to the silence. For the first time, the thought entered his mind. *What if we did kill them all?* He knew better, but he wondered just the same.

"What do we do?" Nicolai asked.

It was Commander Dostoevsky who answered. "We wait for the Tenth." The fulcrum commander said nothing else.

Scott turned to look at Dostoevsky. *You wouldn't have had the nerve to do this, would you? You wouldn't have had the courage. You'd have left Chernobyl a mess for someone else to clean up.*

Dostoevsky looked away.

The wait for the Tenth lasted barely twenty minutes, when word of the unit's arrival came from the *Pariah*. Scott's earlier thought had been correct: an entire crew of scientists had come along, too.

It was another fifteen minutes before the Tenth arrived at the necrilid nest. There were twenty-four operatives from the unit in total, and just under a dozen scientists. None of them reported seeing any creatures on the journey, though it was obvious by their expressions that the sheer number of dead necrilids there stunned them. After the initial uncomfortable silence, an exchange of more jovial nature took place between Viktor, Nicolai, Auric, and their former comrades in the Tenth.

A fulcrum elite approached Scott to begin his own exchange. Scott couldn't see the man's face—everyone was still hidden by their helmets—but he did catch the man's nametag. His name was Axelos. Scott recognized him as the Tenth's captain.

"Remington, how did you accomplish this?"

"We were aggressive," Scott answered firmly. "We came in hard before they could react. We forced them on the defense."

Axelos looked about the room, then turned to Scott. "I have never seen this many dead necrilids before. There must be a hundred."

Scott knew there were not a hundred. But the tally might have pushed as high as seventy or eighty. The significance of the event hadn't escaped him. "We learned a few things. They mimic human sounds. They also recognize danger. That can work to our advantage."

Axelos laughed under his breath, casting a sidelong look to Dostoevsky. After confirming that the commander was out of earshot, he whispered to Scott. "Now that Clarke is out of the way, it is inevitable that the Fourteenth will be yours."

For a moment, Scott was taken aback. He'd completely forgotten about Clarke's death.

"I wish to train my men with you," Axelos said. "If I recall, you used to train with the Eighth. Will you have my unit instead?"

But now Scott's mind was stuck on Clarke. He was shocked by his own numbness to the captain's demise. A familiar knot formed in his bowels. *I did all this after the captain was dead. I didn't even stop to think about it. I didn't even acknowledge his death.*

Axelos had said it so casually. *Clarke is out of the way.* In fact, that was exactly how Scott had thought of it, too. The moment Clarke died only one thing had come to Scott's mind. The captain was out of the way. *He* was in command. It was as if Clarke had been nothing but an obstacle.

Did I really just do that? Did I really just spit on Clarke's death?

He could scarcely believe it. In the aftermath of what had to be one of the most brave and brazen things he'd ever done, he couldn't believe his own heartlessness. It stabbed him to the core of his soul.

Oh my God. I'm really one of them.

Axelos never got his answer. He simply watched as Scott quietly turned away, leaving the Tenth's captain standing awkwardly behind.

Scott walked out of the compound alone. He didn't wonder about the presence of necrilids, outside of a general awareness that they could be near. If they were, they wouldn't attack him. They'd be too afraid.

He couldn't shake Clarke from his mind. He couldn't shake his own lack of remorse. Leaders had to react coldly sometimes, of course. Sometimes it was critical to the survival of others. But this hadn't been one of those times. He hadn't stormed Chernobyl out of necessity. He'd stormed it out of rage.

He remembered the first time he'd met Clarke. The captain had been so pleased to have him there.

How could I have done this? How could I have responded so ruthlessly? Who am I?

For the first time in a long while, he remembered the rest of the world. The Bakma had assaulted northern Europe; they had attacked Stockholm and Copenhagen. They had come with their army. And the Fourteenth had missed it…for this.

Was what I just did worth Clarke's life?

When Scott arrived back outside, the rest of the Fourteenth was there. He hadn't realized it until he hit daylight, but his armor was dripping with blood. He looked like a robotic butcher.

When Scott removed his helmet, everyone's eyes were upon him. Radio silence had been broken the moment Scott had called *Novosibirsk*. His teammates knew what he and the slayers had done without needing to see for themselves. Svetlana stared with total disconnection as Esther struggled to look away. David seemed to have aged ten years.

Gradually the truth dawned on Scott. He had proven David wrong, but triumph belonged to neither man. Scott had shown the Fourteenth that, yes, the Nightmen were on a whole other plane of superiority. And in the process, he'd shown them why. Because they didn't care. They rejected what it meant to be human. Clarke had warned him of that from the start. He'd warned Scott not to let The Machine change him.

But that was exactly what Scott had let it do.

No one said a word to him as he trudged back to the *Pariah* and took his seat, intentionally avoiding looking at the captain's body. His actions in Chernobyl had been comparable to his heroics in Chicago, but the aftermaths couldn't have contrasted more. In Chicago, he'd felt like a champion.

Now, he was a fool.

PART II

17

MONDAY, NOVEMBER 14TH, 0011 NE
1322 HOURS

EDEN COMMAND

ONE HOUR LATER

THIS ONE CAUGHT even Torokin unaware. For the first time in his career, not only as a judge but as a member of EDEN, he was at a loss for rationalization and words. This one scared him.

It had happened so fast—out of nowhere. There wasn't a moment's warning, not a second to prepare. It struck like an invisible hammer blow.

The Bakma had attacked. No, not just attacked. Invaded. Their Noboats materialized, not by the dozens, but by the hundreds. Their Carriers poured into Europe like locusts. Stockholm was razed. Copenhagen was decimated. Half of Europe had been completely overwhelmed. EDEN's response, although no fault of its own, had been totally inadequate. EDEN simply didn't have enough operatives to respond. Legions of Bakma warriors stormed through the cities like ants. Courier fighters fired plasma missiles into buildings and streets. And for the first time ever, Bakma Coneships had bombed. They bombed with a ruthlessness that suggested the war was about to end. The death toll was now well beyond the hundreds of thousands. It was verging on millions. With timing that only the Bakma understood, they had unleashed the full force of a fury that had never before been witnessed by humans.

In a single stroke, humanity had been completely overpowered. The human species had been shown that, even with its near-perfect ability to react, its forces paled in comparison to the alien threat. An entire continent had been thrust to its knees. But that wasn't what scared Torokin. What scared Torokin was what happened next.

The Bakma didn't press forward. They didn't fortify their positions, nor did they make any effort to advance. Instead, they boarded their spacecraft and launched into space. They just left.

That scared him more than anything else.

Never before had President Pauling seemed so embittered or disturbed. He wasn't alone. The entire gathering of judges was at a loss for an answer. Not even Javier Castellnou had words.

The president did not offer them a formal greeting to kick off the session, nor did he request opening statements. The meeting of judges began with one question alone.

"What in the hell is going on?"

Torokin and Grinkov exchanged stoic looks. The same question was on their own lips.

"I'm serious. What in the *hell* is going on?" He glared at the Council members around the table, then focused on Judge Rath. "Jason? Do you know?"

The Canadian offered no explanation.

"Leonid? Dmitry?" Pauling turned to face Archer. "Benjamin? Anyone?"

No one spoke.

Torokin returned to deep thought. The Bakma had them right where they wanted them. They had reached out with their fists and grabbed Earth by the throat. If there was ever a moment to claim a stronghold for themselves on the planet, that had been it. Then for no reason at all, they let Earth go. They released it like a cat toying with a mouse. 'What the hell?' didn't begin to cover it.

Pauling propped his hands against the table and lowered his head. "I am the first person to admit when I'm wrong. I am the first person to admit when I don't know. But God help me, I cannot understand this. This is not like a war. It's like some kind of damned experiment."

Archer looked at Pauling for a moment, then turned away.

"Everything else goes on hold," Pauling continued. "Forget the Superwolf. Forget *Novosibirsk*. Forget everything. Right here, right now, we are going to get some kind of answers. I don't care if we brainstorm for twenty-four hours. There's coffee outside."

Get answers. That seemed obvious to Torokin. To the rest of the world, it must have seemed ridiculous. Nine years of war and no explanations. But what people didn't understand was that this was an enemy that couldn't be explained.

The Alien War had begun like a normal campaign. After Hong Kong, the Bakma turned their sites to near space. Shackleton and Peary—the two lunar outposts—had been destroyed. Malapert Junction, not even an outpost, met a similar fate. CMF-1 was obliterated from Mercurial orbit, and Arsia Mons was annihilated before it began. It made tactical sense: squash man's attempts to spread beyond Earth; stop humanity's expansion. It was a logical first step for a campaign.

But then logic stopped. The Bakma destroyed Earth's orbital telescopes, but left communication satellites untouched. In effect, they were allowing mankind to coordinate and to organize a response. It made no sense.

Pauling pulled out a notebook. Of all the technology around him—wall-sized monitors and computers—the president of EDEN was reduced to paper and pen. "Here is what we know," he said, scribbling as he spoke. "The Bakma and Ceratopians do not work together. The Ithini work independently of *themselves*. No one presses to win."

Still no judge spoke.

"I am pleading with someone to make sense of that." Pauling dropped his notebook on the table. "I'm starting to feel like we're the punch line of an interstellar joke."

It wasn't a joke, thought Torokin. It wasn't a game. He refused to believe that either was true. He had fought the Bakma and the Ceratopians. He had fought the Ithini among both. He had experienced their wrath, fervently fighting for...what? For Earth? They could take Earth if they wanted it—that much was proven in Europe. They wanted Earth for something, but not enough to take it. What were they waiting for? What was the point?

"I want Kang in here, now."

Collective surprise registered around the table.

Pauling pressed in the speaker comm button. "Kang Gao Jing, report to the conference room at once."

A response came quickly, but it wasn't from Kang. It was the voice of a woman. "Sir, Director Kang is in interrogations."

"Then get him *out* of interrogations."

Archer sighed and turned to the president. "Sir, the director is not responsible for this. This falls on our shoulders. It falls directly on mine." Rath stared at Archer oddly. "I have been working hand in hand with Director Kang since my arrival. I have been in interrogations. I am as responsible for our failures as much as anyone else. There's no need to bring him into this."

The woman's voice emerged from the speaker again. "Sir, the director wishes to know if it is urgent."

"He's doggone right it's urgent."

"I'll tell him right away, sir."

As Torokin's mind raced, he ignored the mounting tension in the room. Two extraterrestrial forces, the Bakma and the Ceratopians. Both were working for their own purposes, sharing a common ally in the Ithini. Of late, the Ceratopians had hardly been a factor. Their attacks had drastically slowed since the summer. And as the Ceratopians pulled back, the Bakma pressed harder. Was that a coincidence? It had to be. The Ceratopians and the Bakma weren't working together, which was something the general populace didn't know. The two species weren't allies at all.

They were at war.

It had happened only two recorded times—a Bakma Noboat and Ceratopian Cruiser crossing paths. Both times, the results had been the same: the Ceratopians blew the Bakma out of the sky. No one outside of EDEN Command knew that—they didn't need to.

The speaker crackled on again, and a voice rarely heard addressed the room. "You call for me, Mr. President?"

Director Kang's Chinese accent was unmistakable. Kang: the most obscure man in all of EDEN. A man who didn't exist.

"I need you here, Kang," Pauling said. "Right this very minute."

There was a pause. "I apologize, Mr. President, but I cannot come now. I am making progress with Ceratopian No. 12."

"Ceratopian No. 12," Pauling repeated in frustration. "Refresh my memory on Ceratopian No. 12."

Archer cleared his throat. "Ceratopian No. 12, we believe, is a ranking officer. I've been working with him for some time. Or, trying to, at least. If the director is making progress, well, that's very good."

Pauling looked at Archer briefly, but Kang spoke again before the president could.

"Would you like me to cancel this interrogation, Mr. President?"

For several seconds, Pauling deliberated. After reaching a decision, the older man sighed. "No. If you're making progress…then no." He rubbed his eyes.

"Very well, Mr. President. I will get a report to you soon." The speaker clicked off.

Torokin continued to think. Two species, at war with one another, fighting over the same world. Was Earth the sole reason for their war? Or was this spilling over from something else? Where did the Ithini fit into the picture? Those were questions that had all been asked before.

In the end, those things didn't matter. Humanity wasn't involved with extraterrestrial politics. All that mattered to Earth was survival. If there was one silver lining in the Bakma pullout, it was that it gave Earth time to strengthen a chink in Europe's defense.

He stopped in the middle of that thought. *If* there was one silver lining? The fact that the Bakma pulled out alone was a silver lining. Why didn't it seem that way? It was almost as if the pullout was worse than if the Bakma had advanced. Only because the pullout clouded the waters; an advance would have made sense.

Pauling pressed the speaker again. After several moments, the woman's voice reemerged. "Yes, Mr. President?"

"Get me Carol."

"Right away, sir."

An advance would have made sense. For some reason, that thought stood out to Torokin. Were the Bakma intentionally trying *not* to make sense? What would that accomplish? What would be the point? And why had there been no attempts at diplomacy on the Bakma's part? Or the Ceratopians'? No one wanted to talk.

Judge June's voice came over the speaker. "I'm here, sir."

Pauling wasted no time. "I know you're busy at *Novosibirsk*, but I need to get this to you now. We need a major push for recruitment in Europe. It can't wait until you get back, you've got to start now."

Moments passed before June replied. "Yes, sir. I'll formulate a new recruitment schedule tonight."

"What's our global headcount?"

Her answer was confident and quick. "Our major facilities are still hovering at a half a million. But we've got eighteen million in our city stations. *Philadelphia* is averaging about two million a year."

"What were your percentages last month in Europe?"

Her silence indicated her calculations. Or her hesitation. "Nine percent enrolled."

"*Nine?*"

"Only in Europe, sir," she said. "Global recruitment is *up* seventeen percent. Europe was the only continent that went down."

"And how many phased out in Europe?"

This time her nervousness was blatant. "Over ten percent."

Pauling pounded his fist on the table as the judges near him flinched. "That is *completely* unacceptable! We can't win a war if we're losing more people than we're bringing in. I want fifty percent for next month. Not a fraction less."

Torokin's eyes widened at Pauling's demands. He wanted June to convince half of the people she targeted to enroll? At least? Nine percent was a disappointing number, that was certain. But to have a fifty percent success rate—that hadn't been reached since the start of the war.

June's voice was saturated in doubt. "Yes, sir. I'll...I'll..." Several seconds passed. "I'll get it to fifty by the end of next month. I'll...figure it out."

"Thank you," Pauling answered, closing the line.

Torokin saw the irony. Of all the continents to hit, the Bakma had chosen the right one. Only European recruitment had gone down. Humanity's weakness was exposed. The aliens always seemed to hit Earth that way. But the weakness in Europe, like all others, would be fixed. Carol June was a devil in a dress, but she was a phenomenal recruiter. *Novosibirsk* had drained a lot of her time. She'd hit fifty percent—even if by questionable means.

For the first time, Richard Lena spoke up. "What if it *is* just an experiment?"

Every other judge turned to face him. Evidently, they'd been wondering the same thing. It had always been a question, since day one of the Alien War, but never one taken too seriously.

"We keep thinking that they're after Earth, but what if they're not? What if they couldn't care less about Earth? What if they're simply interested in how we react?"

"The Ceratopians or the Bakma?" Judge Onwuka asked.

"The Bakma. Hell, I don't know. Maybe both."

Torokin leaned forward and absorbed the words. An experiment. What a complete waste it would be if the war was just an experiment. He could not accept that.

"I don't see this being an experiment," said Archer, shaking his head. "I understand the idea, but..."

The other judges waited for the statement to be finished. It never was.

The Bakma must have known what they had in their grasp in Europe. They must have known that they'd hit Earth's most vulnerable region, and what would happen if they relented their attack. Humans would rebuild. EDEN would focus on the gap in their defense. They'd recruit more. They'd build stronger bases. They'd increase their response time. They'd learn—just as they'd been learning from the war's beginning.

This war was like a human body. The Bakma would find a weakness, make Earth hurt, only to have it grow stronger there. Like the building of scar tissue over a wound, or of muscle.

Like the building of muscle.

The thought struck Torokin unexpectedly. Before he could think further, he said it out loud.

"What if they're building us up?"

Around the table, heads swiveled, none faster than Archer.

Torokin collected his thoughts. "Think about this. There must be a reason to retreat. One attacks a weak point to exploit it. You must know what a pullout will do."

He realized that his thoughts were disorganized. He tried again. "Imagine you are a criminal in a city. You know everything about that city. You know where the police are, you know the patrols they run. You have to try to target a place with no police. But you must know—you *must*—that when the crime is finished, more police will be stationed to the place where the crime was committed. That is natural response of law enforcement."

Grinkov rubbed his chin, pondering this new idea.

"The Bakma are not stupid," Torokin said. "On the contrary, they are highly intelligent. They *must* have known what would happen after they left. We would return to the cities in Europe. We would recruit more operatives." He slapped his palm on the table. "Don't you see? That is exactly what we are doing now. They found a weakness in us, and we are making it strong." He paused to let the statement sink in. "What if that is the whole point?"

Grinkov tilted his head. "But why?"

"I do not know. But what other explanation do we have?"

"If you want to capture a planet," mused Lena, folding his arms, "why poke it with a stick and tell it to get ready? Obviously they're not here to help us. When they attack, we die. If they're trying to strengthen us, they're defeating their own purpose every time they kill a man. And that doesn't explain what the Ceratopians are doing."

Torokin was aware that it didn't make sense, but neither did anything else. "Have you ever wondered why the Bakma attack villages in the middle of nowhere, almost completely out of EDEN's protection zones? They attack towns we do not even know exist. But when they attack, we *learn* they exist. And we protect them better. Could that not be what they are doing?"

"I understand what you're saying," Lena said, "but it still doesn't make a lick of sense. What would that accomplish?"

Archer listened intently to the exchange.

"Perhaps," Torokin said, "for some reason, the Bakma want to protect us from the Ceratopians." The moment he said it, he knew it was wrong. But he kept going anyway. "They are at war with one another. Perhaps they want us to be better prepared to repel attacks in general."

"Do you even hear what you're saying?"

The ex-Vector narrowed his eyes. "Yes, Richard, I hear what I am saying. And even as I am saying it, I am thinking it is the most ludicrous idea I have ever heard." He could frankly admit to that. "What I'm trying to do is think in a different direction, because the direction we have been going has gotten us nowhere. What if, somehow, the Ceratopians' and the Bakma's plans contradict each other? What if one specifically needs the other to fail?"

Suddenly Archer spoke up, almost cutting off Torokin's words. "You may be on to something."

Rath threw Archer an impulsively shocked look, but quickly concealed it.

Archer went on. "We have never considered that *we* may very well be the variable. What if one of them solely requires strength on our part to succeed?"

"That could make sense," said Torokin. "You cannot look at the casualties we suffer as proof against this. Casualties take place on a very small-scale level. Per mission, per incursion. They may not be a factor in the larger goal that one of the species hopes to accomplish. Perhaps, in their eyes, casualties are worth it if we are stronger in the end."

"We need to pursue this immediately," Archer said. "Now that it's been brought up, even the start of the war makes sense to an extent. It began with one single attack on Hong Kong, with enough time between it and the next attack for us to form a global military. What if that's all they were trying to do? Make us aware that a threat existed, so we'd prepare ourselves?"

Lena scratched the back of his head. "Who was that Ceratopian you and Kang were talking to again?"

"Ceratopian No. 12. Don't ask me to pronounce his real name." He turned to the president. "We need to look at new avenues of questioning. We've probed in a hundred directions, but to the best of my knowledge, never this one. For that, I blame myself. But nonetheless, this is more than worth looking into."

It didn't take Pauling long to answer. "Do it. Now. You can go."

Archer rose from his chair. "Thank you, sir." He looked at Torokin before turning to leave. "Judge Torokin, would you care to come with me? Perhaps we can plot a course together." He cast a questioning look back at Pauling. "That is, if the president allows."

"I have no objections. Leonid, you can go with him if you wish."

Torokin looked across the table at Archer. He'd never worked hand in hand with the new judge, at least not on a project like this. Offers had been made, but he'd never accepted. This time would be different. "I will join you," he agreed.

The Russian rose from his chair and slid it back into place before stepping away. He glanced briefly at Grinkov and Lena before leaving the room.

Archer snuck a look of his own to Jason Rath. The exchange lasted barely a moment as the British judge made his way out.

Torokin waited for Archer outside the room. "Do you truly believe that this is a possibility?" the Russian asked him.

Archer's bristled pace never slowed. "As you've defined it in there? No. But as a direction to explore, absolutely. You were correct in saying that this is a completely new avenue of study. That may be precisely what we need."

Torokin looked back for a moment, then hurried to keep up with the brisk-paced judge. "What have you learned from your interrogations? Who is Ceratopian No. 12?"

"He's the most promising capture we've ever made. The Bakma seem to embrace psychological torture, as if it were some sort of release. But the Ceratopians simply resist it. Their willpower is as strong as their physical power. Not so with No. 12."

"Not so?"

"He is weak-minded. He can be manipulated, convinced." Archer stopped for a moment, turning to Torokin. "Mind you, by 'convinced,' I don't mean to a great extent. Our ability to manipulate him into cooperation has been minimal at best. But minimal is far better than nonexistent. He is not valuable because of what he knows, but rather because he is not mentally durable. It's the proper way of saying he's daft."

The usefulness of their captives was inversely proportional to their intelligence. It was ironic to say the least. "What have you learned from him?"

"Very little, at least to this point. Barely enough to warrant a report, though that's precisely what I've been working on for the past several weeks. I was hoping to have it finished by our next meeting." He lowered his voice. "You're the first person outside of Kang and myself to hear this, but...the Ceratopians are *desperate* to get Earth. Apparently much more so than the Bakma. You've heard the term, the 'Great Race for Earth.' They mean it literally. Whatever it is they want here, they want it before the Bakma. It may be they want this planet. It may be us. It may be something altogether different. But whatever it is, it's time-critical to an extent we can't possibly imagine. They're desperate to beat the Bakma here."

For a moment, Torokin couldn't speak. He was stunned, not at the information Archer had given him, but at *how* the information had been given. He realized in that moment how much he'd underestimated Archer as a capable judge.

"Of course," Archer said, "I tell you this in strict confidentiality. Everyone will hear it in due time. But for now, it should stay between us. You're hearing a hodgepodge of thoughts, but soon, I should have a formal analysis to present to the Council." He paused as they turned down the hallway. "It's ironic that this attack on Europe happened when it did. We were about to show our headway on this very topic."

Torokin kept pace. "Neither species wants to destroy us." It was more of a question than a statement.

"That is as it appears. Our extinction is not their agenda. Whether some things are worse than extinction—that remains to be seen."

It was one of the first times Torokin had felt actively involved with something new. His role with the High Command had been limited to military tactics in the past—not that he minded. Military tactics were what he did best, even if his expertise was underused. But it was refreshing to take his mind into uncharted waters. At least for the moment.

He had no idea what to expect from Archer's research or what it would be like working in Confinement. But he didn't care. They would be gaining new ground. Time would tell if that new ground was solid.

Anything was better than the quicksand they were in.

18

MONDAY, NOVEMBER 14TH, 0011 NE
1739 HOURS

NOVOSIBIRSK, RUSSIA

SHORTLY AFTER CHERNOBYL

THE *PARIAH'S* WHEELS rumbled on the runway as it touched down. None of the operatives had said a word since leaving Chernobyl.

The flight home had been one of the longest and most unsettling Scott had ever endured. While the Tenth worked to secure the dilapidated nuclear plant, the Fourteenth had been asked to wait outside in case assistance was needed. None was. Despite the fact that several necrilids had supposedly been discovered by the Tenth, there were no human casualties to report. The mission was an on-paper success.

The grotesque remains of the researchers' bodies had been found. Their small dog—the East Siberian laika—was officially orphaned. The animal lay quiet during the entire ride back to The Machine, its nose buried beneath its paws.

Clarke's corpse had been placed in a body bag shortly before the return flight began. It sat awkwardly propped in the corner, where no one had ventured to look for longer than a few seconds. Strangely, no tears had been shed.

It had been one of the eeriest and most uncomfortable flights Scott could remember. Never before had the line between ally and enemy felt so tangible. EDEN and the Nightmen were no longer forced comrades. There was no sense of camaraderie at all.

News about the European attacks had come over the airwaves during their return. Cities had been razed to the ground. Countless homes were destroyed and hundreds of thousands of people were dead. Rumors flew that even several members of Vector Squad had been killed. It had been the worst attack in all of Earth's history.

Still, Scott wished he could have been there.

As the rear door was finally lowered with its familiar mechanical whine, Scott slowly rose. No one else near him stood. He stared at the ground as he stepped past his teammates, his expression a mixture of confusion, anger, and remorse. When he finally mustered the strength to look up, he was already halfway through the hangar. It didn't take him long to find Max. The lieutenant technician was walking toward him from the opposite end of the hangar, where he'd apparently been waiting for them to return.

"What the hell's goin' on, man? I been tryin' to comm you guys for an hour!"

An hour. It felt as if the flight had been ten times longer than that. What was Scott supposed to tell him? Just filler. "I don't know."

"You don't *know*?" He turned his head to the *Pariah*. "Why isn't anyone else getting out?"

"I don't know."

Max watched, motionless, as Scott walked away. After several seconds, he called after him.

Scott slowed to a stop. *Max needs to know. He deserves to know.* "Clarke is dead."

At first, Max offered no response. It was as if he hadn't understood the words. Then his stoic demeanor crumbled. "How?"

"He got killed by a necrilid." He offered the only reassurance he knew. "Only Clarke died."

He waited for Max's response—whether there might be a span of confusion or denial. But there wasn't. Instead, he heard the most collected response from Max since the first day he'd met him.

"We can fix this," Max said, looking Scott straight in the eye. His expression was genuine. "We can try."

Scott's gaze swept past Max's shoulder, back to the ship. Several members of the Fourteenth were removing Captain Clarke's body. The black body bag hovered over the ground as the operatives carried it out.

He felt the same uneasy silence as when Axelos from the Tenth had addressed him back in Chernobyl. And again, he offered the same response—he turned and walked away.

This can't be fixed, Max. Today crossed the line.

Max watched Scott leave the hangar, then turned back to the *Pariah*—to the body bag that lay on the floor. He didn't say anything, nor did indicate to the Fourteenth that he was even there. He just turned and walked away, too.

The rest of the Fourteenth mechanically attended to their myriad tasks. David and Oleg prepared Clarke's body for departure, while Svetlana tended to Derrick's leg. Although she was quaking inside, her hands remained steady on his wounds. She escorted him to the infirmary alone.

Esther remained next to Auric—they were the only pair of EDEN and Nightman operatives in the hangar. But their interaction was strained as they hauled equipment out of the *Pariah* for its standard prep-down. In a similar fashion, Boris worked inside the ship.

The small Siberian laika—the sole survivor of the Chernobyl rescue—lay motionless at the edge of the cockpit door. Of the entire crew, Travis wore the only occasional smile, though it was reserved for the dog. He would occasionally stroke its head in the midst of his prep-down procedure. It was the most meaningful interaction among the whole crew.

The only other member of the team besides Scott and Max to abandon them during prep-down was Dostoevsky. Leaving even his slayers behind, the fulcrum left the hangar as soon as the *Pariah* was parked. He disappeared without a word.

* * *

DOSTOEVSKY WHIRLED around, sending a spinning hook kick across a slayer's face.

Two other slayers behind him lurched forward to grab hold of him, but he was too quick. Grabbing the nearest one by the collar, Dostoevsky jerked him close, using the slayer's momentum to propel himself forward, where an uppercut with his free hand hammered the third slayer in the chin. He threw the Nightman he'd grabbed by the collar over his shoulder.

The scuffle took place inside one of the many separated fighting rooms in the Hall of the Fulcrums. The rooms were as secluded as they were simple: limestone walls, torch lights, and a circle drawn on the floor with red chalk. Anyone inside the circle was fair game. Anytime. It was a common practice among fulcrums to challenge multiple slayers to combative practice. This was one of those times for Dostoevsky.

He had said little since returning from Chernobyl other than quietly recruiting slayers for a fight—a request never refused when issued by a fulcrum. Judging by the condition of the three sprawled slayers, groaning and bloodied on the floor, a refusal might have been worth the punishment.

From just outside the room, from the archway of the open passage, an observer clapped his hands arrogantly.

Dostoevsky placed one hand on his hip, huffing slightly as he wiped sweat from his face. He didn't even have to turn around. He knew the identity of the observer without looking. "What do you want, Strakhov?" The three battered slayers on the ground before him struggled to stand.

Oleg leered from the archway. "Can a good EDEN soldier not talk to his commander after a mission? Or am I not allowed to speak to Nightmen?"

One of the slayers, the one Dostoevsky had punched, assumed a weary fighting stance. He thrust out a jab, but Dostoevsky caught it in mid-air and twisted the slayer's wrist. The slayer cried out and was flipped on his back.

"You need to learn a new move," Oleg said. "You do that one every time."

"Do you have somewhere you need to be?" Dostoevsky asked, still without looking. None of the slayers around him moved to attack.

"Slayers!" Oleg ordered. "Go away. Yuri and I have important business."

The three beaten Nightmen looked at Oleg, then turned their attention to Dostoevsky. After a cordial exchange of nods, the slayers dragged themselves out of the room.

Dostoevsky placed his hands on his hips again, turning to face the eidolon. Though he wasn't shirtless, his muscles bulged through his tight-fitting T-shirt. His black hair was dripping with sweat.

"You are becoming a disappointment, Yuri. After such a tragic mission, you simply leave your unit behind to prep down the ship. That is not how a captain should act."

Dostoevsky scoffed. "A captain. Clarke has not been dead for a day, and you are already talking about his replacement."

"There is nothing to talk about." Oleg stepped into the room, pacing along the edge of the red-chalk circle. "*You* are his replacement. Did you have any doubt?"

"I have not given it much thought."

"Perhaps you should. You have responsibilities now—more so than in the past. Hopefully you will be more effective as a captain than you have been as a commander."

"Clarke is dead, and you talk as if he has never existed. Do you not care?"

Oleg dropped his monotone and answered sharply. "No, I do not care. But you do. That is only *one* of your problems. You have become a liability to General Thoor. Baranov was a respected leader—you are not. When Baranov spoke, those under him listened. When you speak, they insult you behind your back."

"They have their reasons."

"I do not care about their reasons. The general does not care, either."

Dostoevsky's volume increased. "What does this have to do with anything? Why are we having this conversation? Do you not have important things to do?"

"I have been doing important things all day."

"Name one important thing, besides letting the captain die."

"But the captain's death was *very* important."

Dostoevsky's initial reaction was an ordinary stare. But moments later, it changed. His eyebrows furrowed with confusion. His head cocked to the side. "Oleg. Tell me you did not..."

Oleg stretched his arms to the ceiling. "You have not exerted your authority, so we have exerted it for you. Clarke has been removed, and now you will lead."

Dostoevsky's jaw dropped. "Oleg! You killed Captain Clarke?"

"I did not kill him. You did."

Dostoevsky remained dumbfounded.

"You have not shown the general what he requires. You have not shown him the loyalty of Ivan Baranov. You have not even shown him the loyalty of Anatoly *Novikov*, may God curse his soul." The eidolon stepped into the circle. "You have left us with no other options. You have not become a leader by choice, so now you have become one by force. This was our gift to you."

"But why did you do this? Why did Clarke have to *die*? Could you not have asked him to leave? Threatened his life? Explained to him that if he stayed, he would be killed? He had a wife and two daughters!"

"Listen to yourself!" Oleg's words were so loud, Dostoevsky flinched. "This is why you gave us no choice! You are not even the *shell* of the man you once were."

"I—"

"Be quiet! We are tired of your excuses, *Captain* Dostoevsky. You have gone from most feared to most mocked in a matter of months. You are an insult to the uniform you wear. You are almost an insult to EDEN, as pathetic as they are." He went on before Dostoevsky could interrupt. "Consider Clarke's murder your final opportunity, ordained by your own incompetence. Show us that we did not give you this new title in vain."

Dostoevsky fought to express himself. His attitude, once hardened in a default position of coldness, was now broken in horrified shock. "You should have told me what would happen! I would not have—"

"You would not have *what*? Become inconsequential? Clarke died for you and you alone, because your failures deemed it necessary. But listen to my words, Yuri. If you fail again, *you* will be the next name on my list. And for you, I will not come so quietly. You would be a joy."

As casually as he'd first entered, Oleg turned and walked away. When he got to the archway that led into the Hall of the Fulcrums, he stopped. "Perhaps you can take notes from Remington. Spited or not, at least *he* knows how to take control." The eidolon left the room.

Dostoevsky stood silent for several moments in the arena, listening to the sound of Oleg's footsteps receding in the distance. A full minute later, he too walked from the room. But in the middle of the hall, he abruptly stopped—not because someone stopped him, or because he'd suddenly had an impactful thought. He didn't stop for any reason at all.

He had absolutely nowhere to go.

19

MONDAY, NOVEMBER 14TH, 0011 NE
1915 HOURS

LATER THAT EVENING

"DUDE, IT JUST ticks me off," William said through a mouthful of food. "They should have let me go on the mission. If I'd have known it was gonna be *that* big, I'd have stowed away in the landing gear or something."

"Right," Travis said, unamused, "because that would have worked."

The four operatives—William, Travis, Boris, and Esther—sat together at a table in the cafeteria. Of all the men and women of the Fourteenth, only they had grouped after the mission. The remainder of the unit's members were as dispersed as they were divided.

"The bottom line," William said, "is that demolitionists should get called for every mission. You never know. You might be in the middle of recon or something, then *bam*, you get hijacked by aliens."

"...hijacked?"

"Yeah. Then you just gotta blow people up."

Neither Esther nor Boris had been particularly talkative since their return from Chernobyl. Boris had been shaken up since fleeing the facility. Esther was moody and edgy.

William spoke through another mouthful. "So you found a dog—alive?"

"Yeah."

"That's sweet. What're you gonna name it?"

"I don't know. We don't even know if we can keep it."

"Whatever you name it, it better be awesome."

The conversation had been William's alone since the four of them had gone to the cafeteria. He seemed the only one inclined to talk, and Travis exchanged conversation sparingly. William was also the only one eating.

Travis and Boris picked at bowls of borsch, while Esther ignored a full bowl of porridge. There was the unspoken understanding among them that they *needed* to eat, they just weren't particularly in the mood.

Boris was the first to notice Svetlana approaching. The medic walked into the cafeteria alone, her standard uniform replaced with a simple gray and pink sweat suit. As soon as she saw Boris and the others, she approached them.

Travis raised his head in acknowledgment as she neared, smiling faintly. "Hey, Sveta."

Svetlana returned the smile and lowered herself between William and Esther. "Hello, Travis, everyone. How are all of you doing?"

"I guess how we should be," said Travis.

"How's Derrick?" asked William between bites.

Svetlana cleared her throat in an effort to sound professional. "He will be fine. He does not have anything to threaten his life. He will need to recover, but we will have him back in a couple of weeks. They have good treatment for his injury here." She looked at Travis again. "Have you seen Varya?"

"No, why?"

"I was just wondering. I visited Jayden and I thought she would be there."

"How's Jay doing?"

A span of awkwardness ensued before she answered. "He does not realize how bad his condition is. Or he does not want to realize." Her frown deepened. "He told me he was ready to start rehabilitation. I told him first to rest. It was hard to know what else to say. He cannot even move yet." Then she brightened. "I visited Becan, too. He should be back very soon, in limited action. Maybe even in a few days."

Esther continued to stare at her porridge. She had yet to acknowledge Svetlana at all.

"Did you tell them about Clarke?" Travis asked.

"Becan, yes," Svetlana answered, frowning. "I did not think it wise to tell Jayden yet. Not until he recovers more."

"We need Becan back."

"I agree." She allowed the faintest of grins to emerge. "Where is Flopper?"

Travis chuckled softly. "I fed him some scraps. He's still in the ship."

"Who's Flopper?" asked William.

"That's the dog."

The demolitionist looked disgusted. "You named it *Flopper*? Dude, that name sucks!"

Svetlana looked at him a wryly. "It will be good to have *Flopper.* It will be something different. Maybe, I do not know, we can keep him? The poor dog does not have a home." When no one answered, she said determinedly, "I will ask Scott. Maybe having a dog will make him happy. I think it will."

Next to her, Esther's nostrils began to flare. She played anxiously with her spoon.

"This is a hard time for him, for everyone," Svetlana went on, "but we must believe things will improve. In tragic times, sometimes people find strength. I believe things will get better soon."

"You really think so?" asked Travis.

She smiled. "Of course. That is why I am here."

"Good enough for me."

Then it happened.

It was too sudden to predict or prevent. In a single, emotionally driven burst, Esther swept her arm across the table. Her body whirled Svetlana's way. Svetlana didn't even have time to finch; Esther's entire bowl of porridge slammed into her face. A wave of oatmeal crashed over her head.

Everything stopped, from the conversation at the table to the motion in the cafeteria. Travis, Boris, and William's mouths simultaneously fell, as Esther's face twisted with hatred.

"Do you even sodding hear yourself *talk*?" The scout screamed at the top of her lungs as she rose to her feet. "Things will get better because *you're* here?"

Svetlana's mouth hung open in shock. Globs of porridge dripped from her hair and slid down her face. The plastic bowl fell to the floor.

Esther went on. "You're a catastrophe on so many levels, it pains me to think! You've caused nothing but tension with David, you've cut us off from Dostoevsky completely, and if things weren't proper wrecked enough, on the battlefield you're a bloody disgrace!"

The scout pointed at herself. "I am the *last* person to sound supercilious when it comes to performance on a mission. I have made my mistakes. It's called being flustered." Her finger turned to Svetlana. "But in Chernobyl, you were nowhere *near* flustered. Flustered means you get nervous and press the wrong button, or you drop ammunition while loading a gun. All of that is well and understandable. But not so with you. You didn't know how to shoot, you didn't know how to move, you didn't know how to act. You couldn't even tell the difference between a woman and a flesh-eating alien. You could've gotten us *killed*!"

Svetlana's stare remained frozen during the entire outburst.

"Don't think for a second we don't know why you're here. Oh, I'm sure Scott Remington isn't in your lusty little dreams. I'm sure your motives are *completely* platonic." Her sarcasm was only matched by her scowl.

Esther shoved in her chair. "So while you sit here, bamboozling everyone into thinking you're some kind of saint while you doll up for the lieutenant, I'll be busy trying to improve. I'll be trying to salvage whatever dignity this unit has left by working to make myself the best I can be. Because *that*, Svetlana, is what Scott Remington needs." She tightened her lips. "He most certainly doesn't need *you*."

"Enjoy supper." With those words, the scout whirled around and stalked out of the cafeteria. The glass doors swung shut in her wake, as the whole of the cafeteria looked on in disbelief.

The silence in the cafeteria was deafening. Every pair of eyes—and there were hundreds—watched until Esther was out of view. Then they turned on Svetlana.

Porridge still dribbled down her face, sliding in wet clumps from her hairline. When she dipped her head forward, her oatmeal-drenched bangs dangled straight down. Finally, she showed enough self-respect to wipe her face, leaving faint trails of cleanliness behind as she slung the watery clumps to the floor. Her bottom lip tensed for the first time.

William was the only observer to speak. His mouth curved into a blatant grin as his falsetto voice filled the cafeteria. "Wamp, wamp, *waaaaa*!"

Travis and Boris stared at him in shock.

Svetlana maintained her composure. Pushing back her chair, she rose to her feet, turned around, and made for the exit.

Silence prevailed again. Just as all eyes had watched Esther leave, they now watched Svetlana. Only when she was out of view did they find their next target: the oversized southerner. The man who looked as bewildered as they did, but for an entirely different reason. The man who didn't have a clue.

"What?" William asked.

* * *

Since he'd returned to his room hours before, Scott had been at war—with himself. He regretted his reaction to Max in the hangar. It was one of the few times that his fellow lieutenant had ever tried to reconcile anything, and Scott had rejected it as if it had meant nothing. In the wake of Captain Clarke's death, Max had stayed calm and collected. Scott had not, and he felt as though he'd lost all remaining shreds of dignity.

Who was the horrible lieutenant now?

His back began to itch terribly, where the necrilid had punctured him in Chernobyl. The puncture wounds alone hurt fiercely, despite not being too deep. But the itching was almost too much to bear. It wasn't venom or poison—it was a common necrilid scratch side effect.

He recalled the dog they had rescued. Someone would have to drive into the city of Novosibirsk to dispose of the animal. He'd have to find out where there was a shelter. It was just another thing he had to do.

Since returning to *Novosibirsk*, Scott had been exhausted but unable to sleep. It ended up working out better that way. No sooner had he arrived back at The Machine than he was summoned to Confinement by Petrov, the scientist he usually visited. The Fourteenth's Nightmen had challenged necrilids and won, and now *Novosibirsk* demanded to know more. This was fine with Scott. It was another excuse to go to Confinement and do his own kind of searching—the same searching he'd been doing there for months. Now, after winding down from the mission, he was finally ready to make the Confinement trip. He left his room, clutching the manila folder that always went with him.

They're going to ask a thousand questions. What gave me the idea? What thought process was I following? What was my rationale? He sighed. *There's no way they'll understand.* That was the truth. In the hours that followed the Chernobyl battle, the reality—and the insanity—of what he'd done had set in. It all came down to one fact: he hadn't wanted to lose. The entire motivation for his actions was to avoid coming up short. Did that make him admirable or dangerous? In the end, though, it wouldn't matter. The Machine would make its own judgments as it always did. And so, he continued down the hall, rounding a corner onto the main corridor.

He saw her the moment he made the turn.

It was Svetlana, with her unmistakable gait. She walked with controlled urgency, one hand at her head and the other swaying with her steps. Why was she in such a hurry? Where was she going? This was not in the direction of Room 14. When she neared, he saw that her upper body was covered in muck.

"Svetlana?"

Before he could say anything further, she about-faced in the hall and walked away from him, swearing in Russian.

Scott hurried to stop her retreat. He caught up with her from behind. "Sveta! What happened?"

When she turned her head to respond, he saw the dripping cereal that covered her. Her voice was venomous. "I cannot deal with you right now. Please leave me alone."

He kept his pursuit. "Sveta, stop."

To his surprise, she complied, whirling around to point at her face. "Do you see this? Do you *see*?" She shoved him in the chest—unexpectedly hard. His back slammed against the wall. "Is *this* what I have come back for? To be mocked? To have food in my face? To be humiliated in front of the world?"

He was thoroughly baffled. What on earth was going on? "Svetlana, calm down. Just tell me what—"

"Calm down?" She laughed mirthlessly. "Calm *down*?"

"Sveta—"

"This has been disaster since first hour! I cannot be a friend, I cannot fight, I cannot do anything right! I came here to be a help for *you*, and this is what I must endure? Do you even appreciate that I came?"

"Just tell me what happened!"

"It was Esther! 'Polyester,' *whatever* her name is!"

Scott shook his head. This didn't make sense. "Esther hit you in the face with porridge? What'd you do to her first?"

"I hit her with cabbage, what do you think?" she answered sarcastically. "I did to her *nothing*!"

An operative stepped past them in the hall, staring at them curiously before he moved on.

Svetlana's face flushed with deep red. "I'm going. I must clean this off."

Never mind the countless other questions swirling through Scott's mind. Where exactly was she going to clean it off? Room 14 was the other way. "Where are you going?"

"To shower off in the locker room by the pool," she answered, shoving past him. "I cannot go to Room 14. Esther will be there."

Scott pursued her, deviating from Confinement's direction.

"Why are you following me?" she demanded. "To watch me take a shower? Sorry to disappoint, but I am only washing my head."

"Svetlana, please…"

She stopped, turning around to face him fully. "What is it? What do you want?"

"What do you think?" he asked rhetorically. "I want to make sure you're okay. I want to find out what's going on. Do you seriously think I'm just going to walk away now?"

"Why wouldn't you? It is what you do best." The moment she said it, she seemed to catch herself. She winced and turned away. "I did not mean it like that."

Of course she meant it like that—and she was right. Not even he would deny it.

She closed her eyes and ran a hand over her head, slicking back her porridge-caked hair. She faced him again. "I am sorry, Scott, but why do you want to come? Please tell me the truth. Is it obligation? Do you want to follow me for your own curiosity?"

"I don't want you to feel alone."

She sighed, placing her hands on her hips.

"I'm trying, Sveta."

It took several seconds, but finally she nodded. It seemed more out of defeat than anything else. "Then come if you must. But please let me hurry." After an agreeable exchange, she turned and resumed her trek to the pool. Scott followed behind.

They walked into the pool room together, making their way to the woman's locker room door before stopping. Svetlana lowered her head. "Really, Scott, you do not need to—"

"Svetlana," he tactfully interrupted. "I care about you. I know you think I don't, but I do. Take your time, I'll wait outside till you're finished."

She finally acquiesced, nodding but still refusing to face him. Placing his manila folder on the floor, Scott reached out to touch her shoulder and guide her around. "Hey…" Once she faced him, he placed his hands at her sides.

She needed a reason to put things in perspective, to laugh. To realize that in the grand scheme of things, this wasn't such a big deal—regardless of what had spawned it. Reaching out, he brushed one of her plastered bangs to the side. "It's not *that* bad a look."

She managed to laugh through her embarrassment.

"It's got that 'you wear what you eat' thing going for it."

"Are you finished?"

He smiled. "Yeah. Wash up. I'll be outside."

After he left, she walked through the locker room door.

Scott slid to the floor against the outside wall. His legs were bent in front of him, hands draped over his knees. For a fleeting moment it felt like college again.

I used to sit like this all the time in the athletes' dorm. Talking with the guys on the team, right there in the hall. Until three in the morning.

Life was so different now. Responsibilities were so different. Consequences, too. He lowered his head and exhaled a hard breath.

It had been a long time since he'd felt obliged to be a leader off the field—to sort out what was wrong. It had started with his regret toward Max, and now Svetlana was bringing it home. He'd missed opportunities to play peacekeeper before—when David had gone into social isolation, when the tension between the unit and Dostoevsky was tangible, when the chasm between EDEN and Nightmen grew wider. He'd never given any of those situations a moment of concern, even though they were mostly his fault.

He sighed. Mostly his fault. It was a fact he often ignored. This was where it was getting him.

Svetlana's head was lowered beneath the shower's steady spray. She'd already cleaned off her face. Now she was working the mess from her hair. The wet strands dangled as clumps of porridge swirled down the floor drain.

Lifting her head, she pushed back her hair as water droplets trickled down past her ears. Across the room, she could see her reflection in one of the wall-mounted mirrors. She stared at herself as words seemed to echo through the room.

"Nothing good came out of Siberia, Scott! Siberia is why you're a Nightman."

The words weren't heard literally in the locker room. They were the words spoken by David in Chernobyl, before Scott and the Nightmen made their charge. They echoed in her mind; they were etched on her face.

Reaching out, she turned off the shower. She walked across the room toward the mirror, until she was staring at her reflection face-to-face.

"Siberia is why you're a Nightman."

She closed her eyes. Her throat constricted as she sucked in a breath. Propping her forehead against the mirror, she covered her face with her hand as tears began to fall. Gripping the sides of the sink, she cried violently.

It had nothing to do with Esther or porridge, nor her own choice to return to the Fourteenth. It was a verdict—a sentence. It was the connection she hadn't yet made. Until now.

Siberia was why Scott was a Nightman. He was a Nightman because he'd leapt after her.

Scott rubbed the back of his neck. The consequences of Clarke's death were hitting him now in more ways than one, even beyond how he'd behaved in Chernobyl. Now he realized something more ominous—something he couldn't ignore. The unit was theirs. It was his and Dostoevsky's.

In the past, Clarke could always water down the will of The Machine. There was no doubt that Thoor owned *Novosibirsk* and every unit in it, regardless of whether Nightmen were present. But even in a unit with Nightmen, like the Fourteenth, Clarke had always been a buffer between the operatives and Thoor's will. Now that buffer was gone.

There's no doubt I'll be the commander—Thoor would never promote Max over me. If I don't draw some kind of line, the Fourteenth will be completely consumed.

Dostoevsky, himself, Viktor, Nicolai, Auric, and Egor. They made up almost half the team. And with one officer slot now open in the wake of Clarke's death, there was no doubt that a slayer would advance. Three of four officers would be Nightmen.

What could Max possibly do?

Svetlana rubbed the towel through her hair until it was dry. Her golden bangs fell over her face.

Though she'd stopped crying, her expression was still heavy with emotion. Dark stains dotted her sweat suit where the porridge had splattered, but at least she was clean.

Draping the towel over her shoulder, she walked out of the locker room and turned for the pool room door—until something stopped her in her tracks. Sitting abandoned on the floor by the locker room entrance was a plain manila folder—the same one she'd seen Scott carrying in the halls.

For a moment, she hesitated, torn between curiosity and propriety. Curiosity won. Bending down, she took the manila folder in hand.

Scott repositioned himself against the wall as he waited. What was she doing in there? What was taking so long? More importantly, what were they about to discuss? He knew it was coming. It had begun welling up inside him the moment he'd seen her in the halls. Something was coming.

He knew that whatever had happened between Svetlana and Esther was a minor effect of a much larger problem. Svetlana was in the midst of a unit torn on almost every front. The only reason she'd returned was for him—the Golden Lion who became a part of The Machine. She'd come there to answer a call for help that he'd never made. She was doing it for him.

And this is how I've answered.

As Svetlana stepped out of the pool room, Scott rose to his feet. He saw it the moment he looked at her—his manila folder. It was firm in her grasp. He'd forgotten it.

Here it comes.

"Scott, I need to talk to you about some things."

There was no getting away from it now. Everything was about to come out. "You want to go to my room?"

She nodded her head, and they set off down the halls.

Flashes of memories flickered in his brain as he walked. Jumping for Svetlana in Siberia. Losing Nicole. Striking Esther in the face in Khatanga. The entire downward spiral. It made him sick.

Stop thinking of the past and focus on Sveta. She needs you more than you need yourself. Drawing a preparatory breath, he opened the room to his private quarters and led her inside, closing and locking the door behind him.

Svetlana sat on the edge of his bed, her blue eyes on him as he pulled out a chair and sat down. She didn't start with a greeting to ease the tension. She hit him square in his heart. "Many months ago, I made a promise to a man."

He closed his eyes.

"I made a promise that, if this man would be there for me, I would be there for him in return."

He knew what she was talking about; she didn't need to refresh his memory. She was talking about their first night in the lounge, long before she'd left or he'd joined The Machine. And she was wondering what happened to that man she'd made the promise to.

"I am in debt to you in so many ways. I should be dead. I should have died in Siberia, but you saved my life." She broke eye contact. "If I live a perfect life, but die without telling you this, then I will have failed." Her lips trembled. "Scott, I am so sorry."

She was sorry? Sorry for what?

"I am so sorry for running after him." She dabbed her eyes. "Had I stayed back, had I just done what Yuri had told me..."

The hair stood on Scott's arms.

"It is my fault that your fiancée is dead." As the words came out, so did her tears. "Had I not run, had I just helped them escape as he told me, you would not have jumped out to save me. Is that not what made the Nightmen notice you?"

In all his time spent thinking and putting pieces together regarding his fall from grace, he'd never made that connection. Thoor had noticed him because he'd leapt from the *Pariah* to save Svetlana, who was running after her boyfriend. That had set off the whole thing. And now she was blaming herself for being indirectly responsible.

"Svetlana, that isn't your fault."

"It *is* my fault, Scott! There are so many things that are my fault and every time, it is you that has come..."

What was she talking about? Come to what? She said something quietly in Russian that was too low to be understood. It sounded like a prayer.

"Sveta?"

Her breaths became shorter. "I am going to tell you something that I have told no one. I have not even told my own mother. It will not make sense at first, but please be patient for me to get through."

Something was going on that went beyond him as a Nightman. It went beyond everything in the Fourteenth.

"Tolya was my first and only boyfriend. I was stupid...I was *so* stupid," she cursed herself quietly in Russian. "I was with him for a month before you came, that was it."

For a moment, he forgot the fact that he had no idea why she was telling him this. She had been with Tolya only for a month? He was her first boyfriend? Both those things surprised him.

"I made a mistake with him. I made a mistake, and I lost something I can never get back." She laughed self-deprecatingly. "I was *really* a blonde..."

Of course, he knew what she was referring to. He felt something in his heart deflate a little.

She cleared her throat. "I told him, I never will do this again. I told him never to ask me, never to try and convince me, never to do anything. I told him I was not that kind of woman, and he said okay. He said he was sorry. He was ashamed."

Her palms were glistening; Scott could see them from where he was sitting.

"Late one night, when no one else was awake...I went to the lounge."

He already knew what she was going to say.

"I went there to feel sorry about myself. I was such fool. And I thought about Tolya, and why I loved him. I wondered if I had chosen the wrong man." She swallowed and looked up at him. "Then you walked through the door."

Scott felt lightheaded. His heart hit his throat.

"You know what happened in the lounge," she said quietly. "But you don't know what happened after you left."

She'd brought him comfort that night. She'd helped him remember his faith.

"That night, after you left the room, I was in wonder. I am not embarrassed to say it. I was attracted to you."

For the first time, he noticed her scent.

"And I thought, look at this man who just left. What an *amazing* man, his heart is so pure. And it came to me, what if I had waited? What if I had not been so desperate? What if I had waited for someone like you, instead of being with someone like Tolya?" She paused to inhale. "For the smallest of moments, I wished Tolya was out of my life. The very next day, he was dead."

For a moment she lost her restraint and a single, anguished cry slipped out. But she put her hand on her chest to catch herself, holding up the other in a silent request for patience. She composed herself again and continued. "I cannot tell you the guilt that I felt. I felt like I had killed Tolya myself. I went home with that guilt, feeling as if I had killed a man with my thoughts."

Now he understood. That was why she'd reacted the way she had after Anatoly Novikov died. That was why she'd become so distant. It wasn't just remorse, it was feeling responsible.

Svetlana steadied her breathing. "I thought about you every day. I thought about how you saved me in Siberia, but even more than that, I thought about how faithful you were. Even though you were doubting your purpose, you were there for reasons greater than yourself. You were there to follow God.

"Scott, *that* is what you did to truly save me. You showed me what it was like to be an honorable person. It is because of that—because of knowing you—that I made the decision to forgive myself. I thought, maybe if I stop feeling self-pity, I can do something good with my life. Maybe I can find favor with God." She curled her body inward. "You are the reason I opened my Scripture again, for the first time since I was a little girl.

"When I got the letter from Varya, it was like…I cannot even describe it. I had to come back for you. I had to do everything I could to save you. It was not even a difficult decision." She laughed lightly. "It did not take me three months to decide. It took me three months to get back into shape." She sighed. "That did not work so good."

As she paused, Scott collected his own thoughts. The situation was so much clearer now. She'd come back because he'd been righteous. She wanted to be there for him, just as he'd been there for her, not only in Siberia, but in her heart back at home. It made him feel numb.

"I have made so many mistakes," she said. "I have done so many stupid things. But coming back for you is the best decision I have ever made." She blushed. "I think even worth getting porridge in my face."

Scott couldn't repress a small grin, even if only to share in her humor. Her confrontation with Esther seemed so trivial now. She'd gone through much harder things.

She leaned closer to him. "You are a good man, Scott James Remington. I see it in you. I can see it in your eyes, even if only for moments in the midst of your anger. Just like I see it now."

That, he wasn't sure he could believe.

"You are a man of God. You have a chance here. If God only used perfect people, He would have no one to use. He can use our mistakes."

She made it sound so simple. She just didn't understand.

"I know the guilt that you feel. I know you choose to live with it every day." She hesitated, then frowned. "I know what you keep in your folder."

Scott looked at his desk. The manila folder was right where she'd placed it. She knew its contents. It held a life—the one he'd taken.

It held Sergei Steklov.

Scott had begun to collect Steklov's papers shortly after the murder, after reality had time to set in. At first he could only find the basics—official documentation from *Novosibirsk*, unit transfer requests. Nothing personal at all. So he did the next best thing: he researched Steklov's time in the Academy, how he had performed, what his instructors said about him. Scott wanted it all.

That had become Scott's secret quest. He had cut Steklov's life short. He'd placed a period in the middle of an unfinished sentence. All of Steklov's hopes, his dreams—they were gone because of him.

Scott collected the information with the hope of finding something—anything—that Steklov had wanted to achieve. Some dream, some aspiration. Something that Scott had made incomplete. Scott wanted to pursue it in Steklov's stead. He owed the young man he'd killed at least that much. Through all his research, through all his poring over Steklov's files, he'd found only one thing of interest. It may have been of no significance, but it was all Scott had.

Enjoys xenobiology.

From one of his instructors at the Academy, Scott learned that Steklov had enjoyed xenobiology. That was it. The summation of Steklov's known ambitions was limited to those two words.

That was why Scott visited Confinement and attempted to communicate with captives. It was why he took Steklov with him every time he went, personified in a single manila folder. If Scott could learn anything about the extraterrestrials—anything at all that he wouldn't have otherwise known—then he would have done something to honor the life he'd destroyed. It was the only way he could feel even remotely redeemed.

Her voice brought him back to the room. "You are a man who is torn. You are torn between your guilt and your heart. I know this. Scott...you do not have the heart of a Nightman. You are still the man who jumped from a Vulture to save a woman he did not even know. You are still the man who saved men in Chicago. You are still the man who lived a life good enough to touch a *stupid* Russian girl. You are still a Golden Lion."

His closet doors were still partially open, just enough for him to see the armor within. It wasn't golden and it wasn't innocent. It was as black as the sin it was designed to embrace.

Svetlana followed his eyes as he gazed upon the fulcrum's horns. Then she turned back to him. "That is not who you are."

He sighed. "I know how simple it must seem. To forget what happened, to pretend I didn't do what I did. But that would be a lie. That's the part that's so hard to explain. Svetlana, I don't want this. I don't want to be a fulcrum, and it makes me sick to know I'm a Nightman at all. I live with that self-hatred every day. But it's what I am. I did what they wanted me to do, I became what they wanted me to be." He pointed to the closet again. "I hate what's in there. It's a constant reminder of the worst decision of my life."

"Then, Scott, throw it away!"

"I *can't.*"

"But *why*? Why must you live with this guilt? It is just armor! You can get EDEN armor tomorrow if you wish."

"It's more difficult than that. I owe that to Steklov," he said, gesturing to the closet. "For me to take his life, then wash my hands as if nothing had happened—how disrespectful would that be?" It was so difficult to explain. "I don't wear it for myself. I wear it for him. I know this must sound like the stupidest thing in the world, but that armor keeps him alive to me. I can't forget him, Svetlana. I can't devalue his life."

Svetlana wore a vacant expression. Her shoulders slumped.

"Please show me another way to do this, then," he said. "Show me another way to dig myself out. I don't know what to do."

The ensuing silence was filled with mutual understanding of the most painful kind. It was the discomfort of reality, which was a feeling Scott knew all too well.

He knew their conversation was over, even before words made it official. He realized how hard it must have been for her to share her feelings, but he understood why she'd done it. She wanted him to know who she was. She cared about him enough to reveal her deepest wounds, even if they discredited her.

He didn't want her to fail. He wanted her to have the satisfaction of doing something good, even if it meant saving him. She deserved that. He just didn't know how it could be done.

"I do not like myself," she said quietly. She folded her arms over her stomach and looked down. "I have never liked myself. When I look in the mirror, I hate the girl that I see. You made me feel worth it."

Svetlana…don't do this to yourself.

She rose from his bed and went to the door, then turned back. "I will never give up on you."

He didn't know how to respond. He only stared at her, one lost soul meeting another.

After she left, Scott took several minutes to register the conversation he'd just had. All of it—her relationship with Tolya, her negative self-perception, her desire to help him—formed a tangled knot in his stomach. He couldn't stop thinking about her words. He made her feel worth it. She'd never give up on him. How different those were from 'I don't care.'

There was still so much to be done. Scott needed to talk to Esther, but that could wait until tomorrow. Tonight, he had no choice but to go to Confinement to talk to Petrov. Once again, he looked at Steklov's folder. But his thoughts were meant for someone else.

Nicole always said You'd put me where I needed to be. Please, God... tell me where I'm supposed to be now.

It was a scrap of a prayer. More than anything, it was a first call for help. He'd stopped believing in destiny months ago, but he desperately wanted to believe he was wrong. At least that was a start.

20

MONDAY, NOVEMBER 14TH, 0011 NE
2021 HOURS

AS SOON AS THE *Pariah*'s bay door came down, a foul odor hit Max hard enough to make him recoil in shock. "Oh my *God*!" He waved his hands in the night air, stepped back, and looked around. There, laying down in the middle of the ship, a patchy brown and gray dog lifted its head. Scattered in messy piles on the floor, was canine diarrhea. The dog wagged its tail.

"What the hell? Who put a freakin' dog in the ship?"

The animal flinched at his voice.

"Trashin' *Travis*!" He stormed into the ship and stomped at the dog. "Get outta here!" The dog leapt to its feet and shrunk back. Max stomped again and the dog sped past him and out onto the airstrip. He watched it disappear into the night, then looked back at the *Pariah*'s floor. "You've gotta be *kiddin'* me!" He breathed through his nose, coughed, and stepped out, closing the bay door to escape.

"Max!"

He turned at the sound of his name. It was Svetlana; she was approaching from the hangar's side door.

"Hey," he said back. He walked to her and pointed to the *Pariah*. "Who put a freakin' dog in the ship?"

She glared in return. "That is not 'freaking dog.' That is Flopper."

Max blinked stupidly and looked back. "Oh. I'm sorry. I had no idea. How dumb of me not to recognize 'Flopper.'"

"Do not be a jerk. I saved him myself, in Chernobyl. He was the only rescued survivor."

"*You* saved him?"

"Yes. I took him to the *Pariah* myself." She looked past him to the ship. "Is he all right?"

"Uh…" Panic emerged briefly in Max's voice. He quickly changed his tone to disguise it. "Yeah, he's fine. He's sleeping in a locker."

Her face fell. "In a *locker*?"

"On the floor!" he corrected. "He's sleeping on the floor."

"I should check on him."

Max grabbed her by her shoulders and turned her around. "No, no, he's fine. He looked pretty tired. We should let him sleep." He quickly escorted her away, at the same time looking out to the airstrip. The dog was nowhere to be seen. "So what dragged you out of bed?" He suddenly looked at her oddly. "Did you get pied in the face?"

"*What?*"

He shrunk back in defense. "Don't shoot the messenger, just tellin' you what I heard!"

"No," she answered matter-of-factly, "I did not get *pied in the face*. I am not clown."

"Harbinger was talkin' about it back in the room. I was just makin' sure."

"I did not get pied in the face, for your information." She murmured and began to walk again. "It was porridge."

"So it's *true*!"

"There is difference between porridge and pie!"

"Why the hell'd you get pied in the face?"

"Max…"

"Porridged. Porridged in the face."

"That is between me and Esther—this is not why I came out here!" she said, waving her arms. "I came out here to talk about something else. Something serious."

Max watched in silence and slid his hands in his pockets. "This is about *Scott*."

She sighed. "Please do not say it like that…"

"I'm not saying anything like anything, Sveta. Today we lost our friggin' captain. *He's dead*. I wasn't there, because I went and got hurt. Now I gotta live the rest of my life wondering if I'd have made any difference. But fine. Let's talk about Scott."

"You know," she said in disgust, "this is so much like you."

"Contrary to popular belief, I don't hate the guy. I've actually come to respect him, if you can believe it. Hell, I'm almost glad he's a Nightman. I was tired of being the only resident dregg."

"I should slap you in the face for that."

He ignored her. "When Nicole died, I probably felt the worst outside of Scott himself. People actually blamed *me* for what happened. Scott didn't, but a few people did."

"Where are you going with this?"

"I want to know who cares about *me*!" He raised his voice for the first time. "It's always Scott, Scott, Scott. I feel for the guy, Sveta, I really do. I want him on my team. But he's not. He's on some team between us and *them*." He motioned to the sentries in the hangar. "Do you realize I'm the only EDEN officer left? It's Dostoevsky, Scott, and then me. I'm taking a wild guess it's a slayer who'll get promoted."

She waited for him to finish his tirade.

"So what am I supposed to do?" he continued. "How am I supposed to handle this situation? Hell. They're probably gonna kill me to make room for someone *else*."

She put her hands on her hips. "Do you want Scott to be on your team? On *our* team?"

"Yes! Yes, I do. I'm doggone desperate for it, if you want the truth."

"Then do something for me." Her glare melted away. "Do something for Scott. You are the only one who can do it."

"You mean *something* something?"

"Yes, I mean something."

He waved his hand and turned away. "I don't even wanna know."

"Max!"

"I already tried, Svetlana! *Today* I tried! I asked him if he wanted to fix all this, and you know what he said?"

"What did he say—"

"Nothin'! He said absolutely *nothin'*. He just walked away like I didn't exist. I can't help that. I can't fix that. How can I reach out to someone who won't even acknowledge I'm here?"

"Just give him a *chance*!"

"What is it gonna take?" he asked. "The girl is dead, Sveta. Nicole is *dead*. As far as I'm concerned, Scott died with her."

Her shoulders sagged. "Max, please? Give him a chance to show that he can be good again. He wants to be. He does. He just does not know how to show it."

"Then he's gonna have to *learn* how to show it. When he gives me a reason to believe he'll have my back when worse comes to worst, then you can talk to me about favors. But he's gotta show me that first." Turning away, he walked back to the ship.

She watched him for a few moments, then left the hangar without saying goodbye.

Max stood by the side of the Vulture, his arms crossed as he stared out at the strip. His eyes bore into the darkness—straight out into the night.

"Where's that dumb dog?"

* * *

SVETLANA WAS HALFWAY through the halls when she ran into Varvara. The younger woman was walking quickly through the barracks in the direction of Room 14.

"Varya!"

When she heard her name, Varvara flinched. "Sveta! Hello!" she said in Russian. She looked flustered, her hair unkempt and her cheeks flushed. Her breathing was short and irregular.

"Where have you been?"

"Where have I *been*? I went to do some working out. It has been a long day, has it not?"

"Working out in the middle of the night?"

For a moment, Varvara said nothing. Then she brushed back her hair. "There has been so much on my mind—with Jayden, then with everything else. Then what happened with the captain today—it was just terrible when I heard about it. I needed to work out the stress." She glanced over Svetlana's shoulder down the hall.

Svetlana followed her gaze, but no one was there.

"So! How are things with the lieutenant?"

"Do you mean Scott or Max?"

"Scott."

"Things are good..." She stared at Varvara, then her eyes narrowed suspiciously. "Are you sure you were working out?"

Several silent seconds passed before Varvara laughed with apparent fatigue. "Yes, yes. I know that must seem silly. But, it is what I do. You know how I am."

"Yes. I do."

"Will you walk with me back to the room?"

After a moment of hesitation, Svetlana followed.

"I think things will be good here now," Varvara said. "It is so good that you decided to return. You are such a good person. You will help our situation."

Svetlana eyed her from behind. "You were the one who wrote me the letter."

Laughing breathily again, Varvara said, "Yes. Yes, I did. I am sorry… I am tired after working out, you must understand. I am not thinking clearly."

"What are you hiding?"

Varvara stopped and stared wide-eyed at Svetlana. Her hesitation was impossible to miss. "I am not hiding anything. I do not know what you are suggesting. I went to work out, and now I am returning to the room. That is it."

"Since when do you work out with no towel?"

Silence hit.

"Who is it?" Svetlana asked.

"Who is who?"

"You heard what I asked. Who is it?"

"Sveta, I do not know what you mean—"

"If I turn around and walk back, who will I find?"

Varvara shook her head. "I do not—"

"Is it someone from the unit?"

The younger woman looked distressed. All at once, her nostrils flared. "Wait! You are not suggesting…" Her words hung unfinished. When Svetlana said nothing, she gasped. "No. No! I am *not* doing what you think. How dare you accuse me of this!"

"Varya, I am only asking you a question."

"I know *exactly* what you are asking!" Varvara's cheeks exploded with red. "How could you suggest that? How *dare* you suggest that!"

As Varvara's voice rose, so did Svetlana's hands. She whispered, "Varya, it is night, please keep your voice down…"

"I went to work out. That is it! You always think you know what is going on."

Some of the doors along the hallway began to open. Half-awake operatives stared at the two women.

"You are always in everyone's business, thinking you know what is best! You never leave anyone alone." She threw up her hands. "No *wonder* you got pied in the face!"

The observing operatives' heads collectively turned. They followed Varvara as she marched all the way back to Room 14. Then they turned to Svetlana.

Svetlana's cheeks were flushed red. She glared as Varvara disappeared.

For several seconds, she didn't move at all. She didn't turn. She almost didn't breathe. Then, her lips pursed with rage.

She spun around and strode up the hall. She strode all the way out of the barracks.

Right through the cafeteria doors.

* * *

TEN MINUTES LATER

THE DOOR TO Room 14 burst violently open as Svetlana stepped inside. Travis flinched atop his bed, where he had been in the midst of reading his comics. The lights were on in both the bunk room and the lounge. The unit was still awake. Svetlana marched, hands full, right across the bunk room floor. She marched right into the lounge.

Several operatives were already there—among which was Esther. Conversation ceased as Svetlana entered. When the scout saw Svetlana, she sat up erect.

Svetlana's glare was calculated and cold. When she finally spoke, her voice boomed.

"Attention, all who can hear!"

Esther flinched; no one else moved.

Svetlana set a plate on the counter. In her other hand she held a filled-to-the-brim bowl. *"This,"* she said, "is porridge!" Turning the bowl upside down, she dumped its entire contents on Esther's head. The young woman shrieked as oatmeal rained down.

Before anyone else could react, Svetlana reached for the dessert on the counter. "And *this* is a pie." Without warning, she slammed it straight into the scout's face, causing an eruption of white topping to splatter the cabinets behind them. The other operatives gaped.

Esther sat frozen in shock. Whipped cream and melted marshmallow slid from her face. When she finally looked down, the whole mess fell splattering to the floor. Only her ponytail had escaped the messy assault.

"Learn the difference," Svetlana said. Wiping her hands on her sweat suit, she turned and marched out the room, stopping only to glance back at the scout. "Enjoy dessert." Then she was gone.

The remaining operatives stared at Esther as she dragged a hand over her head to slick the porridge back, wiping the filling from her face a moment later. When she spoke, her voice was layered with disgust. "Well, wasn't *that* cute?"

No one answered her rhetorical question. Almost no one answered at all.

Except for one person.

His grin—the sole grin in the room—stretched clear from one ear to the next. His eyes twinkled like a twelve-year-old boy's. When he spoke, his drawl filled the lounge.

"Dude," William said, looking across at Travis. "This unit *rocks*!"

21

MONDAY, NOVEMBER 14TH, 0011 NE
2121 HOURS

THE DOORS TO Confinement slid open as Scott stepped inside. He knew Petrov would still be there, despite the late hour. The scientist had asked to see Scott; he wouldn't leave until Scott came.

It was impossible not to think of the conversation he'd just had with Svetlana, not to feel lost and confused. The manila folder—Sergei Steklov's folder—was tucked underneath Scott's arm. He still felt compelled to bring it along.

Petrov smiled as the lieutenant stepped through the doors. "Good evening, Commander Remington."

Scott shook his head. "Not 'commander' yet."

"Soon enough, my good friend. Soon enough."

The Machine's lack of compassion was disgusting. *Captain Clarke has been dead for less than a day. Is that all he meant to this place?* He knew the answer and hated it. As long as there were Nightmen in the Fourteenth, Clarke would have always been an uninvited guest. Scott remembered his first conversation with William Harbinger a long time ago. William had told him that the Fourteenth was one of Thoor's favorite units—because of Clarke. Now Scott knew it was a lie. Captain Dostoevsky and Commander Remington. That was probably how Thoor had viewed it for months.

"Please, lieutenant, sit down. You have much to tell me!"

Scott sat in the indicated chair, taking a moment to survey the cells. They held many of the same inhabitants; not one of them was new. He looked at his folder. *All my time here, and I've learned nothing.* He fought and failed to quell his overwhelming sense of pessimism.

"Tonight will be wonderful night," said Petrov. "Tonight, we will have an execution. I am very excited."

Execution? Before Scott could ask about it, Petrov went on.

"Tell me what happened when you attacked the first necrilid."

Everything was like that in The Machine. Reveal nothing. Demand everything. He forced out thoughts of executions as he was asked to describe his encounter. "It was like any other necrilid. It appeared quickly, then it leapt to attack." It was strange, but necrilids in general seemed to have slowed down over time. He knew they weren't literally slower. He was just getting used to their speed. "I took a gamble. I attacked at the same time he did. I won."

Petrov eyed him a suspiciously. "Did you believe it was a gamble at the time?"

Scott was silent as he remembered his feelings. Pure vengeance. Pure adrenaline. He had poured out his anger on the necrilid, just as he had with Steklov months before. Unbridled rage he'd never known he possessed. "No."

He watched as Petrov took notes. Rage. In all his life, he'd never felt it before. Not like he felt it now. Not growing up. Not in college. Not in *Philadelphia*. He had needed something to unleash it. The Machine had been eager and ready.

"Then what happened?"

Scott shifted uncomfortably in his chair. "I attacked it. I was tired of losing and being afraid, so I tried something different. I wanted them to fear for a change." He found it hard to believe he'd actually done what he was discussing, and he wondered if he'd have the courage—or the insanity—to do it again. "I attacked it, then I threw it over my shoulder into the room in front of me. I tried to attack it again before it could get up, but it moved away."

"And according to the report, it made a sound?"

"I'd never heard it before. It wasn't normal—it was almost sad." He couldn't think of another way to describe it. "That's when everything changed. They stopped jumping out and attacking and got defensive."

"Describe this in more detail. Tell me how their mannerisms changed."

"Who are you executing?"

Petrov suddenly stopped scribbling and looked up at Scott. "Changing the subject so quickly?"

"You want information. I do, too. I want to know who's being executed." He was on amicable enough terms with Petrov to be able to make such demands.

The scientist watched Scott for a moment, then laughed under his breath. "Tonight, we will set an example in the Walls of Mourning. We will show the other captives the price of uncooperative—"

"The walls of *what*?"

"You do not know of the Walls of Mourning?"

Scott had never heard of it in his life, nor was he sure he wanted to. But now he had to know. "No, I've never heard of it before."

Petrov appeared skeptical of Scott's lack of knowledge. "The Walls of Mourning are within the Hall of the Fulcrums—in the Citadel of The Machine."

That explained it. The Citadel of The Machine. The lair of the Nightman sect. Scott had never set foot there. He'd never had the desire.

"It is…'our' Confinement."

That caught Scott's ears. "You have another *Confinement*? Why didn't you tell me?"

"I am sorry," Petrov said defensively, "I did not imagine you were unaware. You are a Nightman. Do you not walk the Hall of the Fulcrums?"

"No, I don't. What's in this Confinement?"

"Everything we want for ourselves—what we deem important."

"Is it an interrogation room?"

"It is a torture room."

The casualness of the word sent chills down Scott's spine. A torture room. The Walls of Mourning. He should have known. "I want to see it." He had no fetish for torture, but he felt an urge to see this place.

Once again, Petrov sounded confused. "You do not need my permission. You are a fulcrum. You can see it any time you wish."

"I want you to take me there, tonight."

"That is fine."

"Now. You can ask me about necrilids later."

Petrov rose from his seat. "Very well, commander. Let me collect my things, and we will go together."

Scott couldn't believe it. All this time, coming to Confinement over and over again, and not once had he heard of a secondary brig. He realized that must have been intentional. There was probably no mention of a torture room anywhere outside of the Citadel itself.

"Are you ready?" asked Petrov. "Follow me."

For the first time, Scott felt as if he were a legitimate part of the Nightman sect, not just someone who had happened to get caught in their snare. He was entering the Citadel of The Machine. The home of his kind.

To his surprise, the passageway that led to it was one marked as a custodial closet. Scott had passed it many times and never suspected otherwise. When he saw the limestone stairwell and dimly lit walls, the reality of *Novosibirsk* struck him hard. This place went well beyond Old Era—it was almost medieval. He felt strange breezes as he walked, from crevices that couldn't be seen. It was like stepping back through time.

The Hall of the Fulcrums was deathly quiet. No other Nightmen were about, which didn't surprise Scott at all. The Machine was known for keeping strict curfews. When they reached the doorway that led to the Walls of Mourning, the two sentries who guarded it were the first signs of life Scott had seen. They opened up the doors without question.

As Scott stepped through the doors, the putrid and overpowering smell was the first thing to hit him. It was the smell of illness, disease, death, and of exposed, rotting flesh. When the fullness of the room came into light, he actually had to stifle the urge to vomit.

There was blood everywhere. Battered and beaten aliens of all species were segregated in cages like animals. Untreated sores, missing limbs—it was like walking through a grotesque biological junkyard. Or a slaughterhouse.

Petrov seemed completely unaffected. In fact, he appeared almost invigorated by the place. In a way, Scott wasn't surprised. It was a lesson he'd learned several times: a friendly face and charming smile meant nothing here.

There were three other men in the Walls of Mourning, all of whom appeared to be workers. None wore armor, but their uniforms were stained with long-dried blood. When Scott entered with Petrov, the three men turned.

"This is Lieutenant Remington of the Fourteenth," Petrov explained, "soon to be their commander. He has decided to observe our execution."

The workers offered Nightman salutes, which Scott perfunctorily returned.

"Would you like to participate, lieutenant?"

"Not in the least." He felt guilty for even being there. He clutched the manila folder tighter.

"Very well." Petrov turned to the cages and began to walk. "Then allow me to introduce to you our beloved guest of honor."

Beloved guest of honor? Was that how Petrov referred to a death-row prisoner? He was beginning to see the man in a new, twisted light.

"This is Tauthinilaas."

The name meant nothing to Scott. He was only curious as to what it was. Alongside Petrov, he approached the targeted cage. Inside was a Bakma warrior. Its body, frail to the point of near uselessness, lay crumpled on the floor. It was laying face down, limbs splayed awkwardly. It looked to be already dead.

Petrov shouted something in what had to be Bakmanese. He kicked the cage hard and the emaciated alien jumped on the floor. It lifted its head to regard them, looking Scott straight in the eyes.

It was completely unexpected, and it happened the moment Scott locked eyes with the alien. He started back, as his mind surged back in time.

Scott held suppression fire as the last of the Eighth dove into the tower. He watched and attempted to count them as they bolted up the stairwell. Was that everyone? Yes. It was. He whacked his hand over the inner print sensor and it acknowledged him. Security lockout activated. He heaved the door shut.

It stopped within an inch of the frame.

Scott stared at the alien in disbelief. By the look of it, the Bakma was having the same revelation. Scott's memories whirled on.

Scott staggered to his feet. The handgun stayed out. "Do you understand me?"

The Bakma looked puzzled.

"Do you understand me?" Scott repeated.

The Bakma hesitated. "Duthek horu `Uman lkaana?"

What was that word? Scott's mind raced as the gun-checked Bakma stared back at him in confusion. Grrashna! That was it. The Bakma word for self-surrender.

"Grrashna!" Scott said emphatically. He motioned his handgun to the ground.

The Bakma's eyes grew wide with understanding. "Grrashna," it nodded. It lifted its hands above its head and sunk to a knee.

Scott knew exactly who this alien was. "You..."

Petrov shot him a puzzled look. "What?"

Inside the cage, the fragile Bakma attempted to stand. His efforts failed as he crumpled back down.

"Where did he come from?" Scott demanded.

"He was captured during the *Assault on Novosibirsk*. Do you mean to tell me you *recognize* him?"

"Yes, I recognize him." It was unfathomable—surreal. But there it was, collapsed in a heap before his eyes. "I was the one who took him prisoner." It was the Bakma from the assault—the one who'd stormed into the turret tower that Scott and the Eighth were trying to capture. The Bakma whose body had been rippled with muscles. Scott scrutinized its now-frail form. It had dwindled to almost nothing.

Petrov's eyes lit up. "That is amazing! In that case, it must be you. You must have the honor of execution."

Execution? Not on his life. "Open the cage."

Petrov arched an eyebrow.

"Open the cage!"

Flinching, the scientist did as told. The rusty bars of the boxed prison swung open.

Scott wasted no time stepping inside. Bending down, he slid his arms under the Bakma's arms. He propped the alien up against his chest. "Bring me some *calunod*."

"I'm sorry?"

"*Calunod*! Bakma food! Calunod!"

Petrov and the workers stared at Scott from behind, repulsed yet fascinated. Finally, the scientist spoke again. "Is this some kind of last meal?"

Last meal? The Bakma looked like it averaged one meal a week. "There won't be an execution tonight." His next words were for the Bakma. "Or any night. I didn't keep you alive for this." As Scott and the alien moved out, the Bakma appeared to make some kind of noise. It was too weak to speak coherently.

"Lieutenant Remington, this prisoner is scheduled for execution. It would not be wise to go against what is ordered."

Scott glared at Petrov.

"Okay. Okay. Whatever you wish." Petrov turned to the workers. "Bring calunod from the store room."

Scott could feel the alien's bones. Inside, his fury was quickly building. It wasn't the kind of anger that had gotten him into trouble in the past; rather, it was the anger of injustice. What once had been a strong, proud creature was now reduced to something as breakable as glass. Enemy or not, this was egregiously wrong. "We're taking him back to *civilized* Confinement."

"Lieutenant, that is not such a good idea—"

Scott snapped back before Petrov could finish. "Do you have any idea how fast I could kill you? Ask yourself if you should do what I say."

Petrov conceded. "It is better to be your friend than your enemy. We will bring him upstairs."

The journey back to Confinement was difficult. Although there were almost no Nightmen about, avoiding everyone was simply impossible. As Scott and Petrov assisted the Bakma—Tauthinilaas—out of the Citadel and back to Confinement, they were met on several occasions by random passers-by. Word about this would get out quickly. Scott would deal with that when it came.

The transportation was made more difficult for another reason: Tauthinilaas became unconscious halfway through the trip. His malnourished body, though not heavy, was still cumbersome dead weight. Petrov commented that it was doubtful the alien would survive more than a few days. Scott ignored him.

When they arrived in Confinement, the Bakma began to phase in and out of awareness. Its body would spasm and jump. Saliva dribbled from its mouth.

Opening one of the vacant cells—there were only two to choose from—they moved the Bakma inside. The workers had brought calunod, but it was soon obvious that the captive was in no shape to eat. It was simply too weak.

"It is as I told you," Petrov said. "He will not survive. He cannot even consume food."

As Scott removed his hand from beneath the Bakma's head, it rolled limply to the side. For a moment he wondered if it was already dead. But the faint movement of its chest was still visible. "Get me a medic."

For the first time during the entire ordeal, Petrov didn't argue; instead, he obediently stepped out of the cell.

The Bakma's opaque eyes flickered and rolled back. It was the first time Scott had seen the white of any alien's eyes. He hadn't known there was white at all. Bakma were almost bug-eyed—their huge, dark eyeballs unsettled even the staunchest of human warriors.

Scott slapped the alien on the side of the head. "Stay with me, Tauthin." He knew he'd never pronounce *Tauthinilaas* correctly. *Tauthin* would have to do.

Petrov reentered the cell. "There is a medic coming—he is bringing equipment. They are prepared for this sort of thing."

Scott tapped Tauthin again. "Don't go to sleep." If the alien went to sleep, it might not wake up.

"Lieutenant Remington…"

Ignoring Petrov, Scott continued to try and awaken the alien. Finally, he stopped and turned around. "What is it?"

Petrov fought to hold back his frown, but it escaped nonetheless. "What do I tell them when they ask why this has happened?"

Scott thought for a moment. He was asking for trouble doing this—he knew that well. He was asking to be noticed, and that was the last thing he wanted. "Don't tell them anything. Just send them to me." Petrov was putting a lot on the line in satisfying Scott's request. Even his life. "Tell them I threatened to kill you."

Petrov said nothing.

It took six minutes for the medic to arrive from the infirmary. Two nurses were with him, each transporting various instruments and equipment. A rolling bed. Feeding tubes. Things Scott didn't recognize. He wasn't sure how much training in Bakma anatomy the medic had, but he must have had some knowledge. Sometimes aliens needed to be kept alive.

Scott stepped out of the cell as the medical crew went to work. Tauthin was moved to the rolling bed as the tubes were set into place. Several needles were injected into the alien's body. One of the nurses was holding its wrist.

Scott couldn't help but inquire. "What are you doing?"

The nurse was silent for a moment, then answered in Russian. "I am checking his pulse."

"His pulse?" Scott was surprised. That seemed so human.

The chief medic spoke to Scott without looking. "Underneath their skin, they are not so different from us. Of all the other species, they are the most similar to humans, even more so than the Ithini. A medic almost doesn't need special training."

The Bakma were the most humanlike—he'd never considered that. "Is he going to live?"

The medic didn't answer immediately. When he did, he sounded doubtful. "I don't know."

Scott looked back at the alien. It seemed so exposed, so defenseless. He almost couldn't believe it had once been a threat. *Why do I care so much? I have comrades in the infirmary. I have discord in the Fourteenth. Why do I care about this creature?* Scott studied the Bakma as it lay still. Then he looked at the folder in his hand.

Because Steklov might have cared.

He looked at Tauthin again. There were still no signs of conscious activity. But that didn't matter—what mattered was that the alien was still alive. If not for Scott, the execution might have already taken place. It was the second time he had saved the alien's life.

"We have him sedated," the medic said. "We will stay here for the night to monitor him. It is best if we are left alone."

Scott felt a tinge of remorse. He didn't want to leave. Perhaps there was another reason for his compassion that went beyond Sergei Steklov. Perhaps he simply cared.

Tauthin hadn't asked to be born a Bakma. Maybe he hadn't asked for this war. Maybe he's just a soldier—like we all are.

The thoughts were out of character for him, but they felt pure. The realization hit him that Nicole would have been proud.

"Come," Petrov said, escorting Scott out. "I will stay for a while to make sure everything is good, and to explain if anyone arrives to ask questions. We just passed through the halls with a captive. General Thoor will eventually know." They walked out into the hall. "You should go rest. You have had long enough day as it is. We will talk about necrilids some other time."

As Scott left Confinement, he stared at the other captives in the cells. It was the first time he could ever remember seeing genuine curiosity on their faces. None of them were shouting or bore threatening expressions. They all just stared at the scene.

"I will see you again soon?" Petrov asked.

Scott had no choice but to visit again. "Soon enough."

"I look forward to it," the scientist said, waving. The two men parted ways.

Scott returned to his quarters alone as the full day's events settled in his mind. The day felt like several combined. He could scarcely believe he'd been in Chernobyl earlier that afternoon. Or that that morning, Clarke had still been alive.

When he finally shut the door to his quarters and turned the lights off for good, it took no effort at all to fall asleep. Rest came like a welcomed friend.

22

TUESDAY, NOVEMBER 15TH, 0011 NE
MIDNIGHT

NOVOSIBIRSK, RUSSIA

A KNOCK AT HER door caused Judge Carol June to stir beneath her bedcovers. Inside her private *Novosibirsk* suite, awakened from the darkness of solitary slumber, she squinted through tired eyes.

Reaching to her nightstand, her fingers felt until they found the outline of her clock. She looked at the time. She leaned her head back, closed her eyes, and groaned.

Another knock came. Outside, Judge Blake's voice spoke firmly. "Carol, it's me."

With a weary sigh, the auburn-haired woman threw back the covers. Lifting a hand to her forehead, she ran wrinkled fingers through her hair.

"Carol?"

"Yes!" she spat from the darkness. "Yes, I'm coming." Easing herself to an upright position, she groaned and placed her feet into the slippers at her bedside. "Give me a minute to get dressed."

As she donned a robe, she could see Blake's feet beneath her door. She made no attempt to put on makeup or brush her hair. When she opened the door, Blake stood alone in the hallway, dressed in full judge's garb. The Briton stared down at the shorter woman.

"Please tell me this is some kind of advance," she said in frustration, "because if you woke me up at midnight to talk business, I'll be sorely disappointed—"

"We need to talk."

June blinked.

"Meet me outside. South of the barracks. It'll be cold." As he walked away, he added, "I'll wait for ten minutes."

It took all of June's ten allotted minutes to get properly dressed for the cold, from her thick judge's garments to her earmuffs and gloves. Nothing was left to chance in the snow.

As she made her way outside into the Russian night, her body shivered uncontrollably. Teeth chattering, she crossed her arms tightly beneath her breasts and looked up at the moon. Its glow was barely visible beneath a thick layer of clouds. Snow was falling steadily.

In the distance, Judge Blake stood alone in a field several dozen meters away from the barracks. His hands were sheltered in his pockets. Even as she approached him, trudging through the snow that crunched underfoot, not once did he turn.

When she finally came upon him, she spoke. Ice vapors formed in front of her face. "This had better be good."

"Do you remember what brought us to peace, Carol?"

She stared at him with an odd expression. "What brought who to peace?"

"Us. Humanity."

June waited, looking slightly bewildered.

"It was nothing. No political or religious messiah, no cataclysmic event. Our greatest achievement as a species was an uneventful bore."

"Please tell me I'm not here for a history lesson."

"And oh, we do celebrate it," he continued on as if he hadn't heard her. "We hold parades and lift banners. For one day every year, we carry on like merry little children despite the war that rains down from our sky. Peace belongs to our species and we have *embraced* it, regardless of what our alien adversaries do."

He went on before she could interrupt. "I believe humanity is inherently good. I believe peace was inevitable, because I believe we have yearned for it all our existence. It was destined. It required no magical event. It was our soul-written will." He turned to her for the first time. "But what if we had no word for peace? What if such a concept was unknown? What if we worshipped the very act of war?"

She stared at him mutely with growing interest, her anger dissipating.

"There is much you don't know, Carol. But in due time, you will understand. It will not be easy to accept what I am about to say, but you must trust me when I say, we have your best interests at heart."

"Who is *we*?"

He looked down and pulled his gloves on tighter. "There are things in this universe too complicated to be conveyed in a single message. Existence is so complex. That is why we must remember our purpose. We are here to preserve the human species. We are here to ensure that our 'peace,' as boring as it may be, will go on.

"There are times when the simple choice is not always the correct one. There are times when humility must supersede dedication. When compromise must come before loyalty."

"What are you *talking* about?" she finally asked.

He turned away again. "I am talking about responsibility. Sacrifice. I am talking about the fate of our species and our planet." He looked at the stars. "Something is coming, Carol. We have all yet to see it. But it can already be felt."

"Are you talking about the attacks in Europe?"

He stared up in silence.

"Malcolm," she demanded, "*what* is this about?"

He drew a breath. When he answered, his voice was lower than the temperature. "This is not for Thoor. It is not for the Council, nor is it for President Pauling. What I am about to tell you is not for all ears."

The judge shook her head. "What are you about to tell me, exactly?"

He offered no more obscurity and no more playing with words. What he said next was blatantly clear.

"I'm about to tell you why we're at war."

Carol June didn't return to her suite for another two hours. When she did, she entered in silence. The once-tired look on her face was now replaced with something beyond vast contemplation. It was replaced with pure fear.

For ten minutes, she leaned against the inside of her door, staring at nothing. Even as she stripped down and prepared for bed for the second time that night, her mind was elsewhere. Her unsettledness stayed with her the whole while. It was there as she turned off the lights. It was there as she slid under the covers.

It was there in her dreams.

23

TUESDAY, NOVEMBER 15TH, 0011 NE
0545 HOURS

NOVOSIBIRSK, RUSSIA

THE NEXT MORNING

SCOTT FLINCHED AS his alarm clock beeped. His eyelids felt almost too heavy too open. Feeling thoroughly drained, he reached to his nightstand and silenced the clock.

Did I sleep at all? He knew that he had. He recalled dreaming, though he couldn't remember the details. He only knew that he'd lost track of consciousness at some point. In the past he would have leapt out bed and forced himself awake. But for the past few months he hadn't had the energy. Today felt even worse. It was as though the full scope of the previous day's events had all settled upon him during the night, rendering his attempts at rest all but totally futile.

He couldn't shake the conversation he'd had with Svetlana from his mind, even though it made him uncomfortable to think about. Her heart, her purpose in returning, it had all become clear. She was hurting like him.

He forced himself to focus on other things.

The Bakma. Check on the Bakma.

He had no choice about that one. He was solely responsible for saving the alien's life and transporting it from the Walls of Mourning to Confinement. But that didn't bother him—he actually looked forward to it. However, it would still have to wait.

The captain is dead.

Clarke was the next one to enter his mind. Yesterday the captain's death had blindsided them all, but today they would have no choice but to move on. Dostoevsky would never head up the resolution process on his own—at least not with EDEN's half of the crew. Scott hadn't even heard anything about a funeral. Clarke's wife lived right there in Novosibirsk. He wondered if anyone from the unit would go.

Esther.

Private Brooking, their Type-2 scout from Cambridge, England. The moment she entered his thoughts, he felt a knot of considerable size form deep in his stomach.

Esther wanted to go with me in Chernobyl. She wanted to charge the necrilids alongside me, but I told her no. He closed his eyes again. *She always wants to go with me, but I always say no. She's done everything she can to try and live up to my expectations. Even after I hit her in Khatanga.*

His expression grew pained. He had never brought up the Khatanga incident with Esther, instead acting as if it had never happened. He'd hit a comrade out of sheer anger. In a year of bad moments, that one was one of his worst. He'd all but ignored it until now.

She still smiles when she sees you. She still wants to go with you. She still tries her best to make you proud. And you always say no. You've done more for a Bakma prisoner than for her.

He opened his eyes and blew a breath upward. The mere thought of the British scout hurt. In truth, nothing else on his to-do list mattered as much as Esther. Tauthin could wait. As far as the captainship of the unit, that wasn't his problem anyway. But Esther—he needed to deal with her himself. His day would have to start there.

It took Scott fifteen minutes to become fully awake and get in uniform, considerably longer than normal. Nonetheless, he was prepared for the day—at least in body. He was far less confident about his mental readiness. With his tasks set before him, he left the privacy of his room for Room 14.

The plan was to wake only Esther; he didn't want to disturb anyone else. It was a considerable change from former times when he would march into the room, clapping his hands and shouting for everyone to rise.

When he finally reached the room, he opened the door quietly and peered in. His eyes locked for a moment on his old bunk—the one he used to share with David. David was there, sound asleep. *You never used to sleep late, Dave. You used to wake up early with Galina.* There were times when Scott almost forgot the former NYPD officer even belonged to the unit. David had become more of an afterthought than Boris. For that, Scott blamed himself.

To an extent.

He eased far enough in the room to make out Esther's bunk, but he stopped short when he realized she wasn't there. He could plainly see her bed sheets pulled off, with the scout nowhere to be seen. There were no lights coming from the lounge; in any case, she wouldn't have been in there in the dark.

Where are you, Esther? Where would she have gone to get away? Where would she have gone to release the tension of a feud with the new chief medic? If there was one place Esther would go to escape from the world, where would it be?

He didn't have to wonder for long.

* * *

ESTHER'S HEAD BROKE the water's surface as she emerged at the edge of the pool. Dipping her head back just enough to slick down her hair, the British scout closed her eyes and sighed.

"I shouldn't be surprised."

At the sound of his voice, Esther jumped. When she lifted her head, streams of water trailed down her face. She wiped them away.

Smiling as he approached, Scott said, "You're the only girl I know who has gills."

Esther leapt out of the pool. "Lieutenant," she said breathlessly. Her expression showed both surprise and concern.

The irony was not lost on Scott that on back-to-back days, Svetlana and Esther had retreated to the pool, both times to escape one another. "At ease. What brings you here so early in the morning?"

Water tattered the floor beneath her; she fell into attention. "I couldn't sleep. I just wanted to release some stress, sir. I apologize." Glancing at her swimsuit, she frowned.

She apologized, and for no reason at all—as though it had become habit. *This is because of me.* He motioned to a bench against the wall. "Come sit down."

"Yes sir?" It was both an affirmation and a question.

"I want to talk." Scott lowered himself on the bench.

She stared at him uncertainly before sitting next to him. Though she said nothing, she bowed her head and lowered her eyes with the slightly guilty look of a girl who'd been caught in the act of doing something wrong, without being sure of what it was.

"Esther." It was an awkward moment. He could see her apprehensively trembling, but he had to continue. He wanted her to know what he was about to tell her was real. "I am so sorry."

When he said it, she blinked. It was as if she wasn't sure she'd heard right. She tilted her head.

"I am so sorry for what I did to you in Khatanga. You didn't deserve it."

He watched her eyes as they moistened. She took a nervous breath before answering. "No, I'm sorry, sir. What happened in Khatanga was my fault. What you did was—"

"Horrible," he said, cutting her off. "What I did was horrible."

Scott was mentally prepared for what happened next. What surprised him was that it happened so fast. Esther's eyes began to noticeably shimmer as her mouth hung open wordlessly. She was fighting to hold back her emotions. Finally, she lost. As her head sunk, she lifted her hand to hide her eyes.

Scott couldn't help it. His head lowered, too, but for an entirely different reason. *This damage is mine.* He reached out, gently hugging her. She fell apart in his arms.

"I didn't mean…didn't mean to do it wrong," she spoke in heaves. "I thought I was talking to you…"

Scott placed his hand gently behind her head. He wasn't sure of the right thing to say, so he settled for all he knew. "This isn't your fault."

She sniffed hard. "I saw the Eighth, and I saw them see them, and I knew they were ready…"

He listened as she continued. Anyone passing by would have had no idea what she meant. But he understood.

"I was shaking *so much*—"

"Esther," he stopped her again. "You don't have to think about it anymore. It's over. It's in the past. It's not who you are."

She pulled away. "How can you not hate me? How can anyone not hate me?"

Scott remembered the first time he'd met her, in the hangar with Galina the day she arrived. She'd been so eager, so happy despite the downpour. She'd walked through the rain smiling like a child. Because she'd made it. And now, because of him, she was reduced to this.

"I don't hate you. No one does. What you made in Khatanga was a mistake. It was the way I responded that was wrong."

"What you did to me, I deserved," she said through her tears.

"No, you didn't. If anyone deserves to be struck, it's me. I'm where I am and what I am because I couldn't compose myself when faced with adversity. I can own up to that."

Her defense of him was immediate. "Becoming a Nightman wasn't your fault, sir. We know what they did. We know they did it to get you."

None of that mattered. "What I did, I have to live with. The mistake you made, you can let go of. I'm giving you permission to."

She didn't answer.

"I'm just asking one thing in return. Forgive me for Khatanga…for taking my anger out on you."

Esther's brown eyes settled on his face as her breaths began to waver. Once again, saline trailed down.

Scott observed her in silence.

Swallowing again through her tears, she said, "It took every ounce of courage I could muster not to run away after Khatanga." For the first time during that conversation, a small smile escaped. "Forgiving you won't be that hard."

In the very instant Esther's words came out, her whole face changed, as if a weight had been released. Her tears were still there, but there was something else. Her eyes brightened. Her small smile stretched into a grin.

"I don't ever want to disappoint you, lieutenant. I don't want to disappoint you ever again."

"You won't. I know you won't." He actually believed it. *This is what I should have been doing all this time. I've been so wrapped up in my own self-pity and grief.* He had been with Esther for scarcely five minutes, but already it struck him as some of the best time he'd spent in *Novosibirsk*. He felt younger. More importantly, he felt righted.

Esther laughed softly. "This isn't what I thought you were here to talk about."

"Don't worry, we're getting to that, too."

She rolled her eyes imperceptibly. "Must we?"

"You know it." Business was as much a part of his being there as was making amends. He'd considered addressing the cafeteria incident first, though wisdom said to start with Khatanga. He was glad he did; now he could talk with her both as leader and friend. "I just want you know that I believe in you—that I'm not angry for what happened. If anyone has had a right to be angry, it's been you…and you haven't. I thank you for that."

She sniffled. "I could never be angry at you."

Her entire goal had been to learn from him, to be guided by him. He realized he could stand to do some learning from her. He smiled faintly. "Do you need a minute before we talk about the cafeteria?"

"Yes sir, if I may."

"Go ahead."

Esther wasn't gone long—barely two minutes. She returned to the room with a fresh face and sparkling eyes. She smiled shyly and returned to the bench, a white body towel wrapped around her.

"All right, Molly Brooking," Scott said, his tone becoming more formal. "Let's hear about the porridge."

She sighed and looked away. "I admit, it was stupid."

"That's a start."

"We had just got back, and I was still so frustrated. I'm not sure what I was thinking. She said something that got me so mad, and I just flipped my lid."

Scott knew a thing or two about that. Had the culmination of his anger been limited to a bowl of porridge, he'd have been much better off. "What did she say?"

She hesitated. "I honestly don't even remember. That's how silly it was. It was just the wrong thing at the wrong time, and I lost control. It was completely my fault."

He twisted the subject ninety degrees. "What do you think of Svetlana?"

She pondered a moment. When she finally answered, it sounded programmed. "I think Svetlana's very talented. I think we're better for having her. She's an excellent medic."

Scott nodded. "Okay. So, what do you *really* think of her?"

She smiled. "I'm sorry. I must sound so pretentious. Maybe it's just trust. Maybe I have to learn how to trust her."

"Do you want the unit to trust *you*?"

"I do. And I'm aware of how selfish I must sound. I'm hardly someone to speak about trust." She paused. "Maybe she just rubs me the wrong way. You know how women can be—sometimes we're not the greatest at getting along."

He knew that well enough. "What does she need to do for you to trust her?"

"It may just take time…I suppose."

"Then give it time. I won't ask you to like her, I'll just ask you to respect her. Eventually, she will earn your trust."

Esther listened in silence.

"Have you talked to her since it happened?"

The scout eyed him warily. "You could say that."

That actually surprised him. Svetlana and Esther were taking resolution into their own hands? That was good. "How did it go?"

She pursed her lips for a moment, as the corners of her lips slowly curved. After a moment of contemplation, she finally said. "She paid me a visit in Room 14. With porridge and a pie."

"She *what*?" He could feel his face fall.

Esther blushed. "We're quite even, now."

"Elaborate."

"Is there really a need?"

Of course there was a need, for possible disciplinary reasons. But he had another underlying motive—this was getting interesting. "She attacked you with porridge and a *pie*?"

"Black Russian pie, actually. I'd never tried it before. It tastes surprisingly good."

"Okay," he said. "New rule. From now on, if you have a problem, you talk it out or you come to me. Don't start flinging desserts."

"Yes sir."

Though he didn't want her to know it, on the inside he was actually amused. How was it that he kept missing these things?

Esther's eyes widened with realization. "You're enjoying this!"

He tried not to grin.

"I can tell by your face!" She laughed. "You wish you'd have been there to see it."

He gave up. "I'm sorry. I confess. I do." He should have known he couldn't hide from a scout. "But don't misread that," he said seriously, pointing at her for emphasis. "Promise me it stops."

"I promise, sir. You have my word."

Business or not, it felt good to laugh. *This is the kind of camaraderie I've been missing out on. This is what goes on when I'm not around. Is it really that bad?*

"Lieutenant..."

He came out of his thoughts.

"Please come back to the group."

The words surprised him—it was as if she'd read his mind.

Esther looked down. "I know things have been so difficult for you. I can't imagine how the past four months must've been. But we miss you."

For the first time since the start of their conversation, true silence fell between them. Scott wasn't sure what he was supposed to say. He wasn't even sure what to think. When he finally gave her an answer, it was the only honest one he could find. "I'm trying."

She nodded knowingly.

"Thank you," he said, slowly rising from the bench. "We're all going to get through this."

"I know, sir."

"As you were in the pool."

Scott stepped past her toward the door. The moment he walked out, he felt lightheaded. *This isn't what you're used to, but that doesn't make it wrong.* He stopped in the hallway just long enough to settle his thoughts, then resumed his trek through the halls.

Behind in the pool room, Esther stood, statuesque, contemplating the door. Then, she grinned. It was the broadest grin she'd cracked since graduating from *Philadelphia.*

Wandering to the water's edge, she raised her hands, pirouetted, and dove in back-first.

* * *

THE MORNING COLD bit Max as he stepped outside. Despite the fact that it was already seven o'clock, no sunlight illuminated the grounds—it wouldn't creep over the horizon for another fifty minutes or so. But darkness was no excuse for sloth.

Shoving a hand into his pocket, he pulled out his cinnamon-flavored sprig. Its tip glowed orange as he slid it between his teeth and inhaled, exhaling a plume of scented warmth moments later. Closing his eyes, he leaned his neck to the side. It didn't pop, but the slight stretching sound of his vertebrae nonetheless brought comfort.

There were a good number of technicians working in the hangar. That was always the case at this time. As Max stepped into the massive structure, he allowed his eyes to survey the airstrip. Nothing was there. He hadn't seen the dog Svetlana called Flopper since frightening it away the evening before. The *Pariah* was now clean, the stench of dog scat hosed away into a hangar drain. There was no evidence that an animal had ever been there.

Max leaned against the nose of the transport, watching the distant, dark hills. He heard the clattering of technicians' footsteps in the hangar, but paid no attention. He kept his steely eyes pointed ahead.

"I got your message."

Max stood upright and turned to see Tanneken Brunner approaching. Her brown pigtails hung over her shoulders.

"I feel like we are back in *Philadelphia*," she said.

Max observed her for a moment, then turned away. "I could go for some *Philadelphia* right now."

"I am sure that you could."

Tanneken joined him, leaning next to him against the *Pariah*'s nose. Neither looked at the other—they both simply stared at the distance. The Dutch operative sighed. "Why did you call me here, Max?"

He didn't answer her right away. He only squinted as frozen winds whipped over his face. "I don't know."

She chuckled quietly. "Well, here I am."

"Do you ever miss me?"

Tanneken shot him a wary look, moving her fingers through her hairs as the wind blew them about. She held her head high. "If you mean, do I miss your arrogance? Do I miss your horrible manners? The stupid things you say?" She waited, then continued. "If so, then no. I do not miss you."

Max inhaled a breath of cinnamon again, then softly blew it out. When he answered, his voice was deflated. "Yeah, guess that's what I meant."

Her mouth turned downward.

Max cut the sprig off and slid it back in his pocket. "I don't know what to do, Ann. I got a chance to do something good. Maybe. I don't even know."

She crossed her arms. "It sounds like you do not know very much."

"You're right about that."

She smiled faintly, then cleared her throat. "So I am actually right about something?"

"This time, yeah."

Neither of them spoke for almost a full minute. They just stood, side by side, their backs against the nose of the *Pariah*. Her eyes surveyed him for fleeting moments, seeming to find him a buffer between looks at the distant hills. Max's eyes remained far away. For the first time since she'd arrived, the Dutch woman's expression fell soft.

Max sighed and looked the other way. "Sorry I woke you up. You can leave if you want—I know you're worried about home."

"You did not wake me up."

He made no reply.

Tanneken's gaze remained fixated on him, even as he didn't respond. Her green eyes arched sadly as she watched him. Then she turned her eyes ahead. Seconds later, she stood up from the ship.

The American stared on in silence. Even as Tanneken began to walk away, he appeared lost in his own distant world.

There did come a moment as Tanneken made her exit when she stopped and turned around. She turned as if she were about to say something. She even opened her mouth. But nothing came out.

Looking down, she finally made her leave.

Far ahead over the horizon, for the first time, the faint hues of sunrise broke over the hills. Max squinted as he stared through the cold, until another sound caught his ears.

Looking down, Max saw the young dog settle beside him. The technician actually smiled, and a soft chuckle escaped from his lips. "About time. Where you been?"

Flopper wagged his tail and stared up at Max, his tongue hanging out. He swallowed once, then his tongue hung again.

"Yeah," Max said, looking up. "That's where I been, too."

No one else came to find Max that morning, and no one buzzed him on the comm. For the next hour, the lieutenant leaned against the nose of his ship, silent and reflective as he observed the morning light break through the gray. He remained meditative and still, removed from the rest of the world.

Svetlana was cleaning the lounge when her comm beeped. Abandoning her wash rag, she grabbed the device she'd left lying on the table. She stared at Max's name on the display, hesitating before finally acknowledging. "Yes, Max, I am here."

Max's response was so delayed that Svetlana looked at the comm to see if their connection had been lost. Max spoke the moment she did. "What'd you want me to do?"

The corners of her lips slowly curved up. "Max, thank you *so* much."

"Don't mention it. What do you want?"

Closing her eyes, smiling serenely, she whispered a prayer. When it was over, she got back on the comm. "So I have a question."

"Yeah?"

"What can you do with personal armor?"

* * *

THE REMAINDER OF the day passed without incident for the Fourteenth. As the reality of Captain Clarke's death set in, awareness grew that the unit belonged to the Nightmen. By midday, the official word had been relayed: the new leaders were Captain Dostoevsky and Commander Remington. The Fourteenth was under fulcrum rule.

The news brought a new swagger to the slayers of the squad. All four—Viktor, Nicolai, Auric, and Egor—went about their tasks with an air of invulnerability. There was no EDEN captain to keep them in check.

Other news circulated, as well—news of far greater importance than the chain of command. Reports began to pour in from Europe in the wake of the Bakma attack. Despite the fact that *Novosibirsk* existed in its own frozen world, the impact of the miniature invasion would be felt across the globe. The death toll had not reached millions, as had been feared. Nonetheless, almost eight hundred thousand had died. The global economy was in crisis. Political leaders had been killed. Entire cities and towns were in ruin, as relief efforts began to organize across the planet. It was the largest unnatural catastrophe in the history of the world. Even in its extreme isolation, *Novosibirsk* too was affected.

Numerous units, none of which were Nightman in origin, had been transferred from *Novosibirsk* to various bases and stations throughout Europe. Recruiters were hitting the city of Novosibirsk as well. An entire continent needed to be restocked with operatives.

Stockholm had been all but obliterated. The lack of industry in the city diminished the impact of its losses on the rest of the world, but SWEDEN was left in chaos. The financial losses were too high to calculate, and the dual loss of both its capital and a cultural metropolis had crushed the country's morale. EDEN bore the brunt of the anger as spin doctors quickly attempted to deflect attention to the responsible Bakma. Despite their efforts, almost every official estimate contained words like *complacency* and *outrage*.

Copenhagen, on the other hand, had fared considerably better. EDEN forces in Denmark, though still overwhelmed, had made a much larger dent in the Bakma offensive. They had held the aliens off long enough for additional forces to arrive. Though the city had taken its fair share of damage, as had Stockholm, it had not been shut down. It was already even forming a recovery plan.

But beside the loss of a few units, the impact on *Novosibirsk* was still less than that of other places. The global economy was of little consequence to The Machine. Political leaders didn't matter, nor did almost anything concerning the rest of the world

And so the Fourteenth moved on. Soon Becan and Derrick would be returning, if not to active combat right away. Jayden's eye continued to improve. Relations between many of the unit's operatives were more strained than ever. Only a handful were optimistic about the future, though cautiously so. That was the world of the Fourteenth.

It was the only world that mattered to any of them.

24

WEDNESDAY, NOVEMBER 16TH, 0011 NE
2010 HOURS

THE CITY OF NOVOSIBIRSK

THE NEXT NIGHT

FROM INSIDE HIS vehicle, Dostoevsky carefully watched the small gathering of men and women outside the funeral home. He followed their smallest movements while he shifted apprehensively in the driver's seat. His hands—gloved with black leather that matched his jacket—held fast to the steering wheel in front of him.

It had snowed all day in the city of Novosibirsk. Fresh white piles were on the sides of the street and the rooftops of the buildings. Dostoevsky's own vehicle, a polished black Dovecraft hoverquad, was parked against the road a block from the funeral home. He had not had the courage to park any closer. In front of the building, in crudely written letters on an outdoor bulletin board, a simple message was displayed.

Nathaniel Edmond Clarke
7.21.25OE – 11.14.11NE

Dostoevsky was nervous. He had never attended a wake before; he'd never been emotionally affected enough to go. Looking around the street hesitantly, he muttered to himself in Russian.

No one else from the Fourteenth was present—or at least there were no EDEN vehicles to indicate otherwise. Dostoevsky was the only member of the unit who owned a local vehicle. Dovecrafts were expensive, but money was never an issue for fulcrums; they had access to anything they wanted.

Once again he scanned the front of the building. His hand trembled against the door, until he finally pulled the handle. He pushed the door out slightly, and it automatically slid back to open the way. It slid shut in his wake when he stepped out.

The air was frigid, and he slid his hands into his pockets. The sun had set over an hour earlier, and the unhindered arctic wind had come in full force. As he walked, head angled tensely to the ground, icy vapors escaped from his lips.

Dostoevsky was from Siberia. The cold was nothing new to him; tonight, however, it felt particularly uncomfortable—more so than ever before. He intentionally avoided eye contact as he strode up the short stairway that led into the funeral home. As soon as he was inside, he shook the ice from his jacket.

The building was small and modest in appearance. He was standing in a rectangular foyer with two open wooden doors leading into the viewing room. Several people made desultory conversation, and he identified a few British accents. He purposely avoided meeting their eyes.

Inside the viewing room were only two sparse groups of people. One consisted of two middle-aged men, laughing softly at what sounded like business. On the other side of the room, two men and two women appeared engaged in light conversation. But it was the center of the viewing room that caught Dostoevsky's attention. There, next to a simple display of flowers and photographs, he beheld a white wooden casket. He stared at it for several seconds, mesmerized, before he felt a tug on his jacket. Snapping out of his momentary daze, the fulcrum turned around.

A little girl, barely three feet tall, stared up at him with bright hazel eyes, matching his stare with a toothy smile. In her hand was a small card.

Dostoevsky took the card in hand. Flipping it over, he stared at the photograph on its front. It was a picture of Captain Clarke. He was leaning back with a wide, goofy grin, with a red clown nose on his face. Underneath the picture was a poem.

Blessed are they who bring smiles to our souls. Blessed are they who put laughter in our lives. Blessed are they who fill our homes and our hearts with warmth.

Beneath the poem was a single sentence: *In loving memory of Dad.*

When Dostoevsky finally pulled his eyes away from the words, he found the girl still smiling expectantly. After a moment of awkwardness, the Nightman offered an uncomfortable nod. "*Spasibo.*"

The girl grinned and swayed back and forth.

The two groups of guests still chattered quietly. No one seemed to notice him standing there. Sliding the card into his pocket, he ducked his head and walked farther into the room.

There was a funeral planned for the late captain. Svetlana had mentioned to the Fourteenth that it would be held the next night. Dostoevsky wasn't sure how many from the unit were going, if anyone at all. Clarke had always kept himself at a distance. He let everyone be.

Walking hesitantly to the casket, Dostoevsky peered in and saw Clarke's body for the first time. The fallen captain's skin was an odd, waxy white—it almost didn't look human. After mere seconds, Dostoevsky averted his eyes to the photo-laden bulletin board behind the casket.

Despite the banality of the pictures, they were Clarke as the fulcrum had never seen him: a photo of him sitting before a fireplace with what looked like an aging dog at his feet; a photo of a younger, shirtless Clarke, holding a woman of equal age in his arms; a photo of him as a child.

The clown-nosed photo was there, too, though now it could be seen in its entirety. Clarke was outstretched on a sofa, that same goofy grin on his face, as two young girls lay laughing on his lap. The girls' eyes were solely on their father. Dostoevsky recognized one as the girl who'd given him the card.

He tore his eyes away, closing them just long enough to turn away from the casket and find his way out. As he scanned the room instinctively, he locked eyes with one of the women. She appeared quaintly old-fashioned in a simple black dress. Her hair, a mix of burnt auburn and brown, was tied back in a neat coil. She watched him with an unabashed stare.

Dostoevsky almost tripped, but he quickly caught his footing and quickened his pace. Breaking his eyes away from the woman—the widow—he shoved his hands into his pockets and hurried to the exit.

The frozen air bit at his face the moment he stepped back outside. He blew out a breath and rubbed his gloved hands together.

"Wait!"

He knew who it was the instant he heard her. It was Clarke's wife—she was close behind him. He pretended he hadn't heard her.

"Wait! Please!"

Dostoevsky took several steps more, then paused. His car was still a ways down the street—he couldn't escape. But even as her footsteps approached from behind him, he resisted turning around. Only when he heard her stop mere meters away did he finally pivot to face her.

"I know who you are." She looked at him with sympathetic eyes.

Her words caught him off guard. It was the first time he'd seen her before. No one from the Fourteenth had ever seen Clarke's family—at least, not that he knew of. How could she know who he was?

"He always respected you," she said, "even when the two of you didn't see eye to eye." She pressed her lips together softly. "He believed you could be a better leader than he was, if only you could break free."

He didn't know how to respond. He felt more uncomfortable than at any other time in his life.

She took a step closer. "God can forgive every one of us. He can forgive you, too."

Dostoevsky was in shock at her words. Why was she telling him this? He was the worst kind of murderer—a calculated, cold-blooded killer. Of all the fulcrums in The Machine, he had always been among the most notorious. His name and 'God' had never been in the same sentence.

She reached out to gently touch his cheek. It was the most compassionate touch he'd ever felt. His face fell unguarded; his defenses crumbled. He felt his soul snap.

Until she spoke again.

"I am so sorry about your fiancée."

Dostoevsky blinked. He cocked his head as if he didn't understand.

"What they did was a *terrible* thing."

It took a moment for reality to set in. Her sympathy wasn't intended for him, nor was her compassionate touch. Not for him. Never him.

She thought he was Scott.

Her concerned expression lingered for a moment before she slid her hand from his cheek. Offering him a final smile, she turned and walked back inside.

As Dostoevsky climbed back into the driver's seat of his hoverquad, he trembled violently. He shook as he turned on the ignition and pulled out in the street. As soon as his wheels brought him to minimal speed, they retracted and his driftdrive engaged.

He drove for several blocks—past the funeral home he'd just left and around an intersection far up the road—until he could drive no further. Slowing his Dovecraft, he pulled alongside a curb and shifted to park.

Folding his arms over the steering wheel, he buried his face. The first sobs that came out were heavy. They poured out in heaves. Then the worst of it came out.

He hammered his fists against the steering wheel, screaming at the top of his lungs. He flailed his head and thrashed his arms wildly. When his emotions finally ceased their assault, he pressed his fist to his mouth and bit hard. He stared at the bleak cityscape before him, his reddened eyes lost somewhere else.

The Dovecraft remained parked for almost ten minutes, before it restarted, pulled out, and went on its way. At no point did it pull over again. At no point did it deviate at all. It simply drove on until it disappeared down the road—the road that led back to damnation.

Back to The Machine.

25

THURSDAY, NOVEMBER 17TH, 0011 NE
0756 HOURS

EDEN COMMAND

ARCHER MARCHED INTO Confinement from the security checkpoint, not even slowing to acknowledge the guards.

"Judge Archer!" One of the scientists hurried to his side. "I did not know you were coming. Is there something I can—"

"The Bakma I spoke to, Nharassel. Bring me to him at once."

"Yes, judge. Right away."

Within a minute, Archer was outside Nharassel's door. The Bakma had been transferred to a low-end security cell. The low-end cells were smaller and less hospitable than higher-classified ones, and meant for less important captures.

As soon as the cell door slid open, the Bakma lifted its head. Upon seeing Archer, it sat up.

"Close the door. I need privacy again," Archer said to the scientist. The scientist complied without argument. For several seconds, Archer and Nharassel simply stared. Archer's hands were on his hips, his lips pressed together in restraint.

"They hit us, Nharassel," Archer said in Bakmanese. "Harder than ever before. They came in like a swarm. What does that mean?"

Nharassel remained silent.

"I said, *what does that mean*?"

The alien turned away and looked at the wall. Its bulbous eyes were hardened like stones.

Archer paced along the closed entrance. "This was faster than you claimed. Unless you misled me. They ravaged whole cities—almost a million are dead. We've spent the last two days trying to convince the world we're not utter *fools*." His hands were as animated as his words.

"You said less than two full revolutions. How do you expect me to believe that now?"

"That was not the tribulation," the alien said, still looking away.

"How do you know?"

Nharassel turned back to him. "If it were, we would not still be here."

The British judge approached him. He stopped barely a meter away. "Then why? Why strike us like never before? Is it a warning? Are they trying to send us a message?"

"I do not know."

Archer's jaw clenched. His hands remained on his hips. "I need to know what will happen, Nharassel. I need to know what to look for. Does your species stop first? Will there be a lull?"

The Bakma's bulging pupils constricted. Slits of deep black could be seen. "When the Nerifinn appear, you will know. They will proclaim the coming of the Khuladi. There will be no uncertainty. That is the purpose."

"Who are the Nerifinn?"

"They are the declarers."

Archer stopped pacing. "So the Nerifinn come to declare the tribulation? Do they come to fight as well?"

For the first time during the exchange, Nharassel showed a glint of emotion. His gnarled mouth curled up at the corners, exposing a jagged-toothed smile. "If you wish."

For thirty seconds, neither spoke. They both watched each other—one in anxiety, the other in scrutiny. It was Nharassel who broke the stalemate.

"When will I be free?"

Not a muscle on Archer's face moved and he seemed to have ceased breathing. "Not yet." Backing away from the alien, he walked toward the door. "Not soon enough," he added.

As Archer left the cell, the Bakma sat back down on its metal cot. The door sealed it in.

Archer spent no further time in Confinement. Walking past the guards and out of the security checkpoint, he went about his way.

His scowl never changed.

26

FRIDAY, NOVEMBER 18TH, 0011 NE

1230 HOURS

ONE DAY LATER

SCOTT WAS IN the middle of a meal when the mission tone sounded. Though promptness was always standard for a callout, this one required special urgency. It wasn't a call to a crash site, it was a rescue. Two Vultures from EDEN had been shot down.

It marked the unit's first post-Clarke mission, and it rested solely on the shoulders of the fulcrums. Scott had met with Dostoevsky only once during the last two days. They and Max had met to discuss the vacancy at the lieutenant position. It was a brief but heated debate. Scott and Max recommended Oleg, but Dostoevsky's objection was vehement—his choice was Viktor the slayer. A verdict was never reached, and no decision was made. The open lieutenant slot was left for speculation.

That wasn't the only moment of awkwardness in the two-day span; the other had come at Clarke's funeral the day before. Everyone in the unit had attended, with the exception of Dostoevsky and the slayers. Scott had felt obligated to go. The awkward moment came when he met Clarke's widow. She'd given him a peculiar look when he introduced himself, then she opened her mouth as if to say something, only to step away and leave as if she'd changed her mind. The brief exchange had struck Scott as odd.

By the time Scott arrived in the hangar, Dostoevsky was already waiting, along with Travis and Boris and several of the Nightmen. Scott walked to the *Pariah* in full stride.

"Scott!"

Svetlana's voice came from behind him; he recognized it immediately. He waited for her to draw near.

"What is the situation?" she asked.

He hadn't seen her in almost two days, since the talk they'd had in his room. He had not had an opportunity to tell her how his attitude had improved since saving Tauthin and reconciling with Esther. How there was perhaps just a glimmer of hope.

She stood before him now, golden strands of her hair caressing the sides of her face just as they always did. He looked into her eyes—eyes that stared at him expectantly, waiting for his answer.

Two days ago, she'd told him he made her feel worth it. But she didn't need anyone to make her feel that. She was worth it without any help.

"Noboats shot down two Vultures," he finally answered.

"Are there any survivors?"

"Not that I've heard."

It was a Bakma mission yet again, but this time he didn't view it as mundane. Over the past several days, the crimson-purple aliens had become vastly more intriguing—ever since he'd saved Tauthin from execution. He was anxiously awaiting the day the Bakma captive would be able to communicate. He'd checked in with Petrov several times; the alien was still recovering.

Another surprise had come with Tauthin's rescue, this one concerning something that *hadn't* happened. No one from Thoor sought Scott out. No one questioned him about Tauthin's release. According to Petrov, no one had spoken to him, either. Fortunate or not, it struck Scott as strange.

Svetlana interrupted his musings. "Scott, about the other night..."

He gently cut her off short. "Don't say it." He had a feeling she was about to apologize. "You may have been right."

A smile touched her lips.

At that moment, another operative caught Scott's attention. It was Becan. The Irishman was wearing full combat armor, minus the helmet he held in his hands. His typically unkempt hair was now noticeably shorter. It looked freshly cut.

Even Scott couldn't hold back his excitement. "Welcome back, McCrae."

"Wise up, dope. I'm tired o' yeh callin' me 'McCrae.'"

"Then Becan it is."

"Righ'. An' welcome back to you, too."

When everyone was gathered in the *Pariah*, Dostoevsky began the initial brief. Despite his aura of untrustworthiness, the operatives gave him attention. "Two Vultures were intercepted while en route to *Sydney*."

At first, the name *Sydney* took Scott by surprise. That EDEN base hadn't officially opened yet. But the more he thought about it, the more it made sense. It couldn't be more than a few months away from operation; it was probably moving units in early.

"They were shot down north of Nizhnevartovsk, then engaged from above. All contact was lost with one Vulture after it crashed. The other has reported minimal casualties—for the moment. Our job is to engage and extract."

"Who are the units?" Scott asked.

"They are called Frogmouth and Pelican. That is all I know for right now."

An extraction operation. The last time Scott was involved with one of those, it was in the *Battle of Chicago*. Extraction defined his career.

He scrutinized the other operatives. Of his four slayers, he was most pleased that Egor was there. The horse-faced ogre was, of all things, a reliable asset. Scott never wanted to go without him again.

Leaving Egor behind in Chernobyl was Clarke's error. It will never be mine.

Becan and Esther sat side by side in the ship. Scott observed them both. Becan would be rusty, and probably surprised by his own lack of athleticism. That happened when you stayed in the infirmary. *He'd better know his limitations.* Esther, on the other hand, looked sharp and energized.

William and Derrick were also present. Derrick was not in combat shape, despite the fact that he'd returned to active duty early. *There's no way he's leaving the ship—he'll stay with Travis.*

Suddenly Scott's eyes locked on the floor by the cockpit, where the small laika watched the operatives above. The dog's tongue hung from its mouth.

"What's the dog doing here?"

Max leaned against the cockpit door. "Dog's got a name, Scott."

Svetlana smiled at the mention of the animal. "He is good for the *Pariah*, is he not? He matches the picture on the tail wing."

The dog on the tail wing looks diseased, Sveta. This animal looks nothing like that.

Kneeling on the floor, Svetlana opened her arms. The dog eagerly padded her way. "Little Flopper will be good in the ship, won't you? You will watch over Travis and Boris." The dog wagged his tail, licking her face.

"I wouldn't let him do that if I were you," Max said.

She gave him a look. "Do not worry, I am not afraid. He will not bite me." She giggled as the dog licked her more.

"It's not that," said the oily technician. "Five minutes ago, he was eatin' his own poo."

Svetlana's face froze. She pursed her lips in disgust, stood up, and held out her hand.

Max tossed her a wet cloth. "Bad dog."

As the *Pariah* lifted from the airstrip, Dostoevsky addressed the unit again. "Evteev, bring up a map."

A display screen came alive on the wall. The Russian captain pointed at it.

"The two Vultures were shot down approximately thirty kilometers from each other. Frogmouth Squad was shot down to the north, here in the bog. Pelican Squad is east, in the forest. There are several inches of snow in both areas."

Scott listened to how Dostoevsky spoke. He wasn't as eloquent as Clarke, but few people were. Dostoevsky seemed matter-of-fact.

"Commander Remington will lead a team into the bog. This is the Vulture that has given us no communication. It may not have any survivors." He gestured at the Vulture in the forest. "I will lead a team here, to the transport with minimal casualties. There may be Noboats in the area, but if they are there, they are invisible. There could be heavy resistance upon our arrival."

Scott decided to be tactful. "With your permission, sir, I would like to lead the team in the forest. I'm familiar with this kind of thing."

The truth was that Scott didn't *trust* Dostoevsky with an extraction—not with shipwrecked EDEN operatives' lives at stake. Dostoevsky would always put his own safety first.

Dostoevsky thought for a moment, then agreed. "I grant your request. I will take the team through the bog."

Scott was surprised—he hadn't expected acquiescence from Dostoevsky.

"We do not know how many Noboats were in the area," said the Russian, "but the first transmissions indicated two. Three to four are not out of the question. There are Vindicators patrolling above the forest, but they have not had enemy contact." He looked at Scott. "Your contact with Pelican Squad is Captain Rex Gabriel."

Scott affirmed. Now he was waiting to hear the team breakdowns. The fact that both teams would be led by a Nightman made the decision interesting. He had an inkling he knew how it would fall. Dostoevsky was a fulcrum, but he was probably paranoid, too. Scott had a feeling the slayers wouldn't be assigned to Dostoevsky, but to him. He was willing to bet Dostoevsky would want EDEN's operatives at his side to make sure there wasn't a conspiracy to kill him that would be discussed as soon as he was away.

No...he won't leave all the slayers with me. He'll take one slayer with him, just to be safe. Just to make sure someone there has his back, in case the EDEN members decide to kill him off.

"Remington," Dostoevsky said, "you will take Romanov, Goronok, Broll, McCrae, Brooking, and Voronova."

Scott was right. He knew Dostoevsky to the core.

"I will take Ryvkin, Axen, Jurgen, Strakhov, Harbinger, and Yudina. Cole will remain behind with Navarro and Evteev. And...the dog."

So Scott had three of his slayers. Having Becan, Esther, and Svetlana would also be advantageous. Esther—he could use Esther. He was already thinking of how.

His mental planning was interrupted by Becan.

"Remmy," he whispered, "yeh just have to trust me...but I need to go with Dostoevsky's team."

Scott raised an eyebrow.

"I've *got* to go with 'em. I can't tell yeh why. Jus' trust me, please."

Something was wrong. Why would Becan want to go with Dostoevsky? Only one answer came to mind, but surely the Irishman wasn't dumb enough to try that. "Becan..."

"It's not wha' yeh think, I cross m'heart."

"Then what is it?"

"I can't tell yeh."

Scott eyed him warily.

"Yeh know, you haven't exactly been the grandest person on the face o' the Earth the past couple o' months, but I've been with yeh no matter wha'. I'm your friend, an' I trust yeh. Righ' now, I need you to trust *me*. I also need yeh not to ask why."

Scott knew Becan hated Dostoevsky—that was no secret to anyone. There was bad blood between the two. "I'm not ready to be a captain." Scott felt he needed to say it. "Don't do me any favors."

"Tha's fair enough."

After another moment of scrutiny, Scott sought Dostoevsky. "Captain?"

From across the transport, Dostoevsky looked over.

"I'd like to take Harbinger with me. Can you take McCrae?"

For a moment, Dostoevsky tensed. His eyes lingered on Becan's back. "Very well."

As Dostoevsky walked away, Scott turned to the Irishman again. Scott's eyes expressed more than words could.

"Trust me, Remmy. It's not wha' yeh think."

Max and David geared up in silence. Despite the fact that the two Americans sat side by side, checking the same weapons and wearing the same armor, they couldn't have been more emotionally distant. It was Max who closed in the gap.

"I know this don't mean scat to you," he said, closing one eye as he looked down his rifle, "but I don't hold a grudge."

David adjusted his armor in silence.

"We all got reasons for doin' what we do." Satisfied with his E-35, Max slammed a magazine into place. "I know you got yours." He shouldered his rifle and pulled a sprig from his pocket. "The way I see it," he said, flicking his wrist and igniting the tip, "not one of us has been doin' this right." Sliding the sprig between his teeth, he inhaled a deep breath. He closed his eyes and breathed out evenly. "That includes you."

David stopped working and angled his head at Max. But now it was Max who didn't acknowledge him. Opening his eyes again, Max flicked his wrist and the sprig's glow faded away. He slid it back into his pocket. "Just had to get one more good puff."

David listened as Max leaned back, his rifle touching the *Pariah*'s inner hull behind him. He listened as the technician quietly hummed.

Nothing more was spoken between them.

Scott stood prepped by the rear bay door with Auric at his side. He looked back at the troop bay and surveyed the other operatives. His former roommate and friend, David, was still sitting next to Max by the cockpit door.

David avoided eye contact with Scott; in fact, it seemed not even to be deliberate but as if from habit. He'd isolated himself from the unit completely, just as Scott had for months. He was part of the disconnect.

"Ignore him, commander," said Auric. "He would kill you if he had the chance."

Scott turned forward again. "No. I don't think he would."

"Coming down!" yelled Travis from the front.

The bay doors began to slide open.

Scott returned his attention to the mission. Rescue Pelican Squad. Make contact with Captain Gabriel. His first priority upon stepping outside would have to be hitting the comm channels—finding out Gabriel's situation then and there.

The *Pariah* touched down in the middle of a sparse evergreen wilderness with about a foot of snow on the ground. Cold hit the troop bay; Scott turned on his heater.

Svetlana moved to his side. She said nothing, but he could feel her eagerness emanating from her body. She'd had a bad mission in Chernobyl and this was redemption.

"Do you think there are still Bakma here?" she asked.

The obvious answer would have been yes, but the attack on Europe had proved logic wrong. The aliens were inclined to leave at random. "I don't know." He surveyed his team. Three slayers, a demolitionist, a scout, and a medic. That was as diverse as a rescue team could get. According to the last transmissions of Captain Gabriel, Pelican Squad was two hundred meters east. No signs of Noboats had been reported, and Vindicator fighters were actively patrolling. The rest was up to Scott to discover.

As soon as the *Pariah* landed, Scott clamped on his black fulcrum's helmet. It slid into place with a clunk. Hidden behind its featureless faceplate, Scott closed his eyes.

It never fails.

It didn't matter what sense of optimism or revival he sought. When that fulcrum helmet came down—when those horns became his identity—the awareness of his sinful status burned through his heart.

Will this never change?

Scott forced the thoughts from his mind. "My team, out."

Before disembarking, several feet away from Scott, Esther took a second to look back at Becan. The Irishman was already staring at her. They locked eyes for a moment, then she mouthed the words, "Do him in."

Becan nodded his head.

The snow crunched beneath Scott's feet and he sunk several inches, but it wasn't as deep as he'd feared. This was manageable. The slayers were right at his side, and Svetlana and William fell last. William had been surprisingly quiet—probably because he was with Nightmen. William hated Nightmen. As the Vulture lifted away, Scott surveyed the scene through his view screen. Thick forest stretched in every direction. The spruce, cedar, fir, and pine trees surrounding them would certainly provide adequate cover.

"Nothing on infrared in the trees," said Nicolai. The older slayer's head twitched characteristically. Behind them, the *Pariah* lifted off to take Dostoevsky's team to the second drop point.

Scott knelt in the snow. "The transport is ahead, east-northeast about two hundred meters." He thought for a moment. "Auric and Nicolai, I want the two of you spread out to the north. Stay twenty meters away. Egor, spread south, same distance. William and Sveta, linger behind." He trusted Svetlana with William, almost as much as he would have trusted himself. Scott was tempted to take her with him—but there was someone else he wanted instead. "Esther, come with me."

The scout affirmed and joined him, and everyone else took their positions. Nicolai and Auric—they formed as consistent a pairing as could be made. Egor would be fine on his own. Everything was set.

Scott opened a comm channel to Pelican. "Captain Gabriel, this is Commander Scott Remington of the Fourteenth. Can you hear my transmission?"

No reply came.

The first red flags began to pop up. Nothing had been reported wrong with Gabriel's comm. The Australian captain should have heard him. If EDEN had had contact with Gabriel since they'd been forced down, why was there no contact now? "What do you think, Brooking?" he asked in an attempt to keep Esther involved. He already knew what *he* thought.

The scout drew a stout breath. "I believe this is a hostage situation, sir."

Scott blinked under his helmet. He turned to look at her.

"For whatever reason," she went on, "Captain Gabriel is *choosing* not to respond. If there were any outward signs of a fight, not only would we have heard it on the ground, but it would have been seen from the Vindies in orbit. Even if he's under duress from hostiles outside his transport, he should be able to relay that to us." She paused. "I think he has a gun to his head."

That was much more in-depth than Scott had ventured to think. He'd simply reached the conclusion that something was wrong.

The scout continued. "That tells me there are Noboats on the ground, which in turn tells me they're waiting for something—possibly for us to approach. I think it's an ambush. If I may make a prediction, I believe we will continue to have no communication with Captain Gabriel until we've drawn close, literally in the Bakmas' sights. The Bakma are extraordinarily cautious, particularly in ambush situations. They play things remarkably safe, when they can muster up the courage to gamble at all."

Scott stared at her in silence. He had no idea how to respond.

"Bakmanese Tactics and Method." The scout smirked. "It's a 300 course."

Scott looked ahead once again. "Well, there we go."

As the *Pariah* descended with the other half of the Fourteenth, Dostoevsky clamped on his helmet. Max and Viktor stood ready behind him. "We have not heard anything from this transport," Dostoevsky said. "There may be heavily wounded, if there are any survivors at all."

Varvara stared at the ground.

"Travis, ETA?" asked Dostoevsky.

"About fifty seconds!"

Viktor cursed. "Idiot pilot. Must everything always be shouted? Does he think he's in American movie?"

"Watch your mouth when you talk about my friend," said Max, glaring at the slayer-medic.

"Shut up."

"Look at me and say that again."

"Stop it," Dostoevsky said, cutting them off. "Prepare to exit the ship." Moments later, the *Pariah* touched down.

The rear door whined open. The frozen bog of Nizhnevartovsk, a wasteland of dead trees and decrepit earth, stretched to the north. As they stepped out, the stench of iced sludge hit their nostrils.

Back in the wilderness, Scott and his team slowly tracked east. They had yet to encounter any hostiles, nor had they heard from Captain Gabriel's crew. Scott had commed the captain numerous times but was met only with silence.

William and Svetlana remained at the rear. The demolitionist was one step behind her as they quietly pressed on. William's hand cannon was firm in his grasp.

Scott lifted a hand. Everyone stopped and looked at him. "We're a hundred and fifty meters out," he said. "I'm sending Esther to the south to mirror us from farther away. I want everyone on high alert for a possible ambush. Look for any signs of a Noboat."

Several quiet affirmations came and Esther spurted away.

Dostoevsky's team was still moving north through the frozen bog. The snow kept the normally moist ground relatively solid, a rare convenience—the terrain was more passable for them all. Everyone was prepared with their E-35s as they focused beyond icicle-covered remnants of trees. Dostoevsky led with Max and Viktor right behind. Varvara and Oleg took to the middle, and Becan and David covered the rear. Becan had not once spoken to David beside him, nor to Oleg and Varvara meters ahead.

"The ship is not far from here," said Dostoevsky. "Under one hundred meters ahead. We should almost be in visual range."

The team kept onward.

Scott could tell something was wrong by the silence of the forest. A natural evergreen forest was never this quiet, even in freezing temperatures. This silence was overwhelming. Every footstep was amplified to the tenth degree. There were no birds nor any signs of animals. He was still unable to identify the downed crash site, even with his display fully zoomed.

He thought about what Esther had deduced about the possibility of an ambush. What if she was right and this was some kind of trap? There was no reason for Captain Gabriel to go radio dark.

A pair of Vindicators streaked by. It was the only unnatural sound in the woods.

Max's voice emerged through the comm. "Yo, Scott?"

"Go ahead."

"We're within a hundred meters of our crash site. No Bakma contact as of yet."

"None here, either."

"Just lettin' you know." The comm channel closed.

Egor spoke next through the comm. The slayer was still twenty meters south. "There is something very wrong here, commander."

Scott agreed. "Stretch south thirty meters. Romanov and Broll, increase to thirty as well."

"Yes, commander."

"Will," Scott said without turning. "Follow thirty meters behind."

"A'right."

Scott's radio commands carried on. "Remington to *Pariah*."

"*Pariah*."

"Where are you?" He hadn't seen Travis fly overhead.

"We landed five miles to the west, awaiting orders from you or the captain."

"Is Derrick still with you?"

After a moment, Derrick's country-hick voice emerged. "Yeah, I'm still here."

"Stay vigilant. There *have* to be Bakma in the area." Alone, Travis would never be able to defend the *Pariah* if the Bakma landed and attacked them. But with Derrick, they stood a fighting chance. They had the dog, too—that could be a plus. Scott's thoughts stopped right there. *Did I really just think that?*

He closed the comm channel completely. Glancing both ways, he saw that his team had spread out. He gave them the signal to move on.

Dostoevsky's team continued to trek through the bog. They were within sixty meters of the crash site, but still hadn't encountered any Bakma.

Becan caught up with Oleg, leaving David alone at the rear. "I hate missions like this," the Irishman grumbled.

"They are not so bad," said Oleg.

"I hate bein' ou' in the sticks. Give me urban combat anny day."

Varvara chuckled from Oleg's other side. "Last time you were in the city, Becan, you got hurt. You are lucky to be alive now."

"I'd rather die in the city than in the middle o' the bleedin' woods." Shouldering his rifle, Becan nudged Oleg. "By the way, guess who I ran into while I was in the infirmary? Vladimir Lennikov."

"Oh, really?" Oleg asked, still scanning the perimeter. "And who is he?"

"You been here all this time an' yeh haven't met Vlad?"

"Not yet. Was he a comrade?"

"Not a comrade, really," Becan said, slowing his pace. Oleg and Varvara continued ahead. "He's been a lieutenant in the First for three years."

Oleg froze.

It took a moment for Becan's words to set in. But when they did, everyone stopped, equally paralyzed. At the front of the group, Dostoevsky went rigid.

"Wait a minute," Max said, turning to Oleg. "Weren't you…?"

"Weren't you *in* the First before you came to us?" David finished the question.

Oleg opened his mouth, but nothing came out.

Becan aimed his E-35 at the flustered soldier. "Don't worry, Strakhov. Vlad didn't remember you, either."

Dostoevsky lowered his head.

Oleg laughed nervously and began to speak, but Becan cut him off. "I saw what yeh did in the federal building, in Krasnoyarsk. I saw yeh drop a half a dozen Bakma who got the jump on yeh without a second o' warning. I know a little bit abou' scrappin'." His finger hovered over the trigger. "They don't teach tha' kind o' thing back in *Philly*."

Varvara took a step back toward Max.

"But yeh know wha', Oleg?" Becan went on. "I saw somethin' even more tellin' than your knack for reefin' up aliens." He narrowed his eyes with conviction. "I saw the look on your face. An' it wasn't the look we're accustomed to seein'. At least, not from annybody in EDEN."

Max made a time-out sign with his hands. "Hang on, back up the truck."

"Why'd they put yeh here, Strakhov? To make sure everythin' went accordin' to plan? To make sure Remmy fell into place?"

Viktor interjected. "Wait! What do you people try to say? That Oleg is eidolon? He cannot be. If he was, Dostoevsky would know." He turned to the captain.

Dostoevsky was staring at the ground. When Viktor faced him, he lifted his head to match Viktor's gaze. Even with his face hidden by his fulcrum's helmet, his body language said more than words could.

Viktor gasped.

Oleg looked squarely at Becan, his caught-off-guard gape melting away. The glare that replaced it was brazen and clear.

Simultaneously, Max and David lifted their assault rifles.

Oleg shook his head. "You do not know the mistake you just made, Irishman."

"Save it for Thoor," Becan said. "I assume you know him fairly well."

"Yuri, you knew this?" Max shouted at Dostoevsky. "You trashin' *knew* this?"

Dostoevsky had nothing to say.

"All this time, Strakhov," Becan said, "you were here. Sleepin' in our room. Seein' wha' we were abou'."

"McCrae..." Dostoevsky said lowly.

"It was to get Remmy, wasn't it? It was to make sure he did wha' yeh wanted? Everythin' you told us in the lounge, abou' the Murder Rule an' how yeh heard abou' it from a Nightman in the First. Tha' was all part o' the script."

"McCrae, stop."

Max suddenly turned. He no longer aimed his weapon at Oleg, but had Dostoevsky alone in his sights.

The fulcrum began to speak, but Max cut him off.

"I don't wanna hear it, Yuri. You've been let off the hook long enough. I don't care if you didn't kill Nicole. I don't care if you had nothing to do with Oleg. You still knew. You trashing *knew*."

Dostoevsky raised his hands in defense. "Max, you must understand..."

"Shut the hell up."

Oleg's glare stayed solely on Becan. "The repercussions you face cannot be imagined."

The Irishman ignored his threat. "Did yeh murder Clarke, too? Were yeh clearin' the ranks for your good mucker Yuri?"

"I swear upon the throne of God, I will be the last voice you hear."

"Bite the back o' me bollocks—you're exposed. An' we're goin' to tell every man, woman, an' *Nightman* who you really are."

Dostoevsky interjected again. "There could not be a worse time to discuss this." He looked at Max. "We are on our way to a fallen Vulture. There may be lives at stake."

"Yeah, 'cos I'm sure yeh care abou' *tha'*."

"The captain is right," said Varvara. "This is terrible timing. There is a ship, maybe with injured!"

Becan's aim never wavered. "Drop your weapons, Strakhov, if tha's even your real name."

Oleg let go of his assault rifle. He relinquished his pistol as well.

"Now step away."

The eidolon complied.

"Dave?"

David crept forward to claim the abandoned guns.

"Lose the helmet an' armor," Becan said.

Oleg scowled. "You have already made your point."

Becan's finger tightened against the trigger.

The eidolon cursed and removed his helmet. After a minute of unfastening, his armor was discarded on the ground. His insulated clothing was all that remained.

"Give me a reason not to waste yeh righ' here."

"Becan…" David said.

The Irishman's glare remained fixed. "There's nothin' I'd love more than to watch your brain hit the snow. Yours, then *his*." He motioned to Dostoevsky.

"Becan, *don't*."

"Yeh set all o' this up, Oleg. Yeh came to screw everythin' up, you bleedin' hoor's melt."

David's voice grew more stern. "If you do this, you'll be just like them."

"This isn't murder, Dave. It's capital punishment."

"I'll take Oleg. I'll watch him at gunpoint. There's nothing he can do."

Becan hesitated as the others observed.

"Don't become one of them."

The Irishman lowered his gun. "If he sneezes, take off his head."

Oleg turned his glare on David.

Dostoevsky spoke again. "Everyone please listen. This was terrible time for this to happen, but it has already been done. We must continue with the mission. We will take Oleg with us, without weapons." He looked at the eidolon. "He will not cause a problem."

David's aim remained true.

"We have not seen Bakma so far," continued Dostoevsky. "If we are lucky, there will be none. Let us get to the crash site and help as many as we can. Afterward, we will deal with this. All right?" No one answered. "All right?"

It was Becan who broke the stalemate. "Righ'," he said dryly. "Well, lead the way."

Back in the forest, Scott and his team pressed on. At the rate they were moving, they wouldn't get to the transport for thirty more minutes, but he didn't care if it took thirty hours. The Bakma were calculating, and the more he thought about Esther's idea that this was a hostage situation, the more he realized she was likely right.

The transport was within ninety meters, but still nothing could be seen. Only trees and snow covered the landscape.

Casting a sidelong look at the slayers, Scott continued ahead. Eighty meters. Several clearings loomed in the distance, but not to their visual advantage. He scrutinized them just in case, not only looking for Bakma but for any sign of a Noboat. Spatial discrepancies, noteworthy voids of snowfall—anything that could have been a dematerialized ship.

Alien technology was difficult to grasp. Bakma plasma weapons, though generally understood, were troublesome to dissect. Ceratopian neutron blasters were hardly neutron at all—the media simply took that one word and ran. They were more like ballistic reverse-gravity guns. Across the board, from weaponry to armor to mass-defying propulsion systems, alien tech was a mysterious realm.

But nothing was more puzzling than the Bakma Noboat. Nothing about their chameleon ability was understood; in fact, most things appeared contradictory. When they disappeared, they literally disappeared. From visual clues to radar detection, it was as though they ceased to exist. Yet they were there. Even when invisible, they possessed a kind of energy that affected the physical world, enough to be noticed if one looked hard enough. They were there, but they weren't.

It all came down to one thing. In the engine room of every Noboat sat a massive pillar of pure, colorless quartz. No other alien vessel contained one. It was the crux of chameleon technology, but the science behind it was unknown. When a Noboat was shot down the crystal was always the first thing to go, and none had ever been recovered, nor had one been witnessed in use.

But at the moment, none of it mattered.

The crash site was within seventy meters. Instinctively slowing his forward progress, Scott went through a mental checklist. He had several grenades on his belt, his sidearm was ready, and he was prepared for close combat. No Bakma had ever been seen with suits of chameleon-based armor, but he was prepared for that just in case. He was ready for anything.

Sixty meters. His fingers twitched. Though his body was warm from his heaters, he could sense the cold all around.

Within fifty, Egor stopped. Scott caught the abrupt pause in his peripherals. "Commander," the slayer whispered through the comm.

Scott motioned the others to halt.

"The crash site. It is through the trees."

Scott zoomed in again, but he couldn't make out anything. Egor must have had the best angle. "I don't see it yet. Anyone else?" No one replied. "Egor, tell me *exactly* what you see."

"I am too far to make out details, but I can see the Vulture on the surface."

"Did it dig into the ground?"

"I do not think so, commander. I think it is mostly exposed. But I cannot see much."

They would have to move closer. Scott was silent as he took in the woods. *Where are you?* The Bakma were out there somewhere—he knew it. His hand slid to his comm. "We've made visual contact with the transport." That is, one of them had. "Travis, has anything been detected above the site?"

"Negative, sir. Air chatter's been nonexistent. They're just circling around."

"Esther, what do you see?"

"I'm a hundred meters east-southeast from your location. I've seen nothing yet, sir. There's too much tree cover, but I am pressing forwards."

"No signs of Noboat activity?"

"None yet."

"Keep in touch."

"Scott," said Svetlana behind him, "if there *are* wounded, we must reach them soon."

He resisted the urge to argue. She wasn't telling him to hurry, she was just stating the facts. There was a fine line between speed and caution, and they were barely maintaining their balance. He adjusted his comm's frequency. "Captain Gabriel, this is Commander Remington of the Fourteenth contacting Pelican Squad. We have attained a visual on your location. If you copy this transmission, please respond." There was nothing.

He repeated his request. "Captain Gabriel, this is Commander Remington of the Fourteenth. We are approaching from the—"

He stopped. A chill ran down his spine. He let go of his comm. *Don't tell them what direction we're approaching from. Don't even comm them again.* He gripped his assault rifle harder.

"Scott, what is it, man?" whispered William.

Something was wrong—it was like a pricking at the back of his brain. His instincts were warning him. Slowly he pressed on. When he reached the thirty-meter mark, he finally saw the Pelican Squad transport. It had crashed nose-down in the snow, but it wasn't a wreck. On the contrary, it looked like a decent landing, considering the circumstances. "Has anyone detected *anything* else yet?"

"No, commander."

"Nothing, man."

Scott scanned the area again. "Esther, do you see anything?"

"I see the crash site as well, but nothing else."

Scott grimaced. "Exercise extreme caution. Watch everything." He put emphasis on every word.

Twenty-five meters. He could now see the craft well. They were approaching on a straight intercept course for the ship's rear bay door. It was fully closed, and he wondered if it had power at all.

Looking to his right, he scrutinized Egor. The slayer's vicinity looked clear. Panning to the left, he gave the same look to Nicolai and Auric. They looked clear, too, if not faintly distorted from Scott's angle. He turned back ahead.

Then he froze.

Nicolai and Auric were faintly distorted. Slowly, Scott looked back to the left. The slayers came to view, but their forms weren't entirely clear. There was a contour line cutting straight through their abdomens. There was a faint shimmer by their heads. Lowering his eyes, Scott saw the indentation in the snow—right between him and his slayers. It stretched behind and ahead, barely visible, but there. "Everyone, freeze."

A Noboat. They'd wandered right past it from both sides—it had been between them the entire time. He saw Auric turn to face him. *If it's a trap, don't let on that we know.* "Auric, keep looking ahead. Everyone, look like you're scanning the area." Scott moved his own head in mock survey. "Nobody act on what I'm about to tell you. Act oblivious." The last thing he wanted to do was trigger an attack. "There is a Noboat between Romanov, Broll, and myself. If you react to it, the Bakma inside may attack. They are aware of our position." They had to be. By this point, there was no doubt.

"Commander," said Egor, "I see another one ten meters to the southwest." He growled in frustration. "*Now* it is obvious."

That was the infuriating aspect of Noboats. They were notoriously hard to find until they popped up out of nowhere. It was as if the brain had to be convinced they were real.

There are two Noboats. That's at least fifty warriors. We could easily already be dead. He looked at the crashed transport. *They want us to go*

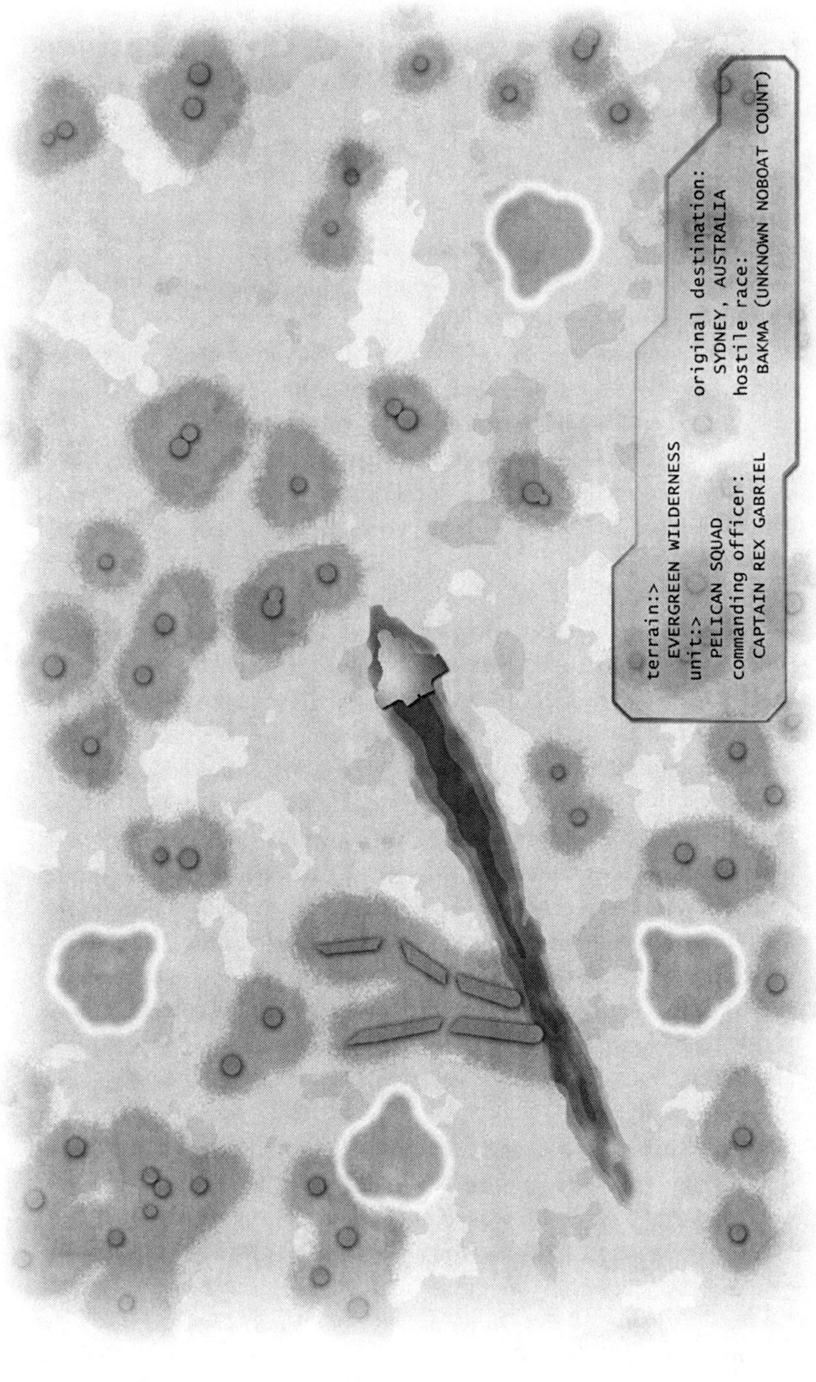
terrain:>
EVERGREEN WILDERNESS
unit:>
PELICAN SQUAD
commanding officer:
CAPTAIN REX GABRIEL
original destination:
SYDNEY, AUSTRALIA
hostile race:
BAKMA (UNKNOWN NOBOAT COUNT)

to the ship. That's what they're waiting for. It's unfolding just as Esther said. They're probably wondering why we've stopped our progression.

Scott adjusted his comm once again for Pelican Squad. He had a theory to test, and a strong suspicion that this time he'd get a reply.

"This is Commander Remington of the Fourteenth, contacting Captain Gabriel. We are twenty-five meters from your position." It didn't matter now if he revealed where they were. The Bakma already knew. "We have come across *no* Bakma activity. We will not proceed farther until you confirm that you're receiving our transmissions. We do not wish to be fired upon." It was a bogus concern.

It took almost ten seconds, but Gabriel answered. "This is Rex Gabriel of the Pelican. We have received your transmission. Please continue your approach."

Now Scott knew that Esther had been absolutely right. Pelican Squad was playing into the trap. Scott had been using the same comm frequency, so there was no reason why Gabriel wouldn't have responded until then. It was all becoming clear.

"I copy, Captain Gabriel," Scott said. "Stand by, and we'll resume our approach shortly." He closed the channel before Gabriel could respond, readjusting his comm to include both the Fourteenth and the Vindicators above.

"This is Commander Remington with an urgent transmission. We are walking into an *untriggered* ambush. We have identified two Noboats on the ground, one within meters of our position."

"*Meters?*" asked Travis, surprised.

Scott continued. "I have reason to suspect that there are Bakma inside the Vulture. If we react outwardly to that suspicion, we may trigger an attack." They could never fight off fifty Bakma, but the Bakma didn't want them dead. If they did, they would have killed them already. "Vindicator flight, are you receiving this?"

"Affirmative, Commander Remington."

It was obvious why the Noboats hadn't been discovered from the air. They'd landed carefully, without damaging the trees. "I am sending you coordinates for the location of the two Noboats." He relayed the positions. "On my mark, engage from above. Make no indication of your awareness until then. You may not hear from me for several minutes—or longer. *Only* if the exterior situation shows open volatility do I request you to fire without my consent."

The pilots affirmed.

"Travis, get airborne. Tighten your orbit around our location, but do not intrude. Be prepared for swift evacuation."

"Yes sir."

"We'll continue our approach until we reach the transport. We have made contact with Captain Gabriel. They've kept us alive for a reason, and I want to find out what it is."

Dostoevsky's voice cut through the comm. "We have reached the other crashed Vulture, Remington. There are no Bakma here. We have one survivor."

"Commander," Esther said through the comm, "I now count *four* Noboats in the area."

Scott's stomach lurched.

"Three are clustered closer to you," she went on. "The fourth is by itself, directly in front of me—I'm coming towards you from the opposite direction."

Esther had circled all the way around. She'd traveled ten times farther than Scott and his crew.

She sighed through the channel. "I'm sorry, sir. I should have spotted them sooner."

Though she couldn't see it, Scott shook his head. "You were right on the money, Esther. This one's on me." He was sure there were smarter approaches he could have taken to the situation, but now they had to press on. "Continuing onward."

They were being lured in by the Bakma. But it was the Fourteenth, not the Bakma, who had the advantage. They had the advantage because they were walking to a trap completely aware, with a flight of Vindicators ready to pounce.

Scott continued to speak to Esther. "Relay the coordinates of all four Noboats to the Vindicators."

"Yes, sir."

Over the past several days, the question had been lingering in Scott's mind: who was he really? He was irritated at Captain Gabriel and his crew—had Scott been threatened as a hostage, he'd have replied with resistance. But more than irritation toward Pelican Squad, he felt outright anger at the Bakma. He was angry at their invisible arrogance. Scott and anger didn't mix well.

He focused on the Vulture's bay door. They were now within meters of the ship's hull. Nicolai, Auric, and Egor closed in behind him; Svetlana and William hung back.

"I don't know who's through this door," Scott said, "but they have *no* idea who we are. Let them think they have us outdone. They think they're in control, so let them be. When I give the word, take control back."

The Nightmen affirmed.

"Commander," said Esther through the comm, "I'm ready to move in."

Scott placed his rifle in the prone position. "Remington to Gabriel—you can open the door."

27

FRIDAY, NOVEMBER 18TH, 0011 NE
1311 HOURS

AS SOON AS the Vulture's bay door lowered, the reality of the situation became clear. Captain Gabriel was kneeling on the floor of the transport, moppy blond hair shrouding his eyes. A plasma rifle was pointed at the back of his neck. He was a hostage.

But that had been expected.

Four Bakma crowded the troop bay, their plasma rifles aimed at Scott and his teammates. Two Ithini were there, as well. The aliens were in control.

But that had been expected.

Blood was splattered on the walls. Several EDEN corpses were piled in the corner. They'd either died in the crash or been killed by the Bakma.

That had been expected, as well.

It was what Scott realized next that he *hadn't* expected—that caught him completely off guard. Captain Gabriel was the only live human there. There were no other EDEN soldiers in the ship besides the captain and the handful of corpses. The six aliens outnumbered the Pelicans, both dead and alive.

"I'm sorry, mate," Gabriel said. "There was nothing I could do."

Assault rifle raised, Scott spoke through his mechanized helmet. "Captain, where is your crew?"

"They're on one of the Noboats, I have no idea why or which one. They were taken as soon as we crashed."

Scott's veins burned with anger. He'd just ordered an airborne assault on the grounded Bakma ships. On his mark, Vindicators would fire. He'd inadvertently given them the order to attack Pelican's captives inside the Noboats.

The Bakma behind Gabriel spat, *"Ta-gash resh. Nakassa tu`shaeck."* It shoved the captain in the back of the head.

Gabriel winced. "They want you to come in and close the door."

"You speak Bakmanese?" Scott asked.

"No."

"Then how do you know that's what they want?"

Scott felt it right then—the moment he posed Gabriel the question. It almost felt physical, but it wasn't. It was almost like a jolt of the mind. He looked at the Ithini to Gabriel's right. Its eyes were slowly widening. That feeling, that mental prod—it was from the alien. "What did you just do?" Scott asked the Ithini. "Did you just do that?"

"Jubeea iche'raal, potaeka."

What happened next defied all Scott's logic. He knew what the Ithini was saying. He didn't understand the alien language, but he knew what the words meant. The aliens wanted him to come inside. If he complied, no one would be killed.

Ithini were the only species known to be telepathic. They could connect with others via the mind. Scott knew in that moment that he was connected. It was the first time it'd ever happened to him.

"What's he telling you, mate?" Gabriel asked.

Scott's mind went numb. It felt used in a way that made him feel nauseated.

The Ithini spoke once again.

"They want us all to come inside," Scott said. "If we do that, nobody dies." He was simply repeating what he felt in his mind. He began to feel lightheaded, but not to the point where he couldn't negotiate. "No," he said to the Ithini. "I will come inside, alone. My teammates will be allowed to leave."

"Scott!" Svetlana whispered behind him.

The Ithini opened its mouth, but Scott held up his hand. "You're on my planet, you play by my rules. We can compromise or we can get nowhere. It's all up to you." The Ithini angled its head oddly at Scott, then Scott felt their connection sever. His nausea subsided.

The Bakma behind Gabriel looked at the Ithini. It was a slender Bakma, but it wore the insignia of a ranked officer. Its black and brown armor bore various designs. But was it in charge, or were the Ithini? As thoughts of the Ithini Control Theory flashed through Scott's mind, the two aliens began to converse.

"Rashae mu'addma. Kon'ribilsib," the Ithini said.

The Bakma's face contorted in anger. Roaring, it grabbed the Ithini by the head and flung it straight back. Scott jumped as the frail alien crashed against the wall.

He realized it right then and there. The Ithini weren't in control at all. They weren't even on equal ground.

The Bakma leader turned to the second Ithini, a somewhat smaller one, and barked out several words.

Scott felt the prick again in his mind, and the sickening sensation returned. He was connected again—but it wasn't an Ithini that spoke to him now.

"You will not advance," said the Bakma. The words were in Bakmanese, yet Scott understood them in his head. It was as if the alien was speaking in English. "Any attempt at coercion will end in death."

Scott's eyes opened wide. The Ithini hadn't connected itself to him; instead, it had connected him to the Bakma. The lightheaded feeling swelled and grew stronger. *What do I do? Do I just speak?* "What do you want?" Scott asked.

"You are unlike the warriors called EDEN."

The Bakma was referring to the Nightmen. To hear the Bakma refer to human military factions was...strange.

"We are to bring you to Khuldaris, where you will be evaluated. *Tu'hessa lach th'en...*"

The alien's words trailed into gibberish in Scott's head. Scott felt his nausea dig deeper as his stomach convulsed. He felt pulled to the ceiling, despite the fact that his feet were grounded. His understanding of the Bakma phased in and out.

"Daash Khuladi l'gnassa ju-kelaas vasch Golathochs' interference. *Tu' will horissa rassha tul-nok salassa. Tu'vich kava* indication *esh* allegiance, *tuush-nae'cennas lae* judgment."

He couldn't make everything out. The Bakma's words, they began to turn garbled. They wanted Scott go to with them. Or maybe they wanted all of the Nightmen. Gathering his endurance, Scott fought through the urge to vomit. "Release Gabriel's men first, and the four of us will go with you." Behind him, the other Nightmen held their stance.

The Bakma cocked its head. It didn't understand.

"Release Gabriel's men first, and the four of us will go with you," Scott repeated. His head felt dizzy. The walls of the transport began to fisheye. The world seemed to lean to the right.

The Bakma's eyes widened as he began to understand. "Acceptable." The connection broke off.

Scott stumbled forward and dropped his assault rifle. The Bakma flinched but didn't fire, even as Svetlana dashed to his side.

He pulled off his helmet and threw up involuntarily. His head spun and his stomach was upside down. His eyes watered and his breath heaved in short gasps, natural reactions to vomiting.

Svetlana grasped him by the shoulders. "Scott, what are you doing? What have you agreed to?"

I've agreed to nothing, he thought as he wiped his mouth and put his helmet back on. He had no intention of going anywhere with the Bakma. This was a way to get Gabriel's men out of whatever Noboat they were in—at least long enough for the Vindicators to strike. But he couldn't say that out loud.

In front of them, the Bakma pushed Gabriel forward. The Australian stumbled out of the ship. As soon as he caught his footing, he turned around to Scott. "Mate…"

"Go," Scott said, reaching up to clutch Svetlana's hand. He needed to steady himself. "Get them and go."

"Scott, please—" Svetlana said.

Subtly, Scott adjusted his comm, in a way that made it appear he was cradling his head. Then he whispered in a barely audible voice, "Tell the Vindicators to prepare for my mark."

"Yes sir," Esther replied.

Nicolai edged closer to Scott. "Commander, what is going on?"

"Be ready," Scott said lowly.

The Bakma raised a device to its mouth—the alien equivalent of a comm. *"Olassi daal ve`cha."* Affirmation came a moment later, and the leader stepped forward. Grabbing Scott by the collar, the Bakma pulled him up.

The fact that Scott had just negotiated with extraterrestrials hadn't hit him yet. Too much else demanded his immediate concern, from Pelican Squad to his own teammates. His stomach was returning to normal.

The Bakma shoved Scott forward, and he stumbled out of the Vulture. He scanned the area where the hidden Noboats resided, but he couldn't locate them.

Suddenly an odd shimmer sparked in the air, as if electricity were surging through glass. The Noboat faded into existence before him.

It was the first time Scott had seen a functional Noboat up close. The only ones he'd encountered before were always damaged and torn as a result of Vindicator interceptions. This one was not.

They were actually fairly sleek vessels, considering their size, with ray-like wings and hulls that almost resembled New Era shuttles. Dual plasma cannons were mounted beneath their forward hulls, and the rear engine resembled the grill of a car. They were fittingly dark gray.

The Noboat's side door opened, and the remnants of Pelican Squad were shoved out. They stumbled to the ground as the Bakma kept them in check.

The Bakma in the Vulture reached out for Nicolai, Auric, and Egor. The three slayers raised their hands to protest, but a sharp word from Scott forced them to comply. They were confused. Nightmen and surrender didn't mesh. They didn't realize what Scott had in mind, but they'd understand soon. The moment Scott's offensive presented itself, the Nightmen would go with it—they always did.

He surveyed the battered operatives of Pelican Squad. He could make out roughly ten of them, but he didn't have time for an exact head count. Svetlana began tending to them, while William watched her from the side.

Take care of her, Harbinger.

The Vindicators were waiting for the order to strike. They knew the locations of the Noboats; they'd fire at once.

The timing had to be perfect. Pelican Squad was headed away from their Noboat, and Scott and his slayers were heading toward it. He couldn't order the aerial assault until they all had some measure of distance, or they'd get consumed in the explosion themselves.

Scott slowed his pace as the Pelican Squadders were escorted away. When the Bakma behind Scott pushed him forward, he fell purposely into the snow. *Stall for time. Take a second or two to stand up again.*

"Nivaash!" the Bakma ordered. *"Tu`etakka."* The alien grabbed him and pulled him to his feet.

It was almost the right time. Scott was still a touch lightheaded, but not enough to stop his combat instincts from kicking in.

We can take them down quickly in the wake of the explosion. They won't know what hit them. We'll hit the ones behind us, then focus on the survivors of the Noboat strikes.

Svetlana was leading Pelican Squad to the forest, but she kept looking back—looking at him. She was doing what he'd told her to do. She had no idea this was a plan.

Once again, the Bakma pushed Scott. Once again, he fell on purpose. Looking up from the ground, he watched the Pelican Squad prisoners. They were far enough away. So were the Nightmen. The Bakma suspected nothing. It was time.

"Mark," he said into his comm, neither loudly nor forcefully. The Bakma behind him waited impatiently.

Scott placed his palms on the ground. His knees were already bent from the shove. He lowered his head.

"Nivaash," the Bakma said. *"Nivaash!"*

Scott didn't rise up or acknowledge. He only waited for the blast.

"Nivaash!"

Then they heard it. It was faint—barely a sound at all, like fleeting whispers of wind. The Bakma looked up.

The first missile struck the farthest Noboat. The next was struck a half-second later. As the fiery booms shook the earth, the Bakma leapt back. When the nearest Noboat was bombarded, Scott was blown back violently through the air. His helmet blew off, as did several pieces of his armor. A deafening ring replaced the sounds of the world.

He hit the ground like it was made of concrete, rolling several times before hitting the Vulture's ramp. There was blood on his face and his hands and his skin burned. He'd been too close to the nearest Noboat. He'd been caught in the blast. As dirt and snow rained on his head, the ringing subsided to gunfire. He shook his head and looked up.

The gunfire was coming from the slayers. They were farther away than he'd been to the alien ships. The blasts hadn't blown them away. They'd taken to the offensive with their own weapons—just as he'd hoped. He pushed up to his feet.

Then it hit him.

The butt of a plasma rifle slammed him right in the face. He felt his cheekbone tremble as his vision blurred, and he landed flat on his back. The next thing he saw was a Bakma towering over him. The alien aimed its plasma gun at Scott's chest.

Scott had never moved faster in his life. He rolled frantically to the side just fast enough to avoid a direct hit. He could feel the heat from the alien weapon, and his vision flashed white. He felt his back burn.

Then Auric appeared. The German slayer dove at the Bakma from behind, knocking it forward into the snow. Scott scrambled to his feet.

The moment the missiles struck, Esther sprung into action. She made a beeline for the fourth Noboat—the lone vessel nearest to her. It had been left alone in the Vindicator attack. "This is Private Brooking to all Vindicators. Do not engage the easternmost Noboat. I repeat, do *not* engage the easternmost Noboat. It's too close to Pelican Squad's Vulture. I am attempting to infiltrate and deactivate."

The Noboat materialized just as Esther leapt against it from the side opposite the battle. Grabbing hold of the side of the vessel, she climbed nimbly to the ship's roof, making her way to the stern section. Readying her pistol in one hand, she used the other to steady herself. She dashed above an obscure impression in the middle of the ship's aft. It wasn't a hatch but a weapons panel where an optional third plasma cannon could have been mounted. But just like a hatch, it could be opened.

Manipulating several of the exterior controls, she leaned back as the panel slid away. She slid through the hole into the maintenance shaft within.

As soon as Gabriel's crew was safely escorted away, William readied his hand cannon. "I'm goin' back."

Gabriel was quick to speak up. "I'm coming, too. Who else is able to fight?" He looked at his squad. Several of the lesser injured stepped forward.

"Go," said Svetlana. "Hurry and help them!"

Scott retrieved his pistol from the ground as Auric and the Bakma wrestled. He could feel scorch marks and burnt flesh all over his body—even on his face. But adrenaline held off the pain.

Something caught Scott's eye out of his peripherals. The fourth Noboat had materialized. Bakma were pouring from its doors. "They're coming from the far one!" he yelled. His face hurt the moment his jaw moved. He forced the pain aside and turned to help Auric. Several gunshots later, the Bakma attacker was dead. The German hurried to his feet.

Dashing into the Vulture, Scott grabbed his previously abandoned assault rifle, immediately gunning down the two Ithini. They'd already invaded his mind twice—that was enough.

From the smoldering wreckages of the other three alien ships, wounded and burned Bakma screamed in agony.

Auric almost ran into Scott when the latter emerged from the Vulture. Nicolai and Egor were not far behind as a barrage of plasma poured from the fourth Noboat. The four men took cover inside the Vulture.

"Commander," Egor said, his eyes widening as he looked at Scott's face. "You do not look very good!"

Scott didn't have time to be concerned. "Meet them head on. Gun for their leaders. Don't let that Noboat lift off." The transport's hull shook with plasma blasts. "Go!"

Bursting from the transport, the four Nightmen turned the corner into the open, firing furiously. That was the difference between EDEN and the Nightmen—four Nightmen could make such a charge, something EDEN could never hope to do.

As they dodged, they fired. As they fired, they acquired new targets. As they acquired new targets, they aggressively pressed on. Plasma bolts neared them and occasionally scraped them, but never hit them dead on. The Nightmen knew how to anticipate. They knew how to get the jump on tactical instinct; they were collectively three steps ahead. They weren't special forces—they were killing machines.

New voices emerged from behind. Scott glanced back, where William and Gabriel ran in tandem. A half dozen others were with them. They fired everything from assault rifles to plasma rifles—whatever they could find on the ground. Pelican Squad was coming to help.

Bakma were plowed down as the tide of momentum reversed. The aliens had anticipated everything but the skill of the Nightmen. Now they realized their mistake, but it was too late. Aliens no longer poured from the vessel, they struggled to escape back into it. Blood spewed as the melee continued until the Nightmen reached the Noboat's main door.

"Bridge! Corridor!" Scott ordered. His words, though brief, had meaning. Nicolai and Auric—paired together since the beginning—would storm the bridge. Scott and Egor would storm the hallway.

Esther's voice emerged over the airwaves. "Ship drive deactivated!"

Scott blinked in the midst of his assault. Surely she didn't mean inside that very Noboat. That would have been impossible. How would she have gotten inside?

When Scott reached the hallway with Egor, he could hear the sound of a lone pistol in the engine room. Esther *was* there.

Scott rolled forward as plasma fire followed him. Egor crouched and fired from behind. By the time Scott was on his knees, Egor had slain two Bakma and raced into the living quarters of the ship.

"Living area clear," he said moments later.

Scott had to get to Esther. Noboat engine rooms were large, but cramped. The quartz crystal occupied the center of the room, with machinery taking up the remainder of the space. The many pipes, devices, and control panels formed snaking, narrow corridors.

The moment he entered the engine room, he saw her. She was firing her pistol desperately at a pair of Bakma farther in the room. A plasma bolt skimmed past her head, and she screamed.

Her vision flashed white, Scott thought. Diving over her, he shielded her body then pulled her behind cover.

Esther blinked hard several times.

Scott knew he was still good on ammunition. He also knew the two Bakma were scared. They'd have to be—their Noboat was being captured. An idea popped into his head. Readying his assault rifle, he screamed aloud. *"Grrashna?"*

"Grrashna!" the Bakma complied.

They were agreeing to surrender. They'd been defeated, and they valued their lives. They were giving up the fight. That was all Scott wanted them to do.

Rising suddenly from behind their cover, Scott swiveled his assault rifle to fire. The two Bakma came into view. *Die, you dreggs.* He pressed in the trigger.

Then she hit him. "Scott, no!" Esther's body collided against his, and his aim was thrown off. A staccato of bullets tattered against the ceiling and wall. The Bakma covered their heads.

Scott released the trigger and the room suddenly went silent. As Egor and Auric turned the corner into the engine room, Scott's focus shifted solely to Esther.

Her eyes were wide open. She wore a mixture of compassion and shock, the former for the state of his mind, the latter for what could only be the state of his face. She addressed him through both emotions. "Please don't."

Don't kill the Bakma. She was stopping him from killing the Bakma—Bakma who'd willingly surrendered because he'd made them say *grrashna*.

All at once it hit him. *I almost did it. I almost cut them down, right then and there. I almost became a monster again.* He'd just saved Pelican Squad. He'd just overcome a Bakma ambush and captured a fully functional Noboat. Yet still the rage was inside him. It had almost overwhelmed all the good he had done.

"Commander," said Nicolai from the doorway. "The Noboat is clear."

Esther stifled a horrified tear. She was still looking at his face.

Auric cleared his throat. "Most of the Bakma have surrendered—"

"Then take them into custody, you noodle!" Esther screamed. She looked back at Scott, but he was already walking out of the room. He didn't look at her again.

When Scott emerged outdoors, Captain Gabriel was standing with his men. The moment the Australian saw him, his mouth fell.

"Scott!" said Svetlana, running his way. She'd returned to the battle scene, too. "Are you okay?" The moment she saw his face, her eyes flashed with an urgent new fear.

"Is everyone safe?" Scott asked. As he said it, he registered his body's pain for the first time. He cringed, stumbled forward, and fell.

The ground was not all that hit him. Something was in his head. His nausea and dizziness returned.

Something is wrong.

Svetlana pulled off her helmet and knelt. "Let me see you!"

His palms were burnt badly, and the rest of his body felt the same. But nothing hurt as bad as his face.

Svetlana opened her medical kit. "Tell me what happened."

He felt around his eye. He'd been hit with the butt of a plasma rifle—he'd almost forgotten. That was when his cheekbone had trembled. The area around his eye was already swollen. He felt dizzy. "I'm fine," he lied.

"You are *not* fine!"

She smeared something slimy and cold into his face. He winced and shrunk back.

"Stop moving," she said, grabbing his arm. "This is cold gel. It will stop the swelling in your cheek."

It felt colder than ice, and wet and disgusting. He clenched his teeth hard.

No sooner had she finished with the cold gel, she coated his forehead with another gel pack.

"I'm not hurt there," Scott said. The dizziness was becoming worse. He felt as though he was being connected with an alien, except to a much deeper extent. He felt as though he was beginning to float.

"You are burnt," she said calmly, taking another handful of the gel and rubbing it on his arms. "This is burn gel. You need a lot of gels."

Gabriel watched from above. "Is there anything I can do?"

Svetlana looked at him. "Contact our Vulture—it is called the *Pariah*. Tell the pilot to land over here." Gabriel acknowledged and moved away.

Svetlana glared at Scott. "That was stupid, Scott. That was *stupid*. You should not have done what you did."

Stupid? Saving Captain Gabriel had been stupid? Capturing a fully functional Noboat was stupid? Scott disagreed. Lightheadedness struck him again, coming in waves, each one subsequently worse than the last. He began to lose awareness.

"You have to be careful..."

He eyes started to roll back. His brain throbbed uncontrollably.

The next thing he felt was her hand cradling his head. When she spoke now, her voice was less scolding. It was soft and compassionate. "I know what you are feeling...do not be afraid. It is normal." She ran her fingers over his hair. "When you awaken, I will be there for you. I will greet you with a smile."

He wasn't hearing her words. His mind had disassociated from everything around him.

Scott fell asleep right there on the battlefield. Svetlana held him long after the healing gels had been applied. She held him long after the operatives began to disperse.

Until the *Pariah* came to take them away.

28

FRIDAY, NOVEMBER 18TH, 0011 NE
1155 HOURS

EDEN COMMAND

ARCHER WAS SITTING at his desk when someone knocked on his door. He answered immediately. "Come in."

"I can't."

The British judge looked up and sighed. Rising from his chair, he crossed the room and opened the door from inside. Every judge's suite had its own security system. Doors could only be opened two ways: by an eye scanner or from whoever was already in the room. Of all the policies, protocols, and assignments in EDEN Command, it was the one thing Archer could never remember.

The Canadian Judge Rath was waiting in the hall. "The door."

"I know. I bloody know." Archer motioned him in.

Rath scowled. "I've been trying to talk to you for days while you've been gallivanting with Torokin. Are you trying to recruit him, *too*?"

"I'm getting him off our back. He's as ignorant as he is obnoxious, but that doesn't mean he isn't a threat. I have not come this far to have an ex-Vector mess it all up."

"What did you tell him after the meeting? Was it the truth?"

"It was my truth. Not *the* truth. They're close, but they're not the same."

"That you spoke to him at all is risky enough."

"Speaking of Vectors," said Archer, deflecting the subject, "I can't talk to you for long. I have a conference call with Hutchin and Faerber in a few minutes."

"Hutchin and *Faerber*?"

"In regards to placing his son."

The Canadian judge sat at Archer's table. "I'm surprised he's not going to *Berlin*."

"Klaus doesn't want him to. He wants him out of the battlefront—he's a very smart man."

"Hutchin is a weasel."

Archer didn't smile. "Brief or not, we have business."

Pulling a sprig from his pocket, Rath flicked his wrist. The sprig glowed to life. "Unscented," he said, sliding it through his lips.

Archer watched the vapors for a moment, then sat down. "Malcolm spoke to Carol."

Rath raised an eyebrow.

"She understands."

"I knew she would."

Archer leaned back, crossing his legs. "She gave me a name for our chief of security: Hector Mendoza. Have you heard of him?"

"Yes, I have. He's someone I'd have never thought of."

"She says he's approachable."

"He's pure scum. And yes, very approachable."

"He'll be here by the end of the month. Inform Willoughby of his imminent transfer. Send him to *Sydney*." Archer's posture stiffened. "Tell me something about *Novosibirsk*."

Rath frowned. "Uzochi found out how they're getting their supplies. There's no money trail because there's no money. They get supplied from small towns and businesses, in exchange for 'police' protection. They have third party forges all over Russia. They run it like the mob."

"A Nightman police force," said Archer. "That's a crime deterrent if I've ever heard of one. Add it to the list of charges."

"I still fail to understand why *Novosibirsk* is so important."

Archer squared his shoulders. "Because the Nightmen breed resistance. Resistance is contagious. I'm curing a pandemic before it begins."

"You do realize that after Europe, *Novosibirsk* won't be the Council's priority?"

"Yes, I do. Europe was awful and ill-timed. But that doesn't matter. The Machine is an obstacle that must be removed." He examined his fingernails. "Pauling will not have the stomach to challenge Thoor. We shall wait until he retires if we must. According to Nharassel, we have two years."

"Two years? What else did he tell you?"

The Briton hesitated for a moment. "Some small bits of interest, but there's a lot more he's *not* telling me. I'm not sure he's aware of how much I know."

"And how much do you know?"

Silence fell between them. As sprig vapors drifted through the room, the only sounds were of the ticking clock and air conditioning.

Finally Archer spoke. "I know time is critical. The Golathoch are sensing urgency and fear. I know no other species will get involved, at the risk of being next on the list." He looked at Rath steadily. "And I know those points are moot if we don't find H`laar."

At the mention of that name, Rath sighed.

"He isn't at *Novosibirsk*," Archer continued. "Wherever he is, he's priority number one, even above Thoor. We are so close. Let us tie up these loose ends. Then all will come."

Rath scratched his head and leaned back. His hazel eyes rested on Archer. "I'll keep looking. We'll find him."

"We must."

The Canadian stood up to leave.

"Malcolm and Carol will be returning shortly," Archer said as Rath crossed the room. "I'll see you again soon enough."

"Right." Rath left, shutting the door carefully behind him.

Once again, Archer's suite fell into silence. The faint clouds of sprig vapor disappeared, and his eyes drifted to his wall clock. His conference call was one minute late, but that didn't matter. For some things, timing was of the utmost importance, but the call wasn't one of them.

Reaching to the conference comm in the middle of his table, Archer input several numbers. After a series of rings, a man answered.

"Hutchin."

"Hello, general, it's Benjamin Archer."

"Ah, yes, judge! How are you tonight?"

"Oh, is it night?" Archer asked, the corners of his lips curving up. "Over here, we're never quite sure."

* * *

NOVOSIBIRSK, RUSSIA

AT THE SAME TIME

JUDGES BLAKE and June crossed the hangar. Their transport, a Vulture from EDEN Command, was ready to take them back home.

The afternoon cold was relentless. Snow covered the landscape in all directions; the airstrip was one of the few areas kept bare. Both judges were dressed in thick overcoats, earmuffs, and gloves. Even so, they shivered.

Blake and June were about to board when a shout stopped them, and they both turned.

It was a Nightman sentry. He was trotting toward them as fast as his armor would allow. He stopped several meters from the ship. "Judges, General Thoor requests an audience before you leave."

"He requests an audience *now*?" asked Blake. "After ignoring us for over a week?"

The sentry said nothing.

"Well, by all means. Lead the way."

The walk to the Citadel of The Machine was quiet. The sentry's pace was purposely slow as he led the judges through the officers' wing and down the hidden limestone stairwell to the Hall of the Fulcrums. While Blake had the look of a man who knew what to expect, June's demeanor was far less confident. It was her first time into the underworld of Fort Zhukov.

Soon, even Blake's familiarity came to an end. As they reached the end of the Hall of the Fulcrums, the corridor narrowed to the point where the flames from the wall torches could be felt. Their fragrance made the air oppressive. The judges stopped when they came to a set of wooden doors, and the sentry stepped aside to allow them to pass.

"The general awaits," he said.

Blake looked at him warily. "He waits in there?"

"Yes, judge."

"What's behind that door?"

"The Inner Sanctum."

Blake and June turned to the door. Besides the one who'd led them, there were two more sentries in front of it—one at each side. "Are we just supposed to walk in?" Blake asked.

No sooner had he said it, a groan of ancient wood cut through the tunnel. The doors swung open. Both judges stared into the lair of General Thoor.

Blake's eyes followed the path of crimson carpet leading into the room. At the end of the carpet, ensconced in the dimly illuminated throne, sat Ignatius van Thoor.

"He sits on a *throne*?" June whispered to Blake. "This can't possibly be serious. How can he look at himself and not laugh?"

Blake scanned the rest of the room. Standing on each side of the carpet, in uniform lines, were two rows of fulcrums. Each was perfectly still, almost as though they weren't breathing. Their dark horns stabbed upward through the dank air of the Inner Sanctum like statuesque, demonic knights, assault rifles displayed at their sides.

"He awaits," said the sentry.

Nothing moved. The two judges looked at each other hesitantly, then stepped inside.

The wooden doors slammed hard behind them, causing both judges to jump. Then the two rows of fulcrums moved. They extended their rifles forward, snapping them to their opposite sides of their bodies. Then all was still again.

"I take it you haven't been here?" June whispered as silence recaptured the room.

"They left this part out of the tour."

All of a sudden, Thoor began speaking in Russian. His autocratic tone reverberated through the room, as Blake and June looked on in awe. When the general stopped talking, he was answered in loud unison by both rows of fulcrums. All went silent again.

"Approach!"

The judges flinched. Thoor's words boomed through the room as if his vocal cords were megaphones.

Blake took a step forward, but June grabbed his arm. "Wait." She pushed him aside and addressed Thoor. "We've been here for nearly a week! Why do you summon us now?"

Thoor sat motionless atop his throne. He said nothing back.

"You should approach," the fulcrum nearest them said. The fulcrum's face was hidden behind his featureless helmet. Thoor still hadn't moved, nor had either row of Nightmen. After a shared moment of apprehension, both judges approached forward.

The room was shrouded in darkness. No torches illuminated the chamber; instead, fires hung from ancient chandeliers. Their flickering was the only sound in the Inner Sanctum.

They stopped meters in front of the throne. Thoor wore a black uniform devoid of almost any insignia, save the Nightman crest. On his head and hiding his eyes was a dark visor hat. A cloak flowed down past his chair.

Blake cleared his throat and addressed him. "General Thoor, why have you ignored our visitation?"

The Terror said nothing.

"We have issued new regulations in regards to interception. As far as our records indicate, you have not complied with any of them. Are you *aware* of these new regulations?"

Still Thoor was silent.

As Blake opened his mouth to speak again, June cut him off and stepped forward. "General, why have we been brought to this place?"

This time, they got a response. Silently, Thoor pointed at the left-hand wall.

The judges turned. As soon as they both faced the wall, the room came alive as torches illuminated what had previously been black. Along the wall, arranged in a single-file line, stood a dozen bound men and women. Aside from the blindfolds that covered their eyes, they were stripped bare. Their hands were tied behind their backs as they nervously breathed.

EDEN's spies.

June's hand shot over her mouth. "Oh my God!"

Thoor barked out a lone Russian word. The fulcrums turned and raised their assault rifles to take aim. They fired before the judges could scream.

Blood exploded into the air as bullet holes burst across the chests of EDEN's agents. Their bodies were thrown against the walls where projectile fire kept them on their feet. The agents' shrieks lasted mere moments, replaced by gurgles of death.

Both judges stood paralyzed in shock.

The firing ceased as the corpses collapsed. Blake turned to the throne. But Thoor was already on the bottom step. Before Blake could cry out, the general's iron-knuckled hand snatched his throat. June screamed as fulcrums grabbed her from behind.

Blake pounded Thoor with his fists, kicking as the general lifted him off the ground and stared into his panicked eyes. When Thoor spoke, the ground seemed to shake. "Our tolerance has come to an end."

Blake writhed in the general's stranglehold. His face slowly turned blue.

The Terror's grip tightened. "You have no authority over The Machine. If you make any attempt to interfere with our operations, you will behold a massacre like none you have seen. We will slaughter your soldiers like sheep."

Still held captive by the fulcrums, June cried out in terror as Blake's eyes began to bulge.

"Do not regulate this facility. Do not send us new personnel. We have personnel of our own." Thoor's voice was monotone. "You will continue to supply us with equipment and aircraft. We will continue to cooperate as we see fit. This is not a declaration of war. That is something you cannot afford."

Blake's eyes were popping out of his head, while his lungs struggled and failed to find air. Then Thoor set him free. The judge fell to the floor, sucking in great, gasping breaths.

The fulcrums released June. She ran to Blake's side.

"Leave my facility," Thoor said. "Do not return."

Blake scrambled to his feet, and he and June fled down the carpet toward the door.

Neither looked back.

PART III

29

SATURDAY, NOVEMBER 19TH, 0011 NE
0653 HOURS

THE NEXT MORNING

SCOTT SAT UP with a jolt; his hand shot up to cover his chest. A plethora of sensations swept over him. His hair was wringing with sweat. His body was sore. His heart was pounding like a drum.

Everything was black. Where was he? What was going on? He knew he must have been asleep because he remembered dreaming. He'd dreamt about screams—screams in his head. That might have been what caused him to wake. But where was he now?

The softness under him gave it away. He was in bed. And not an infirmary bed, but his own.

As the world leveled off, a new wave of sensations overwhelmed him, hitting him from all sides. His hands stung with crustiness, and an excruciating pain burned in his back. His right eye was swollen shut, and that side of his face was numb. His forehead was sticky.

How did I get here? What happened?

The mission—that was the last thing he remembered. He had charged the fourth Noboat in the forest. Then they'd been repelled by the Bakma. No, that wasn't right—they hadn't been repelled. They'd entered the ship. They'd cleared it.

What in the world is going on?

His memory was foggy. He knew he and the other Nightmen had stormed the enemy Noboat and that the Bakma had been defeated. But the details were hazy and few.

He reached up to his face, causing yet another pain to register in his forearm. When he touched his right cheek, he felt his entire eye socket was puffed up. He recalled getting hit by the butt of a plasma rifle.

His brain felt more sore than his body. There was a pain similar to lightheadedness that came with awareness. It was like the echo of deep mental strain.

Groping blindly at his nightstand, he felt for the photograph of Nicole. The movement caused his body to shriek with pain. Instead of the picture, his fingers found a folded piece of paper—one he didn't remember putting down.

Despite the burning sensation on his back, he forced himself upright. He tugged the cord of his lamp and dim light filled the room. Squinting at the paper, he saw that it was a note, placed right by his comm.

Still groggy-eyed, he gingerly unfolded the note. It took a moment for his vision to clear; when it did, he read the note to himself.

Dear Scott,
Please comm me when you're awake. Medic's orders!
—Sveta

He closed his good eye and lay down. Svetlana. He had a fleeting memory of her presence at the end of the mission. She was rubbing his forehead. Why? Reaching up to his hairline, he felt something hard; his hair there was prickly and his skin was tight. It was dried gel.

What happened to me?

She must have brought him back to his room—there was no other way he could have gotten there. Turning to his nightstand again, he looked at Nicole's picture. It was still facing the wall—Svetlana hadn't turned it around. Taking the picture in hand, Scott held it in front of his face. Nicole's smile sent him into a vortex of anguish, just as it always did. He continued to stare at the photo for some time, then placed it back on the table.

He allowed himself several minutes to gather his clarity before he commed Svetlana to let her know he was up. As he waited, the origins of his wounds slowly came back to him. The scorch mark on his back was from the near-miss of the plasma rifle, and the cuts and burns on his hands from the missile explosion. The damage to his face was a combination of burn and battery. Svetlana would have an array of injuries to check on.

As the minutes passed, the other events of the mission returned to his mind. He'd negotiated with extraterrestrials—an Ithini and a Bakma. Captain Gabriel had been held hostage at gunpoint. Then Scott and the aliens had talked. They had connected telepathically somehow through one of the Ithini that he'd gunned down afterward.

He remembered becoming dizzy and throwing up. He remembered bits and pieces of the Bakma's words. The Bakma had wanted to know about him—about the Nightmen. The alien had specifically noted that Scott and his comrades were not from EDEN. They knew who the Nightmen were. Of course they did. They must have. The Nightmen had destroyed their outpost in Siberia.

"We are to bring you to Khuldaris."

Those were the words the Bakma had spoken. The Bakma wanted to take the Nightmen with them. They were willing to release EDEN captives to do it. They wanted to evaluate them, but for what purpose?

Four words orbited Scott's brain. *Interference. Indication. Allegiance. Judgment.* All of them had been said by the Bakma. But what did they mean? He'd only understood bits and pieces.

Finally, a knock came to the door. Without waiting for an invitation, Svetlana opened the door and stepped inside.

Scott smelled food. When Svetlana approached, he saw a plate in her hands. Cradled against her chest was a jug of ice water. He stared at her strangely.

Even through the dimness, he could see she was smiling. "Good morning, Scott."

"What are you doing?" His face hurt when he spoke.

"I am making good of my word."

Making good of her word? What word?

She padded across the room to his bed, placing the plate on his nightstand. She pulled up a chair. "Some time ago, I told a young soldier I would cook for him—in payment for the bad thoughts I had."

It took him a moment to recall, but recall he did. She had promised him in the first conversation they'd had, that night in the lounge months ago, that she'd make him breakfast. It seemed like so long ago.

"I apologize for not bringing you porridge," she said with a self-depreciative grin. "I've had quite enough of it for a while."

Scott had forgotten all about the breakfast. In the midst of his recollections, he actually laughed, but regretted it instantly as the pain seared his face. "You really cooked something?"

She showed him the plate. It was a sandwich—two slices of bread with something in between.

He raised an eyebrow. "That's it?"

"What do you mean, 'that is it?' Do you know what this is?"

He could smell it—an odd mixture of breakfasty things.

"This is a Russian ham sandwich," she said.

Before he knew what he was saying, the words were out. "I could make that when I was six."

She lifted one end of the bread. There was no visible ham; rather, it looked like yellow, chunky paste.

"What in God's name is *that*?"

"It is eggs, ham, butter, and mustard. With pepper and salt. It is blended together."

"Ugh."

She pouted. "Do not just say 'ugh.' This is how it is made here. Try it. You will like it. It is something different."

"That I can see."

"The eggs and ham are very fresh. And you will like Russian mustard."

"Do I need the jug of water to wash it down?"

She allowed herself a wry grin. "Very funny. That is *for* the mustard. Russian mustard is very hot—the hottest in the world. Try it, you will see."

He wasn't intentionally trying to be rude. It just wasn't something he'd seen—or smelled—before. "Thanks." He tried not to sound disgusted.

"Just trust me, doubter. It will be good." She set the plate to the side. "Now let me see your face." Scott turned her way, and she placed her fingers under his chin. "How do you feel?"

"Tired and sore. It's hard to explain."

"What is hard to explain about being tired and sore?" She wiped her hand on a discarded paper towel. "And sweaty." Rising, she walked to his sink.

"I don't even remember what happened. I've never blacked out like that before."

Grabbing a small towel from his vanity, she ran it under the faucet. "You connected with an Ithini for the first time. That has an effect on the brain." Ringing the towel out, she walked back to him. "That is also why you were nauseated."

"That happens every time people make a connection?"

"Only the first time." She wiped his forehead. "The brain is not used to such a connection. There are many things that come with it. Nausea, dizziness, headaches." She smiled. "And yes, passing out. The second time you connect, it will be better. If there is a second time."

He closed his good eye as she did her work. A second connection was the last thing he wanted. "It didn't hit me until after the Noboat. I just fell to the ground."

"You had a lot of adrenaline. When the battle was over, it began to go away."

"What happened?"

"After the mission?" She placed the damp towel aside. Leaning close to his face, she examined his cheek. "Very much. Not all of it will be fun to discuss."

Scott wondered how he looked. He knew his cheek was swollen, but he had no idea just how much. He'd hardly glanced at his forearms and hands. "What happened to Gabriel's crew?"

"Captain Gabriel is fine." Lifting a medical kit from the floor, she pulled out the burn gel. "But there are many from his unit who have died. Eleven from Pelican Squad survived. Only one from the other squad survived—she is in critical condition." Svetlana frowned as she put burn gel in place.

Frogmouth—that was the other squad. Only one person had survived? That was terrible.

Svetlana sighed. "There is something else I must tell you. Promise me you stay lying down."

He nodded.

"Oleg was a Nightman."

Scott's good eye opened wide. "*What?*"

She placed her hand on his chest. "You just listen, and I will continue to work." She moved on to his hands. "Oleg was part of the eidola. It was Becan who found out. I do not know everything, but apparently he met someone from the First and figured out that Oleg had never been there. There were some other things, too, but…I will let Becan explain."

"What…?" The word *happened* never came out.

"He is out of the unit," she answered. "They brought him back to *Novosibirsk*, like he was a prisoner. Then he disappeared. I suppose he has gone back to Thoor, but…he cannot remain with the eidola now. People know who he is. I do not know where he will go."

Scott was in shock. On the other hand, some things now made sense. He'd seen Oleg fight—he fought like no one Scott had ever seen. Nonetheless, it was hard to comprehend. "Did Dostoevsky know?"

"Yes. He too left when we arrived. Nobody knows where *he* went, either."

Scott's feelings toward Dostoevsky were torn. Of course he felt anger, but not enough to strike at him. Even though Dostoevsky had something to do with Nicole's murder, it wasn't he who actually did it. Scott wasn't sure why that had ever mattered.

"I will let Becan tell you everything later," Svetlana said. "Let us get to good news. You have been requested by Confinement again. Apparently you are very good guest."

His mind returned to the alien negotiation—his conversation with the Bakma in the crashed Vulture. *Interference. Indication. Allegiance. Judgment.* What was the meaning of the other words? What was Khuldaris? Was it a planet? A ship? Was it an individual?

She noticed his look. "What is wrong?"

He didn't know how to explain it. "I bargained with a Bakma. He made threats—I think. Did any of you hear it?"

Shaking her head, she pulled the sheets down, exposing his boxers. "No, I am sorry. We heard his words, yes, but we did not hear what they meant. You were the only one with a connection."

Scott had never heard anything about interferences, alliances, or judgment before. Judgment for what? Was this war all about judgment for something? The word *indication* had been used, too. What was being indicated?

"Roll over, away."

Scott painfully complied, and she checked his back. His mind returned to Svetlana's revelation and his summons to Confinement. Petrov would want to speak to him again, but he didn't like or trust the man as much anymore. Their visit to the Walls of Mourning shed a disturbing light on him.

"Okay," she said. "You are good. Now get up, out of bed. To the sink."

"To the sink?"

"We are washing your hair." She stood up. "You must have sweated all night. You feel very gross."

Everything felt very gross. She'd just smeared gel on his cheek. Could she wash that off, too? "Can I walk?"

"Scott, you are not crippled," she said flatly. "You have several burns. Some are bad, others are not. But you do not have broken bones. Now get up—to the sink." She picked up the ham sandwich and placed it in his cooler. "This can wait."

If washing my hair means not eating that, rinse and repeat. Use conditioner. Give me a shave. He cringed in pain as he rolled out of bed. He didn't care what she claimed—his back *hurt.*

As he got up, he noticed his armor was gone from the closet. "Where...?" He turned to find her, but as he did so, he caught a glimpse of himself for the first time in the sink mirror. "Oh my God..."

He looked like a corpse that had been tortured to death. The right side of his face was swollen to the point of deformity. He had a black eye and abscesses on his forehead and temple. His entire face was in ruins.

Svetlana placed her hand on his shoulder. "Do not be scared. I know how it looks." She squeezed his shoulder. "Your cheekbone has *very* minor fracture. It will heal on its own. Scars will be very little, I promise."

Scott stared at his hands. They too had burned and abscessed wounds. So did his palms and forearms.

"Your hands will heal. Everything will heal, in good time. Please trust me, Scott. I would not lie."

Now everyone's shocked reaction to him on the battlefield made sense. They'd seen his injuries when they were fresh. He wondered if they looked worse then or now.

"Your armor is being repaired. It was not exactly designed to survive missile attacks, but it still saved your life."

His fulcrum armor had saved his life. But the armor was his symbol of sin. Deep inside, he wondered if he'd have survived had he worn EDEN's equipment. He was afraid the answer was no.

She urged him to the sink. "Do not look at yourself. It will only make you feel worse."

Scott looked down from the mirror, forcing himself to stare at the sink's basin. Turning around, he sat down in the chair she had placed there.

Svetlana turned on the faucet, placing her hand beneath the water as she adjusted the temperature. "Lean your head back."

He hesitated, but did as he was told. The moment the warm water hit his scalp, a soothing wave coursed through his veins. It was the best thing he'd felt since waking up.

She ran her fingers through his hair. "Not all the news is bad. As much as it pains me to say it, you should be proud of our friend, Molly

Esther. She helped capture a functional Noboat—that does not happen often. She did very well."

Esther had done well in more ways than one. He remembered what she'd done for him personally. She'd stopped him from shooting two surrendering Bakma—she'd held him in check. He was grateful to her and ashamed of himself.

Svetlana squirted a dollop of mild shampoo into her palm, then turned off the faucet. She massaged it into his scalp. "Scott…what I saw you do in the forest, I have seen from you before. I saw a man risk his life to save strangers he did not even know. A Nightman would not have done that."

For the first time, he was not inclined to argue. He allowed her words to sink in.

"It is the truth, Scott. I did not see a fulcrum in the woods. I saw a lion. Things have happened to you, and yes, you have changed. But in your heart, you are still a good man."

He knew she was trying to get him to look at himself positively, but his thoughts were almost solely on her. He was a fallen man in a miserable state who'd made her stay at *Novosibirsk* anything but easy. Yet there she was, taking care of him with a level of caring he'd rarely experienced from anyone. As horrible as he had acted in the past, as awful as he looked now, her compassion had never once wavered. She'd been frustrated, even angry, but she'd always cared. Now she was washing his hair. What medic did that?

"I forgive you for what you have done, Scott. We have all made mistakes. You know of mine." Her fingers slowed and rested against the sides of his scalp. "You have done what you have done, but it does not define who you are. It does not define who you can be."

She turned the water on again, but his mind had already gone somewhere else. Flashes of the past swirled in his brain. Flashes of Chicago—of saving the remnants of Cougar Platoon. Leaping for Svetlana in Siberia. Retaking the turret tower in the *Assault on Novosibirsk* to help fend off the Bakma.

There was a key ingredient to every one of his best moments: none of them were about him.

Svetlana turned off the water and grabbed a towel from the side of the sink, wrapping it over his head. "Lift your head up." He did as told, and she rubbed it gently.

That was the lesson. He'd been doing everything for himself—it seemed so obvious now. His actions should have been about them—his teammates and the ones they were helping in battle. His priorities had been reversed, even in Chernobyl.

"Now," Svetlana said, "here is some burn gel. Apply it to your cheek three times a day. It will help you to heal." She allowed him to rise. "You could be active in as few as five days."

As few as five days? Five days felt like so long. Then he thought about Jayden, and five days didn't seem as bad.

"I am leaving cold gel with you, too. You can apply it at the same time, to your cheek. It will speed up the healing and help with the pain. There is penicillin with instructions in your drawer, to ward off infection."

A strange mix of emotions ran through him. Remorse and irritation with himself, but at the same time hope. It was a new feeling.

She walked to the door. "I will check up on you. And you can always come to find me." She turned with a grin. "Do not forget, in your cooler."

His ham sandwich. He'd have preferred if it remained forgotten.

"It will be good. Just remember, stay close to the jug. I was not joking about Russian mustard—it is hot."

"Thank you, Svetlana."

She winked. "What are medics for?" Reaching behind her, she opened the door. "You know where to find me, if you need."

"Yes, I do."

"I love you, Scott."

The words resonated through the room, but somehow he wasn't surprised and he didn't react strangely. He knew what she meant when she said it—he felt that way, too.

Smiling gently, she left the room and closed the door.

As he sat on the edge of his bed, he was amazed at how little he hurt now that he'd moved about. He wondered if it had something to do with the gel—or maybe it was because of something else.

Turning to his nightstand, he looked at the picture of Nicole. She smiled at him still, as she did every second of every minute of every day.

Drawing a breath, he opened his cooler, where the ham sandwich lay in wait. Taking the plate in his hands, he lifted up the top slice of bread. It wasn't the most appetizing meal he'd ever encountered, but Svetlana had made it for him. She cared enough to keep a promise he'd completely forgotten about. She had not had to do it, but she did. Taking the sandwich in hand, he opened his mouth and took a first bite.

Within five minutes, Scott was back on his feet. He crossed his room without a grimace of pain. He went straight to his sink and turned on the faucet.

He'd finished his first jug of water—his mouth was on fire.

30

SATURDAY, NOVEMBER 19TH, 0011 NE
0759 HOURS

AT THE SAME TIME

THE MORNING WAS snowy like so many others. The eight o'clock sun was on the verge of making its entrance as the lights of the base flickered on to illuminate most of the grounds. Accompanying the steady, gentle drizzle of snow was a contrastingly eerie fog. It hung over the ground as far as one could see. None of it bothered Esther Brooking.

The British scout was not in her uniform. There'd been no morning session to kick-start the day, nor a Captain Clarke to impress with professional garb. Esther simply wore an overcoat over a plain gray T-shirt. Her hair, tied back into her usual loose ponytail, was held down by fluffy white earmuffs. She was a walking touch of class in an otherwise uncaring facility.

She walked with purposeful strides as her brown eyes surveyed the grounds, scrutinizing every male in the vicinity. When she spotted the one she wanted, she veered his way.

David was walking along the outskirts of the base, where only a narrow, little-used pathway ran. Unlike Esther, he was in full uniform, wearing his standard EDEN outfit and coat. When he saw her approach, he stopped and stared at her attire. "Do you have a date?"

"Just with you! Don't tell your wife."

Smiling faintly, David waited for her to get close. "I used to enjoy waking up early," he remarked. "I'm trying to get back into it."

"You've picked a lovely morning to start. At least it's not cold," she said sarcastically as they trod through the snow. "If it's not bucketing down, it's Baltic. Not that I mind being outside."

"A fan of miserable weather?"

"No, it's not that. Svetlana stunk up the room with her disgusting mustard sandwich. I was about to throw up."

The older man chuckled. "Yeah, those Russians and food. What I wouldn't give for a New York strip."

Esther grinned broadly.

"So what brings you out here?" he asked.

She hesitated before asking, "Do you hate Scott?"

David fell quiet and the tranquil look on his face melted away. He sighed and looked away. "Esther, it's not that."

She faced him. "I was with him yesterday, from the beginning to the end of that mission. For the first time since I've been here, I saw a glimpse of the man everyone talked about. The only Scott I've known has been the angry one. But yesterday, he wasn't like that."

David sighed inaudibly.

"He was so heroic and brave. Everything he did was so…so *gifted.* I saw it, first-hand." She frowned. "I also saw him almost lose it in the end. He almost killed two surrendering Bakma. I was lucky to stop him, and that's my point. We can stop him from doing those things. We can change him. You can change him more than anyone else."

David still made no reply.

"I know you have sons. It must've been hard to watch Scott unravel—wasn't he almost like a son to you?" She stopped walking and stood in the snow. "I know it's not easy, but please, David. Please forgive him."

His green eyes stayed fixed on the snow, and he didn't respond at first. He just slid his gloved hands into his pockets. "I don't hate Scott. It's just…"

"It's just that he murdered an innocent young man?"

"…yeah."

Neither spoke for some time. When David did answer, it was almost like a new conversation. "This is going to sound ridiculous, but after he changed, the first thought in my head was, 'I raised him better than that.'"

She let him continue.

"I don't know, Esther. They say time heals everything."

"Then isn't it time?" She was staring at him with stern understanding, as if her words were meant to end the exchange. At long last, he nodded his head. Her lips slowly curved up.

David tried not to smile back. "What is it with you? You know what to say."

"Of course I do. I'm a woman and a scout. I can get what I want."

"So do you want Scott?"

Esther's expression went flat.

"I thought that was it." He briefly glanced away. "Let me give you a little advice, Esther. It's fair, since you gave some to me."

When she didn't reply, he went on.

"Don't go down that road. An infatuation, sure, that's fine, but don't fall for him, yet. He's still got a long way to go."

This time it was Esther who stared into the distance.

David placed his hand on the back of her neck, then gave her a squeeze. "I'm proud of you. Not that my approval means much."

She just stared ahead at the snow-covered expanse. The morning sun had risen now, and the fog was lifting away. At last, she sighed and conceded, "Maybe a little."

He smiled. "I'll take what I can get."

The two resumed their walk across the grounds, though only a few words were spoken after that. Esther was the first one to walk away, leaving David with a girlish kiss on the cheek. She made her way to the barracks. David remained by himself in the fresh morning sun for another full hour, without human or comm interruption. And that was fine with him.

* * *

SCOTT WALKED ALONE to the infirmary. It had taken him longer than usual to dress and leave his room. The burns on his arms, despite being bandaged, made wearing his uniform impossible; instead, he'd donned a loose gray T-shirt. He knew how awful he looked, and if he were to somehow forget, the looks on the faces of those who passed him in the halls served as reminders. But he didn't care how he looked—he didn't care about himself in the least.

The most recent update he'd received about Jayden was the most positive yet. The Texan's right eye had healed to the point where an eye patch was no longer needed, though one still remained over his vacant left socket. Doctors were certain the right eye would fully recover. The rest of his body was healing well, though he'd still be in casts for several weeks. Nonetheless, the prognosis was good—at least, for a semi-normal life back home.

When Scott walked into Jayden's room, the Texan's good eye lit up. His face, though still badly damaged, looked much better than the last time Scott had seen it. He looked like himself again, if not a battered version. He would be scarred for the rest of his life, but not to the extent where he would look disfigured. He actually looked good.

"Hey Jay," Scott said as he approached the bed.

"Hey man," Jayden's good eye followed Scott's movement. He frowned when he looked at Scott's face. "What happened? Did someone beat you up?"

Scott almost laughed. "Something like that." He guessed he must have been the first to visit Jayden that day. Had anyone else, the Texan probably would have known what had happened. "How are you feeling?"

"I feel great, man! I see real good."

It was impossible not to grin at Jayden's optimism. Not once had the sniper complained or wallowed in self-pity during his stay in the infirmary. He'd had his weak moments, and he'd broken down in front of Scott, but his will had never failed. Scott wondered how many people would have such strength. "I got jealous of your one eye," Scott said. "Thought I'd screw mine up, too. I hear Russian women love the Cyclops look."

Jayden laughed. "I kinda like this eye patch they got me wearin'. It makes me look like a pirate." His content look remained for a moment, then faded somewhat. "Have you heard from Varya?"

Scott looked at him strangely. "She hasn't been here?"

"I haven't seen her in days, man. Almost a week."

Scott was stunned. Of all the people who should have been visiting the fallen sniper, Varvara should have been chief. That she hadn't been there was inconceivable.

"She still talks about me, right?"

Scott stared blankly at the Texan, though inside, his heart was torn. "Yeah, of course." It was a natural answer, but it was also a lie. Scott had never heard her talk about Jayden, but then again, Scott was rarely in Room 14 to hear.

"Next time you see her, tell her I love her."

Where are you, Varya? Why aren't you here to hear this yourself? Despite his irritation, he defended the absent medic. "She's got a lot to deal with right now. We've had some rough times in the group." His tone softened. "She'll get back here as soon as she can, but I'll give her the message."

"Thanks, man."

Scott knew he'd have to make a special trip to Room 14 to deliver that message. The last time he'd been there, it had been to discuss the open officer's slot in the wake of Clarke's death. He had a feeling that talking to the unit as a whole was inevitable. With everything that had gone on in their last mission, some things would have to be addressed. Oleg's treachery was at the top of the list.

Suddenly he remembered something. *Dostoevsky tried to talk Max and me out of promoting Oleg. He kept trying to push Viktor instead.* The hair stood up on his arms. *What if Oleg was a threat to him, too? We thought Dostoevsky was trying to fill the ranks with Nightmen when he recommended Viktor. What if he was trying to protect us from Oleg?* He could barely believe he was entertaining that thought, but what if it were true?

"Scott?"

Snapping out of his reverie, Scott refocused on Jayden.

"You all right?"

He wasn't sure how he should answer, so he went with the truth. "We went on a mission yesterday. Something happened. Becan found out that Oleg was part of the eidola."

Jayden's good eye grew wide.

"He's out of the unit. For all I know, so is Dostoevsky." He was surprised when Jayden didn't smile at that. "It might just be Max and me." If Dostoevsky was gone, did that make Scott the unit's captain? It seemed too far-fetched to consider. "Someone needs to talk to the unit."

"Why don't *you* do it?"

The Texan made it sound to simple—so blatantly clear.

"Do it, man. They'd love to hear from you."

Scott wasn't sure what he could offer to the unit. Off the battlefield, he'd been nonexistent; he'd grown accustomed to a disconnected life. Before he could think on it further, Jayden spoke again.

"Do you see things differently now?"

Differently? It wasn't a question he'd expected. Deep questions from the Texan were rare. Did he see things differently? How could he not? So much had transpired over so few months. The death of Nicole, becoming a fulcrum, distancing from his friends. And now this dim glimmer of hope on the horizon. The barrage of changes had never ceased, from directions he could never anticipate. "I feel like I can't see things coming until they hit me in the face."

Jayden's face fell flat. "Are you *serious*?"

That was the best way he could describe it. "I haven't reacted to adversity in the wisest of ways. But it's like everywhere I turn, I get blindsided. I feel like I'm finally starting to learn, but..." his words trailed away. "When

Nicole died, I thought life couldn't get any worse. Now I'm a fulcrum, the unit's a wreck, and it all falls on me. I think I'm finally at the point where I'm willing to accept that, but is it too late to change?"

Jayden didn't say a thing. He simply stared as Scott continued to speak.

"You say to just go talk to the unit, but is it really that simple? If I had handled everything better, maybe so. But I handled it in the worst possible ways. But I guess I can try. Maybe on some level I actually want to. So, do I see things differently?" He shook his head. "I guess maybe I do."

Scott wondered if he was making sense. Everything sounded right in his mind, but he wondered if Jayden could relate to it all. Maybe the Texan was right. Maybe it was just time to move on.

When he looked up at Jayden, he saw a comrade at a loss for words. The Texan simply looked confused. Scott sighed. "If that answers your question at all."

"I meant with one eye, man."

Scott shook his head as if coming out of a trance. "*What?*"

"I meant, do you see things differently with one eye?"

"Please tell me you're joking."

"No, man, I'm serious," Jayden started to laugh. "But all that other stuff was pretty cool, too."

"Oh my God." He fought to find the right words. "Why didn't you stop me?"

"You were just goin' on, man! What was I supposed to do?"

Scott covered his face with his hands, even forgetting for a moment that both were burned. The laughter came out—laughter of sheer disbelief. The more he thought about what he'd just said, the heavier the heaves came. "Well," Scott barely managed the words, "I guess I see pretty good." It wasn't just the hardest Scott had laughed in months, it was the hardest he'd laughed in what felt like years. His stomach actually hurt.

"Dude," Jayden said, "when you said you couldn't see things until they hit you in the face, I was like, 'oh crap!' You gotta tell this to the gang!"

Scott still needed to talk to the "gang" about Oleg, too. Except he looked forward to that now—for reasons that had nothing to do with the eidola. He just wanted to see his friends—to remember what it felt like to be human. "I'm sorry, Jay."

Jayden was still chuckling. "Sorry for what?"

"For letting it get this bad."

The Texan fell quiet.

One moment of laughter couldn't solve all his problems. Nicole was still dead. Her killer was still on the loose—as were many others. Scott was still ranked among them. All those battles still faced him. Outside of a brief prayer about Jayden, Scott hadn't talked openly to God. He still wasn't sure he was ready. There were scars buried deep in his heart—months of trust to regain.

"Just go make it right," said Jayden.

Those words echoed through Scott's soul. *Go make it right.* Maybe it really was that easy. *I need to go talk to the unit. I need to talk to them about Oleg and Dostoevsky—I need to talk to them about myself.*

To tell them I'm sorry.

He wasn't caught up in remorse. On the inside, he was still angry. Anger was something he feared would always be with him—the Nightmen had unlocked it, and now it was free. But maybe, just maybe, his anger could be controlled. Maybe it could be used for something other than revenge.

He realized right then not just what he was, but *who* he was. He was one of the few Nightmen, if not the only one, who could bridge both worlds. Good and evil, freedom and vice, friendship and tyranny. He understood the Nightmen—the Dostoevskys and the Strakhovs—and the depth of their violence. He understood the guilt they carried in their souls, whether they admitted it or not. He'd made the mistake of not only succumbing to them, but becoming one of them.

Rising from his chair, he smiled at Jayden. "Thanks, man."

"Wait, before you leave," Jayden said. "I want to ask you somethin'."

"Sure."

The Texan hesitated. "The doctors said they were sending me home. Do you think maybe you could talk to 'em?"

Scott furrowed his brow. "What do you mean?"

"You know, tellin' 'em I can stay. That I can still be a sniper."

The words hurt to hear. *Jay...you only have one eye.* There was no way EDEN would let him remain. "Jayden, man...don't even think that far ahead yet. Worry about those broken bones first." He didn't have the heart to be honest. "Heal with your family."

The Texan shook his head. "I don't wanna go home, man. I can stay here. I'll rehab, I'll do everything. I'll get better."

"Jay..."

"I don't need two eyes to shoot."

Scott frowned. *But you need two eyes to avoid getting shot.*

"Please, do it for me, man."

Scott placed his hands on his hips. Jayden had no idea what he was asking.

"This is all I wanna do," Jayden said. "That's why I signed up. I'm no good at anything else. I can't play sports, I can't run a business. But I know I can shoot. If they sent me home…man, I'd wanna die."

Scott wanted to be optimistic. He wanted to believe that this would turn out to be a feel-good story—that somehow, Jayden could stay. *I need to at least try. He deserves that much.* Against his better judgment, he agreed. "I'll send a request to Command. I'll give it a shot."

Jayden smiled.

Once I figure out how to do it.

Nothing more was said between them. Scott rose, patted the Texan's leg cast, and turned for the door.

Scott's thoughts were split between Jayden's request and his own imminent conversation with the Fourteenth—what words he would choose, and what he would try to convey. In both efforts, he was preparing to lead as if Dostoevsky were gone. For all he knew, Dostoevsky was.

Scott was halfway out of the infirmary when Captain Gabriel caught his eye. The blond Australian was leaning against the wall, hands casually in his pockets as he turned and caught sight of Scott. Gabriel popped up from the wall and approached.

"Commander Remington," he said, extending his hand. "How do you feel?"

"Not as bad as I look."

"You collapsed not long after everything ended," said Gabriel solemnly. "I've connected with an Ithini before, and I remember how it felt the first time. It was like I had helium in my veins."

Scott couldn't think of a better way to describe it. It also explained why Gabriel hadn't seemed affected at the crash site—he'd gone through the experience before.

"I never had an opportunity to thank you. You saved our lives, mate. I don't think anyone could have done what you did."

"How's your injured girl?"

Gabriel frowned. "She'll recover, but it won't be with us. She'll be going back home." He brushed his moppy hair to the side. "I'm actually here now because of her. I barely took time to know the girl—she just came from *Philadelphia*. Call it captain's guilt."

Scott knew the feeling. He'd felt the same way about Maksim Frolov. "What's her name?"

"Becca Weston. Fellow Australian. She was quiet."

"Give her my regards."

"I will."

"Is your unit still here?"

Gabriel nodded. "What's left of it. We lost our colonel, our major, and our other captain. Half the platoon." He sighed. "We'll be able to leave in a day or two, but I'm staying here until Weston can be moved. There's a handful of others staying with me. If it takes a month, we'll stay. Don't take it personally, but I don't like this place. I don't want her here alone."

"Can't say that I blame you."

Gabriel eyed him for several moments. "So you're a Nightman?"

"Yeah."

"You don't act like one."

The compliment was well-received. Gabriel's gaze held firm.

"If there's anything I can do for you, please let me know. We're all in your debt."

"I will," Scott said. It was a nice gesture by the Australian. Scott felt guilty for having been irritated with him and his crew in the forest. The man seemed to genuinely care. "Thank you."

Gabriel smiled. "I don't want to keep you. I'm sure you're busy."

He was, but he didn't want it to show. Scott extended his hand one last time. "Take care."

"You too, mate." The men parted ways.

Scott was still walking out of the infirmary when he reached for his comm. He sent an initial page to Max, and the lieutenant answered promptly.

"Y'hello."

"Max, is everyone in Room 14?"

"I don't know. I'm in the hangar, washin' the dog."

Washing the dog. Scott should have known. "In an hour, I want to talk to the unit. Make sure everyone's there."

There was a delay in Max's response. "Sure thing, Scott." He sounded as if he was trying not to be surprised.

"I'll see you there." The comm channel closed, and Scott slid the device back into his belt.

He had one hour to figure out what to say and how to say it. One hour to fix three months of hurt. It was better late than never.

31

SATURDAY, NOVEMBER 19TH, 0011 NE
1000 HOURS

THE WALK TO Room 14 felt like an epic journey. With every step, Scott's feet became heavier. It was as though some kind of unseen force was fighting to hold him at bay—to prevent him from moving ahead.

The hour before his meeting had been both a blessing and a curse. It had given him time to collect his thoughts and prepare himself for what he was about to say. At the same time, it served as a doorway for doubt and reservation. Despite his apprehension, he kept moving.

When he finally arrived in front of the door, he stopped. *This is what I have to do,* he thought. *But it has to go beyond that. Is this what I want to do?*

For any other occasion, necessity would outrank desire. But for him—for this—it was different. The very nature of who he was demanded desire. He would be perfectly safe with The Machine. He'd hate himself, but he'd be safe. To do this right—to heal while humbling himself—would require going in with both feet. Was that really what he wanted to do?

Yes it is.

Reaching out, he opened the door.

The immediate absence of operatives surprised him, but he soon saw that everyone was in the lounge. He could hear their rustling and quiet conversing around the tables, and he could see the shadows move beyond the open door.

There was something about the simple satisfaction of knowing his teammates were there that brought him a measure of joy. He fought to restrain it and for the most part succeeded, but it refused to dissipate entirely.

As he walked through the bunk room to the lounge, he glanced at the beds. He could recognize everyone's bed—the neat ones of the women, Travis's strewn with comic books, Jayden and Varvara's matching cowboy hats. David's photos. He stopped there, thinking about the older American who had once been like a father to him. How much things had changed.

He noticed a silence emanating from the lounge. The chattering had stopped and movement had ceased. They knew he was there.

Closing his eyes, Scott lowered his head. It might have been a prayer. Whatever it was, it prepared him. It encouraged him enough to walk forward.

The moment he stepped through the door, all eyes were upon him. For the first time since visiting Jayden, he remembered how terrible he looked with his swollen cheek, black eye, and horrible burns. He must have appeared almost grotesque, but he didn't care. He had a feeling neither did they.

He scanned the room, taking them all in. Max was there, sitting at a table with Travis and Boris. Becan was sitting with Esther, William, and Derrick. Everyone was there—even David and the slayers. But the new captain was nowhere to be seen.

Dostoevsky is gone. For a moment Scott felt disappointed, which almost surprised him. But it didn't matter where Dostoevsky was, or if he was merely absent or abandoned for the long haul. He resumed his scan of the room until he found Svetlana. She smiled at him warmly, her blue eyes sparkling.

Scott smiled back. Her whole purpose in returning to *Novosibirsk* had been for this—to see him redeemed. This was as much for her as himself. She deserved it. Clearing his throat, he began. "Thank you guys for coming…I know this isn't something we're used to lately. I don't really know how to begin, so I'll just start without beating around the bush…"

Back in the bunk room, the door to Room 14 silently opened. Dostoevsky crept inside. He looked at the lounge hesitantly, then quietly eased the door shut behind him.

"I want to ask for forgiveness," Scott said bluntly. At those words, the slayers exchanged perplexed glances. It was impossible for Scott not to notice. All four of them were unmistakably intrigued.

"There is no justification for how I've behaved over the past several months. Not anger, not unfairness. Not personal loss." He could feel the heaviness of the anger and guilt, feelings he'd rehashed repeatedly in his mind. But he'd never addressed them to the unit.

"I went wrong when I stopped listening to you," he said. "The compassion you've shown me when I needed it the most..." He shook his head in wonder. "The way I repaid you was awful." He had to convey his next words straight from his heart, despite their simplicity. "I am so sorry."

They stared at him with a mix of emotions. Some of them looked upon him with hope—Svetlana, Varvara, and Esther chief among them. Some of them watched with respect, while others looked suspicious.

"You deserved a better leader than you've gotten from me."

Dostoevsky was still in the bunk room; he hadn't stepped any farther inside. He stood by the door—hidden by a half row of bunks—as he listened to Scott.

"I realize what I lost," Scott went on, "and that was all of you. I let anger and guilt take over my life, and I ran from the very people I needed the most. I've also been incredibly selfish." No elegant words weaved through his address. He tried to speak plainly. "So far as I'm concerned, I have two options now. I can keep doing what I've been doing, which isn't working. Or I can try to change—work to make myself right. With you, with myself. With this team."

Across the room, every eye was fixed on him. The women's smiles had faded, but so had the looks of suspicion and uncertainty from some of the others. They no longer stared at him like a man awkwardly attempting to redeem himself; instead, they watched him to see where he was going with his words.

"Becan," Scott said, looking at the Irishman. "Esther..." He then went around the room, saying the names of each of his EDEN comrades in turn. When he settled on David, his former roommate and friend, he tried to smile. David's face was blank. "I can stand up here and make a million promises about my behavior, but it doesn't matter what I say. It matters what I actually do." He paused while he formed his request. "Please give me the chance to right what I've let get out of hand. I hope you can forgive me that much."

Outside of the lounge, Dostoevsky's eyes trailed to the floor.

Scott switched his attention from his EDEN counterparts to the slayers. "I have some words especially for you." The room tensed as the Nightmen looked at him. "We've each failed humanity in our own way. We all know the guilt that comes with that."

The slayers' reactions were mixed. Viktor looked wary. Nicolai looked worried. But Auric and Egor seemed to be listening intently.

"Every one of us lives with a vice. I live with anger. You each know what your own vices are. But we need to be different. The way we are now...it doesn't work. Look at Dostoevsky and Oleg—role models for our sect. Neither of them are here.

"We can't segregate ourselves and expect to survive. The things we should be doing together, we *must* do together. Training together, fighting together. Even relaxing together. Believing in each other, together." He no longer spoke to only the slayers.

"We can't afford to be a torn-apart unit. *We* are the Fourteenth of *Novosibirsk*. If any part of this unit fails, we all fail together. We all have a lot of work to do."

At those words, his tone noticeably changed—it became bolder and more forceful.

"Svetlana and Esther." He looked squarely at the two women. They looked back with surprise. "The two of you need to settle your differences. Find the problem, then sort it out. Let it go."

They glanced at each other, then back at him.

Scott turned to the pilot. "Travis, you need to improve." Travis blinked as he was isolated. "Being competent once in a while is not good enough. You need to raise your own bar." The pilot looked genuinely hurt.

"Varya, the same goes for you. Ask yourself if you really want to be here. If you do, crack open the books, get lessons from Sveta, and get Esther to teach you about composure—she's learned that very well."

The room fell deathly quiet. It was as if a hammer of judgment had been hurled tactlessly down.

His focus turned to Nicolai—one of his own. "Nicolai, hear this and hear it well. You will not make perverse comments about your teammates. You will not threaten innocent citizens. The next time either happens, it will be the last."

"Da, commander."

Scott took in their expressions—their surprise and their hurt. Their uncomfortable stares of apprehension. His next words were damning and low.

"Scott Remington," he said aloud. The operatives who'd lowered their heads lifted them again. "You need to stop acting like a child. You need to stop feeding your sense of self-pity. You need to stop your grudging anger and resentment. You need to be the officer you should have been for the past three months." He paused for a moment. "And if you don't, whatever mutiny you receive will be well-deserved."

Scott knew how effective that last part would be. He would have never been able to lay down such criticism of the others had he not chosen to add in his own. At least, that was the gamble he took.

"None of us are above improvement. Especially not me. Let's improve together. Let's be what we should have been all along."

That was it. That was the whole of his speech. He had to show them that he was sincere while showing them that he was still capable of being a respectable leader. Now it was their turn. Without another word, he relinquished his command of the floor—to give them a chance to speak.

Outside the lounge, Dostoevsky's expression remained stoic. Until he overheard the next question.

"Are you and I the only officers left?" Max asked.

For a moment, Scott didn't answer. He knew the issue was unavoidable. Where did Dostoevsky stand? Was he still a part of the unit at all? Scott didn't know. "Until we hear otherwise, Dostoevsky's still the captain of this squad. I know a lot of people here are holding a grudge, maybe none more so than me. But if I can look past what he's done, and give him that respect, so can anyone else here. For the sake of us all, I'm letting it go." The words stung him at first, as if he was giving up an addictive habit. Perhaps he was.

Max's response was less gracious. "I sent him a message about the meeting. I know he knew about it. As far as I'm concerned, this room is it."

Auric, the German Nightman, said firmly, "You are the one we will follow, commander. I believe I speak for us all." The other Nightmen quietly affirmed.

Several seconds later, Scott heard a click come from the bunk room—the sound of the bunk room door opening and shutting in a way not meant to be heard. Glancing into the room, he saw that no one was there. But someone evidently had been moments before. He frowned when he realized who it must have been.

Yuri...did you just hear that? It had to have been the captain. Oleg wouldn't have dared to show his face. He turned his attention back to the room, forcing thoughts of Dostoevsky out of his mind.

His operatives sat expectantly, but Scott simply concluded, "So let's get to work."

Though he stepped away from the front of the room, the unit remained silent. Finally, the first glints of subdued conversation emerged.

Max approached Scott immediately. Though the technician spoke louder than most in the room, his voice was nonetheless low. "That was good, man."

Scott regarded him with genuine concern. The affirmation made him feel good, as if the short speech had been worth it. "I think Dostoevsky was in the other room."

"I hope he heard every word." The chatter around them began to reach normal levels. "How you feelin'?"

"All right. Looks worse than it hurts. I'll be ready again in a few days, so says Svetlana."

"She cares about you, man."

Coming from Max, it startled him. "She cares about you, too," he said, knowing it sounded hollow. Svetlana had never told him one way or the other how she felt about Max. He just didn't know any other way to respond.

"Just between you and me…it'd do you good to get over Nicole."

Scott stared bluntly at the technician.

"Don't take that the wrong way."

He didn't take it the wrong way. He knew Max wasn't being deliberately offensive, he just wasn't sure he was ready to hear it.

"I'm headin' back to the hangar. Givin' the ship a tune-up. Again."

Scott was still stuck on Max's previous statement, but he forced himself to move on. "That dog still in the ship?"

"You mean Flopper? Yeah."

Flopper. Scott couldn't think of a less-intimidating name for a dog. "Toss him a few pillows in the corner of the bunk room. Let him stay here."

"You kiddin' me? I thought we were takin' him to the pound."

"Could you *really* take that dog to the pound?"

For several seconds, Max said nothing. Finally, he sighed, putting his hands on his hips. "No, hell. You know how it is."

Scott knew the sentiment all too well. He'd had dogs, too. "Just housebreak it good. Don't feed it scraps—that'll make it worse."

"As if any living creature could enjoy the junk they serve here, scraps or not," Max said, laughing and stepping back. "Thanks, man. I'll get it set up."

"Do it right." Scott watched as Max left the room, then he surveyed the other operatives. They were all going about their own business, which was probably the best thing that could have happened. For the first time in months, there was no tension in the room. His awkward speech appeared to have struck a chord with the other members of the unit. He'd made it right as best as he could, just as Jayden had suggested.

Suddenly he recalled the message Jayden had wanted him to pass on. "Varya," he said, calling her over quietly. The medic turned to face him.

"Jayden said he loves you."

The look she gave Scott was not the one he'd expected. She didn't smile, nor did she look happy. Her face turned pale. She must have realized how she looked, for in the next second, she faked a grin. It came out looking horrible. "I love him, too." She took a step back and walked away.

It was impossible for the question not to surface in Scott's head. *What was that about?*

Scott didn't stay in Room 14 long, nor did many of the others. Ultimately, only Becan, Esther, William, and Derrick remained behind. "Together" wouldn't happen overnight, but that was something Scott was prepared for. He was now confident that it would come in due time.

As for him, though, he had other business to tend to. He had a reinstatement request to write for a friend. He knew the reality of his chances; they didn't look good. But he didn't care.

Some risks were worth the gain.

* * *

DOSTOEVSKY'S ROOM was like a tomb; only a dim light illuminated the corner. The faint amber glow was just enough to allow the fulcrum captain to see.

He sat still on the edge of his bed in just shorts and an undershirt. Taut, deadly muscles covered his body, yet there was nothing threatening about him at all. He was leaning forward, his elbows bent on his knees and his head lowered. He stared obsessively at his open palms.

He turned his left hand over and stared at one finger in particular. The ring was there—so beautifully innocent, yet so silently terrible. Were it not for the hair-thin sliver that stuck up from its frame, it would have looked like a wedding ring.

No one had knocked on his door or hailed him through his comm since he'd left Room 14. No one had cared, as no one should've. He was alone.

He lifted his head to look across the room. His eyes closed with a determining wince. Then he moved his hand. It drifted to the side of his neck. The ring and its needle—the tool of the Silent Fever—hovered over his skin.

His breathing grew deeper as he held his hand in place, mere millimeters from inflicting the ring's wrath. His mouth hung open as he inhaled and exhaled, his palm wavering but never pressing forward. For a full minute he was unable to move.

Finally he collapsed, his palm falling as he lowered his head. Pulling the ring off with his free hand, he threw the small object across the room. It rattled as it bounced on the floor. He covered his face.

No one had knocked on his door or hailed him through his comm since he'd left Room 14. No one had cared, as no one should've. But contrary to what he'd previously believed, he wasn't alone.

Something else was in the room with him. Something was keeping him alive. It had stopped his hand from moving, as it had told him to go to Room 14 shortly before. It tore him apart, but wouldn't let him die.

It gripped him like fear.

32

SATURDAY, NOVEMBER 19TH, 0011 NE
1915 HOURS

NOVOSIBIRSK, RUSSIA

THAT EVENING

THE DAY PASSED for Scott with an optimistic sense of renewal. As evening approached the world of *Novosibirsk*, he felt anything but ready to turn in. He felt refreshed—as if he'd just awakened from a well-deserved sleep.

After speaking to the unit in Room 14, Scott had looked through the Fourteenth's roster as if he was in command, poring over each operative's history, trying to find new ways to use them. Though he opted not to eat with the unit's members, he did pass them several times in the halls. For the first time in months, he was met with looks of approval and respect. He offered both courtesies back. It was the first good day he could recall in a very long time. But it wasn't over yet.

For the past several days, he'd put off visiting Petrov in Confinement. He knew what the scientist wanted—to drill Scott on his telepathic connection with the aliens. In spite of Petrov's curiosity, Scott had decided not to tell the scientist anything—his trust in the man had greatly diminished. And Petrov wasn't the real reason Scott needed to make the trip, anyway. It had been five days since Tauthin had been saved from execution. That was as long as Scott could go without news.

As soon as Scott entered, Petrov hurried across the room to meet him. "It is good to see you, friend! I was wondering when you would come."

Scott noticed the addition of two new captives right away—the two Bakma he'd captured during the rescue of Pelican Squad, the ones Esther had stopped him from killing in the engine room. He spared them a brief look before looking at Tauthin's cell. "How is he?" The moment he saw the alien, he had his answer.

Tauthin was sitting on the edge of his cot, his wire-thin arms dangling over his knees. His head was down, but he was not unconscious. On the contrary, he looked well—and bored. The moment he saw Scott, the alien looked up, its bulging eyes widening. It was no longer attached to feeding tubes or medical instruments. The alien was garbed in what looked like peasant's rags—plain, brown cloth that hung loosely. It didn't look Bakmanese, but rather like a sack *Novosibirsk* had provided.

From behind Scott, Petrov said, "He had his first taste of calunod yesterday. His recovery has gone very well."

That the scientist sounded pleased disgusted Scott. *He'd be dead now if you'd had your way, you hypocrite.* "Let me in the cell."

"Wonderful! We can attempt to communicate with him again. Perhaps this new turn of events will make him more susceptible to interrogation."

"I want to go in alone. Open the door and let me in."

After a moment of hesitation, the scientist agreed. "As you wish." There was disdain and disappointment in his voice, but Scott didn't care. "Would you like an Ithini to connect you?"

"No. I don't want to connect." If he never connected again, that would be fine. "I'll teach him to talk." He wondered if Tauthin had ever been taught English or Russian while he was in the Walls of Mourning. Somehow he doubted it.

As soon as the cell door slid open, Tauthin rose to his feet. Despite the frailty of his body, he seemed able to move without hindrance.

Scott stepped inside and looked back. "Close the cell."

Petrov reluctantly complied.

It felt odd not to be afraid. As Scott stared at the Bakma, he was struck with how drastically different the alien looked now—how far removed it was from its once powerful stature. Tauthin had almost killed him in the turret tower during the *Assault on Novosibirsk*. It could be argued that Scott had survived by pure luck.

Scott was unfamiliar with Bakmanese emotions. He had no idea how to recognize a smile, a scowl, or even confusion. For all he knew, their expressions meant the opposite of human's. But something looked familiar. The Bakma's eyes were fixated on Scott's face, seeming to take it in from every angle. Then Scott remembered: his face was swollen. He had a black eye.

It looked like Tauthin was actually smirking.

Scott did the only thing he knew how to do—the only way he knew how to greet someone. He extended his hand.

The alien stared at Scott's outstretched palm. His opaque eyes watched the human's fingers intently, then looked up to catch Scott's expression.

Scott felt the urge to explain. "Your hand, in my hand." He motioned with a nod to Tauthin's arm. The alien did nothing.

He has no clue what this means. Scott withdrew his hand and pointed at himself. "Remington." *Start with names.* "Remington." He turned his finger around to point at the alien. "Tauthin." He motioned back and forth. "Remington. Tauthin."

Tauthin cocked his head to the side. He looked interested, but puzzled. When he spoke, Scott was surprised.

"*Remata.*" The alien's voice was raspy and coarse. It sounded either weak or physically injured. Maybe it was both.

Scott gave Tauthin a curious look. *Remata? Is that for Remington?* It had to be. Of all things, Scott found it humorous. He'd coined a diminutive name for Tauthin, so it was only fair that the favor was returned. "Remata. Yes," he nodded.

"*Gaas,*" Tauthin said back.

Gaas had to mean *yes*. The manner in which Tauthin said it, along with the tone of his voice—nothing else would have worked. The realization overwhelmed Scott. *He's just like a human.*

There was suddenly so much he wanted to know, so many questions that burned in his mind. He caught himself in the midst of a pleased moment. *Steklov would be proud. This is something he'd have wanted me to do. This is good.* He realized he'd forgotten Steklov's folder. It was the first time he'd ever done that before.

"*U'nakaassa ta'kuta,*" Tauthin said. "*Una-gaas'talas.*" His words were quick and fluent.

Scott had no idea what they meant, nor any idea whether Tauthin was telling him something or just spouting off. The words didn't sound angry, but they were firm. They sounded as if they had a point.

We have to learn how to communicate. He has to learn English. It would have been impractical for Scott to learn Bakmanese, and he didn't want to teach the alien Russian. *What can I tell him?* As he looked about the room, obvious answers sprung to mind. He pointed straight up. "Ceiling." Tauthin canted his head. Scott pointed down. "Floor." Then to the side. "Wall."

The lesson felt ridiculous even as Scott carried it out; a linguist probably would have been laughing aloud. But all Scott could think of was to begin with words whose meanings would be clear. He pointed to each one again. "Ceiling. Floor. Wall."

Tauthin nodded—a motion so natural, Scott almost missed its significance. *"Cele. Flora. Wao,"* the creature attempted.

Scott grinned. "Yes."

"Yaas. Gaas. Yaas."

This is unreal. When he'd spoken to the Bakma in the forest, he hadn't had a chance to reflect on what he was doing. He'd been in pure survival mode. Now, he could absorb and appreciate it, perhaps even enjoy it.

So where did he go with it now?

Four words surfaced in Scott's mind: interference, indication, allegiance, and judgment. The words he'd heard from the enemy Bakma. He needed to know what they meant. For a moment, he considered getting an Ithini to come in and connect them, but he decided against it. *That would probably be too typical for Tauthin. He's probably been through that a hundred times.* And Scott simply did not want to experience that again.

"Calunod," Tauthin said.

Scott knew the word well. He made an eating motion with his hand. "Calunod?"

"Yaas."

Their communication was at an elementary level, that was for certain. But the Bakma was willing. *He has to know I saved his life. That's got to be why he's receptive. Does that outweigh the fact that I took him prisoner?* He found it hard to believe that, during all Tauthin's time there, no one had persuaded him to speak about anything significant. The alien was obviously willing to learn.

A tap on the glass wall behind him startled Scott. Petrov was motioning for him to come from the cell. Meanwhile, Tauthin was staring at him expectantly.

Petrov's voice came over the loudspeaker. "Commander Remington. I would like to speak with you please, while you are here. Perhaps we can speak first, then you may go back in the cell?"

Scott decided to get it over with. Petrov would not leave him alone otherwise. *I'll give the scientist three minutes, tell him nothing, and get him off my back.* "I'm coming out," he called and looked at Tauthin. "I'll be right back." He knew his words wouldn't be understood literally, but the Bakma would know what he meant.

Tauthin acknowledged. *"Daasvi`danyaas."*

"Dosvedanya," Scott answered, without even realizing it. It didn't dawn on him immediately, but when it did, he froze in mid-stride. Tauthin had just told him goodbye in Russian. He spun around to the alien again. Tauthin stared back in silence.

Something unsettling stirred in Scott's gut, but he tried to dismiss it. The alien had been around Russian scientists all this time. Of course it would have learned a few words.

Tauthin sat back down on his cot.

As soon as Scott was out of the cell, Petrov approached him. "Commander Remington, I would like to talk to you about something."

I'm sure you would. "What is it?"

"Did you connect on your most recent mission?"

There was no point in denial. "Yes, I did."

"Please tell me about that."

"I connected briefly, and they attempted to negotiate a hostage exchange. They wanted to take Nightmen back with them."

Petrov scribbled furiously on a pad.

"That's it. They tried to do a prisoner exchange. Obviously, for them, it failed."

"Nothing else happened?" Petrov asked, sounding surprised. "You learned no further information?"

The guilt of deception tapped on Scott's heart. *Just give him something to chew on. One thing won't hurt.* "They wanted to take us to some place called Khuldaris. To be evaluated."

"What else did they say?"

"That was it." But it wasn't. He was leaving out the four words: interference, indication, allegiance, and judgment. He'd research those on his own. "Then we attacked."

The scientist scribbled again, then suddenly stopped. The pen was still poised in his fingers as he waited for Scott to continue. When he didn't, Petrov spoke again. "Are you *sure* that is it? Nothing else?"

"That's it. Nothing else."

The Russian's skepticism was obvious.

"What do you want to hear, Petrov?"

"I want to hear the truth. I want to hear what has happened so I can tell General Thoor."

He cringed at the sound of Thoor's name. That was precisely why he was keeping certain things hidden. "That is the truth. That's what I heard." It wasn't a total lie, just a lie of omission. Petrov hesitated for a moment, then he sighed. "Commander Remington—"

"Did you teach him Russian?" Scott interrupted.

"What?"

"Did you teach the Bakma Russian?"

"No, we did not."

It wasn't the answer he'd expected to hear. Scott's mind took the thought and ran. Tauthin was smart and the Bakma were crafty. He'd obviously secretly learned some basic Russian. *So what is he learning from me? I'd better be careful how I handle this alien.*

Scott cast a brief look back to the cell. He'd been acting under the assumption that the alien would be grateful to him. But what if it wasn't?

He told me goodbye in Russian. Was that a slip? Or did he want me to know that he knew?

Scott made a quick decision: before he went any further with Tauthin, he needed a better plan of attack. Just walking in and talking wasn't a good idea. He wanted to learn from Tauthin, not inadvertently aid and abet the enemy.

"Why do you ask?" asked Petrov. "Did he speak Russian to you?"

Yes, he did, Scott thought, though he chose not to disclose it. The less he confessed to Petrov, the better. He didn't trust the scientist at all. Without answering, he walked away.

"Commander Remington."

Scott kept walking.

"Commander Remington!" Petrov called out again. This time, Scott stopped and turned around. "The Bakma...he is not your friend."

Scott listened suspiciously.

"You have not been around them like me. If you trust him, you will be deceived."

If I trust you, Petrov, I will be deceived. Yet the scientist's words disturbed him. Turning around, he walked out the door.

Petrov didn't say a thing.

* * *

As Scott returned to his room, his mind raced. He was surprised at his own inclination to give Tauthin the benefit of the doubt. Was it because he'd encountered the alien before? Did he think that somehow

Tauthin would feel he owed Scott something for saving him from execution? Neither argument held much water. He'd captured Tauthin in the first place, and the Bakma were—as Petrov had pointed out—still the enemy. The Bakma had started this war, and Tauthin had still tried to kill him. Whether Tauthin's dedication to the Bakmas' war against humanity outweighed his personal code of honor was unknown. Scott was becoming increasingly uncertain.

This is why xenobiologists do this and not soldiers.

Nonetheless, he had learned something from the encounter. It was the first time he'd communicated to a Bakma in a non-combat situation. He was struck at just how humanlike they seemed. He could not be sure whether that was a good thing.

With all the drama, all that was happening in their personal lives, he reminded himself that they were still in the middle of a war. There were many still things they needed to learn.

He would speak to Tauthin again—and next time he would be prepared. He had to be, for reasons that went beyond his own aspirations. But he would be wary. He would approach the Bakma with caution, not rashly as he'd done minutes before.

Scott entered the officers' wing with a new sense of purpose; there was much he wanted to know. How had EDEN gone so long without getting answers? What things had The Machine discovered? EDEN used psychological torture and nothing else. Did Thoor have the more practical way with physical abuse? It was an unpleasant thought, but one he knew needed consideration.

As soon as he rounded the corner leading to his personal quarters, he saw a man sitting beside his door. He recognized David instantly. He sat leaning against the wall with one knee bent and the other extended. It looked like he'd been waiting for a while.

What was he doing there? Scott watched as David slowly pushed to his feet and approached. As soon as he was within earshot, the older man said, "Hey, Scott." He made no attempt to shake hands or feign a smile.

"Hi, Dave. What's goin' on?" Scott asked, trying to be casual.

David hesitated. "Just tell me you learned."

"What?"

"Just tell me you learned something through this."

He understood what David was saying. He just hadn't expected to hear it. "Someone set you up to talk to me?"

"Yeah."

That answer took Scott by surprise. It was the kind of honesty that stung. He opted not to ask who it was—he already knew it had to be Svetlana. There was no one else who came to mind. He nodded his head. "I learned a lot."

"You're all right with your teammates?"

"Yeah."

"You're all right with God?"

At that question, Scott fell silent. Indeed, God was the final area that needed repair. Scott didn't know where to begin—he didn't even know how to approach it. He wanted to be right with God. At least, he thought he did. Since Nicole's death, there'd been a hole in his faith, one that ached every day. But to be *right* with God? He wasn't sure what that meant anymore. He wasn't sure if God was right with *him*. "Yeah."

David immediately frowned. "Is that a lie?"

Scott sighed and laughed self-consciously. "Yeah."

"That's all right. I lied to you, too." Sliding his hands into his pockets, David took ten steps down the hall past Scott before turning around. "I never stopped caring completely."

Scott realized right then, as he locked eyes with the older man who had once been his closest ally, that the rift between them would never fully heal. This was their new cordiality, their new personal conversation. Few words, with minimal feeling, and just enough compassion to acknowledge the other person. Somehow, it felt okay. Scott lingered in the hall for several minutes after David had disappeared, allowing the conversation to register.

He didn't stay up too much longer, despite the fact that he wasn't overly tired. There was a morning session to be run when the sun came up. For the first time in months, he found himself looking forward to it. For the first time in just as long, he fell into a contented, dreamless sleep.

33

SATURDAY, NOVEMBER 20TH, 0011 NE
1530 HOURS

EDEN COMMAND

JUDGE BLAKE SIGHED with exhaustion as he stood before the High Command. In his hand was a single sheet of paper. "I am afraid, my fellow judges, that the direness of our situation has just come to light," he said, trying to keep his voice level.

Torokin listened eagerly as Blake went on. The two judges—Blake and June—had arrived back from *Novosibirsk* the day before. This was their first big debriefing, the one everyone was waiting for.

The Russian judge had spent the past several days visiting Confinement with Archer, in particular visiting Ceratopian No. 12. It was his first time sitting in on interrogations, and any preconceived notion he had that the quest for answers might be exciting had been summarily squashed. It was slow and agonizingly dull. It felt as if they were going in circles.

He was still looking into his theory—that for some reason, each species needed the other to fail more than they needed Earth—but he had no direction to take it. It was a hypothesis and nothing more.

"Prior to the *Assault on Novosibirsk*," Blake went on, "it was believed that there were approximately thirteen thousand actual operatives at the facility, of which roughly three thousand were Nightmen." He frowned. "In the aftermath of Carol's census, we've learnt we've been terribly wrong."

June listened solemnly to Blake's words.

"By her estimate, the current number of operatives garrisoned at *Novosibirsk*...is over seventeen thousand."

Gasps erupted across the room.

"Of those seventeen thousand, approximately *seven* thousand are Nightmen. Over half of them are completely unregistered."

Torokin was floored, despite the fact that before the meeting had begun he'd convinced himself that nothing should surprise him.

Grinkov looked at him. "*Novosibirsk* is lost to us," he said under his breath.

Richard Lena rose from his chair. "I want to get this straight, because right now, I think I must be confused. Are you tellin' me almost *half* of that base belongs to Thoor?"

"That's correct," Blake answered. "Carol performed a full headcount. She's literally looked at every roster. There are entire *units* that are unregistered—all full of Nightmen."

"You're gonna have to explain to me how this is possible. Last I recall, that base can't house seventeen thousand soldiers."

"Do you recall our spies' report concerning the 'Citadel of The Machine?'"

"Yeah," Lena said, nodding.

"It's an underground labyrinth—the remnants of Fort Zhukov."

"What the hell is Fort Zhukov?"

"It's what *Novosibirsk* was built atop," said Blake. "It was a fort dating back to the Old Era. The underground foundation of the base is very much intact. Unfortunately, I've been there myself."

Javier Castellnou asked, "Were you actually allowed *into* the Citadel?"

"We were allowed everywhere. I've seen their torture chambers, where they keep their own stock of alien captives. I've seen where they thrive. It is worse than you could possibly imagine."

"Were you able to make contact with our spies?"

"Our spies are dead."

The room fell silent. A barrage of wide-eyed stares hit the judge.

Blake continued. "Before we left *Novosibirsk* for home, General Thoor requested our presence. We were then taken to his own personal throne room." At the words *throne room*, several judges raised their eyebrows. "We were attacked physically and forced to watch as our spies were executed by a Nightman firing squad.

"And that is the focal point of my report," Blake went on. "Thoor was aware of our agents, and he murdered them before our very eyes. He attacked us. He grabbed me by the throat and lifted me a meter off the ground. Then he told me—and I remember it word for word—'You have no authority over The Machine. If you make any attempt to interfere with our operations, you will behold a massacre like none the world has seen. We will slaughter your soldiers like sheep.'"

The room was mesmerized.

"'Do not regulate this facility. Do not send us new personnel. We have personnel of our own. You will continue to supply us with equipment. We will continue to cooperate as we see fit. This is not a declaration of war. That is something you cannot afford.'" When he finished, he turned to June. "Was that correct?"

"That was it," she said somberly. "That was the message."

Blake turned to the others. "And that is the gist of my report, as brief as it may be. If you want to read specifics, take a copy of the whole report for yourself. This is the reality of *Novosibirsk*. What happens next is up to the Council."

As Judge Blake took his seat, the room's occupants were plunged into numbness. Suddenly all hell broke loose.

"We must go to war!" Castellnou shouted. "He has declared it, whether he denies it or not!"

"Mr. President," said Archer, "we *must* take immediate action."

Only Torokin said nothing as an onslaught ensued. The judges spoke one over the other. The volume escalated to rarely heard heights.

Lena rose to his feet. "If he has the nerve to murder our agents, to attack our judges, what *won't* he stop at? What if he goes after part of the world?"

"We've got to act *now*!" said Castellnou.

"Everybody be quiet!" Pauling said. "I've heard enough to make up my mind. I am ordering a full scale withdrawal of EDEN operatives from that facility, beginning right now."

The room plummeted into stunned silence.

"Our soldiers' lives are in danger," Pauling said. "Should Thoor choose to do so, he could kill every operative we have there."

"Mr. President," said Archer, "surely we're not giving up the base?"

"That's exactly what we're doing, Ben. Our operatives' lives are at stake."

Torokin couldn't believe what he was hearing. He was too flabbergasted to respond.

"Sir," Archer said, "I understand your anger. But it's not quite that simple a request."

"Nor is it right!" added Grinkov vehemently.

Archer went on. "We've got ten thousand operatives there. It would take days to evacuate them all even if we worked around the clock."

"Then let it take days!" Pauling shouted. "I'm sure General Thoor won't complain! Carol, I want you to look at alternate placements for the evacuees."

This was insane—Torokin could think of no other way to describe it. Pauling seemed to have lost his mind, and the Russian could no longer hold his tongue. "I understand your sentiment, Mr. President, but there are many problems with this solution. I, for one, do not want the Russian people solely protected by the Nightmen. If we leave *Novosibirsk*, it could be a disaster." He was in wonder. He'd never seen such an impassioned response by the president, nor such a poorly thought out one. "There is *Leningrad*, yes, but it is not of the caliber of *Novosibirsk*."

Grinkov spoke immediately after. "I am afraid I must agree with Leonid, Mr. President, and not only for Russia. *Novosibirsk* is the protector of a large region. Mongolia, China, much of the Middle East. We cannot abandon that part of the world. The Nightmen will most certainly *not* have the lives of innocent civilians as their priority."

The next one to speak was Judge Yu Jun Dao. It was the first time in what seemed like months that Torokin could remember the Chinese judge participating.

"I will not support any decision to abandon *Novosibirsk*," said Jun Dao. "I would sooner support military action, despite the risk to our own operatives."

Before Pauling could respond, Archer spoke again. "We must—*must*—respond with military action. If this goes unpunished, how will it look to the rest of the world? We already look like fools for what happened in Europe." He almost scoffed. "If you think recruitment is down *now*, wait until we abandon The Machine. We'll lose potential operatives in droves."

Pauling shook his head. "You all heard Malcolm's report. The moment the general is threatened in such a way, he'll massacre our forces there. We'll invade a base full of EDEN corpses."

"Then don't give him time to react!" Archer answered. "We move our forces into position and we attack. We don't give Thoor a chance to counter. Our forces at *Novosibirsk* could join our fight against him."

"Out of the question. There's too great a risk."

Archer threw his hands up. "Of *course* there's a risk!"

Torokin couldn't believe what he was hearing. As the room again erupted with shouts, he stared at the desperately defensive president of EDEN—the man entrusted to lead the defense of Earth, whose military record was laced with heroics. That was why he had been chosen as president: because he was a strong man. Or, perhaps more accurately, he *had been* a strong man. The past was the past. Almost before thinking, Torokin said above the din, "Perhaps now is the time for you to retire."

The arguments stopped. The glares, the angry retorts—all ceased instantaneously. Every judge turned to face Torokin, who knew the impact of his words the moment he said them. He'd just started a ripple.

"I respect you greatly, Mr. President. I respect all that you have done. Earth is safer because of you, but this is an issue that has gone on for too long already. *Novosibirsk* should have been resolved months ago, perhaps even years.

"We are at war with alien species. We have grown stagnant bickering over General Thoor. I understand there are lives at risk there, and your concern is admirable. You are more compassionate than anyone here. But we will not survive with compassion. We will survive only with strength. If we cannot stand up to one man and his infinitely smaller army, how will we stand up to the Bakma and Ceratopians? You are a good man, and despite our differences, I will always look upon you with respect. But if you cannot resolve *Novosibirsk* and prepare us for the war that truly matters...perhaps we need to be led by someone else."

Pauling glared, and his aged, weary expression began to lift. It was replaced by something fiercer. "I expected more from you, Leonid. I expected more from one of Klaus's best."

The ex-Vector sighed.

"You've missed the entire point of this!" Pauling said. "From a man who once was a soldier, you should know more about loyalty. I don't mean to me, I mean to your fellow comrades at *Novosibirsk*."

Torokin knew what was coming.

"We have to care because we're *not* like General Thoor. You want to go in guns blazing? Well, what about our troops? Where does that leave our men and women there? Dead? Executed in cold blood just like our spies?" Pauling's nostrils flared. "We owe it to the families of every one of those operatives to do everything in our power to keep them alive." He turned his fury to Archer. "You want to give Thoor no warning? Don't you think he'd find out our plan? He found our spies, for God's sake. He'd have our operatives killed before we touched down."

Archer said nothing.

"I will not attack *Novosibirsk*. Not while I'm president, and not under these conditions."

"Sir," Lena said, "we cannot withdraw."

"We can and we will." Everyone was quiet as Pauling surveyed the room. "I retire in four months. I intend to remain president until those four months are over. Contrary to belief, I am not a coward."

Torokin's heart hurt at Pauling's words.

"Before I retire, we will have evacuated *Novosibirsk*. Bit by bit, piece by piece, until the Nightmen are all who remain." The president looked up again. "We will do it by transfer requests. We'll find any excuse that we can, though I doubt Thoor would mind even if we announced our plan to the world. We've already starting moving some units to Europe, and he hasn't had a problem with that."

Pauling breathed heavily and concluded. "In four months, when I walk out this door for the last time, *Novosibirsk* will belong solely to the Nightmen. Our men and women will be safely removed." His expression became rigid with finality. "Then you can all do with The Machine as you see fit."

Torokin knew the damage he'd caused. He knew he'd created a rift between him and the president with whom he'd always gotten along, as well as casting doubt on the president's efficacy. But his words to Pauling had been necessary.

Pauling did not open the floor for discussion, nor did he ask any other questions. Instead, he turned to Judge June. "Formulate a relocation plan. Start tonight."

She nodded.

"Archer, you help her. Blake, as well."

Torokin knew Pauling was incensed. The president never referred to judges by their last names.

"Meeting adjourned."

The exodus was completed in under a minute. The judges rose from their seats and left the room without saying a word.

34

FRIDAY, NOVEMBER 25TH, 0011 NE
1002 HOURS

SIX DAYS LATER

THEY HEARD THE comm sound at the same time: Scott and Dostoevsky from their private quarters, and Max from the hangar. The tone-out spanned the Fourteenth from one end to the other. Only the incapacitated Jayden was spared.

Scott was just stepping out of the shower after a morning session. He had led the sessions every day since his speech to the unit; they'd gone as smooth as was possible given the unit's circumstances. Cohesion would come with time. Only Dostoevsky had been absent from the sessions—he hadn't been seen once all week.

Scott's hands had healed to the point where they no longer hurt. They'd be scarred, but he could live with that. The swelling in his face had gone down, though the bruise had become darker with healing. Shirtless, he grabbed the comm and acknowledged. Dostoevsky did the same from his end.

A voice Scott had never heard before emerged from the channel. It was as monotone as Thoor's, but unmistakably Russian. "All operatives of the Fourteenth, report to the hangar at once." That was all. No explanations, no formal end of transmission. The channel closed.

Turning to his closet, Scott stared at the vacant space where his fulcrum armor had once hung. It had been taken away for repairs after their last mission and had not been returned.

Scott reached for an undershirt and slipped it on. A minute later, he was dressed. Before he walked to the door, he allowed himself a look in the mirror. Despite his battered appearance, the man he saw was quietly assured.

He took to the halls.

Max, already in the hangar, was the first to notice that the Fourteenth wasn't alone in the callout. Several other squads—squads made up almost entirely of EDEN personnel—were rushing to their own transports to gear up. Max did the same. By the time other operatives of the Fourteenth began to arrive, he was in his armor outside the *Pariah*.

Svetlana was the first to approach him. "Max, what do you know?"

"Nothin' yet. I just got the callout."

Behind Svetlana, the rest of the Fourteenth trotted in—Captain Dostoevsky among them. The only one absent was Scott.

Max intercepted Dostoevsky immediately. "So that's it, huh? You just show up again like everything's normal?"

Dostoevsky removed his helmet. "Have you heard anything from Command?"

"You're the captain, shouldn't you know?"

"They have not told me anything. I do not know what to think."

"It's not the first time," Max quipped.

It was at that point when a new set of footsteps emerged in the hangar. Dostoevsky and Max turned around. Soon everyone else did, too.

It wasn't a member of the Fourteenth who approached. It was someone—a fulcrum—none of them had seen before. With the exception of one. Behind his faceless helmet, Dostoevsky's mouth fell.

The stranger was as large as Egor and William. His helmet was in his hands, his face exposed. He was older with a face etched with cracks and wrinkles. His graying hair was pushed up like a tousled mohawk. The EDEN operatives stared in bewilderment.

He marched past Dostoevsky, scrutinizing the fulcrum captain harshly. Then he faced the rest of the unit.

"I am Colonel Saretok," he said, his voice at once peculiar and grating. "You have been placed under my jurisdiction."

After receiving the initial callout, Scott had gone to Room 14 in search of his armor, thinking it had been delivered there by mistake. He'd found nothing. The delay in its return had tried his patience in the past several days, but now it had become a legitimate emergency. Now he needed it and it wasn't there.

He walked into the hangar wearing only his uniform. It wasn't the best way to make an entrance, but what other choice did he have? He couldn't fail to show up at all.

As soon as he neared the *Pariah*, Scott spotted Saretok at the same time as Saretok saw him.

"Where is your armor, Remington?"

Scott had no idea who the man was. Before he could ask questions, Dostoevsky said, "This is Colonel Saretok, Remington. He is one of Thoor's personal guards and overseer of *Novosibirsk*'s security."

Saretok addressed Scott again. "I will ask you again. Where is your armor?"

"It was damaged during our last mission," Scott answered. "It hasn't been returned yet." Why would such a powerful fulcrum as Saretok be addressing the Fourteenth?

"Scott," Max interrupted, "your armor's in the ship."

Scott blinked. Why would his armor be delivered to the ship? It made little sense, but at least it was somewhere. As his mind posed new questions, he entered the *Pariah*.

It was the first time Scott had encountered a colonel at *Novosibirsk*. Colonels ran platoons, which *Novosibirsk* didn't have. The Machine marched to its own squad-based drum. Perhaps that rank was reserved for fulcrums of unique stature.

The young dog Flopper was lying by the door. His ears lay flat as he rested his chin on the floor of the ship. He stared at Scott with observant eyes.

Stepping to his locker, Scott grabbed the latch and pulled the door open. His mind was still churning, even as he registered the fact that his armor was indeed there. *How will the unit react to a third fulcrum? How will Saretok react to them?*

Suddenly, his thoughts slammed to a halt. His awareness was thrust straight ahead, into the locker he'd so carelessly flung open moments before—at the armor he'd only barely perceived until then.

...oh my God...

Outside the *Pariah*, hands clasped behind his back, Saretok began his mission brief. "I will tell you about our operation, then I will tell you why I am here." Everyone paid him attention—except Max and Svetlana. Their attention was solely on the *Pariah*'s troop bay.

Nothing prepared Scott for what faced him inside his locker. His fulcrum armor was as black as it had always been. It still had its menacing horns. But there was something else about it that captivated his eyes.

Something impossible to miss. It caused the hairs on his arms to stand on end. Reaching out, he ran his hand along its glossy surface.

How did this happen? That question was the first to hit his mind, though others immediately followed. Who was responsible? And why?

He registered Saretok speaking, but he didn't hear the man's words. His focus was fixed straight ahead.

"Ten minutes ago," Saretok continued, "two Ceratopian vessels—a Cruiser and a Battleship—entered Earth's atmosphere over Verkhoyanskiy. They were traveling at a very high speed. Vindicators from *Novosibirsk* were sent to intercept them. Something happened before the Vindicators reached them—something we have never seen before.

"Six Bakma Noboats materialized behind the Ceratopian ships. The Ceratopians were then shot down. The Vindicators arrived in time to assault the Noboats. They shot one Noboat down before the others disappeared."

Scott's jaw clenched as he assembled his armor piece by piece, clamping his leg guards around his thighs and ankles, sliding his arm guards over his forearm and biceps, moving his fingers in their metal-laced gloves. Then came his shoulder harness, then his chest plate. Everything engaged with solid metal clanks.

"The Fifty-first and the Forty-second are being dispatched to the Ceratopian vessels," Saretok explained. "We are to engage and capture the fallen Bakma Noboat they left behind. Never before have we witnessed an air-to-air confrontation between the two alien species. Taking prisoners is our primary objective."

The last part to come down was Scott's helmet. As he slid it down over his head, his face disappeared behind a featureless plate. The fulcrum was complete.

Standing alone in the troop bay, his back to the open bay door, Scott angled his head to take in Saretok's words.

Saretok wrinkled his nose. "It has come to our attention that the Fourteenth's leadership is unstable. That is why I am here."

Dostoevsky looked at the floor.

"I am here to eliminate all doubt. Today, you will see what a leader is supposed to be. There will be no question as to who you should follow—" Saretok stopped abruptly, his focus suddenly shifting to the *Pariah*. The operatives stared at the colonel strangely, before their own heads followed his gaze.

Scott was standing on the ramp of the Vulture. His black fulcrum armor gleamed with dangerous luster as he firmly gripped his E-35 assault rifle. His M-19 handgun was attached to his belt. So were two grenades.

The horns of his fulcrum armor were as sinister as ever, spiking back around his featureless faceplate. But something about that spiked half-collar was different. It was the first thing everyone noticed—it made them gasp in astonishment.

The horns were made of gold.

Scott approached Max and Svetlana. His words—amplified by the mechanizations in his helmet—were as much a question as a statement. "You did this."

"Talk to the blonde," Max said, smiling. "It was her idea."

Svetlana's eyes settled on Scott. "You told me you could not wash your hands of this sin," she said. "That it would devalue the life that you took. You told me this was who you were." A faint smile curved up from her lips. "Perhaps you can be something else, too."

Scott glanced at the rest of the unit. Across the board from EDEN to the Nightmen, the operatives looked on with awe. A black and gold fulcrum. It had never been seen.

"Be who you are, Scott Remington," Svetlana said. "Fallen or not."

The meaningful moment was cut short. "Cute, but irrelevant," said Saretok. His attention returned to the others. "Board your transport, Fourteenth. We have a mission to accomplish." No one looked at him; their eyes were on Scott alone.

Turning away, Scott walked back into the ship.

As soon as everyone was inside, Max explained the assignment to Scott. The very nature of the mission demanded Scott's focus—two Ceratopian vessels shot down by the Bakma. Were the Ceratopians and Bakma actually enemies?

Dostoevsky sat alone across from Scott. Even as the *Pariah* rolled onto the airstrip in preparation to lift, he only stared at the floor.

Saretok stood in the middle of the cabin. "We are expecting low casualties from the fallen Noboat. It has not endured heavy damage in the crash." When he looked at the cabin floor, he frowned. "What is *this*?"

The dog stared up at the colonel, paws outstretched as its head lay on the floor.

Dostoevsky cleared his throat. "We took the dog from Chernobyl, colonel. It is ours."

Saretok glared at the animal and then at Dostoevsky. "This is very disappointing, Yuri."

Dostoevsky didn't reply.

Turning to the other Nightmen, Saretok said, "The general wishes to take prisoners alive. Use lethal force for the initial defense. Incapacitate the rest when given the chance."

Restraint. Scott found that concept ironic when presented to Nightmen. Lethal force was what they knew best.

"The crash site is in the middle of frozen plains. Pilot, you will drop off my team thirty meters south of the Noboat's location. You will then hold suppression fire while my team converges." He puffed up his chest. "There is no place for the Bakma to hide. We will attack them outright."

Esther had been listening intently to Saretok, and Scott knew why. "Colonel, Private Brooking is a scout. She could be dropped off in advance to—"

"She is of no use in this terrain," Saretok said, clamping on his helmet. His mohawk was replaced by black metal. "The Bakma will be suppressed by the Vulture until we reach the Noboat. Full participation will *not* be required."

Scott realized it right then: Saretok had no intention of using anyone from EDEN.

"Goronok," Saretok said, turning to Egor, "you will use explosive shells to clear the antechamber. You will then accompany me, Dostoevsky, and the German into the aft hallway. We will sweep the storage rooms, living quarters, dining hall, and engine room." He turned to Scott. "You and Romanov will clear the bridge of the vessel. Ryvkin will remain in the antechamber as backup for both teams."

Scott felt the cabin deflate. This had all been planned from the outset. Why even bother bringing the others along?

"Pilot, what is our ETA?"

"Not long."

Never before had Scott heard Travis so dejected—so uncaring—not even when he'd been criticized in Room 14.

Surprisingly, Saretok accepted Travis's answer. The fulcrum colonel readied his gun.

Scott pondered. This wasn't the way to keep a unit stable. If that's what Saretok had intended, he was failing miserably. As he surveyed his teammates, Scott saw that every head was down except David's. The older man was staring straight at him, the expression on his face revealing his thoughts.

This was not right.

Before long, the *Pariah* reached the crash site. The transport decelerated as its descent began. Once again, Travis's emotionless voice came over the speakers. "Coming down." The Nightmen collected near the rear door.

Snow crunched softly as the *Pariah* landed. The rear bay door lowered.

Customarily, this was when ground leaders offered a final word. But no such word came from Saretok. He stood in silence by the door, his E-35 in his hands.

"Pilot, engage."

The *Pariah*'s nose-mounted cannon erupted. Bullets clanged and sparked against the Noboat's antechamber door.

Saretok burst from the ship with Scott and the other Nightmen fast in his wake, taking an angled route toward the vessel to avoid Travis's shots. The cannon fire was deafening. The heat it produced was in shocking contrast to the frigid air. Bullets peppered the Noboat, tearing a gaping new hole in its closed outer door.

"Hold fire!" Saretok ordered through the comm. He looked at Egor. "Fire your hand cannon."

Egor aimed the weapon forward, sending a projectile explosive toward the alien ship. It detonated, and the antechamber burst into flames.

There was little resistance en route to the door. Within moments, all six armored men were ready to enter. The assault began. Saretok, Dostoevsky, Auric, and Egor moved through the antechamber to the aft hallway. Viktor remained behind, as Scott and Nicolai dashed to the bridge.

Even in battle, Scott was critiquing Saretok's command. *Esther could have come in through the Noboat's top entrance, as she did in the forest. She could have supplemented Saretok's team. Svetlana and Varvara could be here preparing to treat wounded Bakma.* Without even realizing it, Scott had gunned down several Bakma. Nicolai had killed some as well. They were knee-deep in a firefight around the corner of the bridge doorway.

Noboat bridges were not large—roughly the size of a Vulture's troop bay but octagonal. There were six workstations: one for the captain, pilot, navigator, chief engineer, weapons specialist, and a communications officer. At least those were the human equivalents. The ceiling was lower in the bridge, and almost every station was built into the wall.

The crash had been mild, but the room was still damaged extensively. There were four Bakma in the bridge, holding their own against Scott and Nicolai. Scott could hear the battle on Saretok's end.

Darting around the corner, Scott fired a round. One of the Bakma was shot in the shoulder. It dropped its weapon and crashed to the floor.

Nicolai executed a similar attack and a second alien was incapacitated.

Make them surrender. Take them alive and save our medics the trouble.

"*Grrashna!*" Scott yelled from the corner. He knew his Bakmanese was incorrect—technically, he was telling the Bakma *he* was surrendering. But he knew they'd know what he meant. Popping around the corner again, Scott unleashed another burst of gunfire. Intended to be a warning, his bullets tattered violently against the bridge walls.

There was a brief volley of return fire and then the defense effort lulled. An alien shouted from the bridge. "*Grrashna!*"

Scott didn't hesitate. He rushed the bridge, his assault rifle forward.

Two unscathed Bakma threw down their weapons and held their hands in the air. Six more in total were sprawled across the room—two injured and four dead.

The Bakma survivors stared at Scott. It struck him just how different he must have looked with his golden spiked collar. The Bakma probably thought it was some kind of a rank.

This collar...is this why Sveta and Max crafted it, so I could charge into battle and leave them behind? Was this what they envisioned would happen?

Gunfire subsided far behind him; an eerie quiet arose. Saretok's voice crackled over the comm. "Aft section secured."

"Bridge secured," Scott answered. He looked at the Bakma. "Come on. Out." Gathering their wounded comrades, the aliens complied.

Back in the *Pariah*, the other half of the Fourteenth was sitting in wait. Little had been spoken since the assault began.

Travis had his feet propped on the control panel dashboard as his hand pressed idly against his cheek. He had the Fourteenth's comm chatter routed through the *Pariah*'s speakers so that everyone in the unit could hear.

Saretok's voice came over the comm. "Ryvkin, we have three wounded." His words were in Russian. "Hurry and stabilize them."

Viktor complied.

"Sveta, Varya, come help with the wounded," Scott said through the channel.

Svetlana lit up when she heard his voice. Both medics rose to their feet.

"Negative, Remington," Saretok said. "Ryvkin does not need assistance. Prepare the hostages for transfer to the Vulture."

Frustrated, Svetlana and Varya returned to their seats.

The speakers were cut off. "That's all I can take," Travis said from the cockpit. The frequency squeaked and twisted, settling on something altogether different—on Russian voices none of them recognized.

"Fall back, Teterin. We're stuck at the corner."

"One down—where is the technician?"

"Falling back, captain."

Travis looked back from the cockpit. "That's from the Fifty-first at the Ceratopian site. Might as well listen in—it's not like we're doing anything else." He adjusted the volume to background level.

Max tossed down his helmet.

"Do not get upset. This will pass," Svetlana said.

"Hope is a carrot," answered Max. "We're the horse."

William looked at him strangely. "What?"

"It's a metaphor."

"What's a metaphor?"

"What I just said."

"A carrot is a *metaphor*? Is that like a *petit four*?"

Max stared at the demolitionist. "If you're serious, I'm killing myself."

"Noboats! Noboats!" The comm chatter erupted.

Every operative jumped.

"Fall back! Noboats engaging! Pavel, lift off!" There was a burst of static, followed by screaming.

"Is tha' from the Fifty-first?" Becan asked, hurriedly sitting upright.

Travis turned up the volume, as unintelligible statements blared over the speakers.

The operatives swapped frantic looks. "What the hell are they saying?" Max asked Svetlana.

She translated the words. "They're saying, 'Vindicators down!' And now, 'Forty-two down!'—they keep repeating, 'Forty-two down!'"

Max and David said it simultaneously. "The Forty-second's Vultures." Max leapt on the comm. "Scott, get in here now."

Travis furiously worked the communication lines. "*Pariah* to Fifty-one! *Pariah* to Fifty-one!" He looked at Boris, who was already contacting *Novosibirsk*. "There were four Vultures between those two units, Boris. I've lost all four signatures."

"*Novosibirsk*, this is the *Pariah*," Boris said. "We are hearing chatter from the Fifty-first and Forty-second."

"*Pariah* to the Fifty-first, *Pariah* to the Fifty-first, is anyone receiving this?"

A disjointed reply crackled through. "*Pariah*...from the air, by Couriers...Battleship! We're..."

"What the hell does that mean?" Max rushed to the cockpit door. The operatives behind him prepped their weapons.

Travis shook his head. "Fifty-first, I did *not* receive your full transmission. Please transmit again."

This time, the answer was clear. "This is Captain Tkachenok! Bakma Noboats are engaging us *and* the Ceratopian vessels! Our Vultures have been destroyed. We are trapped inside the Battleship!"

"What about the Forty-second?"

"Forty-second is destroyed!"

Max stormed into the troop bay just as Scott appeared from outside. "Get ready to lift!"

Scott ran up the ramp and tore off his helmet. "What's going on?"

"Noboats are attacking the other units. They took out the Fifty-first and Forty-second's Vultures—they've got operatives trapped on the ground."

That was all Scott needed to hear. "Gear up and get ready!" he ordered, clamping his helmet back on. "William, go armor-piercing."

"Aye aye!"

The next voice they heard was neither frantic or eager, but as collected as anyone could have been. "We are returning to The Machine with the Bakma prisoners." Saretok calmly walked up the ramp. "Pilot, set in a course for *Novosibirsk*."

Travis stared blankly.

Scott lowered his rifle. "Colonel, the Fifty-first and Forty-second are under—"

"I know of the Fifty-first and Forty-second. I have already been advised by *Novosibirsk*. There will be no rescue attempt by us or anyone else. Those units are not our concern."

"Not our concern?" Max gaped.

Dostoevsky and the slayers appeared at the bottom of the ramp. Bound Bakma captives were clustered behind them.

"We have captured extremely important prisoners," Saretok said. "We must return them to *Novosibirsk* at once."

Max stared past Saretok to Dostoevsky. "Yuri, we've gotta go after 'em!"

Dostoevsky removed his helmet, revealing a look of total helplessness. "Colonel, perhaps we can leave someone to stay with the Bakma while we—"

"Shut up, Dostoevsky. We are returning to The Machine."

Scott couldn't believe what he was hearing. Over the loudspeaker, the battle continued.

"Ozerov down!"

"Come back to the corner!"

"Captain, we cannot!"

The next words, though Russian, were universally understood. Captain Tkachenok was calling for help.

"*Novosibirsk*! *Novosibirsk*! If you are receiving this, please answer!"

No answer came.

"NovCom's ignoring them," Esther said quietly.

Scott lowered his head in mounting frustration.

"Yuri, take back your unit!" Max shouted. "This isn't right!"

Dostoevsky's mouth hung down in stupor.

"How can you let this happen? You're the captain of this unit, not Saretok! How can you stand there like a coward and do *nothing*?"

Saretok glared at Max. "You have spoken enough."

"You ain't *half* the man Clarke was," Max spat at Dostoevsky. "Clarke wouldn't care *what* this guy said!"

Behind Dostoevsky, the slayers exchanged anxious glances. Dostoevsky tried desperately to speak. "Max, there is nothing I can do—"

"You can do *something*!"

"Enough!" Saretok bellowed, his voice shaking the walls. He looked at Dostoevsky at the bottom of the ramp. "You are pathetic. You command *nothing* here. You are a disgrace."

For the briefest of moments Dostoevsky's eyes shimmered.

They're all going to die, thought Scott. He had no idea who was in the Fifty-first or the Forty-second. He didn't know any of their names. All he knew was that they were in the middle of a battle between two alien species, with no way to escape. Regardless of who won, they would lose.

From the corner of his eyes, he could see his golden collar—his horns. It had been so long since he'd done anything close to heroic that he almost couldn't recall how it felt. He looked at the expressions of his teammates—Max's anger, Travis's terror, David's disbelief. He saw the pain in them all. *Enough is enough.* He turned to Travis. "Set a course for the Ceratopian crash site."

At Scott's defiance, Saretok took off his helmet. "Remington, this unit is *yours.*" He pointed at Dostoevsky. "His time is finished. Do not make this mistake and sacrifice it all. They are not worth it."

Scott faced him dead on. "*Who* is not worth it? What exactly do you mean?"

"Do you think you are saving anything by going to their rescue? Give those units another mission and they will still die. You are delaying the inevitable at the risk of your future."

"I saw Nightmen with those units before we left," Scott answered. "I saw them with the Fifty-first and Forty-second. Not many, but they were there."

"Some Nightmen are not worth saving."

Dostoevsky stared at the debate. Not once did he move.

"You have favor with us," Saretok said. "I speak to you as one fulcrum to another. You have a chance to be relevant." The colonel sighed. "I am urging you to make the smart choice. I do not wish to force you. You are young to have accomplished so much—do not lose it all here."

It all became clear—why Saretok had been there all along. Not to provide temporary stability to the unit, but to find out if Scott was prepared to take the reins. All other motives had been a façade.

Saretok approached Scott in the troop bay until they were standing face to face. "Where Dostoevsky has failed, you can succeed. You wield fear like a sword. You can be strong."

Fear and strength—the motivating tools of the Nightmen. Scott was a Nightman *because* of those two factors.

"That is why you are valuable to General Thoor. You have fire that few others have."

Scott closed his eyes. Fire that few others had—that was why The

Machine cared so much about him, enough to throw the more experienced, and maybe more skilled Dostoevsky in the trash. Scott's violent propensities were more desirable.

"Your rule begins here."

They wanted anger. They wanted force and vehemence and someone who would inflict pain at the drop of a hat. They wanted a lion of their own.

It was time to give them one.

Scott didn't stifle the urge. In a single, fluid motion, he twisted, thrust forward, and kicked Saretok dead in the chest. The colonel flew backward and rolled all the way out of the ship. Everyone else jumped to their feet.

Scott stood at the edge of the ramp. In the thin layer of snow below, Saretok scrambled to his feet. But it was the American fulcrum—the Golden Fulcrum—who closed the debate. "You just told me my rule begins here. Who am I to disagree?"

"Remington!" Saretok yelled.

"Everyone, prepare for ascent. Travis, send a message to the Fifty-first and Forty-second. Tell them we're on our way."

"Remington!"

Scott turned around. Saretok was still standing in the snow, veins bulging from his forehead. "Do you think you will escape from this? Do you realize what you have done? You have destroyed all you have built up!"

"Do me a favor and watch the prisoners," Scott said. "I'm sure they'll send someone for you eventually." He turned to walk away, but paused and looked back down the ramp. "Then again—some Nightmen aren't worth saving."

Every operative in the troop bay grinned.

At the bottom of the ramp, Auric and Egor turned to Nicolai and Viktor. Together, the slayers strode past Dostoevsky into the ship.

Scott had already moved on. *One Cruiser and one Battleship. There could be a hundred Ceratopians. We have no idea how many Noboats there are.* He addressed the crew. "We're dropping into a very hot zone. Travis, I want every ounce of info you can get me."

"Already on it!"

Svetlana touched Scott's arm. She said nothing, but gave him a purposeful look. She motioned her head down the ramp.

Dostoevsky was still standing outside. As the icy winds of Verkhoyanskiy swept past him, his weathered black hair tossed about. He watched the unit that was leaving him behind.

Scott observed the Russian. *Is this how you thought it would be, Yuri? Are you getting what you deserve?* Scott angled his head down in consideration. *Or do you deserve another chance, too?* He stared at Dostoevsky for what felt like a full minute. Then he spoke. "We could use a hand, Yuri."

The other operatives and slayers stared at the abandoned fulcrum. Dostoevsky slipped his helmet back on.

Redeem yourself, Yuri. Make yourself right.

As Dostoevsky stepped into the *Pariah*, Saretok was left in his wake. Behind the colonel, the bound Bakma prisoners looked confused. The *Pariah*'s rear bay door slowly closed.

Max approached Scott. "What's the plan?"

The plan? He hadn't gotten that far yet. "There's no way we can do this alone. We could be outnumbered twenty to one."

"Tanneken," Max said. "She'll come if I call."

Scott thought about it. Tanneken was only a lieutenant; she couldn't dictate the actions of a squad. Furthermore, if she or anyone from the Thirty-ninth came to help, there was no telling what Thoor would do in revenge. She didn't deserve that.

Scott needed someone else. He needed a leader who didn't matter to The Machine. Someone with something to prove. He grabbed Max by the shoulder before he could call anyone. "Wait. Don't call Tanneken yet."

Max stopped in mid-comm adjustment.

"I know someone else."

35

FRIDAY, NOVEMBER 25TH, 0011 NE
0652 HOURS

EDEN COMMAND

AT THE SAME TIME

BENJAMIN ARCHER was brushing his teeth when a knock came at his door. Leaning down, he spit out a mouthful of toothpaste. "Just a moment!"

It was the start of a new day at EDEN Command. With no meetings scheduled with the High Command until mid-afternoon, the morning was open for all the judges. Archer was a punctual 0630 riser.

Walking to the door with a freshly rinsed mouth, the blond Briton pulled it open. Still draped in his dark green bathrobe, he stared at the courier before him. "Is there a problem?"

The courier was struggling for breath. "Sorry, Judge Archer," he said. He extended a hand that held a small letter. "Message from Kang. He told me to run."

"Very well. Thank you," said Archer, taking the letter. He stepped back inside his room and closed the door. Unfolding the letter, he quietly read.

Moments later, the same door was flung open from inside. The courier, still outside in the hall, flinched and turned around. Archer sped past him up the hall, his robe flapping behind him. Clenched firmly in his hand was the letter.

"Jason! Malcolm!" Archer yelled into his comm. "I need you both in the War Room *at once*!" Dodging past the sparse crowd in the hallways, he ran full speed ahead.

A minute later, Archer burst through the doors of EDEN Command's War Room. In the center of the room, a holographic globe of Earth slowly rotated. From various consoles along the walls, staffers turned to the intruding judge.

"*Everyone, out!*" Archer shouted. People jumped out of their chairs and rushed for the doors.

The War Room was the hub of all global operations for EDEN. Every incursion—every incident—appeared on the globe, which could be manipulated at will. It was rare when this special room came into use, but it was always ready. It had most recently been used for the massive attack on Europe.

No sooner had the last staffer exited than Judge Blake burst through the door. He was barefoot in a T-shirt and briefs. "What the bloody hell is going on?"

"Catastrophe," Archer said, manipulating the globe so that it displayed Verkhoyanskiy from every angle. "They had him. They bloody *had* him."

"Who? They had *who*? And who is *they*?"

Just then Judge Rath entered. He was the only judge in proper garb. "What the hell?"

Archer spoke into the console comm. "Security lockout, priority black, requested by Archer, Benjamin, authorization: Tango Delta Foxtrot." The doors along the walls slid shut and their locking mechanisms engaged. The security cameras in the room deactivated themselves.

Rath and Malcolm rushed to the globe.

"They were leaving Earth with him when they got intercepted," Archer said frantically. His voice was shaking. "Thoor's already got two units there."

Blake shook his head confoundedly. "I have no idea what you're talking—"

"H`laar!" Archer shouted. "The Golathoch had H`laar!" Both the other judges stared in disbelief.

"They were intercepted by a squadron of Noboats. Thoor moved in to secure the whole thing." Archer quickly worked the controls. "If he gets H`laar and he is *alive*…" He thrust Kang's letter into Blake's hands. "Read for yourself!"

"Where was he?" Rath asked. "Was he already on Earth?"

Archer shook his head. "I have no idea."

"What time is it there?"

"Late morning, early afternoon."

"Vector," said Rath.

"Vector's too clever. I'm contacting Platis."

Over Archer's comm, a Chinese voice spoke aloud. "Tracking fifth Vulture to crash site."

"Fifth?" Rath's brow arched straight up.

"The first four were grounded," Archer growled as he opened a new comm connection. "General Platis, this is Judge Archer from EDEN Command. I need the Agèma dispatched at once. Sending your orders now." He transmitted the coordinates and parameters.

Moments later, a Greek voice replied. "Orders received."

Archer spoke clearly and firmly. "This is a priority black assignment. You have clearance to engage Thoor's forces if you must. The objective summary will tell you everything you need to know."

"Understood, judge."

The channel was closed.

For the first time in over a minute, Judge Blake spoke. He was still clutching Kang's letter low at his side. "Platis will never make it in time. If Thoor's already got transports en route and on scene…"

Archer ignored him and turned to Rath. "Meet them outside of *Cairo*. You know what for."

The Canadian judge left the room.

Only then did Archer answer his British counterpart. Turning his eyes back to the orbiting globe, he rested his hands on the railing encircling it. "Never doubt, Malcolm. Never doubt."

* * *

"SIR," SHOUTED TRAVIS from the cockpit, "I've got a layout!"

Scott was already in the middle of another task. Adjusting his comm to a frequency he'd used only once before, he placed the call.

Rex Gabriel was in the middle of a cafeteria meal when his comm sounded. The remnants of Pelican Squad—those who remained at *Novosibirsk*—gave the sudden noise their attention as well. The moppy-haired Australian scrutinized his comm display. When he recognized Scott's name, he furrowed his brow and answered. "Gabriel, mate."

"You still want to repay that debt, captain?" Scott asked through the speaker.

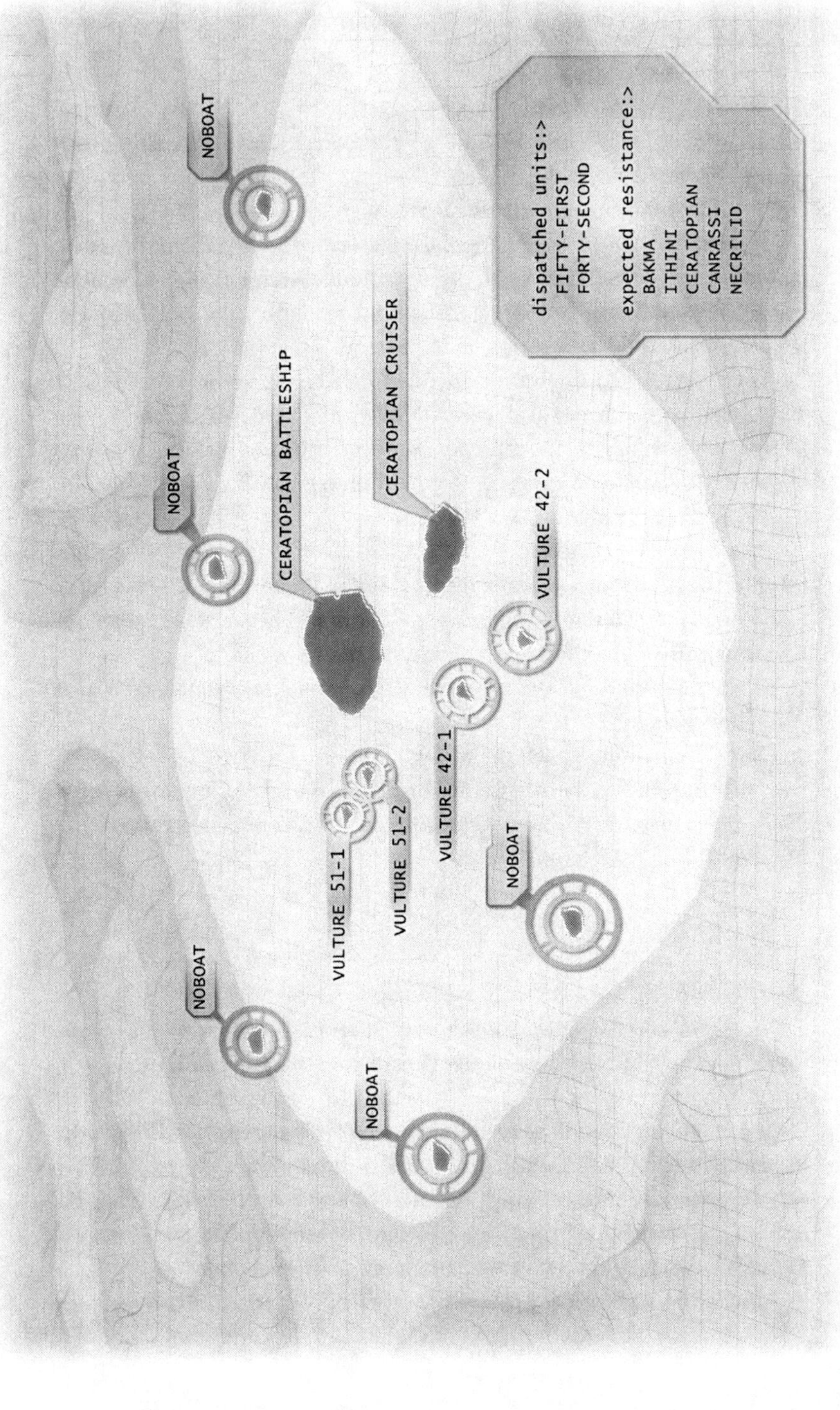

dispatched units:>
FIFTY-FIRST
FORTY-SECOND
expected resistance:>
BAKMA
ITHINI
CERATOPIAN
CANRASSI
NECRILID
NOBOAT
CERATOPIAN CRUISER
CERATOPIAN BATTLESHIP
NOBOAT
VULTURE 42-2
VULTURE 42-1
VULTURE 51-1
VULTURE 51-2
NOBOAT
NOBOAT
NOBOAT

In the background of the *Pariah*, Travis was yelling. "Five Noboats on the ground! I'm getting nothing from the EDEN units."

"Where are you, Remington?" asked Gabriel.

For the next minute, Scott explained everything, from the initial callout to the trapped units' ignored pleas for help. With every word he said, the operatives of the Pelican grew more and more anxious. Gabriel motioned to his crew to get ready, and they rose from their seats.

"Do you have a pilot?" Scott asked.

"Yes, but no ship."

In the *Pariah*'s troop bay, Max tapped Scott from behind. "Tanneken," Max said. "Trust me, man."

Scott had no choice but to give in. "Find Tanneken Brunner," he said to Gabriel. "She's a lieutenant with the Thirty-ninth."

"She's a commander," Max corrected. "She's a commander now."

A commander? That changed things considerably. Max motioned for the comm and Scott handed it to him.

"Gabriel, this is Matthew Axen. I know Tanneken real good..."

Scott didn't hear whatever else Max said. After a third request for his presence from Travis, he went to the cockpit, leaning in between the pilot and Boris. "What do we have?"

"Check out the map. The Ceratopian ships are surrounded."

The wall monitor showed that the two Ceratopian vessels were not far from each other. The Battleship sat in the center of the display, with the smaller Cruiser within walking distance to the southeast.

The four crashed Vultures were split into two pairs. There was a pair to the west of the Battleship belonging to the Fifty-first. The two Forty-second Vultures were west of the Cruiser.

It became immediately apparent why the EDEN units had been overrun. Bakma Noboats surrounded the Ceratopian Battleship in a wide circle, encompassing the Vultures as well. Three Noboats were to the west, and two to the east. Humans were the only barriers between the Bakma and the Ceratopians. They'd been mugged from behind and forced inside the Ceratopian vessels—surrounded by two apparently antagonistic species.

"Do we know who's where?"

"I've had brief contact with Captain Tkachenok of the Fifty-first," answered Travis. "He has two teams at opposite ends of the Battleship. Both teams are cut off from each other. As far as the Forty-second, I've only been able to reach one small team in the Cruiser. Talked to a guy named Torban—he's a medic. He said he's got heavily wounded."

"What are we looking at?" Max asked.

Every crew member looked to Scott for direction—both EDEN and Nightman. He stepped back in the troop bay. "I'd love to give you all a rousing speech, but the Fifty-first and Forty-second don't have time. We need to be perfect." He pointed to the map. "We have *six* locations that require immediate attention—four Vultures and two Ceratopian ships."

As Scott spoke, Dostoevsky watched, his emotions hidden behind his helmet.

"Sveta," Scott continued, "your responsibility will be to treat the wounded in these two Vultures," he pointed to the southernmost pair of transports, the ones belonging to the Forty-second by the Cruiser. "We have to assume they'll have the heaviest wounded."

Svetlana acknowledged.

"Becan and Auric, you're in charge of keeping her safe. Secure the crash sites, hold off the Bakma, and let her do her job."

Scott turned to Varvara. "You're in charge of the Fifty-first, *directly* between the Noboats and the Battleship. Nicolai and Derrick will go with you. Are you okay to go?" he asked the still-wounded Derrick.

Derrick hobbled to his feet. "Just prop me up and gimme a gun."

"I will go too," said Boris. The technician climbed from the cockpit and removed his handgun from his belt. "Four is better than three, yes?"

Scott didn't have time to feel moved. He sought out Max. "You're taking the Cruiser. Your contact is Torban, he's a medic with the Forty-second. He's got heavy casualties."

"Like a day in the park," Max grimaced.

"Take William and David with you. The rest of us will take the Battleship. Captain Dostoevsky..."

All eyes turned to Dostoevsky.

"Captain Tkachenok is trapped in the front of the Battleship. I don't know how many he has with him. Can you reach him with Egor and Viktor?"

Dostoevsky nodded.

It was set. Svetlana had the Vultures from the Forty-second. Varvara had the ones from the Fifty-first. Max would handle the Cruiser, and Dostoevsky would take the front half of the Battleship to find Captain Tkachenok. Everyone had their tasks. Almost.

"Esther," Scott said. The EDEN scout sat erect. "You and I will hit the back of the Battleship alone. There's a team pinned inside by the two eastern Noboats. This is more than two people can handle alone—I need us both to be more."

She gripped her pistol.

"We're making our approach!" Travis cried.

Moving through the troop bay, Scott leaned into the cockpit again.

The battlefield came into view.

* * *

KNOCK! KNOCK! KNOCK!

Tanneken lifted her eyes from her newspaper. She watched her door through a pair of small spectacles.

Knock! Knock! Knock! Knock! Knock!

Removing her glasses, she placed them on the top of her nightstand. She wasn't in uniform; she wore a simple white tank top and black pants, her brown pigtails hanging over her shoulders. She rose and opened the door to find a small crowd gathered in the hall. She blinked in surprise.

"Tanneken Brunner?"

"That is me..."

"I'm Rex Gabriel. We need to talk."

* * *

THE *PARIAH* NOSED down as the warzone appeared. Visible on the ground, the Noboats provided a striking contrast to the endless white snowscape. They surrounded the Ceratopian vessels, neither of which seemed irreparably damaged. The Vultures were also in sight. A barrage of plasma and projectile flew back and forth on the ground.

"Survivors," Travis said, pointing to the E-35 gunfire on the ground, "from the Fifty-first."

In the center of the battle, the Vultures belonging to the Fifty-first were being attacked from the west, where three of the Noboats had landed.

Scott whipped around. "Varya, get ready!"

"How do you want to do this?" Travis asked.

"Descend near the southernmost Vulture." No one was shooting from it, which meant no one was in condition to defend it—if anyone was alive at all. "Suppress the Bakma with cannon fire."

Nicolai, Derrick, and Boris moved to the door. Varvara was right behind them. She exchanged a fleeting glance with Viktor as she passed him.

"Everyone, hold on," Travis commanded. Every operative clutched the handrails as the pilot yanked the controls. The *Pariah*'s nose was slung 180 degrees to face the oncoming Bakma. Momentum carried it over the Vulture crash site.

Travis opened fire. *"Go! Go! Go!"*

Bakma scrambled in every direction on the ground, diving to avoid cannon fire. An entire row of aliens was mowed down.

Nicolai and Boris hit the snow first. Moments later, Derrick tumbled out. Varvara was the last to drop down.

Travis saw the white gleam the moment it launched. It came from one of the Noboats. *"Plasma missile!"* He yanked back the stick and the *Pariah*'s nose lurched straight up. The operatives flew off their feet.

The *Pariah* rode the air like a wave, violently leveling off once the missile hissed past.

"Heading to the Forty-second!" Travis jerked the Vulture southward, and its thrusters propelled it ahead.

Varvara and her defenders took position behind the southernmost wreckage. Smoke rose in black plumes from the hull; the troop bay had been blown into pieces.

Varvara waded through the debris. "Boris," she called out, "help me look!"

Nicolai and Derrick took cover behind one of the wings that was sticking out of the snow like a shark's fin. Nicolai's aim, more careful and precise than Derrick's, panned from Bakma to Bakma like a sniper. With every shot he fired, an alien fell. Ducking back, he adjusted his comm. "Fifty-first unit, what is your condition?"

The northernmost Vulture replied, "There are six of us here. I and another are unhurt. Four are wounded, one is critical."

"Understood."

Derrick was crouched awkwardly on the snow. It was the only way he could function with a bad leg. Pivoting around the corner of the wing, he gritted his teeth and fired.

BACK IN THE *Pariah*, Travis yelled, "Coming down by the Forty-second!"

Becan and Auric readied their assault rifles as Svetlana took her place behind them. The ship lowered to the snow, and they leapt out. The moment they landed, plasma bolts attacked them from both directions—the Noboats and the Cruiser. Becan and Auric suppressed them while Svetlana ran for the Forty-second's northern wreckage.

The first thing Svetlana noticed were Bakma footprints in the snow, running past the fallen Vulture en route to the Ceratopian vessel. The aliens had already been there. Of the EDEN bodies everywhere, half were riddled with plasma.

Becan and Auric pressed against the wreckage's interior hull, leaning around the corners to take outside shots. Becan focused on the Bakma coming out of the Noboats, while Auric targeted the ones by the Cruiser.

"They are dead," Svetlana said morosely. "It is too late."

Svetlana's voice came over the *Pariah*'s comm. "The men here were killed by the Bakma. We are moving to the Forty-second's other Vulture."

Travis drew the transport to a halt, causing Flopper to slide paws-first through the cockpit door. "I'll hold off the ones in the Cruiser, Sveta. Make your run." The pilot pressed the trigger and the nose cannon erupted once more. Bakma around the Cruiser dashed for cover.

Svetlana watched as the *Pariah* open fire. She firmed her eyes on the other crashed ship.

"Leg it!" said Becan. He and Auric dashed from the wreckage with Svetlana behind them. Despite the *Pariah*'s efforts, plasma bolts trained at their heels. One whizzed by the Irishman's head; he lost his balance and fell.

Auric slowed and turned back.

"Keep goin'!" Becan said, scrambling up.

Svetlana was ahead of the pack, running at a full sprint as she fired pistol shots at the Noboats. A flash of white streamed behind her as Auric's head was ratcheted to the side. A plasma bolt had struck him. He toppled to the snow.

Becan saw it happen. Running full speed, he reached Auric's body—but stayed only for a second. The side of Auric's helmet had been completely blown off. His body was sprawled awkwardly like a rag doll tossed to the ground. Becan had seen men like that before: they'd all been dead.

He abandoned the fallen German for Svetlana.

THE *PARIAH* LOWERED outside the Cruiser, where the Bakma had moved inside. Max, David, and William hopped out. "Travis, send me a map of this thing!"

"Sending!"

Moments later, Max had his request. His visor's field of view was replaced with layout of the alien ship.

Cruisers paled in comparison with Battleships, but they were still four times the size of Noboats. All Ceratopian vessels bore bumpy appearances, with exterior sections bulging like abscesses. Despite the damage to the vessel, it had managed to land decently.

A blue dot pulsated where Torban, the trapped medic, was supposedly located. It was a straightforward route. All Max needed to do was take the first hall to the ship's silo. From there, they could get to Torban's team.

Becan's voice came over the comm. "Auric's dead."

Max turned back to the *Pariah* to find Scott. Scott was already staring at him. After a moment of silence, Scott spoke. "Let's make sure he's the only one we lose."

* * *

GABRIEL'S TEAM rushed into *Novosibirsk*'s hangar. None of them wore combat armor—none had any there. The Australian captain scanned the hangar until he spotted a Vulture in the back. "That's the one she said we could take." He avoided the sentries' penetrating stares.

Seth Camm, Gabriel's pilot, hurried to keep up. "I need two minutes, sir."

The sentries intercepted them. "Halt." Gabriel stopped in his tracks. "You are not authorized to be here. Return to your guest quarters."

"Apologies, mate," Gabriel said staunchly. "We need to get to that Vulture."

The sentries aimed their assault rifles. "Negative. Return to your quarters."

Before Gabriel could argue, a voice from behind cut him off. "You must let them through."

The sentries and the Pelican Squadders turned. It was Tanneken—all five feet of her. Two other men, one of them large, followed behind. Gabriel blinked in genuine surprise.

The sentry turned to Tanneken. "Explain."

"General Thoor has ordered us to take them back to *Sydney*," she said, pointing to the Australians. "He does not wish to wait for a civilian airbus."

The sentry pointed his assault rifle at her. "Those orders were not sent here. You will return to your—"

Tanneken snatched the barrel of the sentry's rifle, shoving it away and causing him to flinch. "Get that thing out of my face." She stood on her toes and leaned close to confront him. "Do you think I *enjoy* this, you fool? Do you think I would not rather go on missions than be your pitiful leader's errand girl?"

"I—"

"I am talking, and *you* are listening. If you do not let us through, I will report you to General Thoor, and it will be *your* severed head on a stick. You did not get the order? I do not care. *I* was given the order, and if you do not move, I will bust you in your head and *then* report you. You can take both disgraces to your grave."

Gabriel arched an eyebrow.

After exchanging a hesitant look with his partner, the sentry stepped back and motioned her through.

"Thank you," she spat, then glared at Gabriel's crew. "Why are you still standing here? *Move*!"

The Australians hurried away.

Tanneken watched them walk ahead. Placing her hands on her hips, she exhaled a frustrated breath. "I hate beach people." She and her escorts followed from behind.

The sentries stared as she marched off. Then, very quietly, the one who'd remained out of the conversation snickered under his breath.

"What?" the other sentry asked. "Shut up."

When Tanneken arrived in the transport, the Pelican's pilot was already prepping the ship. The rest of the crew was gearing up with generic armor from the lockers.

Gabriel eyed her. "Can't say I expected *that*."

Tanneken said nothing.

"You weren't supposed to be coming. We only needed your ship."

She slid on her helmet. "I have my own reasons for this. Besides, if I had not shown up for the sentries, you'd already be dead. Sometimes, it takes a woman."

The two women in Gabriel's crew swapped a grin.

"She's primed and ready," the pilot said, turning back around. "Should we get clearance to leave?"

Tanneken gave him a stupid look.

"Right," the pilot said. "No clearance it is."

* * *

BACK IN VERKHOYANSKIY, the *Pariah* was making its final run. The gargantuan Ceratopian Battleship towered before them. They had no way of knowing how many Bakma or Ceratopians were already inside.

Dostoevsky had been uncommunicative since Scott had removed Saretok. He stared blankly at the cabin floor.

"Captain," Egor said.

Dostoevsky looked at him.

"You are still my captain."

Several feet away from the faint conversation, Scott and Esther turned their heads to observe.

Ever so slightly, Dostoevsky nodded at Egor.

"Coming down!" said Travis.

Dostoevsky shouldered his weapon. The troop bay was hushed as he made his way to the rear door. Once it was down, he leapt out, with Viktor and Egor following behind.

Scott and Esther remained alone in the troop bay. As the *Pariah* took off for its last drop-off point, the scout shook her head. "It almost makes you feel bad."

Scott looked at her.

"Almost," she said.

VARVARA AND BORIS were still searching for human survivors in the snowfield. Nicolai and Derrick continued their defensive effort.

Boris lifted and pushed away a hull panel, revealing a survivor beneath. Half of his body armor had been blown off, leaving a charred mass of twisted flesh to be dealt with. Varvara immediately went to work.

FARTHER SOUTH, Becan was providing cover from the wrecked Vulture in the wake of Auric's death. With a troop bay that was still intact, the Irishman was able to take shelter behind the rear bay's exit door. He leaned around the corner to shoot.

Bakma resistance from the Cruiser had diminished after Max's team disembarked, which eliminated an entire direction from Becan's concern. The one direction he faced was challenging enough on its own.

Behind him, Svetlana searched for more survivors. The troop bay was littered with mangled corpses. As she rummaged through body parts, she found her first patient. He was an older man—he looked to be in his fifties. His left arm was severed at the elbow, and his body was shredded and bloody. But he was alive.

"I have you," she said softly in Russian as she opened her medical kit. "Stay alive for one moment more."

Suddenly another sound caught her ears. She instinctively turned.

It was a second survivor. His body was horrifically twisted and barely distinguishable from the mangled wreckage, just like the old man she knelt over now. But there was a difference that made her lock up. The second survivor looked younger than her.

For several seconds, Svetlana did nothing. She only stared wide-eyed at the young man. Then she thoughtfully looked at the older one beneath her.

Becan continued to fire his assault rifle, but Svetlana didn't hear it. She could only stare at the old man's unconscious face as the world around her went still. Slowly, she reached out to touch him. Her eyes glistened. "I am sorry," she whispered. "I am sorry."

Grabbing her medical gear again, she leapt over the old man and away. She dashed to the side of the younger patient.

SCOTT WAS ABOUT to be dropped off at the rear of the Battleship. He readied his assault rifle next to Esther. "First we clear the opening room, then we work our way to the trapped operatives. Follow my lead." He activated his ExTracker and the overlay appeared over his holographic map. The first room on the display was an antechamber with three corridors branching off: one to each side and one heading in.

Scott had never been inside a Battleship; few people had. They had been ubiquitous during the initial Ceratopian attacks, but in recent years they'd slacked off. Visually, they were similar to Cruisers—they bore the same bulbous shape. But their sheer size dwarfed the Cruisers'.

"Coming around!" Travis warned. The *Pariah* fired at the Bakma coming from the two eastern Noboats; they scrambled for cover. "You should beat most of the Bakma inside, but some might already be in! Watch your backs—as soon as I leave they're going to come in behind you!"

They'd have to move fast. Scott leapt from the ship with Esther close behind him. Scrambling to their feet in the snow, they ran for the Battleship. The outer door was massive—large enough for two Ceratopians to pass through. Scott took point and entered the vessel.

He hit immediate resistance in the form of three Bakma crouched next to a left-hand hallway. Firing his assault rifle, Scott dove sideways to avoid their plasma blasts. He wasn't firing to hit them—he just wanted them to fall back. And they did, back down the left-hand hall.

Esther came through the door a half second later, cutting left against the wall by the corner, out of view of the Bakma who'd fallen back. She'd timed it perfectly with Scott's firing. The aliens had no idea she'd come in.

Lure the Bakma back out. Esther can attack their blind side as they pass her.

Esther must have sensed his plan. She ducked back into the corner in preparation to fire. But before they could act on their plan, a new wave of plasma burst out, this one from a deeper corridor. Scott fell back against the corner opposite Esther.

Everything went still.

There are Bakma coming at us from two directions. If Esther or I move, we're in sight.

Letting one hand slip from his assault rifle, Scott grabbed a grenade. Esther watched him closely as he depressed the activate button.

Thrusting his hand around the corner, Scott flung the grenade down the deeper hall. *Boom!* The two operatives cowered as smoke and debris flew into the antechamber. Almost immediately, the three Bakma stormed from the left-hand hall. Their plasma rifles were trained directly on Scott.

Esther cut them off from behind. The moment they emerged, the scout opened fire. One Bakma collapsed as the other two turned to find her. As they did, Scott opened fire. Between the two humans, the three aliens were down. Across the antechamber, Esther looked eagerly at Scott.

According to Scott's ExTracker, the deeper hallway led to the trapped members of the Fifty-first. Adjusting his comm, Scott tried to make contact. A reply came almost immediately.

"This is Lieutenant Papanov. There are three of us left alive here—we are trapped. My commander is here, badly wounded, and we have no medic."

"Where are the aliens relative to you?" Scott asked.

"There are Ceratopians ahead of us. The Bakma have pushed us farther in but they are backing off now."

Scott knew why: the Bakma were falling back to face Esther and him. "I have you on ExTracker. We're on our way."

AT THE OTHER end of the Battleship, Dostoevsky and his slayers were in the midst of a bloodbath. Beyond the massive doorway of the alien vessel, a smorgasbord of hostiles had collided. In all his years both with EDEN and as a Nightman, Dostoevsky had never witnessed anything like this. Bodies of every species—humans included—were strewn along every corridor. The halls were rank with the odors of death.

The Nightmen had also done their fair share of slaughtering. By Dostoevsky's count, he had personally dropped seven Bakma. Viktor and Egor had been equally lethal.

As soon as the first lull came, Dostoevsky knelt down. "Captain Tkachenok, this is..." he hesitated, "...Captain Dostoevsky." Something about saying that title made his voice waver. "We have broken through the rear line of the Bakma. What is your condition?"

"Captain Dostoevsky! We are in—"

The signal cut off, going dead silent. There was nothing else at all.

Dostoevsky shot a look to his slayers. Both men stared back at him. Rising to his feet, Dostoevsky aimed his rifle ahead. "Point—Zulu." Ryvkin and Egor slid into a triangular formation behind him, leaving the fulcrum captain at the lead.

According to his map, Tkachenok's team was forty meters away and one level up. The three Nightmen moved in unison down the hallways. The occasional Bakma they encountered was ruthlessly cut down. Canrassis lasted only slightly longer.

"Necrilid!" Viktor called from the rear. All three Nightmen swung around, where a necrilid was bounding at them from behind. Before they could fire the first shot, the creature leapt in between Viktor and Egor, straight into Dostoevsky. It knocked the fulcrum onto his back.

Rat-tat-tat-tat-tat!

The creature contorted as bullets peppered it from behind. It crumpled to the ground, nerves twitching in its final movements.

Dostoevsky stood as the two slayers stared at him.

"Why did it go after *you*?" Egor asked him. "We were right in front of it."

Viktor answered before Dostoevsky could. "Because they sense fear."

Egor faced Viktor, lowering his weapon, his body language indicating his shock at the blatant words of his comrade.

Viktor said nothing else. He simply readied his rifle for the corridor ahead.

Dostoevsky looked forward again. Carefully, he curled his fingers around his assault rifle to reaffirm his grip. But for the first time, he noticed something different—something about his hands.

He was trembling.

36

FRIDAY, NOVEMBER 25TH, 0011 NE
1121 HOURS

THE CITADEL OF THE MACHINE

AT THE SAME TIME

"IT HAS A FULLY functional crystal," said the technician. "There is no reason it would not work."

General Thoor clasped his hands behind his back. His expression was emotionless but he was clearly deep in heavy thought.

The lone Noboat was dimly illuminated in the underground hangar. It was one of only two vessels there. The other was a simple Vulture transport—the general's personal one.

Another man, this one with a thin salt-and-pepper ponytail, slid a sprig from his mouth, exhaling smoke over his goatee. "You will not find a pilot to do this," he said in a calm, gritty voice. "It is asking for treachery." He was the only man in the room not wearing a Nightman uniform. His jersey bore the emblem of EDEN.

"We have pilots of our own, Antipov," Thoor answered.

Antipov laughed mirthlessly. "You are not serious, general. The Khuladi would destroy us from a million miles away."

Another man chuckled at the remark. In contrast to Antipov, he was outfitted in fulcrum armor, with spiky black hair and a clean-shaven face. "In space, a million miles is not very far."

Antipov exhaled another plume. "You asked for my opinion. This is it. I will do this mission if you ask, general, and I will bring my best men. But what purpose does it serve if we are blown out of the stars?"

Suddenly, the tunnel door to the underground hangar burst open. All four men turned as a breathless slayer approached them. "General Thoor!" he panted.

Thoor frowned and eyed the slayer with a look of displeasure. The slayer bowed apologetically. "Captain Antipov. Captain Marusich. General Thoor."

Antipov chuckled. "You mean *Commander* Marusich, slayer."

"Damn Strakhov to hell," Marusich spat. "He fails, so I get demoted. Only here is that justice."

"Silence," said Thoor, cutting them off. He turned to the messenger. "Why are we interrupted?"

The slayer swallowed before speaking. "General, it is about the Fourteenth." As soon as the unit was named, Antipov and Marusich arched their eyebrows. "They have defied you."

"Defied me how?"

"The message comes from Colonel Saretok. You ordered all transports back to *Novosibirsk*. Commander Remington removed the colonel and fled to rescue the Fifty-first and Forty-second. Now we have just learned that another unit has left *Novosibirsk* to help him!"

Thoor's eyes grew large, but not out of anger. Out of genuine surprise. "What other unit?"

"Commander Brunner from the Thirty-ninth. She and several of her men left with the Australians. They lied to the sentries to gain access to a Vulture. We believe Remington requested their assistance."

"Wait," said Marusich, raising a hand. "What do you mean, Remington *removed* Saretok?"

The slayer hesitated. "He physically removed the colonel from their Vulture. They left him stranded with the Bakma prisoners from the Noboat."

Silence prevailed. A pin could have fallen in the hangar and deafened everyone. No one breathed.

Then it happened—something that almost never happened at all. It caused a physical reaction from everyone else in the room. General Thoor laughed. Not in triumph or in wickedness, but from a genuine thrill. His voice bellowed off the walls.

The messenger said nothing.

"Antipov," Thoor said, "take the Third and rescue Saretok from humiliation. Tell him we will shave his head as punishment. I will mount his mohawk on my wall."

Marusich stared at Thoor in disbelief. "Will you *allow* this, general? Remington has gone against your will!"

"That is what he does. That is why I sought him out. A lion cannot be kept on a leash. I want a predator, not a pet." The general walked to the Noboat, running his hand along its hull. "The perception of freedom is stronger than any chain. Let him think he has defied me and escaped unpunished. That will only make him more effective."

"General, what other man would you let get away with this? He grows more brazen by the day. First he takes prisoners from the Walls of Mourning, and now *this*?"

"What other man has brought me a Noboat with a functional crystal?" After posing the question, Thoor turned around. "Or given me a necrilid hatchery as a gift?"

"It is favoritism just the same!" Marusich shouted, challenging the Terror. "The fact that he is a commander at all is absurd. Remington has not been a soldier for nine months. No other man has been given so much so quickly."

Thoor answered matter-of-factly, "Remington is a leader, and leaders should be put in a position to lead. That is why he is a commander now, and that is why he will be a captain when he returns, should he survive. His actions today, defiant or not, are exactly why I chose him. I require no one else's approval." He turned to the messenger. "Monitor the situation, and inform me of the Fourteenth's progress."

"Yes, general." With those words the slayer turned and left. Only after he'd exited the hangar did conversation resume.

"What will you do with Brunner?" asked Antipov. "And the Australians?"

"Nothing," Thoor answered. "Any punishment she or they receive will cause Remington to hesitate in the future. Hesitation is an unacceptable fault." His face grew sterner as he turned to find Marusich. "Find the sentry who allowed Brunner to leave, and execute him. Resourcefulness is valuable. Carelessness is not."

"Yes, general."

"And mind your tone when you challenge me in the future. I chose *you* for your vehemence—not your tongue."

"As you wish, general."

Thoor turned to Antipov again. "Exercise patience in your retrieval of Saretok. Let him know that he failed."

After an exchange of Nightman salutes, Antipov and Marusich left the general's presence. Turning back around to the Noboat, Thoor ran his fingers over its metallic surface. A trace of satisfaction gleamed in his eyes.

* * *

BECAN DROPPED BACK as a plasma bolt crashed against his cover. He looked at Svetlana from inside the wrecked Vulture. "I migh' need yeh up here!"

The medic was working frantically on the injured young soldier. Several meters away, the older man she'd abandoned began to moan in half-conscious agony. Svetlana continued to operate, her hands bloody but steady.

"Sveta, did yeh hear me?"

"Stay alive," she whispered to the boy. "Please stay alive."

The Bakma were on the verge of storming them; Becan couldn't hold them at bay for much longer.

All of a sudden, the sky above the Irishman roared. He hunched down and peered up to see the *Pariah* hovering overhead. Its frontal cannon opened fire.

Becan fired again. "Travis, can yeh lift us ou' o' here?"

"On my way down—whoa!"

A plasma missile shrieked past. The *Pariah* swished through the air. "Check that," Travis answered. "Apparently they're saving those for me."

"Bollocks."

Suddenly, from the corner of his eyes, Becan saw a distant human-sized movement, dark and awkward. When he turned to focus on it, his face fell with shock.

"Auric!"

The German was stumbling to his feet in the open snow. With one hand, he wildly fired his assault rifle, while his other hand swayed to keep balance.

Becan burst from the Vulture, kicking up snow as he ran toward the soldier. Auric met him on wobbly feet. Once again, the *Pariah* swooped past, providing just enough cover for the two men to move. Slinging an arm under Auric's shoulder, Becan struggled to rush him back to the wreckage.

There was no time for Becan to ask questions or even ease the slayer down. The Irishman threw Auric aside and returned to the defense.

Auric rolled on the ground. The right side of his helmet had been decimated by gunfire; in its place, from the back of his head to his cheek, was a mess of burnt flesh. Half of his right ear was gone. He tried to stand up but failed.

THE DOG FLOPPER slid clumsily in the *Pariah*'s troop bay, his four paws digging out each time the ship veered, and each time slamming against a wall. Travis pushed forward on the stick, sending the transport strafing across the Bakma front. Plasma bolts crashed against the ship's hull.

"Boris, what's it looking like down there?"

"We found one survivor. She couldn't save him."

"Come on, Varya," Travis whispered off-comm.

"We are on our way to the other Vulture."

Below, on the ground, Nicolai and Derrick held cover for Varvara and Boris. The second crashed Forty-second Vulture—the one with actively firing survivors—was a short run away. The moment Varvara and Boris ran, every survivor from the Forty-second held suppression to aid them. Varvara ducked her head and dashed into the wrecked ship with Boris on her heels.

An officer addressed her immediately. Half his armor was gone, and he was bleeding from multiple wounds. He was battle-ready nonetheless. "We have four wounded, one of them critical. What is your name?"

"Varvara Yudina."

He showed her the injured. "We will protect you, Varvara. Thank you."

"'Thank you?'"

"You are saving our lives."

Varvara stared at him as he moved away. The blood from the man she hadn't saved was still on her hands. She stared at the new batch of wounded. The three less injured men were watching her; the critical one was incoherent.

"Help me, God," she whispered. "Help me do this." Swallowing hard, she opened her kit.

IN THE CRUISER, Max, David, and William had little trouble slashing through the initial front line of Bakma. They'd blindsided the extraterrestrials with a barrage of bullets and hand cannon blasts. They were on the verge of reaching Torban, their medical contact with the Forty-second.

They were about to breach the first open section of the Cruiser, a large circular room known as a silo. The two-level room held stations ranging from navigational controls to tactical operations. It was like a separate bridge. Every station was gigantic—every console larger than humans could comfortably operate. The floors were a mud-colored brown; the walls were barely brighter. Typically, the room held many Ceratopians, but it was empty now.

"Three hallways ahead," Max commanded, "at ten o'clock, twelve o'clock, and two. Torban's down two. Harb, stick with AP."

William reloaded his armor-piercing rounds.

"I hear neutron," said David.

Max adjusted his comm. "Torban, we're coming at you from the silo. Don't shoot us."

Torban's affirmation was barely audible.

"Get ready," Max said. David and William positioned their guns. "Go!"

The three men burst into the silo. It was empty, but the hallways were not. The twelve o'clock hall resonated with plasma and neutron. Projectile fire came from the two o'clock.

Max waved off the inter-species clash. "Let 'em fight—we gotta get Torban." The three men jetted down the two o'clock hall.

It took one turn to find human operatives—a man and a woman. Both were hunkered down, protecting the corner Max's team appeared around, their E-35s at the ready. When they saw the men from the Fourteenth, they relaxed their stances.

"Where's Torban?" asked Max.

The female operative motioned around the corner in the direction of a projectile-neutron exchange.

Max saw Torban when he rounded the corner. Four men lay unconscious around him, all of whom Torban was working on. "You *are* here!" Torban cried in relief.

"Who's your gunner down there fighting the lizards?" Max asked, pointing further ahead in the direction of the active exchange.

"Gritsenko. He is alone. We had no one else to spare."

"Harb, go help him."

The demolitionist swept past them and ran down the hall.

Max motioned to the wounded. "Can they be moved?"

"Yes, if it is clear on the way out."

Max turned to the two other operatives—the man and the woman—who were watching the corridor. "The silo is clear, but we've got Bakma and Ceratopians down one of the halls. If I can steal one of your soldiers, we can secure the exit hall."

Torban pointed. "Gavrilyuk, go." The female soldier rose to her feet.

Max detached his technical kit from his belt, swapping it for extra ammunition instead. The kit was abandoned on the floor. "Dave, check on Harb and see if he needs help. If he doesn't, come back in the silo."

"Right."

Max shouldered his assault rifle and tracked down the hall. "C'mon, Gobbledygook, you're with me."

The female soldier stared at him from behind. "Gavrilyuk."

"Whatever."

Farther down the hallway, William and the lone soldier from the Forty-second—an older man named Gritsenko—were in the midst of a firefight with Ceratopians. The two men had taken position where the hallway opened into a living quarters, where numerous Ceratopians were firing their neutron blasters. A dead canrassi, riddled from head to toe with bullet holes, lay sprawled in the center of the hall. The operatives ducked in and out of an adjacent cleansing room, using it as cover while they fired down the hall. William had already dropped one Ceratopian, doing considerably more damage than his less heavily armed comrade. Readying his hand cannon with another set of rounds, he prepared to lean out again.

"Will," David said through the comm, "I'm coming toward you from behind." Moments later, David appeared. "How's it looking?"

William leaned out, launching an armor-piercing round into the living quarters. It blew apart a Ceratopian's head. "Nothin' like a little fun 'n' gunnin'!"

"Can you hold this?"

"Gritty and I got it down," William said. Gritsenko glanced at him.

David nodded. "We're going to secure the silo and start ferrying out the injured. Don't let them press in."

Gritsenko leaned into the open and fired a volley. His bullets hammered down the hall but failed to find flesh.

"Take off, man," William said to David.

"If you need help..."

"I'll call."

David slapped William on the back then turned up the hall.

Max and Gavrilyuk had fortified the twelve o'clock hall in the silo, where the exchange of plasma and neutron was taking place. In the midst of a momentary lull, Max got on his comm. "Travis, where are you?"

"Holding cover for Sveta. What do you need?"

Max looked at the two o'clock hallway as David emerged. "Can you pick up some wounded?"

"No way, man. I gotta stay by Becan, he's holding fort by himself."

"Veck."

"Necrilids!" David screamed behind Max.

Max and Gavrilyuk spun around. Out of the ten o'clock hallway, a pair of necrilids bounded into the silo. All three operatives opened fire. The creatures were gunned down just before they had time to strike.

Without warning, while the three operatives were trained on the necrilids, smooth doors slid down to cover the three main hall entrances. Every hallway in the silo was suddenly sealed off.

Max ripped off his helmet. "No, no, *no*!"

"What the hell is this? This thing had *power*?" David slapped his palms against one of the sealed doors.

Gavrilyuk was already on her comm. "Aleksi! The silo doors came down!"

Torban answered immediately. "We know! They came down all over the ship!"

"All over the *ship*?" Max jumped back on the comm. "Harb, where are you?"

A short burst of static ensued before William answered. "What the hell just happened? We just got cut off!"

"Max," David asked, "can you take control of the ship? Crack into their system?"

"To an extent." Max lowered his gun. "But it'll take me a few minutes—" he stopped. His hand froze over his tool belt, where there had been a technician's kit minutes before. Where there was now an extra cache of ammunition instead.

David's face sank.

"Freakin' hell!" Max screamed.

BACK IN THE Battleship, Scott and Esther were closing in on Papanov's trapped team, leaving a handful of dead Bakma behind in a trek with surprisingly little resistance.

"Lieutenant Papanov," Scott said through the comm, "we should be coming up on you right now. Stand by for contact."

"Standing by."

Rounding a final corner, Scott and Esther found the trapped team. Papanov and his injured commander were hunkered down in what looked like a security checkpoint—a square room that served as a joint for an otherwise straight hallway. Several dead soldiers were sprawled around them.

Papanov was in no position to greet them. He was in the middle of an exchange with a Ceratopian down the hall. Scott joined in the effort, while Esther checked on the injured commander.

"There could be Bakma coming behind us any minute," Scott said. "We circled around some, and there are still Noboats outside." It was unrealistic to think that Travis was watching their backs—the *Pariah* wasn't a fighter, and it was being torn in numerous directions. Bakma could have been storming behind them as they spoke.

Papanov looked at Scott for the first time. When he saw Scott's golden horns, he arched an eyebrow behind his blue-tinted EDEN visor. "Are you a new kind of fulcrum?"

For a moment, Scott had forgotten about his personalized armor. The battle was the only thing on his mind. "Something like that."

"I know a way out of here," said Esther. "There's an exit to the roof from the third level."

"The *third* level?" Scott asked. "Do you have any idea how many Ceratopians are between us and the third level?"

"If you go *my* route, not very many."

Scott stopped firing. He turned around to face his British scout. "Was that a 300 course, too?"

She leered back.

Scott resumed the gunfight. "All right, Brooking. Third level, it is."

Esther picked up an extra pistol from one of the dead soldiers. She now held a gun in each hand. "The Golathoch are brave, but they're not stupid. If I'm right, they've—"

"The *what*?" Scott asked.

"The Golathoch. Did you really think they call themselves *Ceratopians*?" She went on. "If I'm right, they've mustered in one of two places: the stalls with the animals, or the bridge. The stalls are on this level. The bridge is on deck three—where we've got to go."

Papanov felled the Ceratopian in the hall.

"So how do we get to deck three?" asked Scott.

"If we can backtrack thirty meters, we'll hit a maintenance shaft. We can take it all the way up."

Scott grabbed some clips from the soldiers beneath him. "Let's go. Papanov, help your commander to his feet."

"Wait!" the injured commander shouted. He looked up at Papanov from the floor. "The slayer."

Scott arched an eyebrow. "The *slayer*?"

Papanov sighed. "We had two Nightmen in our unit. One of them is dead. Commander Ozerov sent the other ahead, but he got cut off from behind. He is surrounded by the Ceratopians alone."

"I cannot abandon him, Foma," the injured commander said, "Nightman or not."

Scott didn't take offense at the remark. "We'll go get him. Esther, come on." He started down the hall and Esther followed.

Papanov helped his commander up. "The slayer's name is Nijinsky."

Suddenly, Esther stopped. She spun back around. "What did you say?"

"Alexander Nijinsky. He was transferred here two months ago."

The Briton's mouth hit the floor.

"Do you know him?"

When Scott realized Esther wasn't following, he turned around to find her. "Esther?"

She was frozen in the hallway, facing the other two men. Her eyelashes flickered. "I'm sorry, I…I must be thinking of someone else…"

Scott stepped behind her. "Are you all right?"

"I'm sorry, sir," she said, regripping her pistols. "I'm ready to go."

MEANWHILE, THE *Pariah* was in the midst of an air-to-ground battle. Travis had attempted to fortify a hovering position north of Svetlana's team, but the arrival of canrassis and riders cut his efforts short. Their beast-mounted plasma guns weren't as strong as plasma missiles, but they could still tear a hole through his hull. The *Pariah* was hovering sideways like an aerial crab, firing what was left of its cannon ammunition.

"Travis," Max's voice was urgent over the comm, "we have a problem!"

"You're telling *me*?" Travis swung the *Pariah*'s nose toward one of the canrassis. The beast and its rider were blown apart.

"I need another technical kit. The Cruiser has power—the Ceratopians shut all the doors. I'm cut off from the kit I had."

"*What?*"

"They shut the trashin' doors, Travis! The doors in the Cruiser! We're locked in different sections!"

"Veck!"

"I'm locked away from my technical kit—I need one of the backups."

Travis jerked the stick back as a barrage of plasma blasts flew at him. Flopper leapt into Boris's seat.

"Trav, yeh all righ'?" Becan asked through the comm.

"I'm fine." The pilot refocused on Max. "I can't help you, man. If I leave, they're dead on the ground. I got Bakma riding out on canrassis." The low-ammo warning flashed on the console.

"Travis," Becan yelled, "mind your house!"

The pilot checked his rear view screen. One of the eastern Noboats had lifted from the ground and was moving toward the *Pariah*. "Oh, crap."

Max spoke again. "Travis, I don't care what you have to do, but I need that backup kit *now*!"

The *Pariah* had less than six percent of its shells remaining. Inside his helmet, sweat poured down Travis's forehead.

Becan's voice came again. "We got riders…"

In front of the crashed Vulture where Svetlana was working, a spread of Bakmas and canrassis converged. Their plasma cannons trained on the wreckage.

Time slowed down as Travis became overwhelmed. Behind him, a fully-armed Noboat was about to engage. In front of him, a new assault was beginning against the medical team. Inside the Cruiser, Max's team was in trouble. Travis's mouth hung open as everything unraveled at once. His hands grew numb on the joystick. He watched the world fall apart.

Then he looked to his right.

Flopper was sitting upright in the copilot's seat. The dog stared at Travis straight in the eyes; it started to bark.

Travis's eyes suddenly refocused. He turned his stare back ahead. "Becan, I need ten seconds of cover."

"Yeh must be jokin'!"

Travis switched frequencies. "Max, do you have a clear path outside the ship?"

"Yeah."

"Get outside *now*. Your kit's on the way."

Slamming the stick sideways, Travis pulled the *Pariah* to the left. Becan was attempting to fend off the Bakma below; for every shot the Irishman got off, the Bakma got five.

On the weapons display, Travis set the *Pariah*'s auto-fire timer to begin in ten seconds. It immediately began to count down. Pushing the joystick forward, he lowered the craft until it hovered barely a foot off the snow.

Flopper barked wildly.

"All right, dog," Travis said. "Earn your keep."

The timer reached zero, and the *Pariah*'s front cannon burst into auto-fire. It launched an automatic spray of bullets at the canrassis as the ammo percentage went dangerously low.

Travis slammed his hand on the troop bay door button while the ship stayed in hover mode. He jumped out of the cockpit into the back. Flopper followed at his heels.

Reaching for the overhead bins, Travis grabbed a spare technical kit, his hands shaking violently. Glancing outside the open bay door, he saw the Noboat draw near. Flopper barked madly as Travis grabbed a rope and tied it to the kit's handle. The warning klaxon sounded off in the cockpit as the ammo count hit one percent. He tied a loop at the rope's other end, then time ran out. The klaxon stopped sounding and the nose-mounted cannon went still.

Travis shoved the loop into Flopper's mouth. The dog wagged its tail and chomped down. "Max, call your dog!"

Max had just reached the outside of the Cruiser. He skidded as he came to the snow. "Call my dog—?"

"Call Flopper now!"

"Flopper, c'mon! Here boy!" Max clapped his hands and screamed at the top of his lungs from across the battlefield. The shadow of a Noboat passed over him as the Bakma ship beaded in on the *Pariah.*

"Go, Flop!" Travis yelled, pushing the dog out of the ship. Max's voice emerged far in the distance.

Flopper's ears perked and he bolted in the direction of Max, dragging the technical kit behind him in the snow.

Travis looked up and his whole body froze. The Noboat was upon him. Its nose was beading in for the kill. Its weapons charged up.

He had nowhere to go.

Then it happened, right in front of his eyes. The pulse of charging plasma cannons subsided and the sky around the Noboat shimmered with blue electricity. The air crackled. The Noboat was gone.

Travis's mouth fell open. He could still see the faint distortions in the air. It had dematerialized.

"Gabriel to *Pariah*." The comm crackled to life. "We have you on visual contact—do you copy?"

Travis dove into the pilot's seat. His hand fiddled for the comm. In front of him, Bakma riders unleashed their plasma cannons. Bolts of white soared his way. He jerked the joystick back with all the force he could summon. The nose of the transport shot skyward and its rear thrusters rocketed to life.

Then it was struck. Plasma blasts tore through the ship's right wing and underbelly. The cabin erupted with fire.

In the newly approaching Vulture, Rex Gabriel was the first to see it. He quickly shifted frequencies. "Gabriel to Fourteenth—the *Pariah* has been hit. I repeat, the *Pariah* has been hit."

In the Battleship, Scott and Dostoevsky's teams ceased all activity. On the ground, Svetlana and Becan stared skyward. Varvara's crew did the same.

From his position outside the Cruiser, Max watched as the *Pariah* exploded in flames. First it soared skyward, then it stalled. Its nose swayed as its engines gave out. At the same time, Flopper tore through the snow toward Max.

Sirens in the *Pariah* wailed frantically as the auto-extinguishers kicked in. The ship's engines stuttered and shook; the eject button flashed. Manhandling the joystick with one hand while his other grabbed the dangling comm, Travis yelled as the *Pariah* plummeted. "Pelican, this is *Pariah*. Dematerialized Noboat coming your way!"

The new Vulture slowed as it approached. In the cockpit, Pelican pilot Seth Camm spoke to Gabriel without turning around. "Captain..."

Next to Seth, a heavyset girl worked the controls. "I have visual with the Bakma on the ground."

"Take out the riders," ordered Gabriel.

"But the Noboat—"

"We'll find the Noboat, just take out the bloody riders!"

Below, Becan watched as Tanneken's Vulture opened fire. The snow around the Bakma riders blew toward the sky—crimson spurted into the air. The canrassis scattered and fell.

Then the Irishman looked at the *Pariah*. It plummeted toward the ground.

Blood trickled from Travis's forehead and cheeks. His burned hands gripped the controls, the eject button flashing continuously. He pulled back the stick.

Becan screamed over the comm. *"Travis, bail the hell ou'!"*

Boris followed suit. "Travis, eject!"

Travis cried out in agony. He fought the controls. He watched as the earth became large. The stick could go back no more.

Suddenly, the *Pariah*'s engines burst with new thrust. The ground tilted up—but the angle of ascent wasn't enough.

Max watched the *Pariah* make impact as Flopper ran into his arms. The Vulture's belly dug into the snow, as it scraped across the ground like a sled. "Get up, Travis…get up…"

Travis's blood-curdling scream filled the *Pariah*. Sparks hit the cabin again as the ship rocked up and down.

Then it happened. Travis redirected the *Pariah*'s thrust, and the ship suddenly grew light. The jostling ceased. The pilot gasped, holding his breath. His stomach lobbed itself in his throat; he kept on the stick.

The snowscape gave way to sky, and the ship's nose angled up. The *Pariah* charged back into the air.

"Hell yes!" Max pumped his fists as the dog barked wildly. Max grabbed the technical kit, rubbing Flopper with his free hand. "Hell yes, Flopper! That's your pilot!"

Together, they ran back into the Cruiser.

Travis got on the comm as soon as he had the *Pariah* leveled off. "Pelican pilot, you found that loose Noboat?"

"Negative," Seth answered. "We're covering your ground crew. You all right?"

"I'm all right." Travis still fought with the stick, now gently. "She's pulling to the right." He engaged the left rudder to straighten out. "There's not much I can do."

"I'm hot-dropping our ground teams. We're wasting our time looking for an invisible ship."

"Copy that."

There was a brief pause before Seth spoke again. "That was a corker of a recovery, mate. You're going to have to teach me that one."

For a moment, Travis didn't reply. Then slowly, beneath the blood caking on his face inside his helmet, the Fourteenth's pilot smiled.

BELOW, IN THE crashed Fifty-first Vulture, Svetlana finished working on her injured young man. He was as stable as she could get him.

Meanwhile, Auric—deeply wounded—had been mumbling half coherently to himself. Though his words had been slurred at first, he was now regaining his cognizance.

"I will help you, Auric," said Svetlana. "Just wait for me." She was well acquainted with triage measures, and she now turned to the older man—the one she'd left suffering to attend to the younger soldier. When she saw him, her eyes widened. He was still alive. Without a second of hesitation, she dove to the older man's side.

Auric watched her as he continued to mutter intermittently and feverishly. Finally, he grabbed an assault rifle from the ground and stumbled over to Becan. Despite his injuries, he rejoined the defense.

FURTHER NORTH, the battle around Varvara and the wrecked Vulture waged on. The Fourteenth's trio of Nicolai, Derrick, and Boris were holding their own. The Forty-second's able survivors formed a defensive that was sufficient to discourage most of the Bakma from wasting their time.

Varvara worked frantically on the critical man. He was suffering from numerous wounds, ranging from deeply lodged shrapnel to third-degree burns. The medic's hands were full.

HOVERING OVER Svetlana, Tanneken's Vulture came to a stop. A pair of operatives hopped out of the already-open rear bay door and as the Vulture lifted away, they split between Becan and Svetlana.

The man who approached Svetlana was well-built. Tips of wavy dark hair emerged from his helmet. His voice resonated deep. "How many survivors?"

Svetlana didn't look up. "Two in serious condition."

The man got on the comm. "Two for transport."

"Acknowledged, Tristan."

He abandoned her for Becan and Auric, strengthening their crippled defense. The other soldier—a Japanese man—had joined in as well. For the first time since their initial drop-off, Svetlana's team had legitimate protection.

"TAKE ME TO THE Cruiser," Tanneken ordered Gabriel's pilot, Seth. She looked over at her soldiers. "Shavrin, Sokolov, get ready."

"Do you want to take one of my men?" Gabriel asked.

"I do not need your men."

Gabriel watched the Dutch woman walk away. Only when she was out of earshot did he lean over Seth. "I can bed her in two days. Name your price."

"Not a chance in bloody hell. Two hundred, no less."

"Fastest two hundred you'll ever lose."

Next to them, the heavyset girl rolled her eyes.

37

FRIDAY, NOVEMBER 25TH, 0011 NE
1202 HOURS

AT THE SAME TIME

IN THE FORWARD section of the Battleship, Dostoevsky, Viktor, and Egor had fought their way to a mechanical lift. According to Dostoevsky's map, Captain Tkachenok was just beyond the lift on the second floor. They entered and began their ascent.

None of the Nightmen were substantially injured. All three, however, were low on ammunition, their resources having been drained by the combined resistance of Bakma, Ceratopians, necrilids, and canrassis.

As the lift carried them to the next level, Dostoevsky removed his helmet to wipe his forehead. Viktor and Egor studied his face.

The fulcrum leader's eyes were tired and uncertain. Even as he replaced his helmet and shouldered his assault rifle, his body language spoke more than words. His chest was puffed high, his chin was down, and he clenched his rifle excessively tightly.

He was trying too hard.

The sound of projectile and neutron rays emerged as the lift reached the second floor. The projectile was coming from outside, where Tkachenok and his team had to be; the neutron was farther ahead. As soon as the door opened, the Nightmen dashed out.

Tkachenok was on his knees to their immediate right, firing furiously. Farther on, four Ceratopians returned a barrage of fire, using the corners of a three-way intersection for cover. Tkachenok's team had far less cover. Restricted to the hallway that jetted out in front of the lift, they used its corner as their only source of protection.

The Ceratopians ducked back to regroup, and a momentary lull hit the scene.

Tkachenok had three others with him, all of whom struggled for breath. As soon as the Nightmen took over the defense, the EDEN operatives ducked back to reorganize.

Reloading his assault rifle, Tkachenok said to Dostoevsky, "Thank God you are here. We could not go down the lift—there was too much resistance on the first floor. The Bakma forced us to the second level."

"The first floor is clear," Dostoevsky said. "We can ferry you out."

Suddenly Scott cut through the comm. "Captain, it's Remington."

Dostoevsky fired down the hall. "Go ahead."

"Brooking and I are going after a stranded Fifty-first operative. As soon as we get him, we're going to work our way to the third level. We can't backtrack with Bakma behind us."

Dostoevsky ducked out of the fight, and Tkachenok and his soldiers took his place. "What is on the third level?"

"Esther says there's a path to the roof. If we can get there, a transport can pick us up. She knows a safe route."

A third voice cut into the conversation—Captain Gabriel's. "You won't be alone for long, Remington. I'm dropping off two of my best."

"Expect *heavy* resistance getting here, captain..."

"Expected. We're dropping them just ahead of the Bakma front, but it's coming fast. They should beat it to your position by a minute or two."

"Remington," asked Dostoevsky, "what do you advise from your position?"

Gabriel interjected, "Captain Dostoevsky, I'll be en route to you shortly myself. We'll help you move your wounded. No worries."

Scott came across. "My advice is to get out. Take Tkachenok's team back to the first level and get them out of the Battleship. Let Gabriel help you when he arrives."

"Our Vulture will be waiting outside," Gabriel added.

After a round of acknowledgments, the channels were closed.

Dostoevsky stared at his gloved hands. They were still trembling. Not as badly as before, but trembling nonetheless. He clenched his gun harder, and the trembling stopped.

ACROSS THE BATTLESHIP, Scott and Esther were on their way to Nijinsky. Esther hadn't spoken since Nijinsky's name had been mentioned. She simply stayed at Scott's side.

Ceratopian resistance had been light, but the sound of heavier combat echoed down the halls. The large aliens had mustered toward the center of the first floor, as Esther had predicted, not far from the stalls. Esther kept a constant watch on their rear as they continued to press ahead.

The trek had been lengthy, and it was clear why Nijinsky hadn't worked his way back: canrassis. Scott and Esther had encountered several, and between them, they killed the creatures. The feat would have been much more difficult alone.

"Around one more corner," Scott urged. He moved quickly, his assault rifle constantly poised. Esther affirmed. Hurrying forward, Scott rounded the bend and Esther followed suit, her own steps just as quick—until she saw Alexander Nijinsky.

There he was, hunkered down in a three-way intersection, outfitted in battered slayer's armor. Esther went rigid. She watched him through the sky-blue tint of her visor, her eyes wide with disbelief, as if he wasn't real.

Scott went to Nijinsky's side, joining the slayer's defense. Nijinsky glanced at Scott briefly before the Ceratopians seized his attention again.

"Are they your only resistance?" Scott asked.

"No. There are several more farther up the hall. I held them off with the threat of grenades. They will not use them in their own ship. I think they believe they can escape."

Scott spoke through the comm. "Remington to Papanov."

The moment Scott said his last name, Nijinsky jolted back, fumbling his assault rifle and nearly dropping it. He locked his stare on Scott's nametag.

"Papanov here."

Signaling Esther, Scott continued. "We've got Ceratopians in our vicinity. If we fall back to you, they're going to pursue. I'm sending my scout back. Nijinsky and I will hold them off here."

"Understood."

Scott fired around the corner. "Esther, go back. Take them to the third level and get them to the roof."

The scout hesitated, her eyes lingering on Nijinsky.

"Esther, *go*!"

"Yes sir."

Scott positioned himself in front of Nijinsky, giving the Russian slayer a faceless stare. "How many Ceratopians have you killed?"

Nijinsky didn't reply. He stared at Scott as if in some sort of trance.

"*Nijinsky!*"

The slayer flinched and snapped to attention. "One—one or two," he stuttered.

A neutron ray flashed past Scott's head. Aiming his rifle at the nearest alien, he held down the trigger. Bullets peppered the Ceratopian's neck. Scott ducked back to avoid fire. He checked his weapon and readied himself again. "One or two, huh? That's gonna change."

It took Esther a minute to reach Papanov again. Papanov's injured commander was firing poorly from the corner of the security checkpoint; Papanov himself was doing only marginally better. Bakma stragglers had appeared from the hallways behind them.

Esther dove into the fray, firing both her pistols. A Bakma fell before the aliens doubled back.

"Lieutenant Papanov," Esther panted, moving for cover, "we've got to charge through that Bakma front. The maintenance shaft we need to take to the third level is thirty meters away."

Papanov yelled over the sound of his rifle. "A maintenance shaft? Will we all fit?"

"It's a Ceratopian maintenance shaft—quite big enough."

Projectile fire erupted from far behind the Bakma—beyond where Esther and Papanov were crouched. Almost simultaneously, an American voice proclaimed over the comm: "Ladies and gentlemen, the cavalry has arrived!"

Several Bakma stumbled into Papanov and Esther's lines of fire. The two operatives unloaded their weapons and the aliens were gunned down.

From around the corner where the Bakma had emerged, two EDEN soldiers appeared. They ran backward, constantly watching their rear with their assault rifles aimed, even as they came within normal speaking distance.

Both were well-built men, though one favored height over brawn. The taller man, an American, addressed Esther. "This is the part where you thank us!"

"There are at least twenty Bakma behind us," interrupted the other soldier. He was decidedly British. "They followed us in."

"I hate to be the bearer of bad news," Esther said, "but you just came from the direction we need to go."

Bakma reinforcements materialized from down the hall, thrusting Esther, Papanov, and the two new soldiers into another firefight.

The American was on Esther's side of the corner. He shouted between bursts of gunfire. "There's no way all twenty Bakma took the same hall! I'm guessing there's six down there, tops. We can take six if we charge."

"What if you're wrong?"

"I'm never wrong."

Esther looked at his nametag. When she read it, her mouth fell. "*Custer*? Your last name is *Custer*?"

The soldier fired again. "Yeah, so what?"

Esther fell back to the wall. "We're all going to die."

BACK IN THE CRUISER, David and Gavrilyuk—the woman from the Forty-second—frantically tried to open the still-sealed doors. David was straining to his limit to lift one of them. He pressed the full weight of his body against it, the veins in his neck bulging beneath his armor.

The sound of scampering paws caught their attention. They spun to the open exit hall, where a tail-wagging Flopper bounded in.

"A *dog*?" Gavrilyuk asked.

Max burst into the room behind Flopper, a technical kit in his hands. "Get ready! We're raising the doors." Both soldiers grabbed their weapons as Max hurried to a control panel along the wall. Flopper stayed at his side while Max opened his kit and went to work.

David spoke into his comm. "Will, can you read me?"

The moment David's transmission came through, a neutron ray exploded against William's chest. The demolitionist careened backward against the closed door that had cut them off and collapsed face first on the ground.

Gritsenko, the older soldier, grabbed him and dragged him to the cover of the cleansing room. The Ceratopians were in strong force ahead of them; each minute brought them closer.

William forced out a word. "Cannon..."

Gritsenko turned and spotted William's hand cannon lying in the hall. He ran and claimed it for himself, firing a wild burst down the hall. The Ceratopians held their advance.

"Will, come in! Do you copy?"

William groaned and held up his comm. "Medic required..."

"'Medic required?'" David asked in the silo. "Will, for who?" No answer came. "Will? Will!" He turned to Max.

“Doors are opening in five seconds,” Max said. “I don’t know what’s beyond them, but we’re about to find out.”

A new voice called from behind them. “Max!” It was Tanneken. Shavrin and Sokolov were at her heels.

Flopper barked wildly next to Max.

“Ann!” Max shouted. “These doors are about to come up—I can’t slow them down—” He could get nothing further out. Throughout the Cruiser, the metal doors retracted into the ceiling.

Tanneken and her soldiers were in the middle of the silo when it happened. All three were suddenly surrounded by hallways. Ahead of them, a formerly trapped group of Bakma was suddenly visible. A gunfight began.

Everyone dove for cover. Within seconds, every operative in the room had repositioned to meet the alien forces.

“Thanks for the warning, *Max*!” Tanneken hollered.

Back in the cleansing room, William stumbled to his feet, breaking apart his chest plate and throwing it to the floor. His chest oozed with bleeding lacerations and bruises.

“Come,” Gritsenko said, propping William on his shoulder. He clutched the hand cannon in his free hand.

Assistance came in the form of Torban and his team, now freed from captivity themselves. Under their suppressive fire, Gritsenko helped William into safety.

The silo was chaos. Neutron rays blasted into the room, while Max and Tanneken’s teams struggled to hold fort. The initial group of Bakma had been downed, but not by EDEN. Ceratopians lurked farther down the hall. The Bakma had been slaughtered in a human-reptile crossfire.

Torban’s voice came over the comm. “We are moving to your position in the silo. We have your demolitionist. He is badly hurt.”

“Can we get a transport over here?” Max asked the Vultures.

Pelican Squad’s pilot answered the call. “Just dropped off Captain Gabriel, mate. En route to you now.”

“Torban,” Max said, “as soon as you get past the silo, I’m sealing all the doors again.”

“We can capture this ship, Max,” Tanneken advised.

“Screw that. This paycheck’s already been earned.”

“If we do not capture it, some other unit must.”

"I wish 'em the best."

David joined in. "Max, how much can you control with that kit?"

"Don't even think about it, Dave."

"Maybe she's right—"

"Don't even *think* about it, Dave!" Max interrupted him. "If it were that easy to take over a whole ship, don't you think we'd do it every time? I've got momentary control over a limited number of doors that I barely even got to pick myself."

Tanneken glared at the technician. "Interrupt *him*," she pointed to David, "that is fine. But I promise, Matthew, if you interrupt me, I will rip off your manhood and crush it on the floor."

Max said nothing.

"Go back to your control panel and gain access to *all* of the doors. I do not care how hard it is—figure it out. When Torban and the injured are out, seal off the Ceratopians as they did to you. Block them off from each other, and we will strike them one room at a time. This is not a request. I outrank you, and this is an order."

Still Max was silent.

"Did you not hear a word I just said?"

"I was just makin' sure you were finished."

She groaned in disgust.

SCOTT AND NIJINSKY were still holding their own. The lone Ceratopian remaining down the hallway maintained constant pressure. Scott knew there were more Ceratopians around, and if they didn't escape soon, those aliens would overpower them.

Nijinsky's shots were wild and sporadic. Even when ducking to avoid fire, his concentration seemed torn between the aliens and Scott. His whole body trembled.

Suddenly, from the intersection to their left, they heard a canrassi's tyrannical roar. Scott and Nijinsky spun around.

It was a black-furred canrassi—the fiercest variety. It howled through its razor-thin jaws, then charged. Nijinsky was directly in its path.

Everything drew to slow motion. As Scott registered the animal tearing toward Nijinsky, he realized the canrassi attack was exactly the opportunity the Ceratopian was waiting for. It was a priority distraction that would give the alien lizard a chance to advance.

"Nijinsky, *move*!"

The slayer did nothing. He stared at the canrassi as it barreled closer, his arms hanging limp at his sides. Scott had witnessed this before. He'd seen it in Esther in Khatanga and in other places, too. Paralyzing fear. If Nijinsky didn't move, he'd be dead. As Scott watched the slayer stand in imminent death, the realization came to him.

I can let this Nightman die.

Since joining their murderous ranks, Scott had lusted for moments like this—moments when he could watch Nightmen meet their just demises. Butchered like the butchers they were, preying on innocent lives. Lives like Nicole's.

He asked himself the same question every time he met a new Nightman. He'd asked it of Viktor, Nicolai, Auric, and Egor, and of the Nightmen he'd trained. And now, as he stared at Alexander Nijinsky, he asked it again.

What if this is the one?

He watched Nijinsky let go of his weapons. The slayer's whole body swayed as mere meters before him and charging soullessly, the canrassi opened its jaws.

What if Nijinsky had murdered her?

No.

Scott launched himself like a missile. Had a breeze blown, he would have been too slow. But he wasn't. He plowed straight through the battle-stunned slayer, just as the canrassi clamped down its jaws. The canrassi missed them by an inch.

The two Nightmen skidded across the floor past the beast, which lurched around for a second attack. Scott was atop Nijinsky, between the slayer's body and the canrassi's teeth. There was nowhere to go.

The canrassi struck.

Scott flung his hand up to shove the beast's head away, his palm slamming into the canrassi's nose. For a brief moment, his hand slipped inside the creature's jaws. He jerked it out as its teeth clamped down.

His arm was ahead of his instinct, striking at the beast's nose again. Instead of punching it, he grabbed the canrassi in the nostrils, his gloved fingers splitting between the oversized holes. His hand clenched and the beast reared back. Scott was jerked into the air.

What happened next, he couldn't have planned. His left hand still gripped the canrassi's nose. His body was swung around until he landed against the side of the beast's neck. He latched onto its battle armor.

Climb.

With an adrenaline-fueled lurch, Scott propelled himself on top of the canrassi, one hand grabbing neck fur while the other held the beast's nose like a rein. When he clenched his fists, the canrassi shrieked in pain-induced rage.

Giant footsteps boomed from the corner behind them. Scott jerked the canrassi around by the nose, and the animal frantically complied. The advancing Ceratopian emerged.

With his left hand still clutching the beast's nose, Scott unholstered his sidearm with his right. He aimed over his left arm and fired. Bullets pierced the Ceratopian's neck, blood splattered the wall, and the alien fell.

Sparks surged through Scott's veins. Turning his focus to the enslaved canrassi, Scott placed the barrel of his pistol against the top of the beast's skull, pulling the trigger. Blood burst from the canrassi's head, and it toppled forward. Scott stayed on its back the whole while.

For the first time since he had entered the Battleship with Esther, everything around Scott was still. There was no movement or nearby gunfire. He looked at Nijinsky. The slayer was propped clumsily on one elbow on the ground, staring at Scott. He could hear Nijinsky's near-panicked heaves.

"Esther, what's your status?" Scott asked over the comm.

"I'm about to charge the enemy with a man named Custer. Do you really want to know what my status is?"

"I'm sending Nijinsky to you."

Nijinsky exhaled a shaky breath.

"I'm going to hold the hall by myself," he said to Esther. "Take him with you to level three." Nijinsky was more liability than help. The slayer was out of his league. "Esther, did you get that?"

"...yes sir."

Her voice was different, reluctant. That struck him as strange.

More massive footsteps thundered down the hall. Ceratopians were approaching. Scott disentangled himself from the dead canrassi, grabbed his assault rifle, and pulled the slayer up. "I have a scout down the hall with your team. She'll take you to the roof."

Nijinsky just stared.

"Do you understand?" Scott asked, this time in Russian.

"...yes..."

"Go." He shoved Nijinsky away.

The slayer stumbled for a moment, then regained his balance. His featureless stare found Scott again. For several full seconds, he just watched the golden-horned fulcrum. Finally, he turned to retreat.

Scott was alone.

Even surrounded by firefight, Esther was numb. She stared at the comm in her hand. Then Custer spoke.

"Charging in three seconds!"

Esther broke out of her trance. "What?"

"Get ready to go!"

"We can't! Someone's heading for our location right now."

Custer reloaded his rifle. "I hope they can run." Motioning his partner—the Briton named Black—he signaled the charge. Black bolted around the corner. Custer followed and Papanov carried his injured commander behind him. Esther readied her guns and pursued.

Custer and Black cleared the path with reckless ferocity. Like a poorly oiled machine, their haphazard gunslinging forced the Bakma into frantic defense.

With a pistol in each hand, Esther took precision shots behind the frontal assault. Custer fell backward as plasma ricocheted off his shoulder. She slid to his side.

Ahead of them, Black and Papanov pushed the aliens into retreat. Black reloaded his assault rifle and looked back. "Get up, Reg. Scout, take the lead."

Custer's shoulder armor was a melted wreck. He glared at Black. "I'm fine, scat-hole, thanks for askin'."

"Suck it up."

Esther stood up next to Custer. "Are you all right?"

"I'm all right, take the lead."

Esther stoically readied her sidearms. "The maintenance shaft is—"

"Just shut up and move!"

The scout released a laugh of restraint. "Oh, you'll sodding get yours." She said nothing more as she led them through the hall.

On the surface, Svetlana was working frantically on the injured old man, who was slipping in and out of consciousness. Blood stained her armor from her hands to her elbows. Several meters away, the younger injured operative moaned in torment.

Suddenly, the air above her grew deafening. Her shoulders tensed as she looked up.

The *Pariah* hovered, its engines smoking, its hull decimated. "Need a lift?" Travis called. Becan, Auric, and the two soldiers from Gabriel's crew looked up.

"She won't last in a fight, but she's still holding on. I can take some of you guys back to base."

Becan looked at Svetlana. "Go, Sveta. Take Auric with yeh."

Travis lowered the *Pariah* to the ground.

INSIDE THE BATTLESHIP, Esther led her team up the hall. They'd encountered four Bakma during their journey, all of which had fallen with relative ease. More Bakma could be heard in the near distance, drawing closer even as the group hurried on.

Esther stopped in the middle of a hallway, kneeling down against the right-hand wall. She pulled out a small cylindrical laser-cutter.

"What are we doing?" asked Black. The men took defensive positions around her.

"This is it."

"This is it?" Custer asked. "This is a blank wall!"

Esther flicked a switch on the cutter. The laser came to life, searing through the metal wall panel. As she guided the beam into a large square, she explained. "There's no entrance to this shaft on this floor—it's only accessible from beneath the ship itself. It goes up, emptying into level three. From level three we can get to the roof." She stepped back, giving her cutout a forceful kick. The panel fell through, revealing a hollow hole. "There are ladders on both sides of the shaft. The rungs are too far apart for humans to climb, so you'll have to climb the side supports."

"Aliens use ladders?" asked Black warily.

She gave him a look that said *stupid*. "Did you honestly think that in the infinite scope of the universe, we're the only beings who came up with the concept of climbing?"

The Bakma grew nearer. Their menacing grunts echoed down the halls.

She motioned them through. "Wait for me at the level-three access door. I'll stay here until Remington and Nijinsky arrive." As Custer moved to step through, she grabbed his good shoulder. "Custer, wait. Give me your helmet."

Custer did as requested. "What is it—?"

She slapped him dead in the face. The American flinched back. She jammed his helmet back in his hands. "Never tell me to shut up again."

He muttered under his breath as he and the others made their way through.

ON THE OTHER end of the Battleship, Dostoevsky and Tkachenok's teams warded off the Ceratopians. The humans had one thing in their favor: Egor Goronok. The hulking slayer fired his hand cannon relentlessly, staving off any attempt for the aliens to press forward. But as surely as time ticked away, Egor's ammo count fell.

The door to the second-floor lift opened and Dostoevsky and Tkachenok's men spun around.

Gabriel raised his hands in the air. "Don't shoot!" He was flanked by two women, one slender and the other the heavyset one from the Vulture. "We got here as fast as we could."

Viktor glared at Dostoevsky. "We waited here all this time to be rescued by *women*?" he asked in Russian.

Before Dostoevsky could respond, neutron fire soared down the hall. The team fired back in swift defense.

"Get everyone in the lift," Gabriel commanded. "We'll hold off them off while you escape."

Almost everyone in Esther's team had climbed into the maintenance shaft. Only she and Black remained. Just as Black disappeared through the hole, a new set of footsteps appeared. Esther looked up to find the new arrival.

It was Nijinsky. The slayer saw her as soon as he reached her corridor.

Esther went rigid. The hair on the back of her neck stood on end. Her fingers tensed on the triggers of her pistols.

All of a sudden, footsteps emerged behind her. She spun around in the hall, where several Bakma rounded the corner recklessly—as if they didn't expect anyone to be there.

Esther and Nijinsky dove and fired their guns, and the first pair of Bakma was cut to the ground. As the Bakma became aware of them, they positioned themselves for a counter-attack.

A plasma bolt slammed against Nijinsky's shoulder and neck, knocking the slayer off his feet. He screamed and threw off his burning helmet.

The scout's dual handguns were true. She dodged from one wall to the next, firing into the alien force. Two Bakma fell before she was struck. A bolt glanced by the side of her chest plate; though not a direct hit, it was enough to knock her off her feet.

Nijinsky took over. The helmetless slayer rolled forward, slinging up his rifle to fire.

Esther unhitched a grenade from her belt. Activating it, she flung it hard down the hall. It bounced around the corner amid the aliens and when it exploded, blood and screams filled the air.

"Finish them off," Esther said, pointing ahead. Her chest plate was melted, but not breached. She watched as Nijinsky charged through the smoke to the corner, his assault rifle flashing orange, prompting several more Bakmanese screams. Then all was still.

The slayer stood in a mess of mangled flesh, searching with his assault rifle for more life. But there was only the distant sound of Bakma voices not yet near their position. Satisfied, he propped his gun up and turned to find Esther. What he saw made his body lock up.

Esther's eyes were narrowed to slits. Her nose was wrinkled. Her lips were compressed. But that was not what Nijinsky saw. He saw a small symmetrical shape. A perfect circle.

Then he saw nothing else.

The bullet struck him in the center of the forehead, passing right through his skull and splattering the wall behind him with blood. He collapsed to the floor.

Esther stood statuesque, her pistol extended, her breaths controlled. Her glare burned holes through her visor as she took in his final resting place. Alexander Nijinsky—the man who had tainted the lion. *Her* lion.

He would taint no one else.

38

FRIDAY, NOVEMBER 25TH, 0011 NE
1233 HOURS

BACK IN THE CRUISER, Max worked furiously on the control panel, with a firefight taking place all around him. Tanneken, Shavrin, Sokolov, and David were holding down the silo. Gavrilyuk had gone to meet Torban, who was once again pinned down by aliens. The Ceratopians had advanced against both teams. In another minute, they'd be in the silo itself.

Suddenly, Max gasped and let go of the kit. "Holy hell."

Tanneken looked his way. "What is it?"

"Holy hell!" Max leapt on the controls. "I'm in! I control the whole system! Holy hell!"

"Stop saying 'holy hell' and *close the doors*!"

Max screamed in the comm. "Everyone on all teams, get away from the doors! I'm about to seal everything off." He initiated the lockout sequence. Simultaneously, the doors throughout the Cruiser slid down. The firefight was cut off.

The technician didn't slow down. With all doors down by default, he specifically opened the doors between Torban's team and the silo, allowing them a path straight to him. "All right, Torban, follow the open doors!"

David raced to Max's side. "How'd you do that?"

"I made a bunch of mistakes, then one of them worked!"

"What?"

"I don't know! I don't know how I did it, it just happened." He turned to Tanneken. "Ann, I don't know how long I can keep control. If you want to strike, do it now!"

Tanneken stood beside them. "We will attack the central corridor first. When Max opens this blast door, I will throw a grenade. We attack right behind it. What the grenade doesn't kill, we will." She turned to Max. "Are you ready?"

His hands were shaking. "Ready when you are! I can't believe I did this. How did I do this? What did I do?"

"Open it!"

The central blast door rose into the ceiling. Tanneken threw in a grenade. Alien screams filled the corridor as it exploded, and the strike team rushed in behind. Projectile fire littered the halls.

"I gotta figure out how I did this," Max enthused, his hands fast on the controls. "They're gonna name this after me. They'll teach it in books!" He opened the comm to his whole team. "It'll be the 'Axen Technique!'"

He was completely ignored.

WITH SVETLANA AND her wounded safely aboard, Travis steered the *Pariah* over Varvara's site. He lowered the transport to pick her up while Seth covered him in Tanneken's Vulture.

The comm system was interrupted by a new source that overrode everything else. "Attention, *Novosibirsk* Vultures. This is General Bastiaan Platis. We are en route to your position under direct orders from EDEN High Command."

Switching his radar to ultra-wide range, Travis picked up the approaching squadrons: two Vultures and eight Vindicators. The pilot's eyes widened.

"You will cease any and all combat initiatives," Platis said. "Any failure to comply will be seen as an act of defiance against EDEN. Your operatives will begin an immediate withdrawal from the combat zone. Please acknowledge."

Travis stared blankly at the radio. He tuned in Scott on the comm. "Umm..."

"We heard," Scott said. "Tell him we're on our way out. Pick up whatever wounded you can and go back to base."

Tanneken cut in angrily. "We are calling off our strike. Brunner out."

IN THE CRUISER, Max hurled his technician's kit across the room. Flopper scampered to fetch it. "You gotta be *kidding me*! I pull off the technical feat of the century and we freakin' *pull out*? I don't even know how I did it yet!"

David cleared his throat over the comm. "The 'Axen Technique,' right? Is it a tactical retreat?"

Max cursed under his breath.

Dostoevsky's and Tkachenok's teams had fought their way back to the front of the Battleship, escorted by Gabriel and his two female soldiers. The Bakma had all but been cleared from the first floor, leaving almost no resistance in their area.

Dostoevsky had said nothing since they'd left the second floor. Not once during their exit had he faced his slayers.

The entire mission had been a dizzying blur for him. Everything—from Saretok's condemnation, to Viktor's mocking, to the fact that he was almost abandoned before the mission began—tightened the already-tense knot in his stomach.

Viktor had more than held his own. In addition to treating the wounded, he'd fought with intensity. His shots had been true, his instincts sure. Egor had been a one-man force. He had wreaked havoc on the enemy, halting their advances several times.

What had Dostoevsky done?

Ahead, the exit to the outside world appeared. Travis's voice came over the comm. "I'm heading back to base with the wounded. Seth is gonna stick around for Max's team, then he'll pick up you guys."

Gabriel answered him. "Understood. We're almost outside the Battleship. We'll wait for Seth there."

Dostoevsky remained silent.

Scott had been in a shootout with a pair of Ceratopians when he'd heard General Platis's orders. As much as he would have loved to think about the significance of EDEN Command's involvement, the red flashes of neutron rays were a constant reminder that time was critical.

"Esther, how's it looking?"

"We were attacked several times while en route, but at the moment I'm clear waiting for you. Everyone else is climbing the shaft."

"Are there Bakma nearby?"

"I can hear them, sir."

Scott leaned around a corner to fire. His Ceratopian targets ducked away. "Did Nijinsky make it to you?"

Her answer was delayed. "Nijinsky is dead."

Scott couldn't help but think it. *We could have left him here and been out already. He'd have died either way.* He forced the thoughts out. "Go up the shaft without me. Get your team out of here."

"Sir?"

"If you wait for me, the Bakma will catch you. There's about five

Ceratopians on my end, but I can outrun them alone. I'll go to the front of the ship." He could meet up with Dostoevsky and Gabriel there.

"...yes sir."

There was no more reason to stick around and fight the Ceratopians. Turning from the intersection, Scott took a path that led straight through the ship.

Esther was alone by the cutout she'd made in the wall. She could hear the alien voices grow nearer. She holstered her guns and slid through the hole.

It didn't take her long to scale the shaft. "Listen up, team," she said through the comm. "Remington is leaving out the front of the ship. We're going to the roof by ourselves."

"He's not coming?" Custer asked.

"Is that a problem?"

"What if we hit a Ceratopian stronghold?"

Esther climbed beside him. "Then I guess this really *is* your last stand."

DOSTOEVSKY WAS alone outside the ship. Behind him, Viktor tended to Tkachenok's injured men. Each of the others was doing their part.

The fulcrum captain listened to the updates from the other teams. Operatives were checking on one another. Max commed Svetlana and Varvara. Derrick commed William to see how he was doing. Even Egor got a comment from Becan. Dostoevsky heard every transmission.

But no one commed him.

"Captain Gabriel?" The voice was Scott's, through the wide channel frequency. As Dostoevsky heard it, he looked Gabriel's way.

"Gabriel here. Go ahead, mate."

"My scout's on her way to the roof. Can your pilot pick them up?"

"Sure as day."

"Good. I'm heading your way. The first floor looks relatively clear."

The Australian spoke warily. "The aliens are probably all on the third floor. Are you sure your scout know what she's doing?"

"There are Bakma blocking the rear exit and Ceratopians between me and her. The roof route was her team's only option." Scott paused. "Tell Tkachenok we lost the guy we went after. The Nightman—Nijinsky."

Dostoevsky's eyes suddenly grew with interest.

"I'll tell him, mate. Rex out."

Dostoevsky jumped on the comm. "Scott, what did you say?"

"We lost the Nightman we were going after."

"His name! What was his name?"

"Nijinsky."

"*Alexander* Nijinsky?"

"I guess. I don't know. He was a slayer." There was another pause. "Did you know him?"

Dostoevsky was speechless. He stared blankly at the device.

"Yuri, you there?"

Finally, Dostoevsky replied. "Yes. I knew him."

Several seconds passed before Scott answered. "I'm sorry, Yuri. We did the best that we could."

Dostoevsky lowered the comm to his side.

Max emerged on the channel, his voice low and subdued. "Don't worry about it, Scott. I'm sure Nijinsky got what he deserved."

Silence hit. No one else on the channel said a word.

He got what he deserved. Max's words replayed in Dostoevsky's head. He knew exactly what they meant, and why Nijinsky deserved it. Someone else deserved it, too.

Dostoevsky looked up at his slayers. They were already looking at him.

As Esther led the escapees to the third floor, she heard all of it. Her eyes remained defiantly focused as she assisted the final operative onto deck three.

The third-floor access panel opened from the dead end of a hallway. The moment she emerged, she became aware of Ceratopians in the area. They were just as she'd predicted—gathered in the central corridors surrounding the bridge. She didn't need to know how many there were; it was more important that they were avoided at all costs.

Stealthily the team crept through the halls of the ship. As Esther had promised, the exit to the roof wasn't far, and they reached it without resistance.

The exit was strikingly ordinary—nothing more than a hatch in the ceiling. But it was as oversized as the gargantuan halls. Moving to the wall nearest the hatch, Esther accessed a display screen. Depressed ladder rungs, rectangular and oversized, slid out from the wall under the exit. Carefully, she grabbed the first rung.

SCOTT WAS PASSING through the heart of the first floor. He hadn't run into a single extraterrestrial since initially making his break. It was as if that wing of the first floor had been entirely abandoned. That surprised him—but not enough to cause him to let down his guard. He trekked onward with caution and speed, creeping around corners and cutting through intersections with his rifle prepared.

With the action apparently subsiding, he turned on his ExTracker and immediately picked up a signal. The blips were just inside his custom-set detection range of twenty meters, just past an intersection ahead. The ExTracker identified them as Ceratopians. They were moving toward the intersection at intermittent speeds, stopping periodically along the way. Scott knelt and aimed his assault rifle ahead, waiting for them to walk in his sights. When they did, he arched an eyebrow.

It was indeed a pair of Ceratopians—one tan, and one black and green. But they weren't geared up for a fight. On the contrary, both were completely stripped down, devoid of weapons, armor, or clothing. They were tattered from head to toe with various wounds—bruises, gashes, and burns. The tan one hobbled, evidently in pain. They turned and saw him.

Scott held his fire as the Ceratopians froze. He swore he could read apprehension, particularly in the black-skinned one—as if it didn't know how to proceed. Neither creature moved.

Had they been armed, Scott wouldn't have hesitated; he'd have gunned them down, armor or not. But to slaughter them defenseless felt wrong.

The tan-skinned Ceratopian—the one with the limp—held out its hands. *"Dar Achaar veraatat dech."*

Scott's finger lifted from the trigger. *What in the world?*

"Dar Achaar veraatat dech."

He lowered his assault rifle. Was he supposed to know what that meant? The only alien word he knew was the Bakmanese word for surrender.

The Ceratopians entered a brief, quiet exchange. Their body language couldn't have been clearer: they were trying to figure out what to do. The tan one looked at Scott while pointing to itself.

"H'laar."

The alien was telling him its name—there was no doubt. Scott looked behind briefly to check his rear, then turned back to them. He motioned to himself. "Remington."

The Ceratopian nodded its head, clearing its throat. Its words were slow and precise. *"Dar Achaar veraatat,"* it pointed to Scott, *"Rumigtaah."*

Scott couldn't hold back his own words—they just blurted out. "What the *hell*?"

On the third level of the Battleship, Esther hung on the top rung of the exit ladder. Her hands worked the ceiling controls. "All right, get ready." Drawing a breath, she inputted the final command. The door whooshed open with alarming speed, and the sky came into view.

Esther grinned and looked down at her team. "Grab hold of this," she said, tossing down a small line. On her end was a suction device. "Attach the clip to your belts, and I'll lift you up one by one. Commander Ozerov can go first."

The operatives below smiled for the first time. They hurriedly set the clip on the injured commander's belt.

Esther stared at the oversized exit. Holding her breath, she leapt toward it, grabbing hold of its edge. She pulled herself through to open air. As soon as she found her footing, she attached the suction device to the roof.

Looking across the open snowfields, Esther saw the Noboat perimeter. There were still Bakma about but their numbers had dwindled. Far in the distance, she saw Tanneken's Vulture picking up Max's crew. She lifted her comm. "Leaving so soon, David?"

After a moment David answered, "Not a *second* too soon. Let's go back home."

"*Novosibirsk* never seemed like such a nice place!"

"You can say that again."

"Esther out." Closing the conversation, the scout looked down at her team. Ozerov was prepped for his lift. Flipping a switch next to the suction, the device began to pull the line in. It tensed but didn't break with his weight. Ozerov rose from the ground.

The wind felt good on Esther's cheeks. It was a welcomed change to the stale air of the Battleship. Scanning the area one final time, she turned around to catch the view from behind.

Suddenly she stopped.

Something wasn't right. There was a clear area where snow *wasn't* falling, barely twenty meters in front of her. It was distinguishably different from the rest of the air—like an absence of space.

An absence of space.

Esther gasped, her eyes popping. Spinning around, she unclamped the suction. Ozerov yelled and fell to the floor. But she didn't care.

She heard the Noboat materialize behind her. Its electric sizzle crackled through the air as its plasma cannons charged to life. It fired as she dove through the hole.

SCOTT FELT THE ship rumble. The two Ceratopians also felt it, and their bewildered looks said what he knew: they were under attack. Scott lifted his weapon, but not to fire. He motioned the Ceratopians to run.

DOSTOEVSKY, GABRIEL, and Tkachenok raced away from the Battleship. They turned their heads skyward to see.

"That's the Noboat we couldn't find!" Seth said over his comm from the Vulture. "The one that disappeared!"

Still in shock, Gabriel turned to Dostoevsky and said, "Don't you have a crew en route to the roof?"

Behind his helmet, Dostoevsky's face lost its color.

ESTHER AND HER operatives were blown back across the floor of deck three. The blast from the Noboat's plasma cannon had all but obliterated the ceiling above them. Grunting through the pain of a hard fall and a plasma shockwave, the scout forced herself to her feet.

No one from the team had been killed. They were shaken up but able to move. Far down the hall, between them and the maintenance shaft, Ceratopians rounded the bend.

"Everyone, run!" Esther screamed. "Get up and move!"

Everyone—injured Ozerov included—surged to their feet. Behind them, the neutron attack began.

DOSTOEVSKY LISTENED as Esther screamed on the comm. "This is Brooking! We're sealed off from the roof! We have nowhere to go!" The zap of neutron beams verified her words.

Gabriel thrust his comm to his lips. "Seth, can you assist?"

"Captain, we're loaded full of wounded! There's no way we can take on a Noboat."

Dostoevsky felt his heart rate increase. The Ceratopians inside the Battleship would mow Esther and her entire team down. She didn't stand a chance without help.

"We have nowhere to go!" Esther shrieked.

"General Platis," Gabriel said desperately, "we have Noboats engaging from above! Can your fighters assist?"

Dostoevsky turned to the slayers. They were away from the Battleship, watching the sky as the Noboat circled for prey. Tkachenok's crew looked defeated. They were barely able to breath as they recovered from their ordeal. As for Captain Gabriel, the Australian wasn't even supposed to be there—his team had come on their own free will. Everyone had given so much.

Everyone but him.

Dostoevsky's feet became light. His emotions overtook him.

I am living in a nightmare I have created. This shame, this confusion, it is my own.

The knot in his stomach slowly loosened.

God, Your vengeance is here—I can run from it no more.

He closed his eyes and lowered his head.

I give You what life I have left. I pray You are appeased. Have mercy on me, and protect me long enough to do one good thing...

...let me save as many as I can.

He opened his eyes. The slayers were still watching the Noboat. Gabriel was still on his comm. It was as if no time had passed at all.

Dostoevsky loaded a new clip in his assault rifle. He turned to the Battleship's door and launched himself forward.

Nobody noticed him leave.

39

FRIDAY, NOVEMBER 25TH, 0011 NE
1303 HOURS

CHAOS RULED THE third floor of the Battleship. As Esther frantically led her team through turn after turn, time became as much their enemy as the extraterrestrials. They could not reach the second floor without going through the Ceratopians, and the route they'd taken to the third floor was completely blocked. Only so many hallways were open, and they were in no shape to defend themselves.

Every time they rounded a corner, a barrage of neutron was right behind them. If anyone would have stumbled, they would have been dead. The pain of injuries took a back seat to survival.

Esther deduced that the Ceratopians were making a sweep, moving as a unified wave, and not only behind her team. Several times, they'd almost been surrounded. Her knowledge of layouts was saving their lives, but even that would soon fail.

She darted into a storage room, one of three placed back to back that connected two sets of halls on different sides of the ship. Her operatives could pass through the rooms from one hall to the next. If nothing else, it could buy them some time.

Esther hurdled over containers on the floor as the men stumbled in her wake. Ahead, the next storage room came to view, then the next. She could see the hallway across them. Suddenly, she skidded to a stop. In that same hallway, Ceratopians materialized, cutting her path off.

There were no other halls and no other means of escape. When the operatives caught up to her, they dove to the floor to avoid neutron beams from ahead.

"Close the door behind us!" Esther screamed. "Break the panel outside, then close the door!"

Black did as told, bashing the control panel in the hall before sealing the door from the inside. Esther did the same on her end. Both doors lowered, trapping them in.

"How long will this hold?" Black asked her.

"It won't."

SCOTT WAS MOVING as fast as he could. From the moment the first explosions rang out, he and the Ceratopians had made a beeline toward the exit. Hearing Esther's pleas quickened his pace.

These Ceratopians are slowing me down.

It was clear the aliens weren't in good shape. But what could he do? If he let them go, they could grab weapons. If he killed them...that just wouldn't have been honorable.

He knew the only choice he had left, without leaving them free and without taking them along. They were already in front of him, armorless, hobbling, limping.

Render them unconscious. It's the only way.

Scott attacked the larger one first—the black one with green markings. Leaping straight at the alien from behind, he cracked the butt of his assault rifle against the back of its head, beneath the protection of its bone frill. It was a perfect strike, solid and on the mark. There was only one problem.

The Ceratopian didn't fall.

Scott's eyes widened behind his helmet. *Oh, veck.*

The black and green lizard spun to face him. The other one—H`laar—jumped back defensively.

For a second time, Scott tried to slam his rifle butt against the black and green titan. But the Ceratopian, now aware, swung to block. It was as if Scott's rifle had hit a brick wall. Then the alien struck back. Scott was punched squarely in the chest; his feet left the ground. Landing on his back, he skidded down the hall, his assault rifle falling from his hands. He quickly looked up.

The massive extraterrestrial had taken a defensive position between Scott and H`laar. Scott recognized the alien's mannerisms. *He's acting like a bodyguard.* Scott climbed to his feet, reclaiming his gun. *He's capable, but still not in fighting condition. Hit him fast. Go in, dodge low, then uppercut him under the chin.* Bursting forward, Scott's body complied. Ducking beneath the Ceratopian's defensive strike, Scott rose and smashed the butt of his rifle up and into the lizard's jaw. Its whole head rocked backward and it stumbled. It only took one more blow while the alien was disoriented to bring it crashing down, out cold.

Scott focused on H`laar, who raised his hands to protest. But Scott didn't have time. Spinning around, he slugged the alien's face with his rifle. The already-battered H`laar fell easily.

The assault was dirty, but it had to be done. Now Scott could focus on Esther. Stepping away from the unconscious aliens, he bolted full speed down the hall.

OUTSIDE THE BATTLESHIP, a new situation was brewing—the Bakma Noboats were taking off. Gabriel watched as the ships disappeared. "Everyone inside," he ordered, motioning to his crew and the slayers. "Everyone, inside the Battleship!"

Scott appeared by Gabriel from the halls. He stopped as soon as he saw the operatives coming back in. "What's going on?"

"The Noboats took off. We don't know where they are. I've ordered my Vulture to leave."

"You did *what*?"

"It's a sitting duck. They've already got wounded—let them go. We'll wait here until Platis arrives."

Scott disliked agreeing with Gabriel's logic, but with invisible Noboats hovering around, the Australian was right. Anyone outside was asking to be killed. "Esther, give me an update!"

"We're locked in a room and surrounded," she answered. "We've got nowhere to go!" There was a burst of static. "They're beating down the doors!"

That was all Scott could take. Readying his rifle, he turned to Gabriel. No words were necessary.

"You and I," Gabriel said. "Let's go."

They ran for the lift, reaching it within seconds. Gabriel hit the lift's open-door button. They waited.

"Umm…"

"Shouldn't the lift already be on this level?" asked Scott.

"I don't understand." Gabriel hit the button again. "We just stepped off."

"It was working properly, right?"

"Yes! Dostoevsky and I were just—"

It dawned on both men at the same time. They swapped a stare, then whirled to look at the operatives behind them.

The Russian fulcrum was gone.

Dostoevsky slammed the butt of his assault rifle against the lift's control panel, leaning away as it sparked. The lift was now stuck on level three. There was no turning back.

Bursting through the lift door, he charged down the hall. His ExTracker was active—he knew Esther's precise location. Her team was fifty meters from him, past several intersections and turns. She was in the first of three rooms that stood between parallel halls. But he had no intention of going her way. He had another destination in mind.

"Esther," he said through his comm, "get ready to run."

"Captain?"

Dostoevsky rounded a turn onto the main corridor and the bridge came into view, past several junctions and security checkpoints. He could see Ceratopians ahead. It was the place they were most prepared to defend.

That was the point.

The massive extraterrestrials turned in his direction. For a second, none of them moved, as if unable to comprehend what they saw.

Running at full speed, Dostoevsky lifted his rifle. He fired at the closest cluster of aliens. Bullet holes blew through a Ceratopian's face.

All hell broke loose. The Ceratopians collectively turned to fire. By the time they did, the fulcrum had killed a second reptile.

Neutron lit the halls. It came at Dostoevsky like a flood, but instead of flinching or darting back, he dove straight ahead.

Leaping forward, he dove straight through the wave of neutron. He came out clean on the other end, hitting the floor with a somersault that brought him to a kneel with his assault rifle raised. In the second before the next wave of red appeared, his combat senses kicked in.

Kill the next closest to firing. He gunned the alien down. *Keep the nearest alien alive.* His aim found someone else.

There was a reason he didn't want to kill the Ceratopian nearest him. As he continued to rush closer, assault rifle blaring, he remained directly in front of the alien. He was making the other Ceratopians fire around it—they would try to avoid hitting their comrade.

He propelled himself right past the close Ceratopian, leaving it completely ignored. When he landed, he was between it and the ones down the hall. It was exactly where he wanted to be—in the middle of a Ceratopian crossfire.

All neutron stopped. The aliens were aware of friendly fire risks. If any neutron came from either side and missed, one of their comrades would be killed. Caution suddenly applied to every weapon.

Every weapon but one.

Dostoevsky fired at the Ceratopians guarding the bridge. The aliens, unsure whether to fire back, ducked and dove to avoid him. His right hand swept to his belt, unlatching a grenade and flinging the explosive ahead. When it blew up, the aliens' shouts turned to screams of horror.

The crossfire is gone. Spinning around, Dostoevsky aimed and fired at the Ceratopian he'd passed up. He blew its neck open before it could react.

He turned and surged forward. The door to the bridge was before him, but his goal wasn't to enter. It was merely to threaten the bridge enough to warrant more attention—attention that would have otherwise gone to Esther's team.

The door to the bridge was in the middle of a T-junction, and his ExTracker showed Ceratopians around the left corner. Sliding his second and final grenade from his belt, he hurled it ahead at an angle. It bounced around the corner, and he heard it ricochet down the hall. He heard the Ceratopians shout and dive as it erupted, and tortured screams echoed down the hall.

As he slammed his back against the wall and checked to ensure he wasn't being flanked, the surviving Ceratopians barked out loud, short commands, spoken quickly. Dostoevsky knew exactly what they were.

They were calling for backup.

ESTHER'S TEAM WAS still in the storage room, frantically shoving boxes and containers in front of the doors. In the midst of the action, the scout's ears perked as she heard a sound in the hall.

"Everyone, quiet!" She pushed past Custer to get to the hall door, where she stopped and listened intently. "They're falling back. They're leaving."

"They're *all* leaving?" asked Custer.

She hushed him. Listening further, she shook her head. "Not all, but definitely most."

Dostoevsky's voice came through the comm. "I am assaulting the Battleship's bridge. The Ceratopian forces should be coming to me. Work your way back to the hole in the roof and await General Platis. When he has cleared the area of Noboats, lift yourselves out."

Esther grinned. "Yes sir!"

"Can we do that?" asked Papanov. "Can we climb back out that same way?"

"If the Noboats are gone and the Ceratopians leave us alone, yes. It might actually be possible." She readied her pistols again. "Lieutenant Papanov, Black, help me move these canisters from the door. We can still open it from inside." The scout began to push the canisters away.

As the door was cleared, Esther stepped back. "Custer, can you shoot?"

"If I have a gun, I can shoot."

"Any clue how many Ceratopians are left?" Black asked.

"Two to three," Esther answered, "and they'll be proper flustered when they see us attack. Don't spare your ammunition—this is our only chance." She held her hands over the controls. "Get ready…now!" She inputted the command and the door whizzed straight up.

Outside, two Ceratopians were caught unaware. The humans opened fire with the ammunition they had left, and the aliens toppled before they could turn. The hallway was clear.

Dostoevsky was knee-deep in combat. A slew of aliens had emerged from various hallways, cutting him off three directions out of four. The only clear path he had left was directly behind him—the way he'd come from.

A necrilid appeared from around the near corner. Before Dostoevsky could react, it pounced on him, diggings its claws into his armor and knocking him back. Clutching his assault rifle, he contorted his body to throw the animal off. The necrilid was thrown against the wall, only to right itself in the next instant.

Dostoevsky grabbed the creature by its throat. It writhed and clawed in his grasp, striking his chest plate, arm guards, and shoulders. He threw the necrilid off as far as he could, only to watch it land on all fours. He managed to lift his assault rifle and gun it down just as it leapt his direction. Limbs askew, it rolled lifelessly down the hall.

Ceratopians appeared from various halls ahead of him. The fulcrum was directly in line of their fire, with no time to strategically plan and no crossfires to use to his advantage. He had nowhere to go.

Esther trekked through empty halls; not a Ceratopian was in sight. She soon found herself back in the hall with the roof hatch. The ceiling was demolished, but the sky was clear. Even climbing would be easy: half of a wall had imploded, forming a rough hill up to the roof. They would not even need to suction a line.

General Platis announced over the comm, "We have arrived."

The next thing she saw were Vindicators streaking over the Battleship. Their exit was cleared.

OUTSIDE, PLATIS'S Agèma Vindicators captured the skies. Two Noboats materialized to attack, though they fell quickly to the new human arrivals. No other Noboats appeared. A pair of fresh Vultures landed by the Battleship's door.

"EVERYONE UP!" yelled Esther. "Ozerov, Custer, go! Papanov, Black, go!" She waved all of them on while she waited. "Everyone get out!" As they scrambled up the imploded wall, she got on the comm. "Captain Dostoevsky, we're clear!"

NO SOONER THAN Dostoevsky heard the words, a neutron beam hit him square in the chest. Inside his helmet, saliva flew from his mouth as his eyes bulged. His ribcage audibly cracked. He sailed through the air as though weightless.

He landed on his back and slid down the same hall he'd initially come from. He saw the metal ceiling pass overhead and heard the scraping of his armor against the floor. He slammed against the back wall.

Neutron was still soaring at him; the beams hammered the walls all around him. He could feel their energy, smell their particles.

Time seemed to stop as Dostoevsky registered his physical body, from his fingers to his toes. He felt his ribs where they had fractured. Rolling onto his side, he pressed his hand to the floor. With his other hand, he detached his helmet.

This was all I wanted.

Pushing upward, he rose to his knees and lifted his head to the alien mob, surrendering his helmet to the floor.

This was all I asked for.

The Ceratopians fired their weapons. Red flashes pulsed from their barrels.

To save as many as I could.

His fingers relinquished their grasp as his assault rifle fell from his hands. He bowed his head in surrender.

I am Yours.

When it hit him, it jostled his bones. Never before had he been struck so hard. The world spun as he flew through the air. His eyes shot open. Inertia kicked in. He gasped for a breath.

It wasn't neutron that had struck him. It was something much more determined than a Ceratopian kill strike. As the world tumbled in Dostoevsky's view, he registered glimpses above. He saw flashes of ceiling light—then blackness and horns.

He saw gold.

Time caught up with him again. The world sped back up. As neutron gave way to projectile, he focused his eyes.

Scott leapt from atop him and shouldered his gun. "You're *lucky* he's got a good technician!"

Dostoevsky looked at the intersection. A second man stood there—a man in EDEN armor. Captain Gabriel. Dostoevsky watched as Scott joined him to fight.

Scott fired around the corner of the hall, the heat of gun exhaust blowing in his face. Far ahead, the Ceratopians returned fire.

A woman's voice came over the comm. "Platis is here, captain! I'm bringing his team up the lift."

"Good work, Meg," answered Gabriel. "You're getting a raise."

"...right."

The Australian looked at Scott. "I'm counting about nine."

Scott ducked to avoid a near-miss. "Not our problem." They were Platis's headaches now. He and Gabriel had reached Dostoevsky—that had been their only objective.

Once again, the Australian girl spoke. "We're on our way up!"

Scott didn't know the heavyset girl beyond her first name, but she'd singlehandedly saved Dostoevsky's life. She was Pelican Squad's only surviving technician. She'd operated the damaged lift with her gizmos. She'd gotten them there in time.

Edging around the corner, Scott fired again.

Everything had fallen into place. The *Pariah* had survived and was long gone, on its way back to *Novosibirsk* with Svetlana and Varvara's teams. Tanneken was leaving with Max and the survivors from the Cruiser. And now, Esther had led her group to the roof, where the squadron of Vindicators would watch over them. It had all come together as if planned.

This went beyond us. Scott couldn't keep the thought from his mind. *This was meant to happen.*

The lift opened just down the hall. Scott held his fire and turned to see EDEN soldiers rushing out. Their armor wasn't standard silver and gray, but crimson and gold. Whatever this unit was, it was a specialty one like Vector Squad. It had to be.

Scott and Gabriel stopped firing and dropped back as the new operatives took their place in the fight. They didn't hesitate but moved quickly down the hall. At that very moment, Scott realized their battle was over.

"Remington," a Balkan accent came from his comm. "My Agèma will take this operation from here. I await on level one."

Scott pulled off his helmet. Every inch of his armor was bloodstained, from his golden horns to his featureless faceplate. He ran a hand through his sweat-drenched hair. "Affirmative." Wiping his brow, he spoke on. "General, there are two Ceratopians down the second corridor from the lift. You should find them unconscious."

"Thank you, Remington." The comm channel closed.

Scott fell to his knees, closing his eyes. The mission was over. The battle that had begun with a single Noboat—miles from any Battleship or Cruiser, where they'd left Colonel Saretok behind—had come to an end.

A faint smile crept across his sweat-glistening face—a smile of near disbelief. Yet he did believe.

This is what You hoped for, wasn't it? This is what You hoped we would become.

The Fourteenth had done the right thing. Every one of them, from Svetlana to Travis, from Esther to Max. Tanneken and Gabriel, too. Everything had worked.

His smile grew broader; he couldn't restrain it. After everything they'd been through as a unit, after everything they'd endured together, they had finally found their redemption. Every struggle, every trial, every tragedy had brought them to this. Had it been worth it? At that moment, there was no doubt in Scott's mind. It was enough to make him shout with joy.

Bring him to Me.

When Scott registered the words, his eyes opened wide. They were authoritative, a command. But they hadn't been spoken aloud, nor were they his own. They resonated as if from his soul.

It took him a moment to realize who the voice belonged to. It was Someone he hadn't heard from in a very long time—since the day he'd taken Sergei Steklov's life. It was Someone he'd forgotten how to hear. But now he heard. As the realization came to him, Scott arched his eyebrows strangely. *Bring him to Me?* What was that supposed to mean?

It was at that moment when a quiet but unmistakably distinct sound came from behind him. Rasping, breathy releases—the stifling of sobs. Scott slowly turned his head to look back.

It was Dostoevsky—he was curled up in a ball on the floor. His hands clutched the top of his head, hiding his face. His whimpered words were scarcely audible, but Scott could still hear them. They were pleas whispered with impassioned desperation. They were prayers.

Bring him to Me.

Tingles of realization coursed through Scott's veins.

"I gave it to You," Dostoevsky cried, tearing at his hair. "I gave my life to You..."

It took almost ten full seconds for Scott to react. *Is this actually real?*

Dostoevsky whimpered on, "I don't want to run anymore..."

As Scott's heart and mind collided, he rose to his feet. It was indeed real—as real as anything else in the room. He rationalized it as he took it all in. Salvation didn't care who it blessed. It didn't care what they had done. It only cared that they'd sought it out. That they'd reached for something—Someone—higher than themselves.

That they'd surrendered.

Kneeling next to Dostoevsky, Scott placed his hand on the Russian's shoulder. He'd have preferred to be somewhere private, a place where people weren't watching. But this wasn't his plan—and that was fine. He closed his eyes and fought to find the right words, his throat tightening as they finally escaped. "God..." It was all he knew how to say. "...please forgive Yuri."

With those words, the outcry began. Everything inside Dostoevsky poured out as he wailed from the floor.

Meters away, standing awkwardly silent, Gabriel watched the scene.

Scott spoke on. "End this for Yuri, right now."

"...forgive me, my God..."

"Let him know that he's Yours."

Dostoevsky's mouth fell open and emitted a moan that pealed through the halls. It was all things at once—release, agony, defeat.

Then it was joy.

The transition was sudden, but seamless, as if in the span of a single second, the weight of the world had been lifted from Dostoevsky's shoulders. It was as if a reviving breeze had swept through the hall. Scott opened his eyes.

Dostoevsky lifted his head to look through the ceiling. Then he smiled—a broad grin that stretched from ear to ear.

Scott fought to mask his emotions, lowering his head to hide his own glistening eyes. He pulled Dostoevsky close to him; the fulcrums embraced.

Few men were there to witness the scene, but those who did saw a murderer crumble before their eyes. They saw damnation foiled.

Gabriel said nothing during the entire episode. He only watched until the moment culminated, then turned to leave.

EVERYTHING AFTER that was a blur. Gradually the halls cleared out as Platis's unit secured the ship. Soon everyone was preparing to leave.

During their flight back to The Machine, those who knew Dostoevsky couldn't take their eyes from him. Not Esther, not Viktor, not Egor. They were captivated by the murderer who had never met his own soul—the man whose veins had run colder than Siberia itself.

The man who rejoiced through tears all the way home.

40

FRIDAY, NOVEMBER 25TH, 0011 NE
1119 HOURS

CAIRO, EGYPT

TWO HOURS LATER

H`LAAR GROWLED as human hands forced him to his knees in the sand. The tan Ceratopian was beaten and exhausted. It had no strength to fight back.

An EDEN Command transport lowered to the ground ahead of him, blowing a new cloud of desert sand in the air. Behind the alien, General Platis drew a deep breath. He and the Agèma had touched down three hundred miles southwest of *Cairo*, in the Libyan Desert. Despite the lateness of November, a warm breeze blew from the dunes.

The alien struggled to stand once again. As it watched the transport touch down, it grunted through hardened jaws.

The door to the newly arrived transport lowered to the sand. Judge Jason Rath appeared in the doorway. Except for his pilot, he was completely alone.

Platis snapped into attention. The rest of the Agèma crew followed suit. The Ceratopian exhaled a hard breath.

Approaching EDEN's regional general, the Canadian judge said, "Well done, General Platis. This is indeed the one we'd hoped to find."

The bearded Greek took the compliment solemnly. "Thank you, Judge Rath. We took several others alive. Do you require them also?"

The judge shook his head. "This one's the most important. Bring the others to *Cairo*." He looked at the captive. "Did it try to communicate?"

Platis frowned and examined the battered Ceratopian. "It was unconscious for most of the flight. It woke up just before you arrived. It tried to speak, but we did not understand." Rath did not respond. After a moment of thought, Platis lifted his head and leaned closer. "Judge Rath, if I may ask...who is he?"

The Canadian locked eyes with the alien. Ten seconds passed. Neither of them moved. "He's one of their leaders," he finally said. "One of their best. We're fortunate to have him alive. By the looks of it, the crash almost killed him."

Platis scrutinized the alien.

Rath was more concerned about the general. "We'll take him from here. We begin interrogations tonight."

When Platis saw no guards at the back of Rath's transport, he asked, "You will take him alone, judge?"

Rath chuckled. "I can hold my own fine. I don't think he's in condition to fight."

"As you wish, judge."

After an exchange of salutes, the general turned to leave. His operatives in the Agèma followed him, leaving the parched Ceratopian behind. As soon as the alien was released, it toppled forward in the sand, heaving dehydrated breaths.

Rath watched Platis and his men as they boarded their ship. He saw their thrusters kick in as they lifted from the surface of the desert. He watched until they were gone.

Only when Rath was alone with the Ceratopian did he speak. "So you're the great H`laar."

The Ceratopian grunted with all of its strength. It fought to stand but failed.

"You're the one that they fear."

The alien choked and coughed. It strained to push up with one hand. It lifted its horned head to speak. *"Dar Achaar veraatat dech."*

Rath blinked in surprised understanding. He gave the alien a strange, lengthy look—a look that indicated he was caught off guard. But the unnerved expression soon fell. Reaching to his belt, he unholstered a high-powered pistol.

The Ceratopian breathed harder as it struggled fiercely to stand. *"Dar Achaar veraatat dech!"*

Rath disengaged the safety. He aimed the barrel at the Ceratopian's head. "I'm sure he does."

"Dar Achaar veraatat—!"

The alien's last words were cut short. As the pistol discharged, the Ceratopian's bone frill cracked wide open. Blood spewed from its reptilian ears as it fell to the sand.

Judge Rath stared at the massive body before him as the desert winds blew through his hair. Slowly he let down the gun. He engaged the safety and slipped it back in his belt, then reached for his comm.

"It's done."

Several seconds passed before Archer replied. "He's *absolutely* dead?"

"Absolutely dead."

Archer sighed heavily. "It's about bloody time. Very well, then. Come back home."

At first Rath didn't respond; his eyes remained on the corpse. Finally he lifted the comm. "Be thankful you didn't send Faerber."

"What do you mean?"

"It would not have gone well."

Silence ensued on the channel, until Archer replied. "We're being called into an emergency meeting. I'll talk to you when we finish and when you return." The channel closed without further words.

Rath stepped back and turned from the corpse, heading back to his Vulture. He walked up the ramp and slapped the inner hull. The door slowly whined to a close.

The alien's body remained on the ground. As the EDEN Command transport lifted off, a wash of sand flew over it. Almost like it belonged.

No other transports came to the desert, not from the Agèma or EDEN Command. The only vultures that landed were those looking for carrion.

They found it in full.

* * *

EDEN COMMAND

ALL EYES IN THE conference room focused on Pauling. As the president propped his hands on the table in front of him, he furrowed his brow in intense thought.

The High Command had convened in an emergency session in light of the Bakma-Ceratopian confrontation. The Council had kept a tight lid on the interspecies conflict up until that point. Disclosure was now unavoidable.

Torokin observed the president with genuine curiosity. The past few days had been awkward for him, ever since he'd questioned Pauling's effectiveness. He'd become the black sheep of EDEN Command, despite the fact that Rath, Jun Dao, and Blake had approached him secretly to agree. Grinkov and Lena didn't need to approach him in secret—their agreement was understood without words.

"All right," Pauling said, turning to Judge June. "Confirm to the media that it took place. Tell them the situation is 'evolving.' Let them chew on that for a while, while we figure out what we're going to do."

Torokin observed June's reaction. She had the unenviable task of being their official crisis spokeswoman, but for good reason. No one could spin better yarns. June nodded her head.

It was one of the more intimate meetings Torokin ever remembered. This time there were no arguments about policies or plans of action. Besides Pauling's brief reaming of Archer over his rashness in sending Platis to the scene, it had actually been a constructive effort by everyone—with the exception of Rath. For whatever reason, the Canadian judge wasn't there.

Pauling concluded, "We'll meet tomorrow at 0900, after Malcolm and I have had a chance to deliberate. We'll let you all know what we came up with." He looked at Blake. "Malcolm?"

Judge Blake rose and ordered, "Everyone else is dismissed."

Torokin stood and pushed his chair in. Grinkov also prepared to leave—he placed an encouraging hand on Torokin's shoulder in a way only a comrade would understand.

Torokin had no idea how Pauling and Blake would decide to proceed, now that the world knew that the Bakma and Ceratopians weren't friends. He hoped their solution would be agreeable to everyone. Only tomorrow would tell.

He sought out Archer, frowning when he saw the judge making his way out of the conference room alone. The chastisement Archer had received from the president had been scathing. In Pauling's own words, Archer "couldn't have handled it worse." Archer's defense had been that he didn't want Thoor handling such a sensitive situation—a defense that several judges seemed to share, though no one spoke up on Archer's behalf.

Torokin understood the British judge's rationale. Would he have approached it differently himself? Perhaps—he wasn't sure. But regardless of his own feelings, he knew Archer had gone into it with the best intentions. Torokin actually felt sorry for him. Hurrying his pace, he caught up before Archer could leave.

"Benjamin."

Archer waited outside the conference room until Torokin caught up, then the two resumed walking.

"Do not let what happened discourage you," Torokin said. "You did what you thought was right at the time."

"I made a mistake. I handled it awfully. There's nothing more I can say."

"I know why you did what you did. I have done things like that, too."

Archer tried to smile but failed. "You live and you learn. It's a lesson learned the hard way—that's how I see it."

The British judge had a good attitude—better than Torokin's would have been.

Archer changed the subject. "I'll be talking to Ceratopian No. 12 later this evening, if you'd care to come along."

Torokin had been meaning to talk to him about that. After careful deliberation, he'd come to the conclusion that as excited as he had been to assist Archer in interrogations, it wasn't for him. He didn't have the patience for it. "I think I am more of a hindrance than a help. Answers do not come quickly, and...it frustrates me. I trust you to do it alone."

At those words, Archer smiled. "You trust me?"

It took Torokin a second to realize what his fellow judge was saying. That had been his issue with the Briton since the beginning—trusting the man who'd replaced the dead Judge Darryl Kentwood. He'd just told Archer he trusted him without even realizing it.

"I suppose that I do," Torokin confessed. Why it took Archer being corrected in public to warm Torokin up to him was beyond his reasoning. Perhaps it made them seem like kindred spirits.

"I appreciate it, Leonid. Very much."

"You need not mention it."

It had been one of the more tumultuous months that Torokin could recall—from *Novosibirsk* to the invasion of Europe, and now this. The last thing he'd expected was that Archer would turn out to be a bright spot.

Archer offered Torokin his hand. "I hate to cut you off short, but I've got some work to do. I apologize if I'm coming across rudely."

"You do not need to mention that, either." Torokin could give lessons on rudeness. "I do not take it personally."

"I'll see you in the meeting tomorrow."

"Good enough."

There was nothing else on Torokin's agenda for the rest of the day. He was sure something would come across his desk eventually—something always did. But at least he could pretend he was a free man.

Ever since his spat with Pauling, he'd felt the itch to unretire from Vector Squad and return to active duty. That tended to happen any time there was tension in the Council. In the end, the itch would subside—it always did. He'd call Klaus, they'd reminisce on glories past, and he'd come to the conclusion that his hanging up his assault rifle was for the best. Of course, Klaus would have taken him back in a second—he'd told Torokin that many times. But what was done was done. He was a judge for the right motives. One day, he'd make the difference he wanted.

With no other issues to steal his attention, Torokin went his own way.

* * *

SHORTLY AFTER

ARCHER LEANED BACK in the leather chair in his room. On his cherry-stained desk, his audio recorder sat in place. He thought patiently before speaking aloud.

"H`laar has been killed."

He fell silent after just those four words, his eyes distancing into the conch shells on his wall. Twenty seconds passed before he resumed.

"We will have difficulties if you do not get here soon. The Bakma are getting more bold by the week…as I'm sure you now know. The Khuladi will soon have what they wish.

"We are still several months from control. Everything will be in place… but do not underestimate what 'we' in EDEN can do. We may be just strong enough to seal our own fate."

He stopped and pressed his lips together, as if they were on the verge of saying something profound. But nothing came out. He rubbed his chin with his hand while his other hand hovered over the *stop* button. He succumbed to a sigh.

"Benjamin Archer, ending transmission."

He stopped the recorder and removed the disk from its drive. Reaching for his comm, he said, "Archer to Intelligence. I have a priority message to be delivered to Kang. Send a courier to my room at once—five minutes, no less."

"As you wish, judge."

Pivoting around slowly in his chair, Archer looked at the clock. Five minutes. That was always the time he gave; he was always upset when it took longer. But today, if it took a minute or so more, maybe he wouldn't complain. Maybe he'd simply smile. The day had already gone well.

He didn't want to spoil his good mood.

41

SATURDAY, NOVEMBER 26TH, 0011 NE
0454 HOURS

NOVOSIBIRSK, RUSSIA

EARLY NEXT MORNING

SCOTT'S EYES OPENED before his alarm clock went off. As the ethereal realm of dreams melted into the colors of reality, he drew a deep breath. He could sense every rib expand then contract. He could feel the air in his lungs. His body hurt. Pain pulsed in his arms and legs; his battered face still throbbed. But something else overwhelmed all the pains of soldiery. He didn't notice it right away—not until after a full minute had passed. When it finally occurred to him, he sat upright.

He hadn't woken up tired.

Pressing his hands gently against the bed, he surveyed his room. It was dark. There were no sounds coming from the hall. *Novosibirsk* was asleep. Reaching to his nightstand, he deactivated his alarm before it could sound.

Nicole's picture was next to his clock; she was still facing the wall. He'd turned her there the day before and hadn't turned her back. He'd slept the whole night without her smile on him. Rising from his bed, he turned the photo until it faced him again.

He ran a hand over his face. His cheekbone felt numb where cold gel had dried overnight. The gel was doing its job well, despite the swollenness that remained; he'd have a black eye for a couple more weeks. As for the burns—they already looked better.

The aftermath of the mission had been one of the most surreal experiences of Scott's life. He'd spent the entire flight home sitting next to Dostoevsky. The Russian fulcrum didn't stop crying once; they were the happiest sobs Scott ever heard. He couldn't even remember ever being that jovial about anything himself.

Everything about the rescue went beyond words. The fact that it'd even happened was hard enough to believe. He gave his teammates more credit than himself for its ultimate success. Even through odds and injuries, they'd persevered. His mind ran through the long list of wounded.

Travis was being treated for second-degree burns, among other scars. He'd miss a week or two. As for William, after several visits to the infirmary, he had been cleared of any internal injuries. He'd escaped only with a significant bruise. Though Auric's wounds looked the worst by far, they were mostly cosmetic in nature. His helmet had saved his life—and his career. His right ear, while half missing, still functioned. Between Dostoevsky's fractured ribs and Derrick's reinjured leg, almost everyone had some kind of impairment.

But the worst wounds belonged to the *Pariah*, in spite of the fact that it'd returned. Its engines were torched beyond reliability. Its hull was dented and ripped. The feral dog on its tail wing was nothing but char.

Nonetheless, numerous components still worked. The skeleton of the troop bay was intact. The communication system still functioned. Even the controls and navigational circuits could be salvaged. It had fought its most perilous fight, and despite its battle-torn body, it had survived. It was scheduled to be flown to *Atlanta*—for a complete overhaul.

That was a miraculous sign by itself.

The same positive words could not be said for the two rescued squads. The Fifty-first and Forty-second were in ruin. Before Captain Tkachenok had taken ten steps out of his transport, he'd been informed by sentries that he was stripped of command. His unit would be split apart and dispersed. The Fifty-first would be Nightman alone.

No such bad news awaited the captain of the Forty-second, but for a totally different reason: he was dead. Only seven operatives from that unit had survived. Like Tkachenok's squad, the Forty-second's survivors would be dispersed with other units.

Tanneken Brunner received no ill-treatment upon her return to *Novosibirsk*, much to Scott's pleasant surprise. Gabriel received a lecture and no more. Custer was allowed to seek medical attention in the infirmary for his shoulder wound, after which he and everyone from Pelican Squad—recovering or not—would be forced to leave. They would return to *Sydney* again.

The only person whose fate Scott didn't know was Colonel Saretok's. But that suited Scott just fine.

The battle had presented him with many things, from gold-horned armor to strange Ceratopian words. But those things paled in comparison to what mattered most. It had given him his soul back—at least, what little of it remained. A little was better than nothing at all.

Scott was in the middle of brushing his teeth when he heard a sound from outside his door. He turned to see a single white envelope sliding in at the base.

When do I ever get mail?

No one would have written him. His brother Mark would never have sent him a letter. Nor would anyone else outside The Machine. He spit out his toothpaste and rinsed, then walked toward his door to retrieve it.

It was from NovCom, and he immediately realized what it was: his request for Jayden to remain at the base. A knot formed deep in his stomach. Taking the envelope to his desk, he sat down and ripped the top open. He unfolded the letter and read.

The beginning was a stock paragraph dedicated to stating the real contents of the letter. He skipped to the very last paragraph, stopping only at the three words that actually mattered.

...should not return...

The knot in his stomach unraveled, leaving an ache that lingered. He didn't want to read any more of the letter—he wanted to throw it straight in the trash. But he looked at the paper again, forcing himself to read the whole sentence.

Due to the extent of the injury sustained, at the recommendation of Novosibirsk's medical staff, it has been decided that Jayden P. Timmons should not return to active duty.

Scott didn't read any further. Crumpling the paper into a ball, he hurled it against the door. It stopped rolling next to the wall.

Why Jayden? He posed the question to God. *Of all the people to punish, why is it him?*

He hated even the thought of breaking the news—of walking into Jayden's room, looking him in the one eye he had left, and telling him his journey was through. Scott didn't care if there was legitimacy behind the decision. He knew that Jayden wanted to stay to prove himself; the Texan had no further motive or wish.

Scott looked at the paper again. He wanted to pick it up and hurl it down a second time for good measure, but that wouldn't change what it said.

He had planned to wake up and run a morning session, with the intention of starting the day off with something good, but the bad news about Jayden made that impossible. He looked at his fulcrum armor in his closet, cleaned from the battle. Even in low light, the golden horns shone. The new feature was the Fourteenth's reward to him for turning himself around—for giving redemption a try. Where was Jayden's reward for always being the dedicated sniper that he was?

Crumpled in a ball on the floor.

The walk to the infirmary was one of the worst Scott had endured. With every step, he was closer to crushing Jayden's heart. He hadn't bothered to take the letter with him. He didn't want the Texan to see it; he just wanted to get things over with. He'd never be able to concentrate on morning session with the dread of breaking bad news on his mind.

Of all the Fourteenth's operatives, none had earned Scott's trust like Jayden—not even Svetlana. The Texan was the most reliable person he'd ever worked with. So far as Scott could remember, Krasnoyarsk was the sniper's only error. He'd never failed to locate an enemy before. That that one time had cost him his career was cruel.

The infirmary was warm when Scott entered. It was bustling with more activity than outside or in the officers' wing. He walked past the receptionist's desk and down the hall.

Undoubtedly Jayden was capable of recovery. Would it be difficult? Yes. Would being restricted to one eye be a hindrance in the field? Yes. But Scott would take a hindered Jayden over any other fully functional sniper any day. Before he knew it, he was standing outside Jayden's door. He poked his head into the room. The Texan was asleep.

How in the world am I supposed to do this? There was no delicate way to deliver the news, no gentle way to wake up the Texan, stand next to his bed, and say, "Sorry, they don't believe you can do it." But who were they to say what he could or couldn't do?

It wasn't right. It wasn't right to rip away Jayden's sole desire without giving him a chance to prove the odds wrong. None of them knew Jayden's heart. None of them knew Jayden at all.

Scott turned away from the door and stormed up the hall. They didn't know Jayden, but that no longer mattered. They were about to know someone else.

It took Scott all of one minute to find the right door. He knocked calmly, and a small-framed, balding man opened it from inside. He was wearing a doctor's lab coat.

Scott spoke in Russian. "Are you the doctor responsible for Timmons?"

The man looked at Scott's name badge and appeared to recognize his last name. He looked startled. "Commander Remington, good morning. Yes, I oversee Timmons. How can I help you?"

"Is it all right if I come in?" Scott said as pleasantly as he could, offering a smile.

The cordiality was acknowledged in kind. "Of course. Please, come in." Stepping aside, he let Scott inside and closed the door. "Have a seat."

Scott didn't want to have a seat. "A week ago, I put in a reinstatement request for him. I got the refusal back this morning. Was that your decision?"

The doctor hesitated. "Yes, I made that decision. There were too many potential risks to allow him to stay. I couldn't grant the request in good conscience—I am sorry."

"I understand." Scott strolled to the other side of the man's office. He stared at family photographs on his desk. "Am I correct in assuming your approval is all he needs to remain?"

"That is correct."

Scott remained facing away. "I'd like you to reconsider your assessment."

The doctor's chuckle was well-intentioned. "I understand why you're here. I know comrades become very close. You care for your friend, and he wants to stay. I wish it were that simple."

"What if it is?"

"Life is never that simple, commander. Many difficult decisions must be made. I make them every day."

Scott lifted his head. Still facing the desk, his back to the doctor, he stared at the wall. "So do I." He turned his head just enough to allow the doctor to see part of his face. He meant it that way. "Before today, did you know who I was?"

"Oh yes, I know of you well." The doctor smiled. "I have treated many of your fellow Nightmen—the ones that you train. You are quite a dangerous man!"

"Think about that."

The tension didn't hit right away. For several seconds the doctor just stared—Scott could see him in his peripherals. He could see the well-intentioned smile on the man's face. He could see when realization slowly hit. Only then did Scott turn around, allowing the scope of his displeasure to come into view—revealing an edge that wasn't quite gone.

"You said you understood why I was here," Scott said, stalking toward the doctor. "I don't think you do."

The doctor froze with new fear.

"I think Timmons will recover just fine. I think he's shown enough improvement and commitment to persevere through his initial diagnosis. I think you'll agree."

The man gaped, then his entire body flinched as Scott struck for his chest. But not to deliver an attack. Instead, Scott grabbed the pen from the doctor's coat pocket. He held it in front of the man's face. "Now…do I need to grab the letterhead, or will you?"

Ten minutes later, Scott was standing in front of Jayden's door. In his hand was a signed sheet of paper—an official response to his reinstatement request. He stepped inside and tapped on the wood.

The Texan had been sleeping. He stared confusedly at Scott.

"Sorry for waking you up, man," Scott said. "I know you were sleeping."

Jayden stared oddly until his cognition kicked in. "Hey, man." His voice was groggily deep. "It's okay. What's goin' on?"

Scott stepped inside, holding the letter in hand. Then he smiled. "Have I got some great news for you."

* * *

Every step Dostoevsky took made him cringe with pain. He was in Nightman uniform, despite his three fractured ribs. Unseen by anyone else, his chest was a patchwork of bandages and body straps. He had been summoned to the Inner Sanctum while in the infirmary. Injured or not, he had to comply.

As he approached the wooden doors, the sentries at guard parted ways. "Captain Dostoevsky, the general awaits."

The fulcrum nodded and the wooden doors opened. Far ahead, in the darkness of the Terror's domain, the stairway to the throne appeared. Dostoevsky drew a pained breath and stepped in.

Even though shadows surrounded General Thoor, his cold features came into detail. His jaw protruded. His narrow eyes watched Dostoevsky's every step. As soon as the fulcrum was before him, he wasted no time in speaking.

"Your uselessness reeks from the walls."

Dostoevsky lowered his head.

"You have failed as Baranov's successor. You were given an opportunity to grab the Fourteenth by the throat and control it. This was our gift to you, and you have done nothing."

Dostoevsky barely breathed. He simply stood, eyes downcast as the diatribe continued.

"Were you any other fulcrum, you would have already been terminated. That you will walk out of my sight alive is a testament to your dedication in the past." The general's voice maintained its dark resonance. "You are stripped of your captaincy. The Fourteenth is Remington's to lead. You will serve him as commander, as you served Baranov. You will behold the fruits of your own insignificance under his reign. You will witness what it truly means to command. And when—"

Dostoevsky restrained a soft chuckle.

Thoor froze the moment he heard it. From atop his throne, his rancorous eyes bulged.

Outside the Inner Sanctum, beyond the still-wide-open wooden doors, the two sentries swapped a sudden look. They turned their heads inside the room.

"Dostoevsky," asked Thoor, "are you *laughing*?"

Dostoevsky couldn't hold it back. His soft laughter escaped. "I hear you, general. I hear every word that you say. I will forfeit my captaincy. I will serve as commander for Remington. I will do all of these things." There was no trace of spite in his voice. "But I will not tremble at the sound of your voice. You are still my general, as you always have been. But you are no longer my God."

Thoor's mouth fell blatantly open.

The fulcrum offered a courteous bow to the Terror. Then he stepped back, turned, and walked away. The only sounds in the Inner Sanctum were the fulcrum's footsteps as he left. Thoor was left shocked and speechless on his throne. The sentries at the door didn't utter a sound.

Dostoevsky had barely gone ten steps when someone else crossed him in the hall—the next of the general's morning appointments. It was a man Dostoevsky knew well—the new fulcrum captain of the First. As Oleg walked past, both men locked eyes, the fallen eidolon's stare narrowing in displeasure. He passed Dostoevsky without saying a word.

Dostoevsky didn't say a word, either. But unlike Oleg, his eyes only stayed locked for a moment, before his steps carried him past and away. As he turned his head forward, the corners of his lips turned upright.

It didn't matter that his ribs were fractured or that every step brought excruciating agony. It didn't matter that he'd infuriated Thoor or that Oleg despised his very being. Only one thing mattered to Dostoevsky at all. And it let him smile through every pained step he took.

* * *

THE FOURTEENTH WAS waiting outside for Scott. It was already past seven o'clock—late for a morning session. The sky was dark; sunrise wouldn't come for another hour and a half.

Word had already come to the unit: the next time they would see Scott again, he would be their new captain. The revelation wasn't a surprise, but nonetheless brought warmth in the cold.

In the week leading up to the mission, there had been tension between EDEN and the Nightmen. But today there was none. In fact, there'd only been one awkward moment at all, between Max and Esther, regarding a rumor Max had heard. Apparently, a certain slayer from the Battleship had been discovered with a bullet hole in his head. Max asked her if she knew anything about it. She answered without saying a word.

Max didn't complain.

It was a quarter to eight when Scott appeared, wearing his Nightman uniform as he had every day since murdering Sergei Steklov. That part of him would never change.

No one greeted him when he approached. He received no welcoming handshakes, nor congratulatory words about his promotion. They simply watched him, their postures erect, their hands at their sides, as he stopped in front of them.

His face was still bruised, his hands still covered in scars. Standing before them, he gave each and every one of them a direct look. From Max to David, from Svetlana to Esther, from Becan to Boris—no one was immune. Placing his hands on his hips, he finally spoke. "We've got a lot of work to do."

The team remained disciplined. Only Svetlana showed any reaction at all. Beneath the fall of her blond hair, her lips curved.

Flopper barked and wagged his tail in the snow. Scott looked at the small dog and actually smiled—the animal was the only one to receive the gesture from him. Facing his unit again, Scott nodded his head.

"Let's get to it."

It was the twenty-sixth day of the eleventh month, in the eleventh year of the New Era. It was a day the Fourteenth had been waiting on for some time—the day their hero had finally returned.

Eventually, the sun would rise, thawing the earth with its warm orange hues. Morning session would take place then come to a close, but, as proclaimed by their new leader, there was still much to be done. In the wake of their first truly unified mission, the Fourteenth would prepare for the next. And the next.

There was an unspoken understanding among them—one that permeated the weeks and months that followed. It didn't matter that they had overcome their animosities—that they'd persevered over fear. It didn't matter that they'd become proof that light could shine in the shadow of The Machine.

What mattered was that they were not finished. In the aftermath of their victory over strife, they knew that one victory was not good enough. There was more left to accomplish—more they'd been called on to do. They had set a new mark upon themselves. No longer would they be viewed as a decimated squad; no longer could they be. They were the Fourteenth of *Novosibirsk.*

There was more to become.

FOUR MONTHS LATER

WEDNESDAY, MARCH 7TH, 0012 NE
1906 HOURS

YORK COUNTY, PENNSYLVANIA

THE NIGHT AIR was frigid. Curling her fingers rigidly around her E-35 assault rifle, Catalina Shivers stalked cautiously out of the Cruiser. It was the tail end of her platoon's mission; the Ceratopian vessel had been shot down over a stretch of Pennsylvania farmland. Almost every extraterrestrial had been killed.

Almost.

She'd seen it moments before, flitting behind her in her peripherals. Even in the dark, its form was unmistakable: a necrilid. It had scampered out of the Cruiser from a hallway she'd sworn moments before had been clear. Her error was her new obligation—she had to hunt it down. As for why she was completely alone—that error was someone else's.

"I'm gonna kill you, Peters." The words escaped from her trembling lips. "I'm gonna *kill* you." The Canadian beta private's armor was stained with blood. Strands of sweat-soaked black hair dangled from her helmet—her brown eyes were focused. As she left the safety of the Cruiser's interior, she panned her assault rifle to the ship's outer hull. She spoke into her comm. "This is Private Shivers. I'm tracking one necrilid outside the vessel."

The response she got was not a pleased one. "I thought you said your section was *clear*."

"...I thought it was, sir."

"Stand by. I'm on my way."

Something skittered across the top of the hull. Swinging her rifle after the sound, Catalina saw the necrilid bound out of view. It disappeared toward the rear thrusters. "I have visual, in pursuit..."

A female voice crackled through. "Cat, like, didn't the major just tell you to wait?"

"Not now, Tiff."

"But you, like—"

"Not now!" Picking up her pace to track the creature from the ground, Catalina trotted toward the rear of the ship.

It had been the most intense mission she'd ever been on, though that said little considering her inexperience. Nonetheless, five privates had already been killed. She had no intention of being number six. Originally, she'd been paired with another soldier: Mark Peters. They were put together often, and usually formed a capable duo. But not this time. Against her advisement, he'd left her behind to assist another team. He was a good soldier, but he had a rebel streak in him. The two had developed somewhat of a working rivalry—and maybe a little something else, too.

Stopping by the rear thrusters, she put some distance between herself and the Cruiser. The craft had apparently been shot in the rear section, or at least that much could be assumed by the massive holes in its hull. Looking upward, she tried to spot the creature on the roof. But nothing was there.

"Where are you?" she asked the necrilid, swallowing. "C'mon…come down." She adjusted her visor for thermal imaging.

Thump.

The Canadian froze. The sound hadn't come from the roof, or from anywhere near the Cruiser. It came from right behind her. She didn't need to turn to know what it was. But turn, she did—quickly.

She saw it the moment she'd come around. The necrilid's body, warm in thermal imaging, cocked itself back. Its knees bent in preparation to strike. It opened its mouth.

The shot came out of nowhere. The necrilid's head suddenly burst open, erupting in a crimson explosion. The alien's corpse collapsed to the ground.

Mouth still opened in shock, Catalina spun around, aiming her assault rifle at the roof of the Cruiser. No necrilids were there.

"That was the only one."

Even though the voice was familiar, it still made her flinch. Lowering her assault rifle, Catalina forced her stomach back down her throat. Then she faced him. He was walking straight toward her, his sniper rifle still prone. The major.

"I watched it leap right over you from the roof while you were turning on your thermal," Tacker said. "In another second, you'd have been dead."

"I'm sorry, sir—"

"Don't apologize to me," he cut her off. "Apologize to your parents. They lost their daughter because she couldn't follow commands."

Her shoulders sagged.

"Where's Peters?"

She gathered her pride—at least enough to pin the blame on someone else. "He left me to help Pierce and Masters, sir."

"So is this all his fault?"

It was a trick question; it always was with him. "No, sir. I should have listened to you and held my position."

For several seconds, Tacker said nothing. Finally, he nodded his head. "Feathers," he said through the comm, "prep the ship. We won't be here long."

The same woman who'd spoken to Catalina earlier answered him. "Yes, sir."

Catalina knew she was dismissed without Tacker having to say it. He had a way of ignoring those he was done with. She waited several seconds, just to be sure, until his attention went somewhere else. He now stared squarely at the Cruiser's damaged hull.

She walked away in silence.

Inside the Cruiser, Colonel Brent Lilan of Falcon Platoon shouldered his assault rifle. Eleven Ceratopians killed in combat—that made twenty altogether. In a wrecked Cruiser, twenty sounded right. "White, check the bodies. Caldwell, Doucet, clear the silo and signal the sweep."

"Yes sir!"

The colonel pulled off his helmet. His gray crew cut was damp with sweat. He wiped his forehead and spoke through his comm. "What's it like out there, major?"

Tacker's answer crackled through. "We're clear, sir. Sweeper team should be good."

"How'd we do?"

"Five dead, two wounded, one crit."

"*Veck.*" Between Charlie and Delta Squads, that was too many. "Have Rhodes patch up the crit. I'm gonna check out these 'Topians."

A moment passed before Tacker replied. "It's Smith now, sir."

"What?"

"Rhodes was transferred to Hawk two weeks ago. Our medic is Frank Smith, now."

Lilan placed his hands on his hips in disgust. Tacker was right. Sasha had gone to Colonel Young's crew. He'd completely forgotten.

"Sir, there's something else I need to talk to you about..."

"Yeah, go ahead." Lilan's tone indicated his frustration. He couldn't keep track of anyone anymore. Falcon Platoon was a revolving door—a unit whose sole purpose was to wet the feet of new Academy grads. Outside of a few pleasant surprises, like Charlie Squad's Peters and Shivers, he had almost nothing to work with.

There was a lag in Tacker's response. Something was wrong. "Remind me to recalibrate my rifle when we get back to base, colonel. It aims down and to the right."

Lilan stopped walking. Tacker's words weren't a literal statement. They were code. A "recalibration reminder" was a request for his immediate presence. "Down and right" instructed him where: the rear starboard side of the Cruiser. Something was happening that Tacker didn't want on record.

"Will do," the colonel answered. "Lilan out."

The Cruiser had landed on somebody's farmland. In the distance, the farmer was shouting hysterically, angry about the damage to his property. Lilan understood the man's irritation, but he wasn't about to apologize—not for doing his job.

Tacker was waiting at the starboard side of the ship. Donald Bell was with him. With Sasha Rhodes gone, the black demolitionist was the only remaining holdout from the Falcon Platoon of months before—Tacker aside.

"How's it goin', coach?" Donald asked. He always referred to Lilan that way.

"It's going." Lilan shifted his attention to Tacker. "What do we have, major?"

Tacker gave Lilan a knowing look. "You need to see for yourself." He glanced at Donald. "Keep the privates away."

The demolitionist turned to corral the other operatives.

Lilan followed Tacker to the back of the ship. "What am I looking for?"

Tacker motioned to the damaged Cruiser. "I came back here to help Shivers, then I found where this thing got hit in the intercept." At the back of the Cruiser, a hole exposed the engines beneath its hull. "When

I first realized what I was looking at, I thought I had to be wrong. There was just no way this was possible. But I'm *not* wrong."

Lilan scrutinized the hole in the vessel. The hull was dented and cracked inward, where the metal was shredded. "What am I not seeing, here?"

"Look at the edge of the impact zone. Look all the way around. Tell me if you catch it."

The colonel narrowed his eyes in scrutiny. The engine had burst and the metal was torn. That was all typical of a missile strike. The dents, the gashes, the scorch marks—

He stopped at that thought. There were no scorch marks, not so much as a singe. "Wait a minute." He pointed to the scar-less cavities. "What'd we hit this thing with?"

The major nodded. "Exactly. There's not an exterior scorch mark in sight. Every air-to-air weapon we carry creates an explosion. This hull didn't explode—it got crushed."

"How is that possible? There's not a weapon that can do that."

Tacker hesitated. "Actually, there is. There's one weapon fully capable of doing this. I've seen it done before, just not to a Cruiser." Several moments passed while the major stared at the vessel. "That weapon…is a neutron cannon."

Lilan raised an eyebrow.

"I don't think we hit this thing at all, colonel. I think other Ceratopians did."

E P I C • B O O K 4

THE GLORIOUS BECOMING

www.epicuniverse.com

ACKNOWLEDGMENTS

To God: Your mercy and faithfulness are boundless. You have blessed me in spite of me, and You continue to be the God I can never praise enough. Thank You for being my footprints in the sand.

To Lindsey: What a wonderful thing it is to call you my wife! Thank you for standing by me and believing in me. Only you know just how hard this book was to write, but your faith in me never wavered. I am blessed among husbands. I love you.

To Mom & Dad: Thank you for raising me to be a good man—I have never thanked you enough for that. Thank you for your wisdom, your guidance, and your love. I am so proud to call myself your son. Happy birthday, Dad!

To Mrs. Joyce and Mr. Tommy: You have both been such a source of encouragement for me. Thank you for welcoming me into your family with such warmth. I hope this makes up for the *other* book I got you, Mr. Tommy! (you know what I mean…)

To my family: You are an unwavering source of support. Thank each and every one of you for your steadfast love and encouragement. I'm the most blessed grandson/nephew/cousin in the world.

To Arlene, Fiona, Francois, and Justin: None of this would be possible without all of you. If people only knew what goes on behind the scenes of the storyline, they'd realize how much of Epic is due to you four. I know, and it's appreciated beyond words.

To Stevie: It's impossible to describe how awesome it is to have a friend who understands all of this. Thank you for always being there as a source of encouragement, camaraderie, and creative brainstorming. And of course…for incredible maps, too! I truly hope your success surpasses my own. You deserve it.

To Luke: You're about as unsung a hero as Epic can have. Without you, there'd be no Epic community. Thank you for your tireless efforts to keep us all (Epic goers and SPs alike) on the same page.

To Aaron Spuler: You do so much more than maintain a blog. You are as faithful and passionate a fan as any author could ask for. Thank you for your tireless efforts!

To Lieutenant Benjamin Botnick: I'm honored to consider you a friend and fellow coworker. Thank you for being a reliable source of info, and a confidence booster, too.

To Ken Rousseau and Herb Cavalier: You guys have no idea how helpful even a small chat around a table can be. Between you guys and my RN wife, I could almost pass for a medical-savvy author. Or at least not a total moron.

To Peter Hodges & Kate Baker: You guys are an outstanding part of the science-fiction community. Peter, thank you for putting a spotlight on one of the unknowns. And Kate, thank you for the podcasts during Diabetes Awareness Month. That was a blast!

To Alessia Zambonin: One of the unexpected perks of this business has been meeting so many talented people. Thank you for putting faces on some of Epic's best!

To Anita Pedersen: You have no idea how cool it is to wake up one day and find your own Facebook group. Thank you for that fist-pumping moment!

To Maria Belinski: Vielen, herzlichen Dank! You helped me sound a little less dumb.

To Robert Marston Fannéy: Few others understand the behind-the-scenes aspect of all this like you do. Thank you for being a friend in the field!

To Earl & Denise: Your enthusiasm is indispensible. Thank you for being neighbors, friends, and fans. It is appreciated so much!

To Stephanie Police & Greg Zarcone: Thank you for your patience! I wish the extent of our ambitions had worked out, but I consider myself blessed to have found new friends and fans. You are both truly pros.

To the TBBBB: One of the sadder aspects of being an author has been having less time to dedicate to the boards. You guys have been a source of support from day one. Thank you for always being there. You make me hate the Bucs a little less!

To Nova Dog: The time we spent together was short, but so meaningful. Thank you for being my "best friend." I hope Flopper makes you proud. I miss you, girl.

To the fans: Without you, this would all be for naught. Your excitement and enthusiasm keeps Epic alive. Thank you, thank you, thank you for your dedication and support! You've made this one heck of a ride—and boy howdy…what a ride it's about to become…

ABOUT THE AUTHOR

Lee Stephen is a native of St. Charles Parish, Louisiana, and a graduate of Louisiana College in Pineville. Along with writing, he has worked in the fields of education, entertainment, and emergency preparedness. He currently lives in Luling with his wife, Lindsey.

To read Lee's Christian testimony, please visit his website at http://www.epicuniverse.com/testimony/.